Jason and the Sargon

James Collins

This is a work of fiction. Any resemblance of characters to persons living, dead or **mythological** is purely coincidental.

Some license has been taken with the distance between actual places on Symi and there is no military camp where described in this fiction but that's all for dramatic effect. Similarly; I have tried to be historically accurate with the timing of certain events but accurate and reliable records about Symi's history (in English) are… scarce.

Having said that, Stavros Tou Polemou (The Cross of the War) does exist and you can visit it when you come to Symi.

James Collins

James Collins was born in England during the winter of 1963. He holds a Masters degree and has taught theatre and music. He has written several musicals, all performed in the United Kingdom, and has worked on the cabaret circuit. He moved to the warmer climate of Greece in 2002 and has been happily writing novels ever since.

Also by James Collins

Novels and Books

Other people's dreams

You wish

Into the fire

Symi 85600

Carry on up the Kali Strata

These titles are available via www.symidream.com

PROLOGUE
The Panandreas Villa, Symi
October 20th 1882

'What is in the chest papa?'

'Hush Dimitris, let me read in peace.'

'Is it for my name day?'

'It is a very important letter that you have brought me. Go and help your mother on the terrace boy. Quickly now.'

Dimitris was not interested in helping his mother but he could see that his father was becoming angry. He tutted petulantly and shuffled outside into the sunlight where he saw his mother doing something boring with plants.

When the mysterious package had arrived that morning, delivered by one of his father's merchant ships, he had been convinced that it contained something for him. It was a heavy box wrapped in brown paper, tied with cord and sealed with wax. More intriguing though was that it had been sent from Venice. Dimitris had been sure that it was some new and exciting book for him to read or maybe some new music for him to practise, maybe even an instrument. He had gone to collect the package with his father's secretary, Manos Tzankatis. He had wanted to carry it around the harbour and up the steps to his house, but it had been too heavy for him. The secretary had let him struggle with it as they passed some of his father's workers and then he took it back. But he had let Dimitris carry the letter that had arrived with it so the boy had felt like he was on a very important errand. Those sponge workers who still greeted Dimitris with respect had suggested that the package might be a treasure chest but others had mumbled sarcastically that it was Christos Panandreas' latest bank ledger. Dimitris had ignored all the comments as he dodged the piles of filthy sponges and people unloading them from the boats. He had been too keen to rush home and open the unexpected parcel to bother to listen to the workers.

But the delight of discovery had fallen to his father who now sat alone in the salon reading the letter. Dimitris had seen no more than an envelope and a metal chest before his father had ordered him outside.

The servants of the Panandreas household had begun preparing cakes and biscuits for the name day festival and now his mother was cutting herbs for the garlands. Out on the terrace, overlooking the harbour, there was no sign of anything wrapped in shiny material that might suggest a gift for him; nothing remotely interesting to an impatient ten year old; only cakes, flowers and incense.

'What can I do to help mama?' Dimitris asked, hoping that there was nothing to be done.

'If you want to help me, go inside and practise your music,' his mother replied without looking up from the rosemary bush.

Dimitris felt his heart sink. 'But I practised for three hours this morning,' he protested.

'Well I don't know. You are a clever boy Dimitri, you decide what you do. Just keep out of our way. And don't disturb your father again. He has too much on his mind already.'

Dimitris lent on the balustrade, looked down at the harbour and decided to practice his languages. He counted the number of ships in the harbour that his father owned, first in English and then again in Turkish. When he had done that he counted the number of people he could see working for his parents on the quayside. He did this in Greek for, although Symi had been under Ottoman rule for over three hundred years, his parents were always telling him that, no matter who claimed to own their island, it was and would always remain Greek. The island children had been taught that the way forward was to remain loyal to their heritage as one day the island would be part of their country again. It would be part of Greece. And, according to Dimitris' father who was very wise, the best thing Dimitris could do with his childhood was learn as many languages as possible, study his music, and never forget that Symi was a Greek island.

His mind had wandered from his counting and so he began again.

The fleet had begun returning from the diving season that morning and the sound of their arrival had interrupted his harpsichord practise. All day the church bells had rung, flags had been flown from their masts and people had gathered in the harbour to await news of their seafaring relatives. Dimitris could see the huge piles of black sponges being dumped on the quayside and he counted the number of people gathered around each boat. So far only six of his father's fleet had returned, the rest would arrive over the next few days. Then the harbour town of Yialos would become a teaming mass of people all keen to learn how much money had been made and who had collected the most sponges. The women would also find out how many of the men had died at sea. Sponge diving, the island's main industry, had recently become a dangerous business.

As his father sat inside reading the letter, Dimitris counted the number of crippled men and bodies being carried from the boats. He was too high above the harbour to see exactly who the grieving families were but he could make out the shapes of dead men wrapped in blankets as they were passed ashore. He tired of counting them when he reached fifty and so turned to look at his mother again. She, too, was gazing down to the activity below with her delicate hands pressed to her mouth.

'Is that why people hate us?' Dimitris asked. She did not answer him. 'The boys at school say that if you work for father you die. Is that true mama?'

'Of course not Dimitri,' his mother replied. 'Their work is dangerous, it always has been. That is all.'

'But they say that father is to blame. I was told that they are going to throw away his new suit because it kills people. Do they mean the one he wears to church? How does father's church suit kill people?'

'You ask too many questions boy.'

Christos Panandreas appeared on the terrace holding the mysterious metal chest in his arms. As he put it on the balustrade and opened the lid Dimitris noticed that it had no keyhole. Where he expected to see a lock was only a brass panel of three numbers. His curiosity was immediately aroused but, before he could ask what the numbers were for, his mother started speaking and he knew it was impolite to interrupt.

'Who is it from?' Maria asked, returning sadly to her herbs.

'Our friend in Venice,' Christos replied.

'Is it the money he owes us at last?'

Dimitris wondered why his mother was so keen to receive money when they had so much of it already.

'No Maria,' his father said quietly. 'He says he fears that he is dying.'

'Before he pays us what he owes?'

'He may be dead already.' Christos sounded sad but he pulled himself together and clapped his hands. 'Now then, we must prepare for our portrait. Masarakis will be coming soon to start the painting.'

Maria Panandreas paused for a moment while she considered this. 'That old letch can wait. What has been sent to us in place of a debt?' she said harshly.

Dimitris often wondered if it was actually his mother who ran the family empire rather than his father, she always seemed to be the one in charge. She was strict with their servants whereas his father was always gentle with everyone at the villa.

Christos placed the letter in the metal chest. Beneath it Dimitris caught a glimpse of something wrapped in a fine cloth before his father closed the lid.

'Husband.' Maria was glaring at Christos now, her youthful face suddenly older and wrinkled with annoyance. 'What did Richard send us?'

'He has sent us an incredible and priceless thing. A piece of history,' said Christos. He spun the numbers on the combination, locking away the secret and looked down to Dimitris. 'And from now on it is our duty to protect it.'

ONE

SARGO Holidays, Rhodes area office
121 years later
Wednesday afternoon

Andy Slipe clicked shut his mobile phone, pinched the bridge of his nose, closed his eyes and shook his head in disbelief. The combination of these actions was intended to belittle the member of his staff standing before him.

Jason, the cocky young holiday rep in front of his desk, was always the easiest of his team to intimidate. If Slipe had not been so hot and tired he could have gone that little bit further and made Jason cry. But he couldn't be bothered today. To be sure that Jason was suitably bullied, however, and before he opened his eyes to stare at the annoying young man who waited nervously on the other side of the desk, Slipe put on his best *I don't believe you* voice. He added to it a sneer-come-smile and said, 'Jason, this is the third time this season that your grandfather has died.'

From behind his closed lids he could picture the lad trying hard to think up a way out of the trouble he was once again in. He could see him sweating with desperation, trying to come up with another lie to save his career. He could almost feel Jason squirming, getting ready to beg for his job. Slipe enjoyed it when his reps begged. They would do anything to keep their dream jobs in the sun. Some of the younger female reps regularly found themselves faced with the sack; in more ways than one.

He sat back in his chair, let go of his nose and swung his glasses back onto his face. With all the self confidence of a man who knows that he has the power to change lives, he put his hands behind his head, sighed to show his scepticism and said, 'well?' before finally opening his eyes.

Jason had picked up a framed photograph of Slipe, turned away from the desk and was now looking at his reflection in the glass. He flicked strands of his fringe back into place.

This was not what Slipe expected to see.

'Oi,' he bellowed, lurching forward and banging his knee against the desk. 'Damn!'

'It's the sun, bleaches it, dries it… I should get an allowance for conditioner.' Jason tutted, apparently oblivious to the final warning Slipe was trying to give him.

'Did you hear what I said?'

Jason turned back to the desk and smiled.

'Sorry?'

'I said this is the third time this season that your grandfather has died,' Slipe repeated, rubbing his knee and wincing at the pain. 'What do you say about that?'

'This time it's true,' Jason replied innocently.

He put the photograph back on the desk and noticed that the letters in Slipe's nameplate were crooked. He took a moment to straighten them up, wondering how many other words he could make out of the letters, "A Slipe Area Manager."

'So you admit that the previous times you used the excuse to cover your poor performance you were lying to me?'

Jason wondered why Slipe should sound so surprised. He thought for a moment, shifting his weight onto one leg and tapping a finger against his cheek. 'Well, he had always been unwell…'

'Shut it. I don't want to know.' Slipe opened a folder and pushed some papers to one side, sighing heavily. 'What am I going to do with you?'

'No idea boss, but whatever it is do it soon, I've got a plane landing in half an hour.'

Slipe glared at Jason, Jason smiled back at him and winked. *Piles*, he thought silently to himself. *My boss' name is an anagram of Andy Piles.*

'You think this is funny?' Slipe said incredulously when Jason's smooth features wrinkled into a cheeky grin. 'Your sales are down to an all time low and you think it's a joke?'

'Sorry boss.'

No matter how much he hated Slipe Jason knew that he had to humour him. The man on the other side of the desk could end Jason's career with nothing more than a few words. But it would not be as simple as that. There was a history between the two of them and Slipe was not going to fire Jason without first making his life hell. Nor was Jason going to let Slipe sack him without a fight.

Jason had only been a SARGO rep for a month when his original boss, a pleasant woman called Toni, had resigned. Toni had been with the company for several years, managing the Rhodes area team quite successfully until Andy Slipe joined it as a rep. Within his first week Slipe made it clear that he wanted the area manager's job. He started undermining Toni straight away and after two weeks the usually calm and easy-going woman was suffering from stress. Slipe put in false grievances about her to head office and, by the end of week three, the general manger for SARGO-Greece was forced to pay an emergency visit to Rhodes to see what the problem was. Slipe convinced the general manager that the problem was Toni. After only the fourth week of the season she was sent home in emotional pieces carrying more baggage than she had flown out with. Slipe gloated and prepared to move up into her place.

The general manager called a round of quick interviews and all three of the Dodecanese SARGO reps applied for the Area Manager position. Christine from Leros came in third, Jason, who was based on Symi, came second and Slipe, due to some highly polished, unsportsmanlike tactics, came in first. A Kiwi girl, Kate, was drafted in from the Cyclades to cover Slipe's old post and the team was complete again.

But things were not the same. Slipe hated Jason because he was good looking, good at his job and gay. Jason hated Slipe because he had bad breath, a nasty haircut and thought he was god's gift to god. Both knew that it was Jason who should have been promoted. For a start he was actually interested in Greece and its history; Slipe was there for the sun and the women. Jason could speak several languages, including Greek; Slipe just shouted at the Greeks in English until they were battered into understanding. Jason cared about people; Slipe only cared about excursion targets and money.

But even Jason had to admit that Slipe had one advantage over him when it came to working for SARGO.

SARGO catered for holidaymakers over sixty and Jason didn't like old people very much. It kind of made it worse that they, the *wrinklies*, always fell in love with Jason.

'I said what am I going to do with you?' Slipe's shrill voice knocked Jason back into the here and now.

Jason looked at his watch. 'You're going to make me late for my transfer, that's what,' he challenged. He rubbed a foot against his leg to scratch a mosquito bite as he impatiently examined a broken fingernail.

Slipe raised his eyes to heaven and closed the folder. He sat back in his executive chair and swung it around to stare out of the window at the MacDonald's restaurant opposite. He hated Rhodes and he hated Jason. Jason was too popular with the guests, the other reps, the agents on the island and even with the coach drivers. His youthful good looks and friendly manner made Slipe's skin crawl.

For a while now Slipe had been trying various ways to get rid of him, but Jason had proved a difficult person to sack. Each week the old folk handed in their feed-back forms and each week Jason received 'excellent' against the box: 'How do you rate your rep?' And each week Slipe forged a new set of forms and changed the answer to 'poor' or 'adequate'. But still head office refused to accept that Jason should go. Apparently many guests actually phoned or wrote to SARGO about him on their return, saying how much they had enjoyed their holiday and *that nice young Jason who made us laugh and got us all singing Abba songs*. Slipe knew he had to be careful. Recently he had stopped doctoring the feed-back forms, the tactic was arousing suspicion. Now he was looking for another, plausible excuse to get Jason fired. And he had to get him fired.

Jason was a threat to his position.

'This is what we are going to do,' Slipe said in his most patronising voice as he stared at the gormless red and yellow Ronald grinning on the pavement outside. 'I am going to give you a challenge to prove your worth. Succeed and you may see out the end of the season.'

He tapped his fingertips together as he set out an impossible task:

'You are to organise an excursion. Something new, different and financially rewarding for the company.' He knew that there were no new excursions possible on Symi, all possibilities for suitable trips for the over sixties had long been exhausted. Even so he decided to cover all his bases and make certain that it really was an impossible task, one that Jason could only fail. 'You must arrange it for Thursday, tomorrow, and sell it to all of your guests at your welcome meeting tonight.' And one last turn of the screw… 'I will come over to Symi on Friday to make sure you succeeded. If you are not capable of doing this…'

Slipe turned back just in time to see Jason take a sharp step away from the desk in shock. *Good that's panicked him,* he thought.

'Am I clear Jason?'

'Whatever,' Jason replied vaguely.

'I want something spectacular from you. And I don't mean another Taverna night or sunset barbeque. I want something so special that it sets the benchmark for all holiday companies on your island. I want Laskarina and Kosmar to be banging on my door to hire you because SARGO guests have got the best excursion ever on Symi. Do you understand me?'

'Got you babe… boss, got you.'

'And it better be good. This is your last chance saloon, Jason, last chance saloon.'

'Absolutely.' Jason tried hard not to snigger.

'I know that you think you should be in this chair and that it's not fair that I was promoted over you. But life is unfair, Jason, and those are the breaks.' Slipe thought he sounded quite reasonable, almost caring. He checked himself; that would never do. 'Now bugger off out of my sight before I change my mind and sack you now.'

Jason shrugged, hoisted his flight bag onto his shoulder and turned to leave.

'Remember.' Slipe stopped him. 'You only have today to organise it, so get thinking.'

'I got it.' Jason let the words out very slowly as the enormity of the task sank in. It couldn't happen; by Friday he would be unemployed, his career in tourism over. He could hear Slipe gloating already.

'Don't put a foot wrong.'

'No boss.'

But as Jason moved to the door he did put a foot wrong and caught his sandal on a corner of ragged carpet. The toe-strap broke and his sandal flew across the room. He stumbled slightly, swore and hopped around to retrieve it.

'And for god's sake get a new pair of shoes,' Slipe tutted again. 'Remember you are a SARGO rep and SARGO stands for quality, dignity and professionalism. Now piss off and collect your next load of old gits.'

As Jason left the office he stole a glance back at the desk and the nameplate he had altered. He grinned. Slipe's official title was now: *A Piles, A rear Manage.*

TWO

Jason hopped down the outside steps from the first floor office rummaging his flight bag for his deck shoes and wondering why he suddenly felt so cheerful. After all, he had just been set an impossible task that he could not achieve and he would sacked by Friday.

Slipe was a repulsive man. He had a way of making everyone feel inadequate, guests included. He was never subtle and he had no idea how to do his hair, it was always greasy and badly cut. His position of authority, the one that he had lied and cheated to get, had gone straight to his ugly, middle-aged head. None of the other reps liked him and all of them admitted to looking forward to the end of the season so that they could go and work in another resort and be rid of him.

All apart from Jason.

No matter how difficult Slipe made his life Jason did not want the season to end. As he changed his shoes he thought about how the end of summer would bring the end of his dream. He had a simple enough ambition and one that other people had achieved: to live permanently on a small Greek island. But Jason wasn't like those other people. He had no money saved up and no means to support himself once his summer contract ended.

Since first seeing Symi he had loved the island. Arriving by boat on that April morning and seeing the harbour open itself to welcome him, he felt like he had come home. He had found a place where he could belong. As he had settled into his job so he had settled into Symi's hypnotic pace of life. He had been quickly intoxicated by its charm and mystique and ever since then he had wanted to stay there forever.

Admittedly it was not the clubbing, party island that he had first had in mind when he decided that he was born to be a holiday rep. It was quite the opposite in fact and, after being on Symi for only a few days, he had been surprised to realise that he didn't want the hectic, hedonistic pace of life that somewhere like the Canary Islands would have provided. He realised that he wanted something completely different after all. He wanted Symi. It was small, underdeveloped by holiday island standards and quiet. Very, very quiet. There was little for a twenty three year old single guy to do after dark other than drink in a bar or visit one of the two night clubs, neither of which was bigger than a standard, suburban living room. There were no foam parties, bar crawls or sex games on the beach. There were few tourists of his own age and sexuality and no hoards of teenagers throwing up their free shots in the street. And he was grateful for that.

Originally he had applied to be a *Club 18-30* rep but with no joy; they said he was not ladish enough and far too well spoken. So he approached Panorama to become a *Go-Party in Faliraki rep*, again without success; they said he was too intelligent and should try applying to the gay companies. Taking that as a very backhanded complement he went for a job as a *Respect Gay Holidays* team member in Gran Canaria, but they wanted someone with language skills. Apparently they did not respect his ability to speak fluent French and German and passable Spanish and Greek. *Man-Around Holidays* said that he was too young, they needed men, and *Boyz-Around Travel* said that he was too old. *Kosmar*, 'fully staffed', *Laskarina,* 'not quite what we are looking for dear,' and *Olympic* didn't need anyone. *Go-Now* told him to do just that as soon as he arrived for the interview as they were only looking for female staff that season. *First Choice* had been his last choice and he their's apparently but at least they had had the courtesy to suggest the personnel department at SARGO.

SARGO had been his last hope and he went along to the interview as a matter of routine. By then he sensed his career ambition slipping away from him and started preparing himself for a lifetime in a customer-care office with some clearing bank. But a small miracle happened and SARGO snapped him up. Although the interview panel admitted to having had doubts about his application form, (they explained that there had been no need, under 'supporting statement' for him to submit seven sides of A4 on the relevance of Kylie Minogue lyrics to the over sixties) they were impressed by his youth, language skills and dashing good looks. Apparently Jason was just what the elderly traveller liked to see when holidaying in the Aegean islands.

Jason should have been happy but, as he boarded the plane to leave England, he found himself in two minds about his future. SARGO customers were not going to be the partying, young gay set that he had hoped to spend his summer with. *But*, he had told himself when he stepped off the plane at Rhodes airport, *at least I will be living abroad and getting a sun tan.*

As soon as he had seen Symi from the ferry all negative thoughts evaporated. Since then the island's magic had grown over him like a vine, a welcome, safe vine that twisted around his dream, enfolding him deeper in it. He had to find a way to stay.

And that meant he had to keep Slipe happy and arrange an impossible excursion for his new set of guests.

But first he had to find a taxi, and fast. Jason stood at the bottom of the concrete steps and looked at his watch.

Because Slipe had demanded to see him in the area office, his colleague Kate had escorted his departing guests to the airport for him. She had met them all from the Symi ferry with her customary greeting to Jason of 'yasou queer-boy' and bundled the old folk into the coach. Jason had said goodbye to his group of eight pensioners (combined age five hundred and fifty one years) before crossing the main road cautiously. Rhodes was always a culture shock even after only one week on Symi. It had traffic lights, pedestrian crossings that drivers could ignore and two lane roads where cars could get into fourth gear; Symi had one road and lads who drove too fast on their mopeds but, to get out of third, you had to drive up into the middle of the island, put your foot down quickly and then brake before you went over a precipice.

Find a taxi, Jason looked around.

Quiet and slow… just two of the things Jason loved about Symi. He had taken to long walks in the hills where he could stroll for hours singing along to musicals on his walkman as he picked herbs and scared the wild goats. He could scamper across the rocky escarpments dodging boulders and revelling in the fresh air and freedom. At times he behaved like Heidi on acid but that was o.k. There was hardly ever anyone around to see him running wild and free. And if he did meet someone by chance then it was bound to be someone he knew. Having been on the island for a few months he had already come to know many locals. It was that kind of place, friendly, intimate; like living in a quiet English village only with better weather.

'*A taxi? Job to do?*'

Better weather and beaches.

He loved to walk through the valley down to Pedi bay of an evening to have a swim in the clear, cool water; the hotter the day the more rewarding the water. Afterwards he would take a beer at one of the bars, chat to the locals to improve his Greek and then wander back up the road before heading into the village again.

'Pick up the guests! Slipe doesn't need much to fire you.'

The guests. They tended to congregate in his favourite village kafeneion, not far from Villa SARGO and would seek him out to disturb his time off, but he didn't mind. By that time of day he would be relaxed. He would have reminded himself of what his life was all about; taking his time, going slow, only knowing that it was time to eat because he felt hungry, only knowing it was time for bed because he felt tired. And then Slipe would ring on the damn mobile phone and ask how many guests had signed up for the midnight cruise. None. It was a crap excursion. The 'cruise' was a quick dash to a nearby island, 'midnight' was actually seven p.m. and the cost was ridiculous, the trip never sold. No wonder Slipe was putting pressure on Jason to come up with something new and exciting. Something better.

The thought dragged his mind back to his job and the new set of guests who would be arriving in twenty five minutes.

He waved vacantly at a passing taxi. The old man driving it waved back, smiled and drove on.

And then he remembered why he was in such a good mood. He had a special guest arriving today.

His gran.

Another taxi approached and this time Jason lent into the road and flagged it down with his SARGO clipboard.

Suddenly he felt sad. The change in emotions hit him as the car drew up and he slid gingerly onto the hot back seat.

'Aerothromio,' he said flatly to the guy behind the wheel. 'Airport.'

'Yeah, I do speak Greek, mate,' the Taxi driver replied curtly in a thick Australian accent.

As the taxi pulled back into the slow moving traffic Jason again forgot about the time and his rush. He stared out of the window at the nondescript concrete apartment blocks, dusty unmade pavements and tatty palm trees. He was suddenly a mix of emotions and he couldn't decide which one to settle on.

He was excited at seeing his gran, he had not seen her for twenty years, but he was sad because of the circumstances. His granddad had recently died; what he had told Slipe just now had been true, finally. And he was feeling guilty because he had used his granddad's illness as an excuse for bad performance a few times this season. But now the old man had actually died. After nearly sixty years of disability and pain, granddad Stan had finally 'slipped away'.

Slipped away. It was an odd expression for his grandmother to use in her letter. Jason couldn't imagine granddad Stan slipping anywhere. To slip one needed feet, and to have feet one needed legs. Granddad Stan had no legs. He'd lost them in the war somewhere, a very careless thing to do Jason used to think. On the rare occasions that his mother actually spoke about his grandparents she would tell Jason that, 'granddad Stan lost his legs in the war.'

She had first told Jason this strange news when he was three years old. It was one of his earliest memories. That day he had searched the house thoroughly before finally arriving at the tea table in tears.

'What's the matter with you?' his dad growled at him. He hated any sign of weakness in boys, particularly crying for no reason.

'I couldn't find them.' Jason sniffed.

'Find what?'

'Granddad's legs.'

'Betty!' his dad roared over his shoulder into the kitchen behind him. 'Your boy's barking.'

Jason was always 'Betty's boy' or 'mother's boy' to his father. He still called him these things but now he had added 'bum boy' and the more straightforward 'arse-bandit' to the list of pseudonyms for his only son.

'What's he saying?' Jason's mother called back, sticking her head around the door and mopping her brow with the back of an oven glove.

'He can't find Stan's legs.' Jason's father started to laugh. 'What have you been telling him?'

'Oh dear.' His mother also smiled and Jason felt stupid without knowing why. 'You will never find them Jason dear,' she said, trying to keep a straight face.

'I might if I look hard enough,' Jason said hopefully. 'He needs them.'

'Sit down and grow up, you pansy.' His father returned to the back pages of The Sun.

Jason remembered his mother coming to him and crouching down. Her apron was dusted with flour and pulled tight over her round tummy; she seemed to get fatter every day. Her hair was glowing gold with the sunlight that came through the window behind her.

'Granddad's legs aren't here,' she said kindly. 'He lost them far away.'

And then she told him where but it was a place with a strange name and Jason could never remember it.

'For god sake don't tell him about the eyes or he'll be digging up the garden.' Jason's father laughed again, confusing the boy even more.

'Eyes?' he asked, wiping his own.

'You'll find out one day,' his mother said and lifted him into his chair.

But his parents never did explain about the eyes. In fact they rarely spoke of granddad Stan or grandma Margaret after that and Jason never knew why. He only knew that it had something to do with his mother having a baby and his father going into a bad mood that seemed to last for years after. There was a lot about his family that his parents had never told him but now, with grandma Margaret making a special trip to see him in Greece, he hoped that he might find out.

In the back of the taxi Jason opened his flight bag and pulled out the letter that had arrived at the Sargo office that morning. Luckily the taxi driver was of the rare, silent breed and so Jason had peace and quiet in which to reread what his grandmother had written.

Dear Jason

I hope this letter reaches you in time.

It is with a mixture of three feelings that I write to you today: trepidation, sadness and intrigue.

Trepidation. We have not spoken to each other since you were a very small boy and I have no idea how you will take this communication. You are an adult now, you will be twenty three and I find it hard to imagine even what you look like. I picture you as tall, like your mother, strong of body like your father, intelligent and handsome of face like your grandfather.

Jason flicked his hair back from his brow and bit his lip. He wasn't tall like his mother, being only five feet seven against her gangling five feet eleven; he was reasonably fit because of his swimming and running through the hills pretending to be Julie Andrews but he wasn't built like a WWF wrestler like his father. But he did like to think of himself as intelligent, he was something of a linguist and a hoarder of knowledge both general and local. As for handsome? He considered himself as having the looks of the typical 'boy next door'; kind of public school meets youthful catalogue model, but without the posh accent or the polyester underwear. He hoped Grandma Margaret would not be disappointed when she met him. He read on:

And I know that you will be of your own mind and will have your own opinions about your grandmother, whom you have not seen in such a long time. And so my excitement at seeing you is tainted with just a little nervousness at what we both may find. Therefore it is with trepidation that I am coming to see you. I fear I rather took your mother by surprise when I telephoned her just five days ago to pass on my news (see below in a moment) and to discover your whereabouts. I did not tell her why I needed to see you, only that I wanted to and, after a certain amount of beating about the proverbial bush she told me who you worked for. I then spoke to a very pleasant lady and arranged a holiday at the last minute. I shall therefore be one of your guests, arriving on September 8th by an airline with the rather dubious name of Britainair. We shall meet at last!

*Now the **sadness**. A week ago your grandfather, Stanley, slipped away. You may have known that he had not been well for many, many years and his passing came as a release to him. I am left, of course, with a gaping hole in my life that, at my age, will never be filled again. You, on the other hand, did not know your grandfather but he knew you. I am also sad that we never had an opportunity to see you grow up. That is an issue I had out with your mother on occasion many years ago and one which was never resolved. Now, however, with your grandfather's passing, I too find myself somewhat released; from my previous life. I no longer need to spend my days tending to him and, although that is a strange and upsetting feeling, it is also gives me a new lease of life. Therefore this visit to you will be my first, and likely only, trip out* *of the country. I only wish I had been able to make it with your grandfather as he would have loved to have been on Symi again. And he will be. (All will be revealed later.)*

*And finally the **intrigue**. Your grandfather left a will. In it he mentioned only two beneficiaries, me and you. And through it he left only two things: a list of instructions for me and an heirloom for you. I will be bringing your bequest with me. Quite simply put: We both have duties to perform while I am on Symi. I will explain this in much more detail when we meet but in the meantime Stanley left one last cryptic set of instructions for us both. I quote them here:*

"Margaret and Jason: Tell no one of the contents of my will. When you get to Symi do not mention the name on the cigarette case to anyone on the island. The music will guide you. And, above all, trust each other."

There, that is all I have to say at the moment. I am assured by the nice lady at your Sutton branch that I will be well looked after by you and your company on my 'holiday', and I look forward — with the above three feelings excepted — to meeting my grandson again after all this time.

Margaret Rhea (nee De Lacy)

Surrey

'Airport,' the taxi driver grunted. 'Fifteen euro.'

Jason paid the man and insisted on a receipt. While he waited for the paperwork to be done and the under the breath curses to stop, he tucked the letter away and stepped out onto the baking tarmac. He looked around at the coach loads of departing and arriving tourists and checked his watch. His flight was not due for another ten minutes and it would take a further forty at least to get them through baggage reclaim and onto the coach. As long as the flight had not been delayed he would be able to get them all to the ferry in time.

Having snatched the receipt he headed into the terminal building to check in with Kiwi-Kate and make sure his departing guests had gone through into the departure lounge without too many problems.

Long queues of boiled lobster coloured people waited impatiently outside in the afternoon sun, their tempers already starting to fray. After a week or two of nothing but relaxation it took most tourists no time at all to fall back into their old routines. Dads with beer-bellies kicked suitcases ahead of them and grumbled at each other about the wait.

Someone moaned about how the 'Bubbles' (bubble and squeak, Greek) should be more organised. Jason resisted the temptation to point out that over fifteen thousand people a day passed through the airport at that time of year. Mothers broke off their chatting and cigarettes to holler at their children, ordering them to stand still and stop running off while teenagers slouched in small, noisy groups. For the lads their 'Faliraki shagathon 03' tee shirts were already out of date. For the girls the conversation was all about love and how Costas had promised he'd write, and how Michaelis the waiter was *definitely* leaving the family business in the mountain village and coming to live on the dole in Billericay.

As Jason pressed his way into the building, pushing burnt shoulders out of his way, he overheard snippets of conversation.

'Ten degrees in England, aint stopped raining for weeks.'

'I blame the seafood.'

'There'll be snow come October.'

'I was never off the toilet. Same as bloody Spain.'

'Coming back next year?'

'No, the place is full of foreigners.'

Jason sighed heavily as he prepared himself to become a smiling, bubbly yet responsible holiday rep and psyched himself up for another SARGO arrival and transfer.

Had he known what the next forty-eight hours had in store for him he may well have marched straight up to the Britainair check in desk and booked himself on the first plane to Gatwick, rain and all.

THREE

Flight BZ265 approaching Rhodes.
Meanwhile

'Well, it's no secret,' Margaret Rhea said knowingly to the overweight woman sitting next to her. 'The majority of air accidents happen during landing and take off. I remember seeing a documentary about it once on the BBC. So it must be true.'

'If you say so pet,' the large woman replied, tightening her already straining seatbelt.

'I remember also the news coverage of that tragedy in Tenerife, in the seventies I think. Maybe later, can't remember. Many deaths caused by fog and an impatient Dutch captain. Very sad.'

'Tragic.'

'Sad because I have so long admired the Dutch. They have produced some great artists for such a wet country. But they do have rather too progressive an attitude towards certain drugs for my liking. And do you know they actually tolerate homosexuality and allow what they call "gay marriages"? The thought quite makes one feel queer don't you think? The very idea of lesbianism leaves a nasty taste and as for two men...? I mean, it's diabolical. The BBC made a documentary about that particular subject once. Aunty has gone down hill since Reginald Bosenquet died.'

'Look pet...'

For the last four and a half hours the overweight lady had tried vainly to shut out the old woman's constant chatter, but to no avail. Since take off she had twittered on about some inanity or other and since passing over the first of the Dodecanese islands she had hardly drawn breath.

'Look pet, I don't mean to be rude...'

'I do so admire Rembrandt, though I have never seen his museum in Amsterdam. In fact this is the first time I have been outside of Great Britain.' Margaret rubbed her stocking feet on the footrest and pulled her crocheted shawl more tightly around her shoulders nervously. Through the small window she could see a coastline of white hotels and blue water rushing up from far below to meet them. The aeroplane banked the other way and the land disappeared suddenly from view. She noticed that her travelling companion was gripping the mutual armrest and her fingers had turned pale. *Uncooked sausages*, Margaret thought. *How unattractive.*

'If you don't mind love,' the other passenger half turned to her. 'I'd rather not think about plane crashes and the like right now. Landing's the only part of my jollies that gives me the willies.'

'I shouldn't worry,' Margaret continued once she had worked out what jollies and willies might be. 'I read in the Telegraph that, statistically speaking, you have more chance of being killed while having an accident in the home than while flying. And, as I have spent the last fifty odd years hardly leaving my home, I think I am quite a safe person to be sitting next to. I have never suffered an accident in the home. Oh, well once I did make custard using salt rather than sugar but that was hardly fatal. Most air disasters however are fatal.'

The other passenger was desperately trying to think of a way to shut the old woman up and was considering physical assault when the captain interrupted.

'Ladies and gentlemen…' The smooth, calming voice of an ex-public school prefect slipped seductively into the cabin through unseen speakers. 'Once again on behalf of Britainair I would like to apologise for our late arrival. We are on our final approach now, just lining up for what should be a smooth landing. You may be interested to know that the temperature on the ground is a comfortable thirty-seven degrees with a light southerly breeze. There has been a forecast of thundery showers across the Turkish coast, but they are unlikely to bother us here on Rhodes. Please ensure your seats are in the upright position and that your seatbelts are securely fastened. Thank you again for flying with Britainair and on behalf of myself and my crew may I wish you a pleasant onward journey.' A ping and the fasten seatbelts signs lit up. 'Cabin crew to landing stations. So, Geoff, are you up for golf or will you be too busy poking Sylvia… bugger!'

There followed the sound of a microphone being belatedly switched off and a clatter of coffeepots from a horrified Sylvia in the galley.

Margaret clutched at her shawl. 'Well really,' she muttered and raised her hand to the call button so that an appropriate complaint could be lodged. The aircraft bumped on a stray thermal and she decided to make the complaint at a later date, in writing. For now landing was more important; she had never landed before and did not want to miss a moment of the experience. 'I do hope Stanley is not too cold down there in the hold,' she said to herself but out loud.

Even though she knew that a stream of verbal diarrhoea would follow, the woman beside her could not help but ask, 'who's Stanley?'

'My husband dear.' Margaret smiled fondly and pointed a thin finger to her feet. 'They wouldn't let him up here with me on account of his... condition, even though I had all the papers signed and approved. I expect they know what they are doing, and I am sure he is better off down there in any case. Well, not in *any* case, in *my* case, if you see what I mean. I bought a new one especially for the trip. Louis Vuitton sac de voyage. Not a real one of course, not on my pension. But I was assured that the replicas are just as sturdy.'

'So let me get this right,' the other passenger knew she would regret this, 'your husband...'

'Stanley.'

'Stanley is in a case in the baggage hold?'

'I prefer to call it the luggage hold. Yes indeed he is,' Margaret said proudly and then, having checked that they were not being overheard whispered, 'he is the reason for my trip.'

'Really.'

'I would never have dreamt of a holiday, let alone on such a remote island as this, if it were not for Stanley.'

'Rhodes isn't that remote.' The large lady heaved a sigh as weighty as herself. She was travelling on to Symi. At least there she would be free of this nutcase.

'Not that island.' Margaret nodded her head towards the window where Rhodes was now even closer. 'This island.'

She held up a brochure open at 'Symi', and beside her a fatty heart sank.

'Are you with SARGO?' her companion asked, sausage fingers blanching further.

'Yes dear, are you?'

'Uh hu.'

'Delightful! Then we shall be travelling on together. Oh I *am* pleased.' Margaret offered a polite hand to shake. 'Margaret. I am on a mission.'

The other woman refused to let go of the armrest but nodded a reply. She heard a mechanical thud, the floor beneath her feet shuddered and her buttocks clenched like a car-crusher.

'Just the wheels dropping,' Margaret reassured her. 'I believe they call it the landing gear. Sometimes, though rarely, they can become stuck and the aircraft lands on only one set of wheels, one wing and several prayers I imagine. Now *that* kind of disaster is survivable as long as there is not too much fuel still held in the wing tanks. In ninety-three a 737 landed with only one set of wheels and with half its fuel still on board and a mere fifteen people burned to death. Quite remarkable when you think about it.'

'What kind of a mission?' The blanched passenger could feel her in-flight lunch about to make a reappearance and desperately tried to change the subject, even if it meant more inane chatter.

'Oh that. Well it's a bit secret, but as you're SARGO I can trust you. I am to find the place where Stanley lost his legs. And to find out more about… what was his name? I have it here.'

Margaret rummaged in her handbag and pulled out a tin of boiled sweets.

'Ah, no, that's not it,' she muttered and rummaged deeper. She pulled out a silver cigarette case and held it in the palm of her hand, running her thin fingers shakily over it.

'This was given to my husband during the war,' she said proudly. Her eyes became moist as she studied an engraving on the back of the case. 'By… that's the name there.' She suddenly snatched the case away from her travelling companion's gaze and hid it beneath her shawl. 'But I can't tell you what it is, I am not allowed. Anyway we have never been able to open it but Stanley seemed to think that it was of importance.

Such importance that he bequeathed it to my grandson and instructed me, through his will, to ensure that I took it to him personally. I am going to give it to the boy as soon as we land. And I should not have told you any of that either. Oh lord, this whole travel thing is just too unsettling. When I am unsettled I do chatter so. Would you like a boiled sweet for your ears? I saw a programme once about ears, apparently the drum can burst under pressure and a sherbet lemon can save you from deafness. But that was on ITV, so I would treat the information with caution. Better safe than sorry though.' She popped a travel sweet in her mouth and cheerfully offered the tin.

'No ta, pet. Me ears are fine.'

'Excuse me for asking, but are you from the north?'

'Bolton, originally, but I've lived all over.'

'How brave. I am from Surrey. I didn't introduce myself fully. Margaret Reah, pronounced *Rear* unfortunately. I am a Rotarian.'

'The name's Harriet. I'm a lesbian.'

To Harriet's relief Margaret was strangely quiet for the rest of the landing.

FOUR
Rhodes Airport – Coach park
5.00 pm

'Right,' Kiwi-Kate announced firmly, snapping shut her file with equal force. 'That's fifty of mine to dump at the Plaza and only six going over to Symi with you. Think you can manage, queer boy?'

'Have I ever let the team down babe?' Jason looked at his colleague and stuck out his tongue.

'Oh, now let me think...'

'Bog off.' Jason pushed her playfully and Kate span away from him laughing.

'Just make sure you get my guests to their hotel before you get on your boat. You've got an hour, even you can mange that.'

Jason boarded his coach and wandered to the back counting the number of blue rinses and bald patches. There were fifty five clients, with a combined age of about three thousand years and still one guest was missing. He made his way to the front again where the driver, Dinos, was checking his watch.

'We miss the boat.' Dinos grinned through a face full of beard. 'Then you stay in Rhodos the night and we go out for jig-jig.'

'I'm not jig-jigging with you Dino, I've told you, you're too old for me.' Jason didn't look at him as he climbed down onto the tarmac again.

'Not with me malaka.' Dinos crossed himself. 'With pretty ladies.'

Jason ignored him and scanned the car park. Lost somewhere in the airport complex was guest number fifty-six, his grandma. He noted the time again. The ferry for Symi left promptly at six and would not wait. It was now five past five. With the drop off he had agreed to do for Kate in return for her favour that morning, the journey would take forty-five minutes. He wouldn't put it past Slipe to have kidnapped a guest in order to make him miss the boat, another nail in his career coffin. He dialled Kate's number on his mobile.

'What now queer boy?' The Kiwi greeted him cheerfully from somewhere inside the arrivals hall. 'What's up?'

'Have you got one of mine?' Jason asked, heading back towards the terminal building.

'No. Who have you lost?'

'A Reah from the Gatwick flight.'

'It's all you think about,' Kate laughed back down the line at him. 'What is it with you poofs and rears? Well, all mine checked through and there's no rears here wandering around looking lost.'

'Oh bona!'

'What?'

'Got her. Bye.'

Jason snapped off his phone and quickened his pace towards an old lady sitting on a concrete bollard. She was looking down into an open travel bag and at first Jason thought she was being sick.

'Mrs. Reah?' he called, waving his clipboard to attract her attention. 'Grandma?'

The old woman looked up suddenly and then down again. She appeared to be talking to the contents of her luggage as Jason trotted up in front of her. *Yup*, he thought, *taking to her Louis Vuitton. She's with SARGO.*

'Grandma Margaret?'

'Grandmother,' the old lady corrected him and looked up.

Margaret closed her case, locked it and stood up.

'Grandma?' Jason said again, hardly believing that he was finally meeting his elderly relative.

'*Grandmother.*'

Jason looked at her closely for the first time in twenty years and saw bits of himself looking back. He could tell that he had inherited his grandmother's eyes, blue and sparkling.

'You look just like your photograph,' Margaret said pinching his cheek and pulling him down to her. 'Kiss your grandmother like a good boy.'

Jason felt her powdery cheek touch his as the old lady kissed the air beside him. He noticed that he had inherited her jaw too; strong and in need of a shave.

'Mind you,' Margaret said cheerfully, 'in the only photograph of you that I have you are eighteen months old and naked. But still you haven't changed.'

'I was sorry to hear about granddad.' Jason looked at his watch again as he straightened up. Whatever he felt about this reunion would have to wait until his guests were securely on the ferry.

'Grandfather.' Margaret tutted. 'We have so much to do...'

'Later. We are in a bit of a hurry just now.'

He grabbed her imitation Louis Vuitton luggage and started dragging it towards the coach. It was heavier than he had expected and he wondered what on earth she had brought with her for a seven night stay. The kitchen sink, it felt like.

'Slow down dear. And do be careful with that,' Margaret said as she followed him. 'Your grandfather is inside.'

'Sorry love, but we'll miss the boat.'

'Love?' Margaret was shocked.

'Grandfather!' Jason even more so.

He dropped the imitation Vuitton as if it had turned red hot in his hand. Margaret overtook him.

'Come along dear, there is much to do.' She winked at him as she hurried past.

By the time Jason reached the coach he was hot, out of breath and praying that he had misheard. His grandmother had taken up residence in the front seat and Dinos was revving the engine. Jason tried to fit the bag into the overfilled luggage hold. He checked that his grandmother could not see him, said 'sorry granddad,' and gave the case a hefty shove with his foot wedging it in under a pile of Samsonite. He slammed the hold shut and came around to the door.

'O.k. Dino, we can go. And step on it.'

'Is Grandfather Stanley quite safe?' Margaret placed a hand on Jason's arm as he boarded, she looked concerned.

'He's just dandy love,' Jason replied, turning to adjust his highlighted hair in the wing mirror and check that his tie was just so.

'Thank you, he's not travelled for such a long time.' The old lady sat back in her seat and drew her handbag in close. 'When can we talk?'

'Later. On the boat.'

Dinos took the microphone, clicked it on and announced: 'good afternoon loidies and men. I am your driver Dino and I get you to the harbour quick. Normal day is fifty minutes. I do it for you today in thirty. Please no smoking,' he lit another cigarette, 'and no spitting. You do good for me and I do good for you and you give me big tip. Ha ha Tony Blair.'

Jason grabbed the microphone from him. 'Just drive,' he ordered and was relieved to hear the door swing shut with a hiss and a clunk.

He pulled down his centre aisle front seat, flipped open his clipboard and ticked off the last name on his list. All he had to do now was drop off Kate's guests and he'd be heading for the ferry and back home to Symi.

As he sat he glanced over his shoulder to his grandmother. She was looking out of the window, her handbag clutched on her lap and her eyes wide. She seemed to be taking everything in while, at the same time, staring into space. Jason wondered why his mother had not contacted him to mention the visit and his mind flashed briefly on old family history.

His grandparents had been at the house on the day his mother returned from hospital. Jason remembered the day, it was a warm one and he was at the front of the house on a large lawn playing with two Action Men while he waited for his parents to come back. Granddad Stan was sitting in his wheelchair behind him on the porch, sleeping. Grandma Margaret was inside cleaning the house. The sound of the vacuum cleaner was droning on in the background. Jason had been looking forward to the day because it was the first time he was going to see his new brother or sister. His father had explained that Jason's mother would be going away for a short while because she was fat and, when she returned, there would be a new baby in the house. This was that day.

He remembered seeing a taxi pulling up and his father helping his mother from the back seat. She was crying, her face was red and her nose was running. His father took out a small suitcase and Jason worried in case the baby ran out of air. It had to be in the suitcase because the taxi pulled away and there was no sign of a new brother or sister. His parents walked straight past him and into the house, ignoring his pleas to see the baby. Inside the house the vacuum cleaner stopped droning.

'Are they back?'

His granddad had woken up but he hadn't moved. He never moved much and, because of that and because his eyes were always hidden behind dark glasses you could never really be sure if he was asleep or awake.

Jason didn't have a chance to reply. A low, frightening wail started inside the house and he froze in terror. The sound got louder and Jason started to cry. Something was terribly wrong.

Within minutes of his parents marching into the house his grandma came running out hoisting her handbag onto her shoulder. She kicked the bottom of granddad's wheel chair, releasing the break and causing the old man to protest. Without even saying goodbye to Jason she bumped granddad Stan down from the porch and raced him through the front gate. Her face was screwed up tight and she too looked like she was crying.

That had been the last time Jason had seen his grandmother.

She looked different now; older, obviously, and much smaller. She was not frail though and she had a determined look about her and, he suspected, a strong will.

Jason turned back to his clipboard and his duties. The coach pulled out of the airport and turned left towards Rhodes Town. He set his mind back to his transfer and prepared to give his welcome speech.

He had made it so many times during the season that he didn't have to think about it any more. He simply opened his mouth and the words came out. This usually allowed him time to think of other more interesting things, like Britney Spears and Greek men, but today his mind was full of his grandmother's visit, her strange letter and the promised 'heirloom'. *Let's hope it's valuable*, he thought, *then maybe I can sell it and stay on the island for the winter.*

He tapped the microphone to ensure it was working properly.

'Well, good afternoon ladies and gentlemen, or as we say here in Greece, Kalispera!' A silence followed. 'Kalispera!' he repeated pushing himself into smiley SARGO mode.

There were a few weak attempts at a response from behind him. He stood up and faced his audience.

'Bravo. That's better. So: my name is Jason and I will be one of your SARGO reps during your holiday in the lovely land that is Greece. SARGO, as you should all know by now, stands for Sensational and Relaxing Getaways Overseas. I am the sensational part…'

No one laughed.

'And you are here to get away from it all and relax. Are we all ready to relax?'

Silence.

This was not a good audience. Jason continued cautiously. His grandmother was looking at him from beneath his left elbow and he felt pressurised to perform well for her.

'Shortly we will be dropping some of you off at the Plaza hotel where your resort rep, Kate, will be meeting you later. For the rest of you, those who are coming with me to Symi, we will be catching the six o'clock ferry from the harbour.' His inner mind butted in, *that is if Dino doesn't kill us all first.*

The coach rounded a corner and Jason was sure he felt two wheels lift from the ground. He grabbed the driver's seat beside him and tried to appear calm. 'Now then, if I can just see a show of hands for my group? Hands up who is going to be having a riot on Symi with me?'

His Grandmother waved proudly at him and he counted another four hands dotted around the coach. *Only five? Oh bugger, who's missing?*

'I was supposed to have six,' he muttered to himself and the microphone picked it up.

'You have pet,' a husky, northern accent piped up from further down the coach. 'There's another one behind Pavarotti here.'

Jason looked up to see who had spoken. A large woman in a gaudy shirt was signalling to him and pointing to an equally fat man across the aisle.

'You calling me fat?' The fat man tried to turn to the woman who had spoken but was too firmly wedged into his seat to move. 'That's bloody pot and kettle that is.'

Jason saw a wiry arm pop out from behind 'Pavarotti'. The arm was covered in yellow plastic and followed by a small face. A man wearing a cagoule and sunglasses peered out into the aisle like a surfacing mole and waved timidly.

'Ah ha!' said Jason. 'You must be Mister Simpson.' He only had one male guest this week, this must be him. 'Glad we found you,' he added, ticking his clipboard and returning to his speech. 'When we arrive at Symi we will be taken to our villa by complementary transport and we will have our welcome meeting this evening before dinner.'

During which I will sell you an excursion I have not yet invented…

'Excuse me.'

Oh hell, they've started already.

'Yes grand…'

It was his grandma who had spoken. Was she to be treated as a guest or as family? He decided that she was a guest. After all, he knew as little about her as he did about the other people on the coach.

'Yes love?'

Margaret frowned as she lowered her hand. She cleared her throat and lent forward. 'It's *Grandmother*. If a person has a title you should always address them as such. Now then, may we stop en route for the little girl's room?'

'We will be at the harbour soon.' Jason tried to smile. 'Thanks to the delayed flight there is no time for stopping.'

'Oh dear.' Margaret sat back and looked worried. 'We don't really need a *harbour*, just something with a pan, lid and flush. We would prefer somewhere more private.'

'Toilets,' Jason announced cheerfully to the others over the airwaves. 'The question was about toilets…'

'And we need one very soon,' Margaret insisted.

Jason looked down at the empty seat beside her. '*We?*'

Margaret shifted uncomfortably. 'The detail is immaterial, the necessity however is important.'

'As we are on the subject of toilets...' Jason's routine had been thrown but all he needed to do was swap a few paragraphs around and he would be back on track with his SARGO script. 'I should say a few words about Greek plumbing.'

'The best in the world.' Dinos laughed, swerving the coach violently onto a roundabout.

'The plumbing in Greece is what is known as "small bore",' Jason went on.

His confidence was slightly undermined when he heard someone whisper, 'how appropriate,' loudly enough to be heard by the front five rows.

'Which means that the pipes are very narrow.' *Like the minds of some of these guests.* 'And this in turn means that nothing must be put in the toilet bowl unless it's been... man made.' He emphasised the last two words to ensure that there was no doubt about what he meant.

'In what sense man-made?' A woman in a straw hat raised a hand and lent into the aisle.

This lot are definitely going to be trouble, he thought. *Everyone knows about Greek toilets.*

'I mean that nothing goes into the bowl unless you've... well unless it's been made by man,' he tried to clarify. He didn't like this part of the speech at the best of times but usually got away without having to go into details.

'So plastics are acceptable then?' the straw hat woman queried, taking out a notebook and pencil.

'Plastics? Not that kind of man-made no...'

'Well make up your mind,' someone grumbled and a ripple of dissent could be felt spreading around the coach.

'Hon?' An American accent pierced the air from behind a pair of huge sunglasses and heavy make up. The thin faced woman clicked her fingers over her head. 'I'm confused already. What constitutes man-made?'

Shit, thought Jason, but before he could open his mouth straw hat woman had chipped in again.

'If you don't consider plastic to be man-made I would like to know exactly what you do mean.' She was taking notes.

'Bakelite is man-made,' the timid mole man pointed out, gaining confidence. 'But why would you want to flush that away?'

'Do we *have* to put these things in the toilet? It seems rather strange,' straw hat asked the people around her.

'I don't think he knows what he's talking about,' big sunglasses whispered to her companion. She spoke with such perfect clarity that her voice sliced through the muttering which had started in the middle rows.

'Give the lad a chance,' the rough voice from up north boomed and the bus fell as quiet as if they had just sensed the far off rumble of an earthquake.

'What I mean,' Jason said when he thought he had control again. 'Is that nothing goes into the toilet unless you have produced it yourself.'

'I say Cassie,' the companion to big-round-sunglasses also spoke with projection and clarity, 'just like your last show.'

'Bitch,' the sunglasses replied.

'O.k.' Jason thought it was time to move on. 'So if we are clear about that, I will now tell you about…'

'Not yet!' Straw hat woman raised her hand and waved her pencil in the air. 'This is very confusing. What must we *not* put into the toilet?'

Jason was getting bored with this. His inner mind whispered to him like a tempting devil. *Tell her exactly what you mean babe, that'll shut her up.* 'What I mean exactly,' he said slowly and deliberately, 'is that you must not put anything into the bowl except natural waste. Number twos for example. Things like your used toilet tissue, sanitary towels and condoms must go into the little bins provided.'

All muttering stopped and a deathly hush befell the coach.

'Condoms?' Someone whispered the word as if it was blasphemy.

Without warning Dinos slammed to a halt at some traffic lights, jolting the passengers suddenly forward.

'Do you mean to say,' straw hat went on, oblivious to the false teeth that skidded past her along the aisle, 'that the toilet paper in the bins has been used?'

'Jackpot! Free glass of Retsina for the lady in the straw hat.' Jason tried to repair the fractured atmosphere as he regained his balance and caught the teeth beneath a foot.

'Oh dear.' Straw hat woman had turned pale. 'I thought it was a strange place to keep it.'

'I read about that in a Gerald Durrell,' mole man lent over to her and said helpfully. 'So I brought some quilted Andrex.' He passed her a roll. 'Now that's suitable for the lavatory surely?' he enquired of his rep.

Jason shook his head. 'No.'

'Only poo and pee-pee in the pan pet,' the big northern woman clarified for everyone once and for all. 'Now let the lad finish.'

'Thank you,' Jason tried to smile at her but her helpfulness was only acting to further undermine his authority. 'We will shortly be stopping at the Plaza…' *You've done that bit.* 'For those of you….'

'Can I smoke?' Northern woman interrupted him.

'Not just yet…'

'I say?' Margaret had raised her hand a while ago and now lent forward to tug at the hem of Jason's shorts. 'All this dreadful talk of the W.C. only serves to remind me that we need to pay a visit.'

'We will be at the boat in a few minutes.'

'Does the boat have a toilet?' Someone asked.

What is this obsession with toilets?

'And does the rule, vis-à-vis the quilted Andrex apply on the boat?' straw hat asked, licking the lead in her pencil.

'I must insist,' Margaret said apologetically and Jason could see that she was in trouble.

'If you are very quick you can pop into the Plaza when we drop the other passengers off.' Jason gave in. He was, after all, there to help.

'Are they clean?' Margaret whispered back conspiratorially.

'They have individual hand towels.' Jason winked and this seemed to satisfy her. *Best shut up now and leave the rest of the speech,* his little voice told him. 'Good idea,' he answered it aloud. 'So, if there are no more questions about toilets…'

Several hands shot into the air and he ignored them all.

'Good. So on behalf of SARGO holidays may I thank you for choosing to travel with us and wish you a happy stay. Now, just shit back and enjoy the rest of the journey.' *You said shit back. I know, but I think I got away with it.*

Margaret's eyes widened and not just because of her urgent need for a W.C.

Her grandson, on first inspection, seemed hardly up to the task that Stanley had set them both.

She suddenly feared for her mission.

FIVE
Symi
1890

The century was drawing to a close and the days were changing. Christos Panandreas had become moody and sullen, his sponge business, though thriving, was causing him great concern. Divers continued to use the new diving suit despite a recent protest by the women of the island, a protest which had taken their grievances as far as the Ottoman Sultan. The Sultan, who until recently had allowed the island unmolested independence, was now starting to tighten the screw. The suit, he said, must be banned. Christos' divers were currently still using it; its use made him more money. But its use made widows of the island women and even from his lofty terrace up at the villa he could feel their hatred of him.

All this was having an effect on his health. He was suddenly older now, his hair had started to turn grey and his face had begun to crease, showing permanent heavy lines that once only appeared when he was angry. His travels had lessened. He visited his Paris offices only once a year now and London even less. He had not returned to Venice in over eighteen months, his secretary there had been ordered back to Symi to discuss the business. Christos seemed to have lost all enthusiasm for the empire he had built. Something had changed.

Dimitris stood in the salon with a suitcase in his hand and looked at the family portrait. In it his father was regal, assured and stood as proud and solid as the new buildings in the harbour behind him. In the painting his mother was as radiant as the sunlight that lit the sea. Her eyes were as dazzling as the clothes she wore and her face as beautiful as the composition itself. But even she had recently changed. She used to move through the villa like a dream, directing the household, brushing her fine hands over the furniture and making the place sparkle as she glided by. Now she haunted the rooms, walking slowly, sighing as she picked her flowers as if every move was made only out of tradition. She seemed not to enjoy anything anymore. She no longer sat beside Dimitris at the harpsichord when he practiced. Something was wrong.

Looking back at him from the family portrait was a small boy. A ten year old anticipating his eleventh name day, a cosseted, cared for boy who stood proudly beside his parents preparing himself to carry on the Panandreas family, innocently anticipating the responsibility to come. In his hand he held a piece of music manuscript paper, holding it towards the viewer to show what he had achieved.

He had achieved nothing. The paper was blank.

Dimitris heard slow heavy footsteps approach from behind and smelled the faint scent of cigar smoke. He felt a tired hand on his shoulder.

'Are you ready?' his father asked.

'Almost,' Dimitris replied and put down his suitcase.

'Your trunk has been taken down to the steamer. Shall I have this taken?'

'I will carry it papa.'

Dimitris looked deeper into the painting. He saw the sponge fleet tied up along the quayside, he saw the workers cleaning the sponges in the sea and he saw his island portrayed as prosperous and thriving. It still was. The fleets still sailed after Easter and returned in the autumn, trade was still good in Europe, people still had livelihoods. But even the island seemed changed now.

Or was it? Maybe it was he who had changed. Maybe this is what happened when you reached eighteen and left your island; you felt different. You noticed things that had always been there, your parents, how they had aged. Maybe you started to see yourself as you would be one day and you started to realise that your youth had gone and that you would never know it again.

'What's wrong?' Christos asked. 'You are troubled.'

'I am leaving home. I imagine I am nervous.'

'You have a right to be. The future of our family lies with you.'

His father always spoke to the point. Dimitris expected nothing else.

'And is the future of our family to be found in Paris?' he asked.

'Its future is to be found in you. Wherever you take it.'

'I should be going to London with you,' Dimitris said. 'I should be learning the business and preparing to take over from you when you die.' He could be just as blunt as his father.

'When I die?' Christos laughed and Dimitris felt his shoulder squeezed. His father's grip could still be strong. He would be around for a while yet. 'You will have a long wait boy. And while you are waiting you will follow your heart. Follow your talent. That is what our family does best. I had a talent for trade, your mother for loyalty. Yours is for music.'

'But music will not bring us prosperity,' Dimitris said glancing up and over his shoulder to his father.

Christos too was staring at the family in the portrait. He appeared to be studying it as if trying to work out who these people were, his brow wrinkled as he thought. Then he smiled and shot a sideways glance down to his teenage son.

'Music will make your fortune,' he said and let go of Dimitris' shoulder. 'You should look at what is behind that painting.'

'At what is behind it?'

'One day I will explain.'

Dimitris had a question and he had wanted to ask it for a long time now. His boat was due to sail within the hour and, if he didn't ask the question now, he may not get another chance. Something told him that when he returned to his island it would have altered completely. He was to be away for three years, anything could happen in that time.

'Father?'

Christos was over at the table now, sorting through papers.

'Yes son?' he replied distractedly.

Dimitris could sense that he was now thinking of something other than the family portrait. Perhaps he was trying to take his mind off the fact that his only child was leaving home.

'Something about this portrait has always troubled me,' Dimitris said turning back to look at it again.

'Don't tell me. You look fat?' Christos was hiding whatever he was feeling; Dimitris could hear him smiling as he spoke. 'Your mother always complains that Masarakis painted her to look fatter than she is. Than she was. Masarakis, as we all know, likes his women big.'

Dimitris laughed a little too. It was true what his father was saying about the old letch Masarakis. Now well into his sixties he was still chasing the divers' wives. His sport lasted all summer until the bells rang to announce the return of the diving fleets. Then, suddenly, the old artist would retreat to his shack at Marathunda for the winter, locking himself away at the other end of the island to work, as he put it. Everyone knew he was hiding from the husbands and taking regular walks over to the monastery of Panormitis to pray that none of his plump conquests had fallen pregnant.

'What's wrong with the painting?' Christos asked, still searching his desk for something.

'It's my music,' Dimitris said, pointing to the blank paper in the boy's hand. 'Or rather the lack of it.'

'What do you mean?'

'Why is the manuscript paper blank?'

'Ah ha!'

Dimitris heard his father locate whatever he was looking for and felt him come to stand behind him again.

'You don't remember?' Christos asked, but Dimitris could not.

He remembered when Masarakis had come to start the painting, the same day as the strange package had arrived from Venice. The artist had arranged the three of them in a group, taking particular care and far too long to manually position Dimitris' mother. He had then suggested that they each hold something dear to them, something that defined them. He remembered what they had each chosen and the evidence was there staring back at him. His father had said that he would be shown holding his most treasured possession, his wife. His mother had blushed and said the same thing, she held her son. Dimitris had asked to hold his harpsichord but it was too cumbersome to be dragged onto the terrace and besides, as his father had pointed out, the sun would do it no favours. The boy had settled for a piece of music, a piano sonata by Mozart. He reminded his father of this now and asked again why the manuscript paper was blank.

'Because,' Christos replied, 'you ordered it to be painted that way.'

'I did?' Dimitris had no recollection of that at all. He sensed that his father was lying for some reason. 'I don't recall...'

'It was a long, boring afternoon for you,' Christos said. 'You were desperate to get away to our church to prepare for your name day. You don't remember because you had other things on your mind.'

As did you. Dimitris thought.

He remembered his father's eyes straying to the mysterious metal box. The artist Masarakis had to keep reminding him, politely at first but later with more annoyance, to keep his head still. At one point Christos had broken his pose and gone to whisper in the artist's ear. Masarakis had looked at Dimitris for a long time, and had then rearranged the sonata in his hand to show the page as flat, not rolled as it had been. If anyone had changed the painting it had been Christos.

'It was Mozart I was holding,' Dimitris said, 'not a blank sheet.'

'At first.' His father's voice suggested hat he was tiring of this conversation. 'But then you said to paint it blank as one day you would write some fine music on it. You said it was to represent your achievements yet to come.'

'I did?' *I did not.*

'And what will those achievements be I wonder? Here, I have something for you.'

Dimitris felt himself being turned around. His eyes and his memory left the painting as he faced his father.

'Two things actually,' Christos said. He held up a letter. 'Here is a letter of introduction to a friend of mine in Paris. His name is Charles-Marie Widor, he is organist at the church of Saint Sulpice. You will make it your first duty, after registration at the Conservatoire, to seek him out and introduce yourself. He will be expecting you. You are to give him best regards from the Panandreas family of Symi and this letter. Understood?'

'Monsieur Widor?' Dimitris' heart skipped a beat. He knew of the composer but had no idea that his father knew the great man. 'I am to meet him?'

'You may well be studying under him,' Christos smiled. 'I hear that old man Franck is unwell and that Charles is tipped to take over as professor of organ at your Conservatoire. Be polite,' he emphasised.

'Thank you father, yes of course I will be polite.'

Maria Panandreas stepped in to the room, her long skirt settling a few seconds after she did. She coughed slightly.

'The steamer is preparing to leave,' she said.

'It will wait,' Christos replied without looking.

'Indeed. I will remind them who owns it,' Maria said with a placid nod and then she was gone.

'The other thing,' Christos went on, his eyes still fixed on his son, 'is something for you to take with you and to keep. A going away present from me.'

He handed over a small, silver box and Dimitris took it with a quizzical look.

'But I don't smoke father,' he said. 'I mean, thank you very much it is beautiful, but I don't smoke.'

'You don't need to smoke to own a case for cigarettes.' Christos sounded slightly affronted but kept his manner benevolent. 'You could keep notes in it, or your pencils. I don't know. I had it made especially for you in London. Here, your name is on the back.'

Dimitris turned the case over in his palm and saw his name engraved in italic script. *Dimitris Panandreas, 1890.* The precious metal of the case felt cool in his hand and the box was smooth. Its corners were rounded and there were no protrusions or contours apart from his engraved name and two tiny hinges on one edge.

'Open it,' his father said, his face breaking into a smile.

Dimitris traced the side of the case opposite to the hinges expecting to find a clasp or switch. There was nothing but a barely perceptible join between lid and case. He tried to insert a fingernail into it but even this was too wide. There was no way to prise the box apart. He looked at his father and feigned annoyance.

'It's a puzzle box,' he said. 'Impossible. I can't open it.'

His father tapped him on the head playfully. 'If you don't smoke you don't need to open it.' He laughed and took the cigarette case back. 'Here, let me show you.'

As soon as Dimitris saw how the box opened he was in awe of its simplicity. He would never have thought of doing that.

SIX

The Plaza Hotel, ladies room

5.35 pm

Margaret completed her toilet, washed her hands and was pleased to see that individual towels were indeed supplied. She heard a flush and quickly turned to leave, not wanting to get involved in an in-powder room discussion. Too late, Harriet emerged from a cubicle adjusting her shorts.

'Hey up Mags,' she bellowed cheerfully. 'Feel better for that?'

'It's Margaret.'

'So what do you think to our young Jason then? Seems a bit camp.' Harriet looked at herself in a mirror before diving into her back pack and rummaging around. 'Had a rep on Lesbos once, looked like him, all hair-do and no sense. Bit of a mummy's boy I reckon.'

Margaret did not feel comfortable having a conversation in a toilet. From what she had seen on television it was the kind of thing that only teenage girls and rough women from Liverpool did at discotheques.

'Actually he is the grandson that I told you about on the aeroplane.'

This seemed to floor the big woman. But only briefly.

'Fine young lad he is too and no mistake. This is your first time in Greece you said?'

'Yes, my first time abroad actually.' Margaret had her hand on the door handle. It felt uncomfortably wet.

'You'll love it, pet.'

'Excuse me?' a voice called out from behind a cubicle door. It sounded like the woman in the straw hat. 'Can anyone tell me what this sign means?'

'Go ahead,' Harriet called back, throwing her lipstick back into her bag and adjusting her bosom with her forearms.

'Well there's a rather dainty hand holding a piece of material. I think it's Gingham but I couldn't swear to it, and beneath there appears to be a frowning toilet seat. Any ideas?'

'No paper in the toilet, pet. Were you not listening on the coach?'

'It's all so confusing,' the lady in the cubicle muttered.

Harriet raised her eyes to Margaret as she turned to the door. 'Best not keep young Jason waiting,' she said. 'Don't want him to split an end.'

Margaret had no idea what she was talking about but held the door open for her out of politeness.

Outside at the coach Jason stood with one foot on a step and one on the pavement. His clipboard was pressed tightly to his chest and he was curling his fringe nervously with a finger. The late afternoon heat had brought on an uncomfortable sweat and his deodorant had started to lose its strength. His nervousness did not help the situation. He had less than fifteen minutes to unload his guests onto the ferry and now he was three people short, grandma included.

Dinos slammed shut the door to the luggage hatch and climbed back into his seat. 'Ela,' he called to Jason and pointed to the hotel doors. 'Or as you say, *hey up babe*. Ha ha. Poustis.'

'Thank god,' said Jason as two of his party emerged from the hotel. He ignored Dinos' insult and called, 'quickly ladies, we're causing a jam. Any sign of Mrs. Shaw?' He peered out hopefully as the women boarded. Behind the coach the traffic was backing up and car horns were starting to blare.

'Think she's almost done pet,' Harriet said as she heaved herself into the coach. 'She was at the wiping stage when we left her.'

'Oh dear.' Margaret blanched at the remark as she took up her seat again.

'Everything alright now gran… grandmother?' Jason asked as she arranged her handbag on her lap.

'Quite satisfactory thank you,' Margaret replied with a smile.

Jason checked his watch again before noticing mole-man's raised hand. 'Yes, Mister Simpson?'

'Do I have time to fetch some chips?'

''fraid not.'

'Not even a small portion?'

'You can get a snack on the boat.' Jason bent down to scrutinise the hotel doors.

In their seats the lady with the huge sunglasses and her companion were looking across the street to a fast food outlet.

'Now tell me if I am wrong,' the companion was saying, 'but when we did that Greek thing at the National with Sir Peter there was no mention of hamburgers.'

'Polly, it was Antigone. I guess Sophocles never heard of fast food.'

'Well it's not what I expected from Greece, "mega-burgers" and... what does that say? "A long, slow, comfortable screw against the Acropolis?"'

'I had one of those once,' sunglasses mused.

'And how was it?'

'Quick and uncomfortable.'

Polly laughed charitably. 'I'll write that one down. Seriously though Cassie, I thought there would be much more culture.'

'If you looked in the kitchen you'll probably find plenty of cultures. Boom, boom!' Cassie laughed loudly at her own play on words but Polly didn't consider this attempt at a gag worthy even of a smile.

'You will have to do better than that,' she said, 'if we're to get our show written in this heat.'

'Hey!' Cassie turned to her companion and peered over the top of her glasses accusingly. 'It was you suggested we took the trip, not me.'

'To be precise it was Barry who suggested it,' the companion replied. 'I'd much rather have stayed and worked in Brighton.'

'O.k. So it was your agent who insisted, but it certainly wasn't me. Anyhow, we're here now so we should make the most of it. We need characters.' Cassie put on a plastic sun visor and turned to look at the other passengers.

'What do you make of that one Polly?' She nudged her friend and indicated Harriet who was squeezing past.

'A Sappho reader I dare say,' Polly whispered back with a wink. 'Could do with losing a few stone.'

'She'd have to chop off a leg. And the fussy old bird in the front stalls?' The sunglasses were tilted towards Margaret who was riffling through her bag.

'Could be an interesting subject. Small, intent, slightly dotty.'

'That'll be your part then. And our rep?'

'Reminds me of a hoofer.' Polly's eyebrow rose as she studied him. He was frantically waving straw hat woman on board with his clipboard while sniffing his armpit.

'You'll have to elucidate hon,' Cassie replied, fanning herself now with a guidebook. 'Sometimes I have no idea what script you are reading from.'

'Well.' Polly sat up a little in her seat. The combination of heat, nylon seat covers and silk culottes was dampening her behind. She shuffled to find a drier spot before explaining her impression. 'You remember how it was when you actually *worked* in the theatre rather than just reminisced about doing so? No, probably not... Oh lord.'

Polly was momentarily distracted from her explanation. At the front of the coach straw hat woman had stopped just long enough to let everyone see that she was back. She adjusted the tilt of her hat for the umpteenth time and made slow, deliberate progress to her seat as if the aisle was a catwalk. She passed Cassie and Polly and nodded to them graciously.

'Say hon,' Cassie called after her in her brash, Californian accent. 'You're tucked in at the derrière.'

Mrs. Shaw hurried to her seat pulling her skirt free from her underwear.

'Sensible knickers, now that's what I like to see,' Polly said, loudly enough to make everyone else react.

'Say Pol,' Cassie said dryly. 'You nearly got a laugh.'

'I was elucidating.' Polly narrowed her eyes at her friend and went on with her explanation. 'Our rep the hoofer. Imagine this: It's 42nd Street. The show's producer advertises for twelve dancers and three singers. Five hundred hopeful young hoofers turn up for the auditions, me included, and an equal number of ambitious singers, yourself included, queue around the block. After endless recalls, routines, interviews and auditions we get a part in the chorus…'

'I was *never* in the chorus,' Cassie said pointedly.

'Rubbish,' Polly cut in immediately. 'We met in the chorus.'

'You were chorus hon. I think you'll find I was principal.'

'Yes, forgive me,' Polly smiled. 'And what was your one and only line in that particular production?'

Cassie shifted uncomfortably in her seat. 'It was still a solo.'

'I hardly consider four words as entitlement to call yourself principal, darling.'

'They were four vital words, they set the whole piece. You will remember that I started the entire show with my solo.'

'I remember it clearly.' Polly was enjoying this little exchange. Such banter made their friendship work and they both enjoyed recalling their glory days in *the business*. '"Five, six, seven, eight." Wasn't it darling?'

'Which, I will remind you, had to be said in time, clearly and on cue,' Cassie said, wagging a slender finger. 'Otherwise you hoofers wouldn't get off on the right… hoof. Cloven in your case, *darling*.'

'And remind me how you delivered those four vital words on opening night?'

'That's not fair. Get on with your explanation.' Cassie clutched her guide book and fanned faster.

'"Nine, ten, eleven, shit!" I think was the count you gave. And not just to us but also to the assembled audience of critics, colleagues and angels.' Polly's well made up face had expanded with such a wide grin that her foundation was in danger of cracking.

'We were young,' Cassie tried to defend. 'It was my first real solo.'

'The rest of us had to tap through the opening number without laughing, and without music. The conductor was in such hysterics that he actually grabbed his sides. The orchestra took his baton movement to mean "cut" and fell silent. All that could be heard was twelve pairs of tap shoes clattering out what sounded like rain on a tin roof and the director being given the kiss of life off stage right.'

'He recovered.'

The two women looked at each other and mischievous smiles were exchanged.

'I got a mention in The Stage didn't I?' Cassie said proudly, lifting her sunglasses and winking.

'I think the word they used was "unforgivable".'

'Get on with your story you old bag,' Cassie said nudging her friend and suppressing her laugh. 'Tell me why our young rep is like a hoofer.'

'Well,' Polly went on, banishing Cassie's youthful faux pas to that part of her mind where she stored other people's embarrassing deeds as ammunition. 'He's been through his auditions and his interviews. He's rehearsed his lines and he's got through his opening night. Probably without causing the show to be stopped and restarted...'

'Enough already!'

'And here he is, five months into his tour, doing the same old performance day after day, week after week. The excitement of the initial run has gone. It's become a job. He's looking forward to his day off once he's got Worthing and Hastings over and done with. You see where I'm coming from?'

'Victoria station? My English geography is not as parochial as yours.'

'I mean that he's stuck in a routine. Just as all chorus boys are in their first real job. He covers it well, I don't doubt that he's a good actor, but he's lost his spark of enthusiasm.'

'And what's that to me?' Cassie thought she understood but couldn't see the relevance.

'You asked me what I made of him and that's my answer. He's a handsome lad who's found himself stuck in a rut.'

'You want to know what I think?' asked Cassie.

'Not particularly.'

'I think he's a fruit.'

'Well there you are then. We agree. He's just like a chorus boy.'

'Not all chorus boys are fruits.' Cassie winked knowingly.

'I'm not going to get that tired old Oklahoma story am I?' Polly whined. She had heard the story of *Cassie in the surrey with the chorus boy on top* a hundred times before.

'It's a corker,' Cassie protested and enthusiastically prepared herself to tell the anecdote yet again.

The coach started off with a jolt taking them by surprise.

'Ow!' the Californian singer yelled as her head snapped back into the head rest. 'He could have warned me.'

'Oh good,' said Polly. 'There's the punch line. Now you don't need to tell me the rest.'

Jason tried to learn the names of his guests as Dinos raced them towards Mandraki harbour. He put a tick next to Mrs. M. Reah, he knew his grandmother's name. He hadn't found time yet to ask her more about his grandfather's death, the will and the cryptic instructions that she had quoted in her letter. He hoped to get time on the ferry to discover the full story and to get hold of the heirloom she had promised. He associated the word *heirloom* with the word *priceless* preceding it. Perhaps it would be worth something and he could finance his dream. Priceless heirloom, remote cottage on a Greek island, peace, tranquillity, solitude…

'Malaka poustis re!' Dinos swore loudly as the coach narrowly missed a priest.

Now was not the time for dreaming. Jason returned to his checklist.

Mrs. Shaw, from Epsom. She was the blue rinsed bimbo wearing the straw hat and M & S underwear. She was given a tick, as was Mister Oliver Simpson. Travelling as a lone male in a party of women he was an easy name to remember, he also stood out because of his silly cagoule. The large loud woman from somewhere up north was probably the Harriet Smith from Bolton, which left the only guests that week who were travelling as a pair. A Miss Cassie Devereaux and a *Ms* Polly Arnold. He looked at the couple of well dressed women sitting together and sniggering like school kids. That would be them then.

The coach entered the main seafront road and turned right, cutting across the oncoming traffic. Dinos ignored the blaring horns, his target was in sight. Although Jason now had less than ten minutes before the Symi Two left, he calmed a little. He could see the ferry through the trees and the clutter of the other boats moored along the quayside. They were only a minute away. Dinos would park the coach as close to the boat as he could and it wouldn't take long to transfer his six guests. He clicked on his microphone.

'We're just approaching the ferry now folks,' he announced. 'The Symi Two, you can see it with its back down just up ahead. That's where you get on. Dino will take care of your bags and I will take care of the tickets. We are running a little behind so straight to the boat.'

He took a deep breath and told himself to slow down. Everything was on track, nothing would go wrong now.

But, as the coach drew up opposite the ferry, he saw Slipe tapping his watch and shaking his head.

SEVEN

Mandraki harbour, Rhodes

5.54 pm

'Get them on to the bollocking boat!' Slipe shrieked as Jason jumped from the coach. 'Where the hell have you been?'

'We had an unscheduled piss-stop,' he said as he dashed around to open the luggage hold.

What the hell was Slipe doing there? He never came to the harbour. At this time of day he should have been at one of the hotels making someone else's life a misery. *He's checking up on me.* Thought Jason, *great!* He had less than five minutes to get everyone and their baggage onto the boat before Captain Phil left them stranded for the night. Jason looked around for help.

Dinos had clambered down from his cab and had wandered over to converse with another driver. They were now leaning against a tree and arguing over whose cigarettes they should smoke.

'Dino, cases!' Jason yelled but the driver ignored him.

'You're a fiasco,' Slipe screeched loud enough for the guests to hear. 'I'll sort the luggage, you get the guests.' He barked his order at Jason who had just opened the hatch and had already started pulling cases from within.

'What?' Jason turned to Slipe.

'Get the guests!'

Jason stood back suddenly thinking of Elizabeth Taylor. 'What film is that a quote from?' he asked out loud. '*Let's play get the guests...*'

'Move.' Slipe pushed him out of the way, knocking Jason into Cassie who had appeared behind him.

'Sorry Mrs... Er...'

'Virginia Wolfe.' Cassie said with a smile. 'Or Richard Burton.'

'Eh?' Jason didn't have a Wolfe or a Burton on his guest list.

'Who's afraid of Virginia Wolfe,' Cassie repeated. '*You've got great tits Martha.*'

'Well thank you very much but the name's Jason.'

'Who's afraid of Virginia Wolfe. The film, the quote. *Get the guests.* Never mind.'

'That's' it!' Jason beamed at Cassie. 'I knew I knew it.'

'A classic hon.'

'Get the guests!' Slipe roared as he threw a piece of luggage out onto the pavement.

'Enough with the movie quotes already. Pass me my valise doll.' Cassie stepped forward to try and help but a wall of flab suddenly blocked her.

'Out of me way love,' Harriet commanded. 'I'll get it.'

She elbowed Slipe in the ribs, knocking him back against the coach and hoisted her bulk into the hold.

'Mind that Vuitton Mrs. Smith,' Jason called, wishing he had the gall to shove Slipe like that. 'My granddad is inside.'

'You what pet?' Her voice echoed inside the underbelly of the coach. 'And that'll be *Ms* Smith I'll thank you.'

'Get the bloody guests!' Slipe coughed, winded. He looked even more furious.

Jason left Harriet and Slipe to fight among the cases and returned to the front of the coach where Margaret was now helping mole-man down from the steps.

'If we can be quick folks,' he called past them to Mrs. Shaw who was dawdling at the back. 'Our ferry is just there. Please, if you could all get yourselves on board.'

'I just need to find some crisps,' Mister Simpson announced and started off towards a kiosk.

'No time... Oi!'

Jason dashed after him and led him back by the arm.

'But I must have my carbohydrates...'

'No time. On the boat.'

Margaret had made her way to the luggage hold and was fussing over her new sac de voyage. Slipe was not best pleased.

'Yes o.k., I *am* taking care alright?' The manager roughly grabbed two cases in each hand and started towards the boat.

'He's never been very mobile, not since the war,' Margaret explained as she trotted to keep up. 'I have to take extra care of him, so if you wouldn't mind...'

'Look, will you just let me do my bloody job,' Slipe yapped back.

Margaret stopped in her tracks. 'I am only trying to explain...'

Slipe bellowed back over his shoulder, 'Dino! Get your lard arse over here. This is your job. Bloody Greeks.'

'What a disagreeable person you are.' Margaret decided that she did not care for this little man, whoever he was. She made her way towards the ferry making a mental note to write a strongly worded letter to SARGO on her return.

Jason had manoeuvred Mister Simpson as far as the gangplank and was herding him up it into the stern. 'There's a bar inside,' he said giving the mole-man a little push of encouragement.

'Do they sell newspapers?'

'I thought you wanted crisps?'

'Both. Do you know what flavours they might have? I can't be doing with anything but salt and vinegar.'

'No idea.'

'English newspapers of course. But I might get away with cheese and onion if it's the same language. Do they have bilingual snacks?'

'Please, just get on the boat Mister Simpson!'

Jason turned to see Slipe behind him, angrily throwing cases at a crew member before steaming furiously back to the coach.

Harriet was approaching, two suitcases under each arm, two in each hand and one being pushed ahead of her with her foot.

'I've got them pet,' she called as Jason tried to help. 'I'm used to dead weights. Used to be a porter in a hospice.'

Jason was horrified.

'Just me sense of humour,' she added. 'Hey up, you should keep an eye on that one.'

Jason looked in the direction she indicated and saw a yellow cagoule dodging through the crowd back towards the kiosk.

'We will be talking about this.' Slipe spat the threat at the young rep as he threw another bag aboard. 'If you can't run a transfer after five months on the job do you really think you're suitable material for…'

'Mister Simpson!' Jason ignored him and ran after the cagoule.

Around him dithering tourists were moving towards the ferry. The crew had started unwinding the tethers and he heard someone shout a one minute warning. He pushed through the crowd and grabbed mole-man by the arm of his cagoule.

'Please Mister Simpson we will miss the boat,' he pleaded.

'You must call me Oliver,' mole-man said quite calmly. 'The bar didn't have salt and vinegar only oregano flavoured. Can you imagine it! Oregano.'

'Please hurry.'

'I'll be with you in a moment. I must have an English newspaper. Today's if they have one.' Oliver headed deeper into the crowd.

Jason turned to see if any of his passengers were on the boat and was relieved to see that his grandmother was now aboard. He saw her heading towards the salon, looking all around her at the wonder of it all. Big *Ms* Smith from up north was merrily tossing cases to the crew. The theatrical duo was already up on the highest deck surveying the scene from its stern rail and looking as if they were settling into the Royal Box for a command performance. There was just runaway Mister Simpson to get on, and where had he gone now?

The ferry sounded its claxon drowning out Jason's voice as he called for his guest.

Suddenly Ms Smith was beside him. 'I see him pet,' she panted as she rushed past. 'Leave it to me.'

'Oi! Queer boy!' Slipe's voice cut through the turmoil. 'Get here now!'

Jason hated him even more just then. Only Kiwi-Kate was allowed to call him queer boy. He threw up his arms and ran back to

Slipe, stopping in front of him with his hands on his hips and his face taught with anger.

'What.'

'Are they all aboard?'

'Well they would be if you'd let me do my bloody job,' he started but Slipe's look silenced him. He took a quick, deep breath. 'O.k. yes. Look, three upstairs...'

From the corner of his eye he saw a commotion ripple through the crowd on the quayside. Out of it burst Ms Smith with Mister Simpson tucked under her arm.

'All under control,' she called, flattening tourists beneath her as she thundered past. She was aiming for the ferry like a Quarterback heading for a season winning touchdown.

'Two more boarding now,' said Jason, impressed. 'And... oh bugger, where's my Laura Ashley?'

He turned to see Mrs. Shaw alight from the coach as if she had all the time in the world. Oblivious to the commotion around her she paused on the bottom step and placed a sailor's hat on her freshly combed hair. Her Laura Ashley print skirt had been replaced by a two piece, blue and white sailor suit and Jason couldn't remember seeing those white ankle boots before.

'Over here quickly Mrs. Shaw,' he called and she gave a lazy wave in reply. 'Dino!'

Dinos looked up from under his bushy brow, saw where Jason was signalling and licked his lips.

'I will call you later,' Slipe snapped. 'We obviously need another talk about your place on my team. This whole transfer has been laughable. Not what I expect from my staff. I will get you...'

'Yeah, yeah, and my little dog too.' Jason was too concerned about getting himself and Mrs. Shaw onto the boat to listen to any more.

'I am not joking. Look at me when...'

Jason had had enough. He rounded on his manager, shaking with anger.

'You want me to miss this boat don't you?' he shouted in Slipe's blanching face. 'You ordered me to do the extra drop off even though you knew my flight was going to be late. You've been looking for an excuse to get me sacked all season. Carry on victimising me and I'll give you the chance.'

He stormed away as tears started to well up in his eyes. He vaguely heard Slipe's shrill voice screaming after him as he headed back towards the coach.

He was met half way by Dinos and Mrs. Shaw sauntering arm in arm like a promenading couple on a Sunday outing. Dinos was peering into the cleft of her bosom and nodding his head.

'How you say... pert? Yes, very pert.' He licked his lips again.

'This lovely man was just escorting me...' Mrs. Shaw began as Jason rushed up to her.

'No time love.' The rep pulled her by the hand and dragged her towards the boat. 'Next week Dino. Yasou!'

She clutched her hat and called back over her shoulder, 'we will meet again!'

Dinos just raised his head, tutted and went back to his comrade to continue his conversation.

Up on the top deck, leaning on the stern rail, Cassie and Polly had been surveying the scene. They watched blithely as Jason jumped aboard, followed by the woman who had previously been wearing a straw hat.

'She wasn't wearing that outfit when we left the hotel,' Polly noted with suspicion. 'Must have changed on the coach.'

'She's a three costume a day girl if you ask me,' replied Cassie. 'Looks like Reno Sweeny from "Anything Goes".'

'I saw the Elaine Paige production,' Polly said. 'And believe me darling, everything went.'

The Symi Two blasted its horn for a final time. The ropes were dragged aboard, the tailgate lifted and water started churning up around the stern as it began to pull away from the quayside. All SARGO guests and their rather sweaty rep were aboard and accounted for.

Down below Jason lifted himself heavily onto a bar stool, slammed his clipboard onto the counter and dumped his flight bag at his feet. With his head buried in his hands he let out a long, low moan and wondered if he really did want this job after all.

He felt someone sidle up beside him and caught a whiff of Lilly of the Valley. It was a strange scent that calmed him in a mysterious way and brought back a memory of childhood. A memory from a time before he could remember faces or images; just a presence. He had smelled the scent when he had been a baby and the person wearing it had been watching over him, caring for him. He opened his weary eyes and turned his head.

His grandmother was smiling back at him, blinking.

'I need to talk to you about a couple of things dear,' she said sweetly but then dropped her voice to a sharp whisper. 'Your heirloom and a man called...'

'Hi gran,' Jason interrupted her gently. 'Tell you what, give me half an hour to recover and I'll meet you up top. O.k.?'

Margaret looked at him blankly for a moment and then smiled. She could see he was tired. 'It's a lot to take in,' she nodded. 'You have a milk shake or similar and I will be waiting.'

As soon as she was out of sight Jason ordered a very large Vodka and Tonic.

EIGHT

Aboard the Symi Two, crossing from Rhodes to Symi
7.28 pm

'Shall I read to you what is says about Symi in our complimentary SARGO helpful handbook?' Cassie asked as she stretched out as best she could on her plastic seat.

'Darling that would be delicious.' Polly adjusted her sunglasses and sipped from a can of ice-tea through an orange straw.

'"The magical island of Symi,"' Cassie began after clearing her throat theatrically, '"lies twenty-four nautical miles north east of Rhodes and two hundred and fifty five miles from Piraeus."'

'What's the difference between a nautical mile and a land mile?' Polly enquired.

'No idea hon, probably the same only wetter.'

'I see, go on.'

'"The island is mountainous and arid and the majority of its inhabitants used to be employed in the sponge industry, shipping, fishing and small scale farming. Now, however, the main industry is tourism, but, because of its lack of water and steep hills, not the mass tourism we see on Rhodes."'

'Oh dear,' Polly sighed.

'What's that hon?' Cassie looked over the top of her sunglasses to her companion.

'I'm sorry darling, but it sounds like this is going to be a boring soliloquy and has put me in mind of a dreadfully tiresome actress I worked with once many years ago.'

Cassie put the handbook on her lap and waited for her friend to get something off her chest.

Polly went on. 'We were engaged to perform something experimental by Beckett. Can't for the life of me remember the name but it was a few years before I moved, more successfully, into musical theatre. I worked with this Yank who delivered each speech as if it were something worthy and meaningful. She had no idea. Everyone knows Becket doesn't mean a thing and, if you must perform it, you get on, say your words and get off to the bar as quickly as possible. It was a dreadful production and she was a dreadful, so-called, actress to work with… Oh.' Polly suddenly remembered something and blushed slightly under her Leichner foundation. 'Sorry darling, that was you wasn't it?'

Deciding to ignore her friend's lack of memory and tact, Cassie picked up the guidebook, cleared her throat once more and carried on reading.

'"The main habitation on the island is in Yialos, the harbour area, and Horio (pronounced Horio), the village. The village is located above the harbour and is accessed by a long passage of steps known as the Kali Strata. (Pronounced Kali Strata.) There are over three hundred steps," presumably pronounced *steps*, "leading up to the village and, due to the island's hilly nature both Yialos and Horio have, between them, somewhere in the region of three thousand steps." Oh my, Polly, your knee!'

'Well I also have a hip.' Polly sat up and paid attention. No one had told her that she would need to climb so many steps.

'How will you manage?'

'I will cope,' Polly said determinedly, rubbing her hip and feeling the plates within. 'Doctor Simon says I'm a wonder of medical science. But one more high kick and I could be done for.'

'You should never have tried to outdo Dora Bryan in Seventy Girls Seventy,' Cassie chided.

'She was so difficult to work with.' Polly remembered the tour. 'I had to show the director that only I could save the production and take over from her when we got to Bournemouth so I did my splits. Got carried off by four dancers like I was a plank of wood. Huge applause.'

'I missed the performance,' her friend said sadly. 'But I read your review in The Lancet.'

'What else does it say?' Polly encouraged the American to change the conversation. It had been a few years since her hip was replaced and she had not danced since. Only at home, in the privacy of her own living room had she waltzed with Rex Harrison to *I could have danced all night*, and spun in a Polka with Yul Brynner to *Shall we dance?* She could still have out-danced both had not her leading men been dead and she herself been nearing seventy.

'"The pretty neoclassical houses that jostle up the hillside from Yialos bear testament to the wealth that the island once enjoyed,"' Cassie continued reading. '"While the smaller houses in the cramped village, where the poorer workers used to live, show us a glimpse of what life on Symi used to be like..."' She skimmed through a few pages. 'Ah,' she said at last, 'this is more like it: "Villa SARGO is one of the fine merchant-built villas and enjoys spectacular views of the harbour. Originally commissioned in 1880 by Christos Panandreas, it was passed on to the occupying Italians in 1915. After the First World War it fell into disrepair and was badly damaged by German forces in 1944. Now SARGO Holidays Ltd. is proud to be the owner and has lovingly restored the villa to its former glory..."'

'Yes, yes,' said Polly impatiently, 'all very interesting, but does it say how we get to it? Our rep mentioned complimentary transport.'

'Nothing in here about that,' Cassie replied after a quick search. 'Why don't you ask him?'

Jason approached, his flight bag slung from his shoulder and his clipboard tucked under one arm. Cassie waved him over and noticed how his expression changed from dull boredom to feigned enthusiasm when he saw her. *He's a pro,* she thought.

'Kalispera ladies,' he chirped as he sat side-saddle on the neighbouring seat and placed his clipboard on his lap. 'Enjoying the crossing?'

'A bit choppy coming out of the harbour,' Polly replied. 'But quite calm now.'

'It gets very rough at times,' Jason said. 'We're lucky today. I have had people lose their lunch over the edge before now.'

'How charming.' Polly put down her can of ice tea.

'But we do see dolphins from time to time,' the rep enthused.

'That's swell hon but we were wondering about the villa and how we get to it?' Cassie waved the guidebook at him. 'It don't say zip in here.'

'Your complimentary transport is all arranged,' Jason replied and a wicked smile crossed his lips. 'Your bags are taken up by truck and delivered for you and you will be taken up... by other means.'

'You're hiding something from us,' said Polly.

'It's a surprise.' Jason winked at her. 'I'll call you later when we are about to arrive. The view of the harbour from the front of the boat is the most spectacular way to see the island. Wouldn't want you to miss it.'

'I'm delirious already,' said Polly sarcastically.

Jason's expression didn't change. He simply nodded, rose and wandered off to find his grandmother. Now refreshed by his Vodka and Tonic he was keen to discover, at last, what his priceless heirloom might be.

Margaret was sitting to one side of the top deck, trying to keep away from the other tourists. By leaning seaward slightly she could watch a large, grey lump of rock advance towards her through a dark blue sea. Behind the island she could see the sun setting; the sky was turning to a dusky pink and the breeze was becoming cooler as they made their slow progress towards Symi. She held the silver cigarette case in her hand.

'We are nearly there Stanley,' she said quietly to herself running her fingernail along the join where the lid of the case met the body. 'Maybe soon we will find out what this is all about.'

Just as she had done a thousand times before, she tried to prise the lid of the case open. Again it was impossible. There was no catch, no clip, nothing to suggest how to get inside. She felt the engraving on the back and the indent on the corner where a piece of shrapnel had struck and she felt a mixture of emotions.

Back in 1944 the army doctor had told her that if her fiancé had not had the case in his pocket he would have been killed in the explosion that maimed him. A piece of metal had struck the case, causing the dent. It was probably only small, the doctor had said, but large enough and travelling at such a speed that, if it had struck Stanley, it would have pierced his flesh and imbedded itself into his heart. The army doctor had examined enough shrapnel injuries to know what he had been talking about. If this Dimitris Panandreas had not given Stanley the case then he would have not been carrying it that day. Presumably, if Panandreas himself had not been given the case in, she checked the date again, 1890, then it would not have been his to pass on. She wondered who had made it and marvelled at how fate had destined its path.

A small cigarette case, no bigger than a packet of modern cigarettes, had found its way, from London in 1889, where the hallmark showed it had been made, to Symi and thence, fifty-five years later, to the breast pocket of a young army private from Surrey. Once it had saved the young man's life it travelled back to England where it had lain forgotten in a dressing table draw for a further fifty nine years. Now, over a century since being created, it was finding its way back to the same island and would soon be passed on to another young man. Perhaps it was destined to save Jason's life in some way? Margaret didn't know. All she did know was that it had changed hers.

She had often pondered on how her life would have turned out if Stanley had not been carrying it, wondering how her life would now be different.

For a start they would never have married. Stanley would have been returned to England dead at the age of eighteen. And, if he had died out here, she would not have shared over fifty years of married life with him. She would not have spent those years caring for him, bathing him, helping him on the toilet every day, reading to him, being his eyes and legs. She would have had a life of her own. On her own. Stanley was her only love since they were children, she would not have married anyone else.

But she *had* had a life and she had never been on her own. It had been a life with Stanley; the paraplegic, blind and damaged love of her life. And what a wonderful life it had been. He had been a brilliant musician. At the age of fifteen he had performed a violin concerto for Churchill and the cabinet. Aged only eighteen he had played in concert parties to cheer his fellow troops and the islanders of Symi after the British had liberated them. But then he had been so damaged by his war injuries, mentally and physically, that he had never been able to read music again, and he had not touched an instrument since.

Well, Margaret thought, *at least this little silver box saved part of his life.* She smiled. *Life goes along its own path.*

And her path was leading her to Symi, returning Stanley to the last place on earth he had seen before he was blinded, according to his last wish. And, according to the same wish, she was bringing the cigarette case with her, to hand on to their grandson. A boy she had not been allowed to see since he was three years old.

In his will, Stanley had instructed her to find Jason, give him the case and return Stanley's ashes to Symi. He had also said if Jason could open the cigarette case all that would follow should be self-explanatory.

It was a magical twist of fate that their grandson happened to be working on the very same island where Stanley had fought and been maimed. It tied in well that she could knock down two birds with one stone, deliver the ashes and the cigarette case at the same time. But it had been a painful journey.

After the reading of the will Margaret had been forced to speak to her estranged daughter for the first time in twenty years. She had told her of her father's death and listened to her indifference at the news. She had carefully asked about Jason's whereabouts without giving anything away but her daughter had not been helpful, only saying that he was working for a holiday company called SARGO and was away somewhere. Margaret had used all the detective skills she had learned from watching *Murder She Wrote* and *Miss Marple* to track him down.

Then she had organised the trip and the necessary permissions to travel with the ashes. There was the rush up to London to get a passport in time and the frustrating day spent waiting for service in an uncivilised Civil Service waiting room. She had spent money she couldn't afford to spend and been on an aeroplane for the first time. Now she was travelling by boat, another first, and preparing herself to complete Stanley's mission.

And it all came about because Stanley had been given this cigarette case.

None of it made sense to Margaret apart from the scattering of the ashes. She could understand why he would want that. But the locked cigarette case was a mystery. If she was unable to open it how would Jason? Did Stanley intend for him to damage it? Was there something so important inside that the thing would have to be destroyed before revealing some secret?

'You're a silly, stubborn old bugger, Stanley Reah.' She smiled to herself fondly as she whispered it. 'You always were.'

She saw her grandson approaching and slipped the heirloom back into her bag. Telling herself to be strong, she sniffed and adjusted her posture, sitting up in the hard plastic chair and crossing her legs at the ankles.

Silently Jason sat next to her appearing more relaxed than before. They looked at each other for a moment before Margaret had to give in. Without warning she threw her arms around the lad and hugged him hard. She felt a tear rise in her eye and she tried to force it back.

'After all these years,' she said quietly, pressing her cheek against his. 'How grown up you are.' She pulled herself together. 'And how handsome.'

She sat back and let him go, but only for a moment. Grasping his hands and giving them a healthy squeeze she shook her head. 'And how much like your grandfather you look.'

'I hope you don't mean how he looks now,' Jason said. His face suddenly screwed up tight and he bit his bottom lip. 'Sorry, didn't mean…'

'Shh, Jason.' Margaret placed his hands back in his lap and gave them a tap. 'We have much to talk about.'

'It's all been such a rush today,' Jason said. 'I feel like I haven't even had a chance to say hello.'

Margaret looked him over, smiling. She saw all the necessary traits that confirmed he was family. He was not as tall as she had expected but he was as handsome. He had a scrubbed clean look that she approved of and the local climate must be agreeing with him. He had a healthy tan.

'Hello dear,' she said and she felt happy. 'Can we talk?'

'We have about half an hour before we round the headland into the harbour,' Jason said. 'Long enough?'

'For now,' Margaret said and nodded once. 'Then let's to business.'

She could sense Jason's eagerness. He fidgeted like an expectant child on Christmas day, waiting for his best ever present. Margaret reached into her handbag and felt the cigarette case. She paused.

'This is so strange,' she said and had to look out to sea for a moment. She realised that she was about to give away the only thing that Stanley had ever been able to call his. This was the defining moment. Stanley was dead, he was gone and, once she handed the case over, there would be nothing left.

'I'm a silly old bird,' she said, turning back to Jason. *I will have Jason from now on*, she thought.

'It's not an easy time for you,' Jason said and patted her hand.

She was grateful for that small gesture. No one had touched her since Stanley had died.

'I mentioned a few rather cryptic things in my letter,' she said, resolving to pull herself together. 'I apologise for the secrecy of my tone but it is what your grandfather wished. Firstly I think I mentioned your bequest.'

She saw Jason's eyes light up momentarily and caught him repress a look of keen anticipation.

'In your own time,' he said.

'Very well. Then firstly I should tell you about his instructions.' She saw his face fall again. He would have to wait to see what he had been left in the will. 'Stanley asked me to bring his ashes to Symi.'

'Ah now I get it,' Jason nodded. 'That's what you meant about him being in your suitcase.'

'Quite. His ashes are indeed in my sac de voyage.'

Jason looked concerned and so Margaret tried to reassure him.

'He is in an urn of course,' she added quickly but he still looked uncomfortable. 'I have the necessary paperwork so all is in order.'

'Fine, fine.' Jason waved a hand. 'Whatever. Sorry, just the thought… I've never seen someone's ashes before.'

'Well, he wanted me to scatter them at a certain place. The place where he met with his accident actually.'

'Mum told me the name of that place once,' Jason said remembering his very early childhood and the hunt for granddad's missing legs. 'But I don't remember. I didn't know it was here.' He pointed towards the island now looming even nearer. 'It's spooky isn't it?'

'It's also convenient,' Margaret admitted. She didn't mention that she too found it rather unsettling that fate had given them all Symi as a common factor in their vastly different lives. 'So, while I am here you and I must see to it that we scatter Stanley as he wanted.'

'O.k.' Jason said trying not to grimace.

'And the next thing.' Margaret could feel the silver inside her bag turning warm and damp in her hand. 'Your heirloom.'

'No rush. When you're ready.' Jason was definitely trying hard to sound disinterested as he shuffled in his seat.

'Very well,' Margaret said as she withdrew her hand from the bag. 'We will talk about that another day.' She looked Jason directly in the eye and saw his face crumple in disappointment. 'Now what say you we go and find a nice cup of tea?'

'O.k.'

Margaret made the pretence of gathering her things, tightening her shawl and looking around to find the best way of going down to the salon. From the corner of her eye she saw Jason fussing with his flight bag, pretending to check that he had it done up. Her face started to break into a smile and he caught it.

'Just like your grandfather,' Margaret said, beaming and reaching back into her bag. 'You are as impatient as each other.'

'You're wicked!' Jason pouted and crossed his arms, pretending to sulk.

'And how like your mother too.'

The old woman felt a sudden chill then. Once the excitement of the heirloom had died down it would not be long before Jason started asking other questions. Why had he not seen Margaret for the last twenty years? What had happened to his sister? She was not looking forward to that conversation. She shrugged off the uncomfortable feeling and took hold of the cigarette case again.

'Now you are not to be disappointed,' she warned. 'I don't think it is particularly valuable.'

She watched him intently and saw his expression change. He was clearly disappointed to be told this news but still eager to see what this mysterious thing was. At last she drew the small artefact from her bag, turned her hand palm up and showed him what he had inherited.

Jason looked at the small lump of metal in his grandmother's hand and saw his dream crumble. It was a tatty old piece of tin, dented and turning black in places. But then he remembered that the old girl had come all this way for this moment and tried to look enthusiastic; it was what she would have wanted.

'What is it?' he asked, peering closer. It looked like a paperweight.

'It's a cigarette case.'

'But I don't smoke.'

'You don't have to smoke to own a cigarette case,' his grandmother replied. 'Besides, it doesn't open anyway. Take it.'

Jason wondered what the use of a non-opening cigarette case was to a non-smoking cigarette case owner and then suddenly a ridiculous thought hit him. He was gay, gays were also known as fags, this thing was meant to hold cigarettes, they were also called fags. Perhaps granddad Stan had had a warped sense of humour. But then he remembered that Stan would not have known Jason was gay. The last time his granddad had seen him he was sitting on the lawn playing with two Action Men. But Stan had not actually seen him then either. Stan had been blind.

He blew the thoughts from his mind as he took the case from his grandmother. It felt lighter than he had expected, clearly it was not a paperweight. As he examined it he noticed the two small hinges on one side and tried to prise the thing open.

'You'll never do it,' Margaret said. 'I've been trying for days. I've pressed it, poked it, tried to get the lid away from the box but to no avail. I think it's some kind of puzzle box. I am sure it can be opened, it's just a question of how.'

'Weird.'

'I thought perhaps there might be someone on the island who could help us?' Margaret said. 'Perhaps a museum with a similar thing? I am fairly sure that there is something inside.'

Jason looked up at her and cocked his head. 'Inside?'

He shook the case by his ear. Sure enough there was something in there. He heard a very faint movement.

'Someone's last cigarette maybe?' he asked.

'No idea,' Margaret replied. 'Stanley never mentioned this to me. Well, only once when he first returned from the war. He told me that it had saved his life and then he put it away. I never saw it again until after he died.'

'Saved his life?' Jason was examining the case again, in more detail. He turned it over.

'The dent came from a piece of shrapnel.' Margaret pointed to the small indentation on one corner. 'It dented the case but the case prevented the shard from entering Stanley's chest. Maybe it is because of the dent that it now will not open?'

'Well tickle my tits 'till Thursday.'

'I beg your pardon!'

Jason realised that he had spoken out loud and tried to cover his tracks. 'Sorry gran, I just noticed something,' he said by way of apology. 'Something that's *really* weird.'

NINE
The Panandreas Villa, Symi
1914

Dimitris sat by his father on the bed and knew that this would be their last conversation. Christos had had his bed moved downstairs into the salon. The room, once the lightest and grandest in the villa was now dark and depressing. Dimitris looked at the array of medicines and bottles that now cluttered the room and saw just how bad things back home had become in the time he had been away. He had been travelling for many years now, following his career around Europe while his father had remained on Symi, trying to save a dying business while fighting a dying body.

'You arrived just in time boy,' Christos whispered. His breathing was shallow and his words as difficult for him to form as they were for his son to hear.

'Europe is in a mess papa,' Dimitris said. 'It takes time to travel these days.'

'How is London?'

'They no longer have the mind to appreciate my music, any music. Nowhere does, thought is only of war. Two months ago I played the Rachmaninov in Venice. Delius was in the audience but the audience hardly paid attention, they whispered about war throughout. I shall not be going back for some time.'

'I was right to make you practice, eh?' Christos turned up a corner of his mouth in a painful attempt to smile. Cancer was everywhere. Each muscle seemed affected and even blinking hurt him.

'I am grateful papa,' Dimitris touched his father's hand gently and the old man flinched.

'I hear that the war has begun,' Christos said. 'There will be no time for music now.'

'It will pass. Maybe I will return to the concert stage, take their minds off these times and continue to make you proud of me.'

'I have always been proud of you boy. But...'

A spasm of pain shot through the dying man's body, starting at his chest and shooting out to his fingertips. His body stiffened and his pale skin tightened.

Dimitris held his breath, only releasing it when he saw his father breathe out. Minutes passed as he watched Christos recover enough to open his eyes.

'I have so much to tell you papa,' Dimitris said, his own eyes unfocused through tears. 'About London, the tour, my music...'

'Stop.' Christos moved his hand; a slight tap against the bed sheet with skeletal fingers. 'Not now, there is something you must do. Something I must tell you before...'

'Just tell me what I must do papa and I will do it,' Dimitris interrupted. He knew what the end of the sentence would have been, *before I die.*

His mother had called him back to Symi urgently and stated the two reasons. Her letter had been specific and business like-as she had always been. *'Your father is dying. He must talk to you. Come now.'*

Dimitris Panandreas, concert pianist and composer of popular chamber music had performed Debussy's newest set of Preludes at the Wigmore Hall, taken his applause and boarded a train only an hour later. He had instructed his agent, by wire, to cancel all other engagements until further notice and, thanks to family wealth and connections had been back on Symi seven days later. His luggage, his music and his career had been left in limbo back in London.

Christos signalled for water and his son poured a few drops between his lips. Some spilled onto the man's untidy beard but Dimitris left them there to catch the light from the oil lamp and glitter like diamonds. He looked away as his father cleared his throat and spat blood amid skin-tearing rasps from his lungs. When Dimitris looked back the diamonds of water had turned to rubies. His father was paler, his skin more grey but his eyes had taken on a new determination. Whatever he was about to instruct was of great importance.

'You remember boy,' Christos began quietly but surprisingly clearly. 'When you were ten we received a package from Venice? It came just before your name day and you thought it was for you?'

Dimitris thought back thirty odd years to the previous century. He recalled his childhood; privilege on a prosperous island. His father, the richest of the sponge merchants had the grandest villa looking down onto the harbour. They had the most servants and the most money. The poorer people who worked for his family lived where Dimitris never went, in the crowded village below the Castro. These people had worked and died for Christos so that Dimitris could be educated and sent away to music school. He remembered long summer days at their house by the sea, warm evenings at the harpsichord, a beautiful mother and a powerful father. He remembered walking down the wide steps of the Kali Strata to promenade along the waterfront and inspect the fleet of sponge boats with his father. People bowed their head to them, and people thanked them. A lifetime so far removed from the troubles of the world now. He remembered his parents as tall, elegant people, respected and important.

He nodded to the withered man who had once looked like his father.

'I remember the package papa,' he smiled. 'It contained a metal chest with a strange lock. You would not let me see inside. And then it disappeared.'

'I hid it,' Christos said trying to smile, but his time for happiness was over. 'I had to hide it from you or else you would have tried to break in to it. You always had to know what things were, what they meant. Well now, now it is time for *you* to protect it.'

Dimitris could still recall the mysterious chest in all its detail: black iron with riveted silver bars running across the lid and joining on the front so that, when closed, the bars appeared to encase the chest without join. On the front had been a panel showing three numbers, the combination lock. No key, only numbers. He had not seen so intriguing or well crafted a lock before or since. It was easy to remember it.

'Must I hide it papa?'

'More than hide it. You must protect it, Dimitri.'

'Where is it?' Dimitris scanned the room quickly. Amid the clutter of icons, crucifixes, gilt edged paintings and lamps he could see no chest.

'It is where it has always been,' Christos raised his eyes to the furthest wall. 'But it will need to be moved before long.'

Dimitris did not understand and shrugged. His father continued.

'Listen and, for once, ask no questions. When I received that box I knew that its contents would one day be valuable. The man who sent it to me owed me money but had none, and he thought he was dying. Instead of money he sent me the box. I have kept it for you, for all people like you. And I have kept it away from you, from everyone, even your mother, because of what it is. I was waiting. Not for it to increase in value, we have never needed the money that its sale would bring. But I was waiting until such time as you, and the world, would understand its significance.

'But now… Now that Europe is preparing for war and the world is standing on the edge of its civilised cliff and about to throw itself over, well now is not the right time either. It will not be valued now, not appreciated. It would even be destroyed for what it represents, what it says. The world, as you know, has little time for beauty these days. If the secret in our box comes to light now it would not be understood. And believe me boy there are people who would stop at nothing to destroy it if they knew of its existence. If they only knew.'

Christos breathed in as deeply as his failing lungs would allow. His eyes still flickered with a last twinkle of excitement but his body was slowing down. Dimitris burned with questions but obeyed his father's wish, bit his bottom lip and remained silent. Christos forced himself to continue.

'Whatever happens in your life you must protect what is in that chest. Protect it with your life if necessary. It is more important than you, Dimitri, more important than me. It is history. You must protect history.'

'But father, I don't understand you…'

A low growl from somewhere deep inside the dying man brought Dimitris back to impatient silence.

'When you open the box you will understand.' Christos coughed and the sound brought fear to his son's heart.

Dimitris closed his eyes and waited for the attack to die down. Once again Christos recovered but this time it took longer and, afterwards, his breathing was desperately harsh. He raised his eyes again to the furthest wall and his son followed his gaze.

He was looking at the family portrait. He remembered standing for it while Masarakis, the old man who smelled of oil, painted it. It was the same day that the mysterious box had arrived and the fleet had begun its return with the annual sponge haul. But the picture showed no signs of the rebellious divers who, by then, were refusing to use Christos' new suit, the skafandro. Dimitris vaguely remembered the pressure his father had been under at the time, pressure from the families of the divers who were brought back dead or sick from hugely successful expeditions. As the men died the Panandreas wealth grew and Dimitris remembered with guilt how he had counted the bodies in various languages as a way of improving his vocabularies.

Beside his father, in the painting, stood Maria Panandreas wearing her finest clothes, her jewellery and a proud smile. She rested china like hands on a small, round eyed boy. Dimitris was pictured wearing his best church clothes and holding a blank piece of music manuscript paper in one hand and a quill pen in the other. He remembered how hot the afternoon had been, the sun had been on his back for hours and his feet had hurt. Once his face and outline had been painted he had been allowed to join some friends at the church where they prepared for his name day festivities. And there the memory faded.

'Take it down,' Christos instructed and Dimitris rose to cross the room.

The heavy painting still hung on wires from the high picture rail where it had hung since Dimitris was ten; dusted but never moved. Until now. He carefully lifted the portrait towards the ceiling and heard the wires slip from their hooks on the back.

'Put it to one side, carefully boy.'

With the painting resting against his mother's dressing table, Dimitris turned back to the wall that it had covered. The decorated wood panels were the same as the others around them but, where the painting had been, the paint was brighter, clearer and unaffected by the years of sun and dust. He looked at his father, whose eyes were still fixed on the ghostly outline of where his family had once been.

'The centre panel, pull it downwards.'

Dimitris did as he was told. He found a finger hold between the centre panel and the one above and gave a small tug. The panel came away without resistance and he was able to lift down a square of painted wood about two feet across. He had never seen this before. Confused and intrigued, he placed the false panel on the floor by his feet.

Behind it, cut into the stone wall, was a plastered, dark void.

And in the void was the Venetian chest.

The young musician had a hundred questions yet to ask. What could be in the box that was more valuable than money? Who had sent it to them? Papa had kept it for people like him, what people? Why would some people want to destroy it? How could a piece of history be kept in a box such as this? And why must he now take over its protection and guard it with his life?

He thought all of these questions but dared not ask them as he carried the black iron chest across to the bed. It was smaller than he remembered, at least it appeared so. He remembered the words of his father's secretary who had delivered it to the house. He had suggested that it might contain a bible. It was large enough to hold a proper, church bible, but not heavy enough to contain gold or other priceless treasure. He remembered that the thing inside had been wrapped in cloth, and hadn't there been a letter in there too?

'Your questions will be answered,' Christos said as if reading his son's thoughts, 'when you open it.'

Dimitris looked at the panel of three numbers, set to three noughts, and could now see that the combination lock was made of brass. The box was, for all intents and purposes, impenetrable save for the combination. Whoever had made the box did not want anyone getting at what was inside it.

'It was made by the same man who made your cigarette case,' Christos said quietly. 'And you remember how hard that was to open.'

'So how do I open it papa? What are the numbers?'

Christos turned his head to look at his son and instead saw himself standing there. He had been forty when it had arrived from Venice, Dimitris was now forty two. Where had the last three decades gone? He closed his eyes and saw his divers, his sponges, his offices in London, Paris and Venice. He saw his wife in their English apartment arranging flowers in a vase, he saw Dimitris parading the icon of the saint around their small mountain church. He saw his villa being constructed, the portrait being painted and he saw his life as buildings and possessions. And he saw Dimitris as he set off to the Paris Conservatoire as a boy, and saw him graduate as a man. He heard his son's music, saw his fingers flashing over the piano keys and scribbling notes onto manuscript paper. He could smell his wife's perfume and the secrets of the sea that surrounded his island.

And then he saw his divers being dragged dead from his boats, their new metal suits hanging like snake skins from the rigging. He saw crippled boys and men glaring at him with dark eyes as they sat on hard chairs in bare Kafenions. He saw widows cursing him as he paid them coins for dead husbands. He smelt the noxious breath of divers as they hauled precious black sponges from the sea bed for him, for his business, for London, for the rich of Paris and Italy. He smelt death and prepared to meet again those people who had died so that his family could live in their villa, could have their portrait painted, wear fine clothes and study music.

From somewhere on the edge of his life he heard his son's voice.

'How do I open it papa? What are the three numbers?'

The pain stopped. The release was intense, the dark room was all at once light and cool. The sky outside was blue again and the air was clear. Christos could taste the sea on his tongue.

'Two hundred and forty men died for me in the year this arrived on Symi,' he said and the clarity of his voice shocked Dimitris.

'What?'

'It was a good year. Only two hundred and forty,' Christos repeated and his son understood.

Dimitris turned the dials on the combination. The lock fell into place and the lid sprang open a fraction, released. Dimitris was once again the inquisitive ten year old. He opened the lid and saw the letter, beneath it there was the something still wrapped in material that he had tried to look at thirty years earlier. He took out the letter, opened the brittle envelope and read.

By the time he had finished reading he understood completely. All his questions were answered and his father was dead.

TEN

On board the Symi two

7.40 pm

'What is so strange that it causes you to use such language?' his grandmother was asking.

But Jason was not really listening. He was staring at the name on the back of the cigarette case and trying to figure something out.

'Did granddad say who gave him this?' he asked, finally looking up.

'Yes,' Margaret replied. 'The man whose name is engraved on it. They were good friends.'

'Granddad Stan knew Dimitris Panandreas?' Jason asked incredulously.

'They played in a concert together, just a few days before… before the accident. Why, does the name mean something to you?'

'Just a bit,' Jason said half under his breath. 'Gran do you realise…'

Jason suddenly became aware that someone was standing right in front of him. A large shadow fell across his hand and the case. He looked up.

'What you gunna do about this?'

The large woman from Bolton was bearing down on him, looking very cross and gripping a rolled up newspaper. Jason flinched.

'You seem rather agitated Miss… Harriet, dear. Is something wrong?' Margaret asked, trying to stall any attack on her grandson.

'I'll say Mags, I'll say.' Harriet planted both fists on her wide hips and stood with her legs apart.

Jason recalled a picture of the Colossus of Rhodes but managed to flick it out of his mind. He pocketed the cigarette case and stood, edging out from underneath Harriet until he was in a less vulnerable position.

'What's the problem Ms Smith?'

'Someone's vandalised me paper.' Harriet waved it directly in his face.

'I'm sorry?'

'Me paper!'

Harriet was looking around the deck to see if she could spy the culprit. Her chins took several moments to catch up and settle as her head flashed from left to right.

'I don't quite follow you,' Jason said, slipping into customer care training situation number one: how to deal with an angry guest. 'Perhaps if you tell me the whole story I can help?'

Harriet looked at him and took a moment to calm her self. 'Sorry pet, a bit wound up.' She waggled the rolled up newspaper and recounted her story. 'I was in the toilet. Now then, when I'm at work I usually take me paper into the khazi for a bit of a read, as you do. But, seeing as I am on me jollies, I thought no I'll not. I'll take a break from routine, so I left it on the table in the bar. When I come back some bugger's... well look! And I brought it all the way from Heston Services.'

She opened the Daily Mirror to somewhere near the middle and turned it to show Jason and Margaret.

At first Jason could see nothing wrong but then he noticed and was outraged.

'No way!' he protested loudly. 'The Spice Girls are making a come-back?'

Harriet whacked him on the top of the head with the newspaper.

'Look closer lad.'

Jason did just that, rubbing his crown and squinting. On closer inspection he realised that part of the page had been roughly torn out. Amid a slough of sensational stories of celebrity antics, a gaping hole showed half a picture of Hannah Gordon on a stair lift from the page behind.

'Well, well,' said Margaret thoughtfully as she also studied the page. She had no idea how to react to such news. 'Does Hannah Gordon really need a stair lift?'

'You what?'

That was obviously not the point of Harriet's discontent. It suddenly dawned on Margaret what Harriet was so upset about. Wanton vandalism of a tabloid. 'Perhaps it was a coupon or similar?' she suggested. 'I am sure the person who took it must have thought the paper was abandoned.'

'It were on the table with me knapsack and beer. It were obvious I hadn't finished with it,' Harriet protested.

'Well I always think,' Margaret ensured that her voice was calming, 'that if someone is desperate enough to steal, then they obviously need the thing more than the owner.'

'Crap!' Her words had not helped calm Harriet. 'It's not stealing, it's vandalism is this!'

'Step over here for a moment,' Jason said calmly, aware that other tourists and the Manos rep were watching the incident. 'Let's just you and I talk about it in private eh?'

Margaret nodded approvingly at him; maybe he did have sense after all. Maybe he would be up to the tasks Stanley had set them both. She watched as he led the large lady to one side. As Harriet moved out of her line of vision, letting back in the last of the sunlight, she saw the small man in the yellow cagoule walking towards her. Margaret raised an eyebrow; why would someone wear a cagoule in Greece in early September? Was he in disguise?

The man in the inappropriate clothing approached waving half a sandwich.

'I believe we are travelling together,' he said when he had arrived and swallowed a mouthful. In the distance Harriet was still brandishing the newspaper and Jason was holding up both his palms to keep her at bay.

'It would seem so,' Margaret said, drawing her attention back to the man.

'My name's Oliver,' he said and held out a hand. Margaret saw that it had what looked like marmite on it and so she only held his fingertips by way of greeting.

'Margaret Reah,' she said.

'That lady seems a bit upset.' Oliver nodded to the disturbance going on behind him.

'Someone has assaulted her Daily Mirror,' Margaret explained. 'Apparently people from the north find that kind of thing quite distressing.'

'Oh dear,' Oliver replied thoughtfully. 'Perhaps I shall see if I can find her a replacement when we arrive. Are you going to the front to see the view? Jason says it is quite spectacular as we come in.'

'Yes, I will.'

'Then may I accompany you?' Oliver said through his last mouthful. 'As we are to be spending a week together it would allow us the opportunity of getting to know each other.' He brushed crumbs from his hands before whipping out a packet of biscuits from a pocket.

Margaret was slightly uncomfortable at his suggestion but told herself that it was born from politeness and had no inappropriate overtone. The man was shorter even than her and mostly covered in yellow plastic so she doubted he meant anything suggestive by it.

'Certainly,' she said casting a last look at where Jason had calmed Harriet and was now leading her towards the bow. 'We don't want to miss the first sighting of our holiday home, do we?' she added and only flinched slightly when Oliver took her by the elbow.

When they arrived in the bow Cassie and Polly were already leaning on the front rail as if they were in a bar. Each had one foot resting on a lower rail and fresh cans of ice-tea swinging between their fingers.

'I can see that Reno's gunna be one to keep an eye on,' Cassie said nodding her head along the row of tourists all watching the approaching island.

Polly turned to look and saw the woman in the two-piece sailor suit ambling along the deck. She had added an accessory to her outfit; a young, extremely attractive, Greek soldier was now on her arm. He was listening to whatever the woman was saying to him but his face displayed distinct signs of bemused politeness.

'She's a vamp,' Polly smirked.

'As long as she doesn't start bringing strays back to the accommodation and keeping us up all night with creaking bed-springs,' Cassie mumbled. 'The poor boy is no more than twenty I'll bet.'

'Darling, she may look only forty but she must be at least sixty to have come on a SARGO holiday.'

'And you think us old birds can't make the bed springs creak?' Cassie said her eyes wide behind her sunglasses.

'It's more likely to be the creaking of bones that disturbs your much needed beauty sleep than the grating of metal, I fancy,' said Polly.

'Speak for yourself,' Cassie shot back and then added, 'or were you referring to your hip?'

The lady in the sailor suit arrived at their side and nodded graciously to both before turning to her young man.

'Thank you Lieutenant,' she said in a very slow but well spoken voice. 'Or should I say *a-ferret's-toe*?' She threw her head back, laughed coquettishly and then squeezed his arm. 'You will have to give me more Greek lessons. When we are *alone*.'

The Lieutenant, who could speak English perfectly and was actually only a private, pretended he had no idea what this woman was saying. He touched the front of his cap, bowed slightly at all three ladies and then beat a hasty retreat.

'Such a nice man for a Greek,' the sailor suit said, watching him go. She turned back to Cassie and Polly and her smile faded when she saw their blank faces and their mouths hanging open. 'Now don't be jealous girls.' She smiled playfully and pursed her lips. 'I am sure there will be plenty of young men for all.'

'Absolutely,' Cassie agreed. 'And after all, twenty goes into sixty more times than sixty goes into…'

Polly kicked her.

'Does it? Oh yes, how interesting,' the sailor suit said with a bemused nod. Maths was clearly not her strong point and she missed the relevance of the comment entirely. She got herself back onto firmer ground quickly. 'And I must confess to my weakness for uniforms. My first husband was a military man and from him I took a passion for khaki and shooting. Of course I also took the house, the timeshare and the

Land Rover but needs must. The name's Lesley Shaw, hello. We are all staying at Villa Sargo I believe?'

'Aint this gunna be an episode of the Waltons,' Cassie said under her breath.

'Polly Arnold.' Polly gave a small wave of her can.

'She won't be competition,' Cassie chipped in.

'And this is my friend, Cassandra Devereaux. Ageing spinster and cow.'

'Nice to meet you.' Lesley was already searching the crowd for her next conquest. Her attention was brought back to the two ladies when Polly said, 'Cassie wants to know who your plastic surgeon is?'

Lesley took that as a compliment. 'Oh I don't use one of those,' she laughed. 'Just exercise and a healthy diet.'

'Of what? Virgins in the full moon?' Thanks to her years of vocal training Cassie's aside was projected across most of the upper deck.

'Whenever possible,' Lesley said seriously, winked and nudged her arm.

'Well hon,' Cassie returned the nudge more forcibly that was necessary. 'I can see that this week is gunna be a blast.'

'I do hope so,' said Lesley. She adjusted her jacket to allow more cleavage to catch the eye.

'Here we all are then! Lovely.'

The three women turned to the voice. Jason had arrived with the other SARGO guests and he mustered them all into place along the rail, ensuring they were to get the best view.

Once they were in the right place Jason stood behind his guests and took a deep breath, preparing himself for rehearsed speech number two.

But it was a long time before he let the breath out again.

As he looked along the line of guests he saw a young soldier standing against the fading sunlight. He was half silhouetted and Jason could not see all the features but he could make out enough of the guy to see that he was good looking. Good looking and different. Jason had not seen him on the island before. He was new.

And he was perfect.

He wore a dark green outfit that Jason recognised as the Greek National Service uniform. He must be returning from duty Jason thought. And then his heart gave a flutter.

The soldier was gawping back.

The eyes of the vision in greens were in half shadow but Jason could sense that he was being studied as closely as he was studying the soldier. And for once he did not back down. He held the stare. Not being able to see the guy's expression gave him more confidence. If this soldier didn't like being gawped at he didn't show it. The ship tilted slightly as it turned the headland, but the Greek guy held his position, supported by two solid legs that strained within his uniform trousers. From his wide, powerful chest his body narrowed to a slimmer, tight waist.

As Jason blatantly looked him up and down he felt his own legs go weak. There came a rushing sound in his ears and his vision started to blur with the dreamy perfection of what he was looking at. He was falling in lust.

'Breathe, pet, breathe.'

Harriet's coarse voice shot through him like an injection of steroids, jolting his lungs back into action. Jason gasped for air.

'Good lad.'

Jason shook his head and remembered that he had guests. They were all now staring back at him and waiting for whatever gem of information he was going to give them. Only his grandmother looked perplexed and tried to see where he had been staring.

'Yes, right,' Jason stuttered, trying to remember where he was. He glanced to his right but the vision was now descending the steps. His heart sank but he put on his happy holiday voice as he launched himself back into the real world and into his script. He rattled it off at top speed, missing out unimportant words, keen to get below and catch another glimpse of his Greek god.

'In a moment you get your first sight of Yialos, main port of Symi,' he blurted. 'As we come into harbour, look left, see Villa Sargo, can't miss it, big, yellow and purple thing. *Who was that?* We dock by the clock tower, that's by the police station, post office, Coast Guard blah-di-blah. Get off, *gorgeous*. Quite a throng, busy time of day, go to clock tower, wait there. *While I search for mister right.* Luggage on truck, us on complimentary transport, up steps to accommodation. *Dreamboat's in Jas.* Here you go, look, Symi.' His guests were still focused on him with blank expressions. 'There! Behind you, look. Yes there. *Must find him, must find out who he is.* See you on land. Must go and check his packet. *Packet?* Your Bags. I must check your bags. Oh forget it!' And he was off, tripping down the steps with his heart bouncing in his chest and lustful thoughts bouncing in his head.

Margaret was slightly perplexed. It was obvious that her grandson had been staring at someone and was keen to get away all of a sudden, but she could not quite see why. *Perhaps it was an old friend,* she thought. *Someone he has not seen for a while.*

That thought satisfied her for a moment and then she remembered that he had still not told her what had made him shout out, what was it? 'Tickle my....' Never mind. That would have to wait. She was finally arriving at the island and did not want to miss a thing. She turned back to face the view and gasped.

She was hardly aware of the cameras that flashed uselessly around her in the dusk. Ahead of the boat she could see the harbour cutting deep into the island. The houses, yellow, ochre and cream appeared like faces, looking down at them from the steep hillside. Their light brown roofs pointed to the approaching night above where a lone star had appeared. Behind the town a mountain towered overhead. The fading sunlight lit one side of the scene with a deep pink while the darkness on the other caused the lights from tavernas and shops to glitter on the calm water.

To Margaret it looked like a time-unchanged fairy tale of a place. She imagined the seafront full with service men and pictured Stanley as a youth in uniform, resting a foot on a bench, watching the flat sea and dreaming of his safe return to her. She wondered if things had changed since Stanley had set foot on this place and decided that little had. It looked just as he had described it to her, beautiful and extraordinary. Over to her left she could see the ruined windmills he had talked about, and a large round stone circle he had said was an ancient burial ground. She caught sight of the red domes and wedding cake spires of the churches where he had gone to search for those in hiding. She saw the rows of houses that he had helped lead the rightful owners back to after liberation. And she saw, behind all this, the dark, brooding mountains that had been the location of his destiny. A cold shiver whipped down her back and she shuddered. It was as if Stanley was sailing in with her, as if he was standing behind her, touching her on the shoulder and encouraging her on.

If only he was, she thought.

If he had been, then the two days that lay ahead would have been a great deal easier for all of them.

ELEVEN
Symi harbour
7.50 pm

Harriet pushed through the crowd of tourists and headed for the nearby clock tower. She was still bitter about her vandalised newspaper and worked off some aggression on a party of Germans, wading through them and knocking them aside like skittles. She saw a couple of men taking the luggage from the boat and putting it into the back of a truck. Having checked that they were coping and didn't need her help, she approached Jason.

'Hey up pet,' she greeted him cheerfully. 'Think the others got trampled. Want me to go back and see if I can drag them out?'

Jason was taking no notice of her.

'Hey lad, you with us?'

Jason was looking beyond her, back towards the ferry and the throng that was teaming around it. He was rooted to the spot and taking no notice of Harriet. She looked over her shoulder, then back at him, checked his direction and looked back to the crowd again. Then she saw who he was staring at.

Amid the madness created by two hundred disembarking passengers, men trying to load luggage onto four trucks, an army lorry, a group of soldiers and several donkeys, one person was standing dead still. Like a rock in a fast flowing river he stood staring back at Jason, oblivious to the teaming masses around him. A tall, well built lad in his early twenties. Dark hair, dark skin, a proud almost ethereal expression and an aura of calm she could sense even from that distance. He wore a tight, military shirt that moulded itself around a wide, strong chest showing off every muscle and even tighter trousers that did a similar service to other parts of him.

Harriet looked back at Jason. His jaw had dropped open and his eyes were wide. A slight breeze caught in his hair and, where the hair gel would allow movement, a few strands blew across his forehead. He instinctively pushed them back into place. His hand trailed from his fringe, down his cheek and came to rest on his shoulder. He looked, to all intents and purposes, like Michelangelo's David, but dressed in a blue and yellow uniform, and with his tongue hanging out.

'I get it,' Harriet said but he still didn't hear her. She spoke louder. 'It's alright pet, your secret's safe with me.'

The spell was broken. Jason looked at her and blinked, trying to remember where he was.

'Sorry love?' he said and immediately looked back to the soldier.

Harriet turned to stand next to Jason, folded her arms and also stared at the other boy. He still had not moved, he continued to gaze at Jason and it looked like they were staring each other out, preparing for a fight. Only the looks that they exchanged spoke of lust rather than aggression.

'I said you're secret's safe, pet. He's a bit of a catch if you ask me. Who is he?'

'I have absolutely no idea,' Jason said slowly, forgetting that he was talking to a guest. 'But I'd like to find out.'

'I'll ask shall I?'

Harriet started off towards the lad in the crowd. Her action seemed to knock both young men back into the real world. The soldier saw her advancing on him and turned his head. Jason noticed the movement and realised with horror what was going on.

'Ms Smith!' he called desperately, but it was too late. She was already out of earshot.

Jason could only watch helplessly as she strode up to the vision in tight greens. He saw him lean down to her, look up at Jason, his face set with polite confusion and then he stood up straight again. Then he laughed, slapped a powerful hand on Harriet's shoulder, said something and shook his head. Jason felt his blood freeze with embarrassment. But the guy looked at him again, smiled and waved.

Jason waved back but his smile turned to concern as he saw someone else come up behind the guy.

A huge Greek man who Jason vaguely recognised slammed a palm down on the boy's head. The younger guy flinched, his expression changed and he turned around. Harriet moved away as the older man pulled the younger one roughly to one side. Some kind of argument was taking place and it was obviously about Jason, both men glanced at him several times. The ugly older one was clenching his fists, the cute younger one was waving his arms about and both were shouting. Jason thought he could hear their raised voices through the noise of the harbour. But within a few seconds it was over.

The brutish looking man pushed the lad towards a battered old truck before stomping around to the driver's door and getting in. The last Jason saw of his dream personified was the young man's face as he lent out of the passenger window, staring back at the red faced rep. The truck nudged its way through the crowd, revving angrily and eventually disappearing around the corner.

'Well now pet.' Harriet was back. 'What was all that about?'

'I don't have a clue,' Jason replied. Now that the moment had passed he tried to focus on his job. 'I hope they didn't upset you Ms Smith.'

'Call me Harriet, I'm a lesbian. So you're safe with me lad. Hope you don't mind me being so forthright,' she added as she straightened her bright Bermuda shirt. 'I like to tell folk how it is right from the start. That way men don't get any funny ideas.'

Jason looked down at her round, saggy face, her cropped hair, her khaki shorts and white trainers and wondered what kind of ideas men might have, funny or otherwise.

'Don't like to get hassled. Hence I lied about me age to get on the SARGO trip. I'm only fifty-nine,' she added before cracking her knuckles and whispering, 'want to know what his name is?'

'Who?' Jason said innocently. He was looking into the crowd now, trying to locate his other guests.

'Who? Come off it lad. The only thing missing just then was the band thumping out the theme from Shaft. Get it? *Shaft*. Who my arse.'

'I think I see our party,' Jason said trying to change the subject. He had not only heard a band but an entire orchestra and the theme wasn't Shaft, it was Love Story. Whoever this guy was, Jason felt sure that he was *the one*.

'His name is Michaelis,' she said in a harsh, penetrating attempt at a whisper. 'Can't remember his second name, sounded like Tzatziki but it wasn't.'

'What did you say to him?'

There was no way she was not going to tell him and, as the other guests had now seen him and were coming over, he wanted to get the conversation over and done with quickly. He was also keen to learn what he could about the young soldier who had turned his knees to jelly.

'Word for word,' Harriet said. 'I says: "hello pet, my friend fancies you."'

'You never!' Jason was half shocked and half delighted. He was suddenly a teenager with a crush again.

'Straight up.' Harriet smiled.

'What did he say?'

'He said something like: "I don't understand."'

Jason's heart sank.

'Then he said: "your friend is very nice."'

Jason's heart surfaced.

'So I says: "what's your name and where do you come from?" Felt like Cilla a bit.'

Harriet dug him in the side with a flabby elbow and snorted a quick laugh.

'And what did he say?' Jason was in too deep now to leave things alone, but the others were almost on them. 'Over here,' he called.

'He said: "you sound like Cilla Black." And then he laughed. And I laughed 'cos I wouldn't have thought someone as lives here would know Cilla Black. But he said he'd heard of her.'

'And?'

'And he said his name was Michaelis Tzatziki or whatever and he was from Symi. Just finished his national service. He started to ask who you were when this old geezer turned up, swore at him I think and… well you saw him drag him away. Don't think he was that chuffed to find his lad lusting after you.'

'He said he was *lusting* after me?' Jason's heart was suddenly out of the water, soaring through the air like a dolphin leaping before the bows of the Symi Two as it cut through a mirror flat sea...

'Well, he didn't say as such, no.'

...and plunging back into the cold, dark ocean.

'But I can tell, pet. As I say, your secret's safe with me.'

'Is there anywhere here I can find some Pringles?' Oliver had arrived.

'Don't know about Pringles, pet, but Jason here has seen something he'd like to get his lips around.' Harriet's ample belly wobbled as she laughed. Then she realised what she had said. 'Shan't tell another soul pet.'

The other guests had joined them and Oliver was looking around for snacks. Jason pulled himself together as best he could and addressed the group. Rehearsed speech number three.

'If you will follow me I'll take you to our complimentary transport.'

'Or some Chipsticks?'

'There will be supper waiting for us up at the villa.'

Jason held his clipboard high and headed off back towards the ferry. Now that the crowd had thinned all that remained was the army truck and the harbour officials.

And seven rather weary looking donkeys.

TWELVE
Meanwhile

'What were you doing?'

The man driving the truck was chewing on raw pipe tobacco. As saliva built up in his mouth he spat it out through the open window with no thought for the people crowding the road.

'Nothing uncle.'

'Nothing?' The man gave a blast on the horn. Tourists were in his way, luggage and people banged against the side of his battered truck and he was tempted to run over a few just to show he meant business. 'Who were you staring at like some poustis, malaka?' He spat again.

Beside him Michaelis ignored the insult and reached for a packet of cigarettes with shaking hands. He glanced sideways at his uncle and tried to avoid the subject.

'How have you been?' he asked as he searched his pockets for a lighter.

'What do you care? You want to know?'

'I've not seen you for over a year…'

'Because you've been having parties and getting young girls pregnant in Crete. You have forgotten your family. '

'I have been in National Service…'

'Bah! A holiday for weak boys. You serve only your family. Why are you touching yourself up now, what are you doing?'

Michaelis was still searching for a lighter. He was sure that he had had one on the ferry. Then he remembered lighting a cigarette for the old English woman who had accosted him. He must have given it to her, or she had kept it.

'I need a light,' he replied to his uncle, stretching his legs as he dug deep into his trouser pockets.

'In there.' The driver slapped the dashboard above the glove compartment.

Michaelis opened the flap and papers spilled onto the floor, unpaid parking tickets, fine notifications. No lighter.

'Useless malaka!' the driver cursed and blasted his horn again as he slammed on the brakes. 'Stay here.'

His uncle had stopped the truck by the Customs House. The rush of new arrivals from the Symi Two were dispersing now, a couple of flat beds piled high with luggage manoeuvred past the stationery Mazda, their own drivers cursing and slamming their hands onto its rusty roof. Michaelis slid down in his seat, aware that just the sight of his uncle's truck angered his fellow islanders.

He was cursed with his family name and his only family was his uncle Aris who was now arguing with the man in the kiosk. It was unlikely that Aris was buying him a lighter, more likely securing himself more tobacco on credit. Michaelis left his own cigarette hanging unlit from his mouth as he rested his arm on the open window and watched the tourists filter past.

He had been away from his island for almost three years, except for two short return visits; one Christmas and one Easter. If the Christmas had been bad, the Easter had been almost unbearable.

He had left his barracks on Crete and taken the overnight ferry to Rhodes with a few other Symi lads who had been with him in his barracks. They had grown up side by side on the same island, attended the same schools, had taken part in the same festivals and shared the same childhood. They had learned to fight together, learned to fire a gun, they had practiced unarmed combat on each other and had got drunk together. They had shared their homesick nights and their secrets, shared rooms, chores, their name days and military exercises in the cold mountains. They had bonded and become like a band of brothers in their time away from home.

In the army he had found friends, some of them had already returned to Symi, some were still away. But as for the rest of the islanders...

When he had returned to the island last Easter he had tried to renew old friendships with other islanders and other school friends, with other lads who drank in the village bars and danced in the tavernas like he had done. But not many wanted to know him anymore. He was practically ostracised on his own island and all because of his family name.

On Easter Saturday he had attended the service at the church of the Virgin Mary up at the Castro. It was not his church but it was popular. He had gone so that people would see him there. He wanted them to know that he was not with his uncle and that he was distancing himself from Aris. But, even in the joyous Easter moment as the Papas announced Christos Anexi, *Christ has risen*, faces turned away from him. As the solitary candle in the blacked out church passed its light from God to priest, priest to person, from person to neighbour to friend, his candle remained unlit. His fellow islanders presented their backs to him and passed the light elsewhere rather than be the one to share Christ's resurrection with the nephew of Aris Tzankatis.

Tzankatis. A name once revered and praised on the island was now worth less than the scraps that his uncle fed to their livestock. His name was his curse.

But it had not always been like this. The Tzankatis family had been known for their bravery and their resilience. Hundreds of years ago they had resisted the Knights of Rhodes, later they had fought the Turks. They had been the best divers in the Dodecanese, proud and strong captains of the fleet, diving deeper and for longer to bring prosperity back to the island. And they had not been afraid to stand up for themselves. During the last century it had been the Tzankatis women who had led the rebellion against the use of the skafandro, the metal diving suit that cost lives. A rebellion that took them to the Sultan in Constantinople and returned them to the island as heroines, the death suit was banned and even the likes of Panandreas took notice.

Michaelis' family name used to be respected. Now it was filth.

Because two years ago his only surviving relative and guardian, Aris, had killed a man.

Killed a man and got away with it.

Everyone knew the story and the feud. It was a long standing fight between two families that had been raging for over four hundred years. But it was ridiculous. All that time ago two families had become sworn enemies, now it was only the likes of his uncle who persisted in keeping the feud going. And the people he was angry at were not even direct descendants of the other family. The man he had killed was a very distant relative of an island woman called Maria Kalaris. Over one hundred years ago Maria had been married to one of the wealthiest sponge merchants on the island, Christos Panandreas. But her immediate family had died out during the war and the only relatives left were distant half cousins who farmed out at Marathunda.

One day, two years ago, while Michaelis was back on his Christmas leave, he had been out walking at Marathunda when he slipped and badly sprained his ankle. He was unable to walk and night was closing in, the air was cold and the wind near to freezing. Stelios Kalaris had heard Michaelis' yells for help from his smallholding in the valley and had come with his dogs to help. Having inspected the injury, treating it and declaring it nothing but a sprain that would heal in a few days, Stelios had helped Michaelis into a truck and driven him back home. As they pulled up at the end of the road closest to his remote home, Michaelis had told Stelios to drop him there. He knew that his uncle did not tolerate visitors, he guarded his small piece of land jealously and everyone knew that no one was allowed to trespass there. Particularly not someone whose ancestors had married into the Panandreas family. Stelios had protested as the track got rougher, pointing out that Michaelis would not be able to walk it, especially in the dark.

They finally approached the end of the track and Stelios supported the lad as he limped the last hundred metres up towards the courtyard. The night was black by then, the wind stronger on top of the mountain and Michaelis had begged old Stelios to leave before Aris discovered him.

Stelios had refused, unable to understand how the lad's uncle could object to a Samaritan helping a relative in need. Stelios did not know the depths at which Aris' hatred of all visitors ran and so he practically carried Michaelis, protesting and in agony, through the courtyard.

Neither had seen Aris appear in the shadow beside the chapel and neither had heard his warning. The wind battered their faces and all they could hear was their own breathing and their own thoughts.

But Michaelis heard the gun shot as he felt himself fall to the ground. A sharp pain sheared through the side of his head as stray pellets bounced off Stelios' skull and hit him.

The next day Aris had explained to the police how Stelios had been trespassing, trying to steal his goats and had been carrying a weapon. He cited Michaelis' wounded ear as proof that the intruder had fired first. He had also told Michaelis that if he did not back up the story he would go the same way as Stelios. Michaelis knew he meant it, he knew his uncle well enough to fear for his life.

The police had no other evidence and there was nothing they could do. Michaelis knew that he held his uncle's fate in his hands but he had nowhere else to turn, nowhere else to live and no other family to support him should he ever find the courage to turn his uncle in. He had been waiting for his National Service to be completed. Then, he had hoped, he would be able to find a way of escaping his uncle's maniacal grip. Even if it meant leaving the island he loved.

Now he sat brooding as he stared blankly out of the truck window. He was still unwanted. He had done his service for his country and now that was over. But where was he? Back with nowhere else to go but his uncle's home in the mountain, back at square one, only in a worse position. The resentment for his family ran deeper now. People who might have become his friends in time had all turned their back on him because of what his uncle had done, and because they all knew that Michaelis could simply go back to the police, tell them the real story and have his uncle sent to Kalymnos gaol.

But Michaelis didn't dare. Here he was, now a trained soldier, twenty one years old, a man. He could leave the island, he could do more or less anything he wanted but he was still trapped. Trapped by his loyalty to his family and a name that had once been great.

'Need a light?'

The sudden intrusion into his thoughts caused him to blink and look up. He saw the round belly of a donkey and a bare, human leg a few inches in front of his face.

'Eh?' he grunted, peering out of the window and up.

'I said do you need a light?'

The Englishman in the strange blue and yellow uniform sat straddling the donkey and leaning down. Next to him Michaelis could see a fat lady spread across another beast. She seemed to be egging the Englishman on.

Michaelis felt his heart skip a beat and, at the same time, felt himself go cold. He glanced over his shoulder nervously. His uncle was completing his transaction at the kiosk. If he came back and found Michaelis talking to a foreigner…

'Here,' the lad on the donkey said and reached down to offer a lighter.

'No,' Michaelis replied, backing into the cab and taking the cigarette from his mouth. 'Go.'

'He were only being friendly pet,' he heard the fat woman say.

'Take it,' the Englishman insisted.

'Please go,' Michaelis implored. He saw his uncle returning to the vehicle, examining his tobacco pouch carefully.

The foreigner had put his hand on the roof of the truck and was bending lower to look inside. Michaelis shrank in his seat, terrified of what Aris would do when he caught him.

Suddenly the truck rocked with a great thump and the door to the glove compartment fell off. More papers spilled onto the floor and Michaelis' heart froze. He heard a stream of swear words gush from his uncle's foul mouth as he continued to slam on the roof and curse at the Englishman, ordering him to leave his property alone.

Michaelis knew what property he was referring to. Him.

'Well don't get in a huff,' the young Englishman was saying. And then he said something that made Michaelis laugh: 'Who rattled your cage?'

It was the first time he had ever heard anyone answer back to his uncle and the thought of Aris in a cage was spot on. He should be caged like the other wild animals.

More cursing and swearing followed, this time with added threats of violence. Michaelis heard the word castration in there somewhere and he hoped that the funny English guy did not understand.

But obviously he did. He swore back at Aris in fluent Symi slang, giving as good as he was getting. Michaelis was impressed and yet terrified. At any moment Aris would attack the lad and then, once he had finished, he would start on Michaelis. This was not going to be a good homecoming.

A handsome, tanned face appeared at the window and the Englishman lent in to Michaelis. He handed over a cigarette lighter with the smile of a stupid schoolgirl.

'There you go mate,' he said, again in Greek and winked.

Before Michaelis could think about it he had taken the lighter and the other lad had gone. His uncle slammed the roof of the truck one final time and ripped open the driver's door.

'Why are you speaking to that poustis?' he demanded as he threw himself into the seat.

'He was speaking to me,' the young soldier tried to protest but a thick hand slapped across his head, silencing him. He had expected worse and ignored the pain.

'They are scum.' Aris spat. 'They try to take our island from us again. You speak to him and I'll kill you.'

As the truck set off around the harbour Michaelis looked straight ahead. He ignored both his uncle and the lad on the donkey as they overtook him.

He could not ignore, however, the strange feelings that were now racing around inside him. Somehow he knew that he would see the Englishman again. And when he did it would not be an easy encounter.

THIRTEEN
The Kali Strata
8.10 pm

On Symi the thoroughfare that leads from the harbour town of Yialos to the village of Chorio (pronounced 'Horio') consists of a series of stone steps. During the prosperous years of the nineteenth century the Kali Strata, *the good steps*, were improved and widened as affluent merchants had their grand villas designed and built in the neoclassical style on either side. Previously this path from the working harbour to the residential area of Chorio consisted of a donkey path, similar to the one still tucked away at the back of the village out of sight. But the rough cobbled paths were unpalatable to the wealthy businessmen of the eighteen-hundreds and so the Kali Strata developed. The Bourgeoisie could use the new path, with its shade and grand facades, while the workers could keep to the back steps which remain to this day roughly cobbled, in the glare of the sun and difficult to climb. Although the main route of the Kali Strata is obvious, various other smaller tributaries of steps join and leave it en route, heading both up and down to the hundreds of lanes and alleys that make up Chorio. No one in their right mind would ever conceive to count the exact number of steps that can be taken from the harbour to the village. There are so many different routes, so many paths to choose that when the guide books state a number it is purely guesswork. It depends on which way you go and how lost you get.

The edges of many steps have been worn smooth over the years and can prove treacherous. When it rains on Symi it rains hard. Water pours down from the mountain and gushes through the hillside village, gathering momentum as it finds its way to the sea. The Kali Strata changes from a grand stairway to a torrential rapid and can be impassable in places. In the summer, when the sun bakes the slippery stones and the locals keep to the shadows, it is no less dangerous. Several visitors have succumbed to a latent heart condition, heatstroke or an asthma attack while walking up, or slipped and broken an assortment of bones while walking down.

If the paths and steps of the village could talk, and some people still believe that they can, they would tell of the many historic sights they have witnessed. They would gossip, just like the locals do, about the famous people that have trod them; from eighteenth-century pirates to Hollywood stars, (it is rumoured that Mel Gibson once tripped on the step outside the butcher's shop). And they would talk fondly of how every important Greek had at one time climbed the Kali Strata, from soldier to singer. (Nana Mouskouri took a cab, actually, but…) The steps would talk of the battles, bloodshed and liberations they had witnessed as the island ownership passed from Ottoman, to Italian to German to English and finally to Greek.

And they would tell of the new, twenty-first century phenomenon, the SARGO Wednesday procession; probably the strangest and least historically interesting sight of all.

Tassos, a wiry old Greek man with a moustache too big for his crumpled face, led his seven donkeys around the grand corner where the Kali Strata Bar overlooks the harbour entrance. Jason sat on the lead donkey examining the heirloom his grandfather had left him and pondering the strange connection he had recently discovered. He was only half listening to the chatter of his guests as their donkeys, displaying an air of dignified boredom, zigzagged their way slowly up towards Villa Sargo.

'Well there is nothing about this in our handy SARGO handbook,' Polly said through gritted teeth as her beast lurched up another step.

'I think it's rather exciting,' Margaret called back. Her knuckles were white as they gripped the saddle and her last meal was sloshing about somewhere inside her but she was determined to enjoy the ride. 'The last time I was on a donkey was on Blackpool beach in nineteen thirty eight when my father took me on a weekend's holiday.'

'It's playing havoc with my hip,' Polly moaned. 'This animal has no sense of rhythm.'

'I wish you would stop quoting your own reviews Pol.' Cassie laughed over her shoulder.

'Look at all these lovely buildings.' Margaret was concentrating on the scenery to take her mind off the sore that was developing *down below*. 'Jason dear, when were all these built?'

Jason twisted to face her as best he could. 'Mainly in the nineteenth century,' he shouted back, 'by rich sponge merchants and businessmen.'

'You'd have thought they could have installed a stair lift by now,' Polly mumbled.

Jason forgot about the cigarette case when he noticed that the last donkey was now without its passenger.

'Has anyone seen Mrs. Shaw?' he asked, feeling a wave of panic wash over him.

'She was right behind me in the harbour,' Oliver announced also glancing behind. 'Maybe she fell off.'

'Probably stopped to change into a suitable outfit,' said Polly dryly. 'Yashmak or similar.'

Jason asked the man who was leading the animals if he knew anything and his face fell when he received a reply. He looked cross for a moment and then turned back to the group. 'It's o.k.,' he said feigning a smile, 'all under control.'

'Are we nearly there yet?' Oliver asked meekly, pulling his cagoule tighter around him. 'All this motion is making me feel a little queasy.'

'Not far now,' Jason reassured him and the donkeys turned a sharp corner.

As he twisted back in his wooden saddle to face front the cigarette case was jolted from his hand by the lurch of the donkey. He tried to catch it but only succeeded in juggling with it like an inept circus performer until it escaped him. He swore and tried one last lunge as it headed to the ground, right in the path of his donkey's front hoof.

'Ella! Oopah!' Tassos the donkey man saw it coming and deftly caught it in his free hand.

'Thanks Tasso,' Jason said gratefully. He reached out to take it back but Tassos held on to it, examining the engraving. 'Er, hello, Tasso?'

The old man's moustache twitched as he considered the name on the back of the case, then he looked up at Jason and shook his head before handing it back.

'You should be more careful with this,' he said as Jason took it.

'You should be more careful with your donkeys,' Jason mumbled back at him.

'That is something that could fall into the wrong hands.'

'What do you mean?'

But Tassos just spat and fell silent leaving Jason with the realisation that what he'd always thought about the donkey man was true: he was as barmy as he was uncouth.

They had left the main steps and were headed along a narrow, flatter path that ran parallel with the harbour way down to their right. On both sides of them doors to houses and courtyards opened onto the alleyway and the buildings gave way, here and there, to open areas of oleander trees, wild rosemary and vines. In these openings between the houses the group caught sight of the harbour far below them and could see the ferry that had brought them now lay dark and empty. Along the harbour the tavernas lit up in a blaze of multicoloured lights as darkness fell quickly over the island. In the trees cicadas played their legs with a sound like brushes on a snare drum and somewhere a cockerel with no sense of time was crowing.

'This is a very special place,' Margaret said contentedly to herself. 'You were right to tell me to come here Stanley.'

'We are approaching our villa now,' Jason called back along the line. 'Is everyone enjoying the complimentary transport?'

'It's not complimenting me at all. I doubt I will sit down for a week,' Polly called back.

'Hey up pet.' Harriet had been laughing and whooping all the way up, thoroughly enjoying the ridiculousness of the situation, but now sounded concerned. 'I think me mule's suffering under me weight, should I carry him for a while?'

It was difficult for Jason to tell if she was being serious or not so he just laughed back and then returned to his thoughts. There were suddenly so many.

He looked down at Tassos the donkey man. *This is something that could fall into the wrong hands.* Whose hands were wrong hands and how could it fall into them? It was only a cigarette case. But there was no point asking Tassos for a further explanation, Jason knew from previous journeys that he didn't do conversation. Instead he turned to the next thing on his mind: how to actually open the cigarette case. He had conceded that the thing itself was of no financial value, not unless dented nineteenth century silver fag boxes were highly sought after these days. He doubted it. But there was something inside it and it was that that was occupying his mind. Ever since he was little he had always wanted to know how things worked, what was inside them, what their secrets were. He had often destroyed his toys in an attempt to discover their inner secrets; what made Buckeroo buck? How come Barbie's hair got longer when you combed it? How could a Rubik's cube move in all those directions? He had so driven his mother to distraction by repeatedly asking why Action Man didn't have a willy that she had banished him to his room for two whole days.

'You always have to understand, don't you?' she had said. 'Why can't you just be content to let things be? Why do you have to know why all the time?'

'Why did you ask me that?' he replied and received a thick ear for his trouble.

He wanted to open the cigarette case to find out not only what was inside but also how come it was so hard to open. It was a puzzle and puzzles were there to be solved.

And here was another one: The handsome soldier from the boat and the evil looking man who had dragged him away, what was that all about? And another: What was the soldier's staring competition all about? From Jason's point of view it was nothing short of a bare faced cruise. Had he been in a gay bar or night club, or just innocently hanging out on the edge of Clapham Common, he would have said that the look the soldier gave him earlier was definitely a cruise; that silent, flirtatious and scaringly enjoyable overture that promised a night of rampant bonking. Jason had never been stared at like that by a local man before. What was the other guy thinking about? Was he looking back to intimidate or to attract?

Obviously he hoped that it was to attract.

Ever since he could remember he had dreamed about living in a secluded place in warm weather, with clear seas to swim in and wild hills to walk in. As a boy, not so many years ago, he had pictured himself sitting under an olive tree, drawing, reading a book and taking life easy. And, as he had grown, so the fantasy had developed with him.

In the most recent edition, the unabridged version that he reprinted and published in his mind every night before he went to sleep, he was living on Symi. At least that part of the fantasy was real, albeit temporarily. But in the ultimate portfolio, gold edged, leather bound collector's edition he did not have to return to England at the end of the season to work in a bar, or an office. In this version he stayed on the island, lived in a remote house, walked in the rain through the forests, drank morning coffee at the village kafenion, chatted in Greek to his local friends and spent the evenings… Well, that's where the handsome guy from earlier had just got written in. He would spend his winter evenings with Michaelis sitting by an open fire, wearing thick, woollen jumpers and drinking whisky. They would play Tavli together, discuss the small-holding that they worked together and then head off to bed in their tiny, rural cottage to keep warm the best way they knew how. And in the summers they would swim, take a boat to a deserted bay, have picnics, sit beneath olive trees, draw, read or do whatever couples do beneath olive trees when they are hopelessly in love. This was Jason's dream. This, and only this, was all Jason wanted.

'I want the bathroom,' Oliver called out and broke into Jason's daydream. Reality smacked him in the face and snug warm thoughts of Michaelis vanished.

'Not long now Mister Simpson.'

He fiddled some more with the case in his hands. He, like his grandmother, had tried pressing it on the sides, in the corners, on the top and the bottom, where the clasp should have been. He had pulled, gripping it with only his fingertips, until his hands ached. He had tried pressing the hinges, pinching them and pulling them, he had even tried swearing at it but all to no avail. He shook it next to his ear again and was just contemplating throwing it on the ground and getting his donkey to step on it when Harriet rolled up beside him.

'Anything in that lad? I'm gasping.'

'Hi Ms Smith. Sadly no,' he replied shaking his head. 'At least there is but I can't get it open.'

Harriet cracked her knuckles and flexed her thick fingers. 'Want me to have a go? I'd do anything for a fag right now. No offence.'

Jason wasn't sure. He was determined to see inside the case but wanted to be the one who finally solved the puzzle. Besides, if Harriet started banging it about it might get crushed beyond all recognition and whatever was inside could be damaged and rendered worthless.

'Thanks, but you've been helpful enough already today,' he replied with a smile. It sounded sarcastic but he didn't mean it to be. 'I mean giving me your lighter to give to… you know.'

'Hey lad.' Harriet put her hand on his shoulder and almost knocked him from his saddle. 'All you needed was a little push in the right direction. Next time you see him you'll have something to talk about. You can smooch up to him and say, *hey up pet, I know you've got a light, now all you need is a fag. Here have me!*' She laughed loudly and her donkey jolted with surprise beneath her. 'Secret's safe with me though, shan't tell a soul. Nor any other fish. Gerrit?' She winked at him and pointed to the cigarette case again. 'Sure you can't get in, I need a smoke.'

You need something alright. 'I think I saw Miss Arnold smoking,' Jason said. 'Perhaps you could bum one off her.'

'Well done lad, ten points for unnecessary use of the word bum. You and me have the same sense of humour. We're gunna get along like bosom buddies. Hey up, ten points to me for gratuitous use of bosom. Your turn.'

Jason had no idea what she was laughing about. He turned to the women behind him. 'Miss Arnold do you have a cigarette that Ms Smith could borrow?'

'No, but I do have one that she could have,' Polly shouted back.

'Ta pet.' Harriet yanked her reigns and the donkey farted in protest. 'Weren't me. Not that time.'

She turned her animal around and headed back down the line, leaving Jason alone again.

As they arrived at villa Sargo a few minutes later Jason couldn't get over how weird it was that his heirloom had found its way home.

Margaret felt herself being helped from her donkey. 'Thank you,' she said not looking at her helper but at the side of a grand building before her.

'You're welcome pet,' Harriet said, a lit cigarette now between her lips. She moved on to lift Oliver down.

They had approached the villa from the side. The path they had taken now turned sharply to the right and carried on back down the hill, the imposing end of the building effectively forced it to do so. There was nowhere to go from here but down or, if you could scramble over the boulders, it might have been possible to climb up to the next row of houses behind the house. The walls of the villa were not so much yellow, as they had appeared from below, but were more of a dusty, sandy colour. The architraves and shutters were painted in a mixture of blue and purple. Directly ahead Margaret could see a pair of black iron gates open to a long pebbled courtyard and, along the back of the courtyard, seating had been built into a wall. There was a walled garden lush with plants. Trees hung heavy with oranges and lemons and the whole area was protected from above by a vine. It looked very pleasant indeed, even better than it had in the brochure.

'If you'd like to follow me inside folks we'll have a drink on the front terrace while we sort out rooms and keys.' Jason led the way through the courtyard and into the back of the villa.

Behind him, in the lane, Tassos the donkey man turned his train around and headed back towards the Kali Strata. No one saw him take out his mobile phone, look furtively over his shoulder and dial. And no one but the man on the other end of the line heard his conversation, even when he spat out the name Panandreas as if it was a curse.

As they entered the villa the guests marvelled at the highly decorated ceilings, the wood panelled walls and the old, dark furniture. Cassie noted the display of stringed instruments hanging on the wall above the fireplace and Polly instinctively ran a finger over the back of a chair to check for dust. She was pleased to find none. Harriet marvelled at the bar that was stocked with every kind of bottle and immediately offered to mix everyone a drink.

Oliver, forgetting his queasy stomach, ignored the exquisite renovations, the attention to original detail and the stunning views from the French doors and made straight for a packet of peanuts that lay unopened on the bar. The room was buzzing with sounds of admiration and approval when, suddenly, everyone froze.

Two uniformed soldiers entered from the terrace, rifles slung from their shoulders and their camouflage caps pulled down firmly on their heads.

They stopped, looked at the group and nodded. Then they walked quickly through the room and out into the courtyard. In the stunned silence that followed Cassie and Polly exchanged glances.

'Three guesses,' Cassie whispered, removing her sunglasses and rolling her eyes.

'There you all are. I was about to send out a search party.'

Lesley appeared from the terrace and draped herself against the French doors. She had somehow found time to change into a cocktail dress that had hints of vivid blue sequins but was otherwise virtually transparent. Lamplight from the terrace filtered through the material silhouetting her figure which, even Cassie had to admit to herself, wasn't half bad for someone over sixty.

'*She may very well pass for forty three in the dusk with the light behind her,*' Polly sang quietly to her friend and the two actresses smirked knowingly at each other.

'The boys offered me a lift,' Lesley explained. 'They took pity on me when they saw me being paraded around the harbour on that beast like the Virgin Mary. I hope I wasn't naughty.'

'Did she say virgin?'

'Down Polly!'

'No, that's fine, Mrs Shaw.' Jason forced a smile.

'One of my husbands was a Marine so the boys and I had much to talk about.' Lesley raised an arm and dangled a cocktail glass from her fingers. 'I gave them a tipple as a thank you.'

'Well, we are all here now.' Jason put his flight bag down on a table and headed towards the doors. 'Come through to the terrace and see the view everyone,' he called back as he tried to squeeze past the vision in blue.

Lesley didn't move to let him pass; she just eyed him seductively as he brushed against her feeling slightly uncomfortable and very vulnerable.

'I'll bring out a tray pet,' said Harriet making herself quite at home behind the bar.

'And a refill for dear Miss Shaw,' Polly called, raising an eyebrow at Lesley. 'She must be panting for a fresh bowl.'

'Thank you but I have my Blue Bols,' Lesley replied, the sarcasm missing her by a mile. She held her glass in front of her frock. 'I always like to coordinate my fashion with my cocktails.'

'What was that drink we saw in Rhodes, Cass? A long slow comfortable…' Polly raised her eyes to heaven and pushed past Lesley. She was the first to join the rep on the terrace. She went straight to the balustrade and looked down into the harbour below.

'Look at this view Cassie and this terrace! I feel like I am in something by Coward.' She clapped her hands together in delight. It was the first time Jason had seen her happy all afternoon.

'As long as it's not *Nude with violin*,' Cassie replied, looking at Lesley as she stepped outside. 'Why all the musical instruments in the salon hon?'

'The villa used to belong to a musician,' Jason informed her. 'When SARGO renovated it they put it back to how it used to be, adding the instruments as a kind of tribute.'

Oliver and Margaret had managed to negotiate Lesley but it took Harriet and a tray of drinks to finally dislodge her from the French windows. Lesley joined the others, taking up a seat at a small iron table and arranging her dress around her knees as she sat.

'Does anyone have a cigarette?' she asked generally. 'The boys took my last one.'

Polly belligerently threw a packet onto the table and it skidded to a halt by Lesley's glass.

'You're a lifesaver.'

'Feel more like a charity worker,' Polly muttered back. 'Did any of you other smokers actually think to buy cigarettes, or am I the only one here with foresight?'

'O.k. folks,' Jason banged his clipboard to indicate that he wanted silence. He sensed group politics starting already. Polly and Lesley were both vying for group leader position and he could see a conflict arising if he didn't assert himself. Add to this the fact that his party would be hungry and tired and he had a recipe for disaster should he not show them who was boss. They had been travelling since early that morning and were probably usually in bed with their Horlicks by now. Their routines had been upset today and he knew from experience that old folk out of kilter were nothing but trouble.

Once he had their attention he put on his organisational voice, similar to the one Julie Andrews used when lining up the Von Trapp children to sing for their father.

'I will now allocate your rooms, give you your keys and then you can have dinner.'

'Are we having potatoes?' Oliver asked hopefully.

Jason looked at him blankly. 'I'm not sure. The cook comes in during the afternoons, prepares a meal and leaves it for me to serve. I'm always in Rhodes on a Wednesday so I have no idea what she's made for us, it's always a… surprise. But if you don't like it you can, of course, eat out. You remember where we turned right, off the steps? Well if you go back to there and carry on up a few more steps you'll be in the village square. There are restaurants up there and many more down in the harbour.'

'Can I check on bathroom arrangements?' Lesley fished her notebook out from a sparkling clutch bag and thumbed through some pages.

Here we go again, Jason's inner voice, now as hot and bothered as he was, piped up. 'Bathroom arrangements?' he said warily.

'Vis-a-vis plumbing?'

Jason sighed. He knew that daydreams of Greek soldiers and puzzling cigarette cases would have to take a back seat for the next half an hour at least. He looked at the expectant faces of his new guests and put on his SARGO smile. His jaw ached.

'Yes you have a toilet, no you can't put your quilted Andrex down it, and yes, Mr Simpson dinner will be along very soon.'

FOURTEEN
Symi
November 1915

Dimitris had made his decision the previous day; the chest had to be moved, it was no longer safe at the villa. Things had changed dramatically in the eighteen months since his father had died.

The Italian administration, who had taken over the island during their war with the Turks three years before, had started claiming huge pieces of land around the harbour, taking buildings and businesses from the local people and claiming them for the municipality. It was obvious that, to survive on the island now, one had to make some kind of deal with those in power and Dimitris had done just that. Although Symi had been allowed some degree of independence in recent years, the word now was that the Italians were clamping down. Other islands in the Dodecanese were having their independence stripped away and it was expected that the small backwater of Symi would soon have to toe the line. The new administration wanted to stamp its mark everywhere. The schools were now teaching Italian, the traditional island costume was now outlawed except at certain, prominent religious festivals and then was only to be worn with permission. And, the last straw for Dimitris, the islanders had to prove ownership of their property or lose it to the Italians.

Because there was no recognised ownership paperwork pertaining to the Panandreas *houses*, (there had never been a need), the summer house in Pedi had already been lost to the administration. The grand villa on the hillside was next. Dimitris had been preparing; it was all but empty now. Things had changed dramatically indeed.

Only three months after Christos had died, Maria followed him. The Greek doctor said she died of a broken heart. The Italian doctor said it was simply a heart attack, he wrote this in his ledger before crossing out her name once and for all as if she had never mattered. With her death what little remained of the Panandreas empire had fallen, like the island, to the Italian government.

The Panandreas sponge business had been declining during the first years of the new century. Divers had left the island in search of a better life in America before the war broke out. Now that the war was raging around Europe there was little call for sponges, and very few men left on the island to dive for them. The Italians had commandeered the boats for their own uses and fishing and shipping embargoes made diving virtually impossible. Once proud divers and their families now became soldiers and widows and a once wealthy island was becoming a poor, starving one. C. Panandreas and Co. Direct Sponge Importers had been forced to close its offices in London, Paris and Venice. Maria Panandreas had been seeing to the loose ends of the business when she collapsed and died on the villa terrace.

And for Dimitris, sensitive son of a once wealthy family, the burden of it all was starting to show. Life simply was not the same. Much of the exotic furniture, collected from places around the world by his father in his glory days, had been sold to pay off the business debts. Maria's collection of jewellery and fine dresses had been sold to pay for food and all that remained in the villa now was the portrait, a few items of furniture and Dimitris' musical instruments.

Dimitris paced the terrace, his shoes crunching on the dead vine leaves that blew around in the wind. In his hand he held the gift from his father, the silver cigarette case given to him on the day he left for the Paris Conservatoire and the start of his musical training. He remembered how his father had laughed at him when he had first tried to open it.

'If you don't smoke you don't need to open it,' he had said. But his father had shown him the secret and Dimitris had had to agree that it was so simple it was perfect.

He smiled to himself as he remembered his father and his thoughts turned to the other puzzle, the iron chest.

He could leave the island with it, take it to London or America and try and sell what was in it. But now was not the time, no one would be interested in what was in there. The chest itself was probably more valuable than its contents in these war-torn days. Besides, he could never sell what was in it. It was his job to protect it, for the future, for a time when it would be appreciated and understood.

And its contents were also politically dangerous at the moment. If it was brought out into the open it would either be used as propaganda or destroyed. The Italians would claim it as their trophy if he showed it to them, or they would just take it from him and claim that it had been theirs all along and that he had stolen it. Then, when they took the trouble to understand it, they would realise what it implied and would destroy it, pretend it had never existed and a priceless piece of history would go up in smoke.

No, no one must know of it just yet, it was too vulnerable.

It was virtually all that Dimitris had left but it could not be sold. The chest, the church in the mountains and the villa were all that remained of the Panandreas fortune. And very soon the villa would pass from the family forever too. Dimitris had decided that it would be politically wise to offer the villa to the Italian Governor before he took it; talks had been held and papers signed. He had two days left to vacate, two days to find a secure place to hide the chest.

While sorting through his mother's effects after her funeral, he had found documentation that clearly stated his right to his inheritance. There was nothing about the villa or the summer house but there were papers that proved that the small chapel of Stavros, high up on the hill at Manos, near the centre of the island, was his. The papers showed how the land had passed down through the Panandreas family for the last four hundred years. They also showed quite clearly that after Maria's death the land must pass to the eldest child. Dimitris was the only child and the last surviving member of the family; there was no question of who owned Stavros. It was far away from the harbour and of no interest to the Italians. It was virtually inaccessible but for a long walk and a difficult climb, the outhouses were small, there was not much grazing land and even the ancient well had dried up. The Governor had allowed him to keep it and had even provided him with a document stating that it was his and would not be taken from him. In return for this affirmation the Italians had got the finest villa in Symi, the summer house in Pedi and whatever was left in both properties.

The war had ended Dimitris' musical career and had made travel virtually impossible, even for those that did have the means. Now he had moved himself into a one room building in the village, along side the families who once worked and died so that he could be sent to Paris to study music. He had no water there but his neighbours, sympathetic to his plight because it was as harsh as their own, gave him water and food when they had it. In return he played for them in the evenings, local folk songs or classical pieces, dances and cheerful tunes to lift their spirits. He had gone from being a concert pianist to a busking minstrel in less than two years. But this was his life. He had decided to stay on Symi to protect the contents of the chest, just as his father had wished it.

He pulled himself from his gloomy reverie, slipped the cigarette case into his pocket and headed back into the villa. His footsteps echoed on the bare floor, the sound bouncing from the cold plastered walls to the high painted ceiling.

He took down the family portrait, wrapped it in a blanket and stood it by the door. Then he removed the secret panel, reached inside and pulled out the chest. He resisted the temptation to open it again, to touch what was in there and marvel at how such a thing could be so beautiful and yet so dangerous. Now was not the time. It could not stay with him in the village, he had to get it away from the villa to somewhere safe. He had thought of another place for it. Somewhere where no one would go and where no one would ever find it; unless he wanted them to.

He replaced the wooden panel carefully, making sure that it fitted back into place perfectly. Then he covered the chest with another blanket, tied it with string and carried it and the portrait out into the cold morning sunlight. There was no one else in the street as he closed the iron courtyard gates behind him and headed off towards the Kali Strata. He didn't look back.

He thought only of hiding the treasure and protecting history.

FIFTEEN
Villa Sargo
8.45 pm

By the time everyone had been allocated a room and had their keys, the luggage had arrived. Most of the guests headed off to unpack before their late supper. One of his duties, Jason had explained, was to ensure the guests were given breakfast and an evening meal. He was now in the kitchen, a small out-house on the far side of the back courtyard, clattering around with crockery and unpacking a selection of local dishes that the cook had prepared.

Only Margaret now occupied the front terrace. She sipped her second orange juice and drank in the view. The fresh evening air smelled of Jasmine and the thought struck her that she had finally travelled. After years of hardly leaving the house, let alone the country, she was on her first holiday. But it was not quite a holiday. She remembered her mission. To find the place where Stanley had met with his accident, scatter his ashes and unlock the secret of the cigarette case with her grandson.

Jason was not what she had expected.

But then she had not known what to expect. It had all happened so quickly. As soon as Stanley had died a mad scramble began. She rushed through the days after his death in a blur, organising the funeral, returning the medical equipment to the hospital, going through his papers and talking to their solicitor. Stanley had never mentioned his will since the day he dictated it to their solicitor, the same day that they had banished their daughter from their lives.

It was the same day that she had last seen Jason. He had been playing on the lawn as she stormed from her daughter's house, calling for her as she wheeled Stanley towards the car. She had been in such a rage that she had not answered him. She remembered an urge to scoop him up and take him with her but it passed quickly as she helped her husband into his seat. If she had taken Jason then his mother would have had cause to contact her again and, after what Margaret had just learned within the house, she wanted nothing more to do with her daughter.

After telling Stanley what had happened, the drive back to their small terrace house was conducted in steely silence. Neither spoke, both were deep in enraged thought. Margaret calmed herself with thoughts of her grandson.

'I don't have much,' Stanley finally said as Margaret wheeled him back to their house. 'But anything I do have must go to that boy. Am I right?'

'Of course Stanley.' Margaret squeezed his hand, a little too tightly. 'You always are.'

'From now on I'm going to do everything I can to make sure that boy gets a good life,' he carried on. 'I know that woman is our daughter Margaret, but what she and that husband of hers have done is… well it's beyond… beyond… From now on they don't exist as far as we are concerned. Only Jason matters.'

'Whatever you say dear, let it rest now.'

Angry though she was at what she had learned when her daughter returned from hospital that day Margaret secretly wanted the rift to be temporary. Families had rows, wounds healed. In time each party would forgive the other and life would go on as before.

'I can't Margaret,' Stanley said, thumping the side of his chair with his fist. 'If I wasn't stuck in this damned contraption I'd march back there and knock their lights out, both of them. How could they do it Margaret?'

'They said that they…'

'It's bloody lies,' Stanley fumed on. 'They only needed to ask us, we would have helped.'

'What do we have to give? Your war pension and handouts from the state…'

'Let me finish.'

An outburst from the mild mannered Stanley was as rare to Margaret as a decent bottle of German wine and so she let him finish. She wheeled him gently into his downstairs room and prepared the sofa for him as he ranted on.

'Even if they come crawling back to us for forgiveness we will not give them the satisfaction. I can never forgive what they have done. And nor can you so don't pretend that you can. But it's not the boy's fault, he knows nothing about it. But he will. One day we will tell him, we will explain to him what his parents were really like. Until then I am going to guide his life.'

Margaret lifted her husband from his chair and placed him on the sofa, arranging the cushions behind his back.

'How are you going to do that darling,' she said quietly. 'We have no means and I told you what they said.'

'I'll be watching.' Stanley quietened a little, he was plotting now. 'Not with these pathetic eyes of mine, but I have friends. We have friends. Somehow we will keep a watch over the boy and, when the time is right, I have a way to help him. We'd have him here now if we could wouldn't we love?'

'Certainly but his mother would never allow it.'

'I can't believe we brought that woman into this world.'

'Time heals,' Margaret said and immediately regretted it.

Stanley threw off his dark glasses and pointed to the scars where his eyes had once been. 'Time heals nothing,' he said, his voice harsh again.

'I'm sorry Stanley…'

'Fetch the yellow pages and find a solicitor,' he ordered. 'I'm going to make my bloody will. That woman gets nothing.'

As it turned out, all that Stanley had to leave anyone was the cigarette case.

When Margaret had handed it over on the boat earlier, she had wanted to tell Jason about the day she had turned her back on her own daughter. She wanted to explain to him about his parents and what they had done, but she had not had the courage just then. She decided not to think about it until the morning. In the warm light of day she would spend some time with him and find out what his life had been like so far. If he wanted to ask about his family's past she would tell him, otherwise she would not mention his parents and their differences. He seemed so happy here, and she found it such a peaceful place, that it would be a shame to bring those old feelings back. His parents were well and truly out of Margaret's life now, she had no reason to talk to Jason's mother again. Now that she had passed on the news that Stanley had died, and now that she had found Jason, there was nothing to talk to her daughter about. That was the end of that story.

And the start of the next and possibly last, chapter of hers.

She had enjoyed her day. She had decided to enjoy every day now that she was no longer tied to Stanley's sick bed. And she was seventy six years old, she reminded herself. She felt like she was living on borrowed time. She felt as fit as she ever did, she still felt only thirty years old, but occasional aches and pains, things that took longer to heal than they used to and a certain lack of memory all combined to remind her that she was not getting any younger. Each day could be her last and therefore each day was to be lived to the full.

How proud Stanley would have been if only he'd still been around to see her. Sitting here on a terrace, watching the night sky over Symi and feeling that something extraordinary was about to happen.

Jason's daydream of his perfect life with Michaelis the stunning soldier continued as he prepared the meal. Michaelis had just been about to suggest to Jason that they hold some kind of unorthodox wedding ceremony high up on a deserted hillside when the sound of a mobile phone playing *'we're all going on a'* (pause) *'summer holiday'* shocked him back to reality.

'Yeah, hello,' he answered, leaning back against the worktop with a bread knife in his hand.

'I've been reviewing your previous sales against targets and am not happy.'

'Kalispera to you too,' Jason said with a sigh. Did this arsehole never let up?

'As you know, you're sailing very close to the wind, dangerously close,' Slipe went on, hardly pausing to breathe. 'So I've made it official. I've emailed head office and they will agree with me. Consider today as your last warning. Your sales improve, you bring in more excursion payments for SARGO or that's it. So, how many places did you sell for your new excursion at your welcome meeting tonight?'

Jason was suddenly wide awake and he had no answer. With all the business about his inheritance, seeing his grandmother again and then the vision in army uniform, Slipe's challenge had been put on the back burner. He had to think fast. If he told Slipe that he'd not thought of anything yet he would go ballistic, probably get the next ferry over and sack him on the spot. And he didn't want his grandmother to see that.

'Enough,' he replied hoping that being vague would work and satisfy his boss.

'Enough being…?' His boss was rarely satisfied.

Jason tried to think quickly. What trip could he organise that no-one else on the island was selling? There were loads of trips already available to his guests in any one week, all of them virtually impossible to sell to SARGO clients. Long walks across the hills to Saint Emilianos, only popular with the very active in the cooler months of May and late September; an evening walk to Nimborio to see the ancient Roman mosaic and watch the sunset, something no one ever wanted to do after a hard day on the beach; the traditional Greek night at one of the harbour tavernas, usually his only chance of making a sale and only then if he had guests who were not fussy about food. He needed more time to figure this thing out and so decided to lie.

'The new trip is full,' he said and screwed up his eyes knowing that it would never happen and that he'd certainly just sealed his fate.

'Oh really?' Slipe almost sounded as if he believed him. 'That's only because they're an easy bunch I suppose, and there's only six of them. Try and rope in someone else's guests, do a bit of poaching from Laskarina but don't tell anyone. Do a deal with that Manos rep but don't give her a kickback. I expect to see full details so fax the paperwork through tomorrow and I'll check it out on my way over on Friday.'

'Will do.'

'Where are you now?'

'What?' What business was it of his where he was?

'I said where are you? Have you started dinner yet?'

Jason tried to keep his voice calm. The pleasantly warm and erotic images from his daydream had shrivelled the moment he had heard Slipe's nasal moaning, now they were banished completely and he was left feeling frustrated.

'I am in the toilet,' he lied again just for the hell of it.

'On SARGO time?' Slipe sounded genuinely exasperated. 'Save it for your time off. Christ, when I was a rep I was up every day at five thirty, I put in the extra hours and my guests appreciated me more for it,' Slipe lectured. 'Your guests won't appreciate you taking a crap when you should be working. You've really got no idea have you? Get a move on.'

And Slipe rang off. Jason resisted the temptation to do something criminal with the bread knife and covered his eyes with his arm, breathing deeply to control his shaking.

Margaret thought she heard someone crying in the distance as she finished her orange juice on the terrace. She cocked an ear but the sound stopped. Shrugging she returned to the dreamy vision of the glowing harbour. It certainly was a picturesque place. Neatly painted houses stood out proudly amid mysterious ruins, the granite grey hills acted as a backdrop and highlighted the colours of the illuminated buildings below. The sea reflected the lights from boats magnificently as they lined up against the quayside. She could make out, even from that distance, a number of shop keepers and restaurant owners outside their businesses, greeting people, showing menus and enjoying their work. Tablecloths were being shaken, tables arranged and people were moving to and fro in all directions, calmly but with a purpose. And in the distance she could hear a bell ringing from a church somewhere above and behind her.

She was wondering again how much or little had actually changed since Stanley's time here when Jason appeared from inside the villa.

'Are you o.k. gran?' He greeted her cheerfully but his face was red and his voice cracked.

She was surprised to see that he had changed into casual shorts and now wore a tee shirt, no uniform. That was a shame. He had looked almost dashing in his blue and yellow.

'I am fine dear,' she replied. 'But are you?'

'Dandy,' her grandson replied and slipped into a chair opposite. 'Dinner's almost done. Did you see your room?'

'Yes thank you. Such a charming view.' Margaret waved her hand in the general direction of the harbour.

'It's a charming island,' Jason replied without turning to look. He'd seen it before. 'Now then, I was going to tell you this weird thing, remember? We were talking on the boat but I completely forgot what with the transfer and Ms Smith's newspaper. Wednesdays are a long day for me, and I'd had some trouble with the boss.'

'That weasel of a man with the glasses who was so rude to me?'

'That's him.'

Margaret shuddered and banished the memory of Slipe. 'I am sorry if my presence here came as a shock to you and added to your troubles,' she said kindly. 'I thought your mother would have mentioned that I was asking for you.'

'She rang a couple of days ago but only said that granddad had died, didn't mention you.'

'Hmm.' Margaret didn't doubt it. Her daughter had never been a great communicator even when they did communicate. And she could well believe that she wouldn't want to talk about Margaret.

'Well,' Margaret pulled her shawl more tightly around her shoulders. Thoughts of her daughter had chilled her. 'We will talk about that anon. What were you going to tell me? Was it about your inheritance?'

Jason brought out the cigarette case and placed it on the iron table. The outside lights reflected in its dull sheen.

'It's the name,' he explained, turning the case over and showing the engraving.

'Yes, the man who gave it to your grandfather. What of him?'

'Come with me.'

Jason stood up and encouraged his grandmother to do the same. He slipped the cigarette case into his back pocket and led her inside, to the salon.

The room was furnished in the old Greek style with hard backed sofas and tapestry covered chairs. A long dining table of dark wood occupied the centre of the room and a large dresser stood against one wall. On it were an arrangement of ornaments, plates and an icon.

He watched as Margaret looked around the room. They had all walked through it a little while ago when they had first arrived but he doubted that anyone had noticed its fittings.

'What am I looking for?' Margaret asked

'It's what you are looking *at* that is important.' Jason smiled back and nodded towards the far wall.

Margaret took a moment to work out what he was talking about.

'Is that him?' she asked, her eyes wide now. 'The man in the painting?'

'Er no,' Jason corrected, drawing her near to the large portrait. 'The man is his father. This painting was done in 1882. But the boy is Dimitris Panandreas, the one who gave granddad my cigarette case.'

He watched as his grandmother studied the detail. She seemed not to have noticed that the view was the same as from the terrace where she had just been sitting even though little had changed. She looked closely at the boy's face.

'He looks like he was a confident little chap.'

'He was about ten years old then,' Jason explained.

This was not one of his rehearsed speeches and was not from the SARGO script. But, when he had first taken the job and moved into the villa, he had wanted to know more about it so that he could furnish his guests with accurate historical information. Over the last few months he had visited the museums, learning about the island's history while practicing his Greek by chatting to the curators. What he had learned had not always been pleasant and there were some things that he did not tell his guests. The history of the villa, it's ruination by the Nazis in 1944, its restoration in the early 1990s and sketchy details of its previous owners were all that he ever told his guests.

'So if he was ten in 1882 he would have been how old when Stanley knew him?' Margaret was asking.

'Seventy two.'

'You have inherited your grandfather's gift for sums too I see,' his grandmother said, impressed at the speed at which he had worked it out.

'I wondered where I got it from.'

'Seventy two is quite old for those days you know.'

'Not on Symi,' Jason informed her. 'The island supposedly produces some of the oldest living people in Greece. They are known for their longevity.'

'I see.' Margaret stood back from the painting to take in the whole picture. 'And why is this painting here?'

'Well that's the thing,' Jason said. 'You see, this villa used to belong to the Panandreas family.'

'Of course!' Margaret patted her fingers on her mouth, the realisation dawning. 'That's the view from outside.'

'Christos, him here with the bushy 'tache and pocket watch, had it built. 1880. There's a stone above the courtyard gates with the date on.'

'I didn't notice.'

'One of the few things the Nazis didn't rip down or take,' Jason said and Margaret looked at him sharply.

'What were *they* doing here?'

'Searching.'

'For what?'

'No idea. All I have managed to find out is that they sent a search party to the island towards the end of the war specifically to search the Panandreas properties. They ripped up the floors, tore down the ceilings, this painted ceiling is new but renovated to as close to the original as the architect could establish. What they didn't destroy in this place was blown apart when the English attacked the island in forty-four. The castle above was blown up and rubble landed on the roof, bringing it down. The place was a ruin.'

'Forty-four. When Stanley was here?' Margaret was remembering something. 'He mentioned the explosion at the castle. But no one knows why they ransacked this house?'

'No.' Jason shook his head. It was one of the few mysteries about the villa and the Panandreas family history that he had not been able to discover. 'All I know is that the SS soldiers who did it were sent here with express orders from Hitler himself.'

'You are such a clever boy.' Margaret pinched his cheek. 'To know all this.'

'It's a hobby,' Jason admitted. *More like an obsession.*

Margaret turned her attention back to the painting again and examined it closely. 'How strange,'

'What?'

'What is this here?' She lent forward and scrutinised a particular part of the picture. 'Has this portrait been restored?'

'No,' Jason answered confidently. 'It was found, in perfect condition, at the family chapel up on the mountain. When they restored the chapel they found it hidden beneath the altar. It was well wrapped and hardly affected by the damp winters. That was in, let me think, 1954 I believe. SARGO bought it by way of a large donation to the museum when they bought the villa. Why do you ask?'

'So this is…?

Jason moved closer and looked at where his grandmother was now pointing. In the bottom right hand corner was the initial 𝓜.

'That stands for Masarakis,' he said. 'The artist used only his one initial on his paintings. He's got more pictures in the museum if you want to see one day.'

'I see.' Margaret was obviously not satisfied with this answer.

'It's quite common,' Jason explained, 'using just an initial as a signature.'

'Yes I know,' she said. 'But is it so common for an artist to sign his name twice, or add to a painting long after it is finished?'

Margaret pointed to another part of the picture.

'Well tickle my… I never noticed that before.'

Sure enough, if he looked closely enough, Jason could make out another letter 𝓜. This one was written on the piece of music that the young Dimitris held proudly in his hand.

'That is strange,' he said.

'And stranger still,' Margaret said, 'is that he has signed on a ledger line.'

'A what?'

'Stanley tried to teach me about music,' she explained. 'He was a great musician but refused to play again after his accident. He would, though, often talk about music as we listened to the light classics. And some heavier works as well. He had a passion for both Mozart and Wagner, one extreme to the other in my opinion. Wagner is so Germanic don't you think? What's that Oscar Wilde quote that Stanley used to say…'

'Yes gran,' Jason prompted. Her eyes had become watery and he feared she was going to go off on one of those old people's reminiscences about how life used to be when the world was sepia toned and there was rationing. 'What's a ledger line?'

'Ah yes,' Margaret pointed a bony finger to the tiny letter M on the music paper. 'You see that the letter has a line running through it?'

'Yes,' Jason saw it. *M* 'It looks like it's been crossed out. Maybe it was a mistake?'

'I don't think so,' his grandmother answered. 'You see the letter is exactly where the note of middle C should be. And you always have to put middle C on a ledger line. Otherwise it would be a different note entirely.'

Jason didn't quite follow. 'And? Why is that strange? Maybe the artist was just being clever.'

'Oh no dear,' Margaret said and stood back to examine both signatures. 'The artist didn't write that letter. Nor did he paint this music. Look closer.'

Jason studied where she was pointing. The paper that young Dimitris held in his hand had a list of instruments written on the left. To the right of them were scribbled lines representing music, no notes just zigzags. Above the lowest, otherwise empty, stave of music, was the letter M with a line through it. The music looked like hurriedly scribbled graffiti.

'How do you know that the artist didn't write this?' Jason asked after he had squinted at it for a while.

'For one thing,' his grandmother explained, 'the penmanship of the two Ms is completely different. And secondly, the instrument names have been written in ink. No dear, I am fairly certain that two different people have contributed to this portrait. The questions therefore are who and why?'

SIXTEEN

The monastery of Stavros
June 1915, 11.50 p.m.

Dimitris approached the iron gates with a lantern held before him lighting the way. He pulled gently on the rope that he held in his other hand encouraging the donkey up the last few steps to the churchyard. It had been a long walk up from the village, over six hours and at night, and he was exhausted now. The donkey, on the other hand, had been quite happy to plod on and Dimitris had had trouble holding it back at times. He now tied the rope to a tree and let the animal graze in the darkness.

He could sense that he was alone. All around him the night closed in, jet black and warm. Only the lantern and the stars lit his way, no other lights. Only the sounds of a slight breeze in the fir trees, the rustlings of nocturnal creatures and the lazy chewing of the donkey broke the silence. There would be no one up here at any time of day or night, no one would see what he was about to do. He was quite alone and his secrecy was assured.

He drew out a framed document from the bag slung across the donkey's back and examined it by the yellow light of the lantern. It was very specific. Written in Italian and Greek it clearly stated that this monastery and all land within its boundary, as marked on the document, were the property of Dimitris Panandreas. Not only was that now written and sealed by the Italian Governor but it was also stated that the land would remain in Dimitris' family for as long as the Panandreas dynasty continued. This made Dimitris smile, sadly. He was the only member of the family, he was married to his music and he had no intention of marrying anyone else. He would pass on the land, though, to someone who would care for it, when the time was right. He would make some sort of arrangement before he died.

But that would not be for several years yet, he hoped. He had no intention of dying in the foreseeable future and had agreed with himself that, until the troubled world settled down, this would be the best place for him to hide the iron chest and the treasure it contained. In a few years he would either retrieve it and divulge its contents to the world, or he would leave the island with it and live elsewhere. In the meantime the notice, once fixed to the gate, would keep out trespassers and let everyone who might venture near know that this small part of Symi was, and would always be Panandreas property.

Satisfied with his plan he nodded to himself and stepped up to the gate. Taking a small length of wire from his pocket he attached it to the back of the frame and tied it around one of the scrolls on the ironwork. Here it would stay, protected from the sun by the ancient tree that always shadowed the gate and from the winter rains by the glass. Should anyone try and remove it and claim the land as theirs, there was always the ledger entry in the registry book in the Governor's office.

He returned to the donkey and untied a water skin from the wooden saddle. After pouring some into a dish for the animal he took a swig himself before replacing it. Then he turned his attention to the other canvas bag slung over the donkey's back. This he untied and, using the leather straps that had held it in place, slung it over his shoulder. Inside the canvas the iron chest banged against his back as he stepped up to the gate.

The gate opened inwards silently and, still with the lantern held before him, he made his way up and into the courtyard of the monastery.

The place had the feel of death about it, death and history. He briefly remembered the summer panagias of his youth; playing his instruments after the service, taking around trays of bread and cakes to the congregation and being complimented by the adults. Over the years, as his father's fortune grew and his workers suffered, the congregations dwindled. When Dimitris returned from Paris, during his holidays, he found less and less people rejoicing with his family and thanking God at their chapel until, five years ago, only he and his parents celebrated there.

The lantern lit the stone ahead of him and cast weird shadows on the derelict buildings. Dark shadows that danced about him as his school friends had done all those years ago.

He shrugged off the memories. All that was in the past, there was no point in dwelling there. He had a job to do and, once done, he could forget about this place for a while at least.

He approached the centre of the courtyard. To his left the once white walls of the small chapel were now grey and ghostly, set before the summit of the dark mountain behind. To his right the other buildings stood like mourners, sad and hunched looking down on a circle of rocks no more than three feet high. A man-made rim that marked the location of the deepest well on the island. His mother had always been concerned that someone would one day topple into the well and his father always replied that there were worse ways to get to God than through the Panandreas well. It was not until Dimitris himself had once almost fallen in that his father agreed to a sturdy, metal covering with a lock.

As Dimitris knelt down beside the well now he could see that the covering and the lock were gone. He held the lantern over the hole and looked down into the abyss. He could see nothing. Just as he had done when a child he picked up a pebble and dropped it into the hole. He waited to hear it bounce from a wall and then land. It never did. When he was young he used to imagine that, if he had fallen into the hole and into the ground, he would still be falling now. Down through the earth, under the sea, through the centre of the world and on, into space, into heaven.

Suddenly he was leaning forward and grabbed the stone wall to stop himself from falling in. He shook himself, brought himself to his senses and set about his task.

From the canvas bag he took a long length of strong rope and a second lantern. Having lit the light he tied it securely to one end of the rope and began to lower it into the well. The light spilled out onto the rough, earthy wall as it descended. There had been no rain for three months but the lower the lamp went the shinier the walls became. Further down it became damp where the rock gave way to a pocket of muddy soil and below this, when the light was no more than a pin prick, he thought he could see bedrock again and knew that that was too deep for his purpose.

He withdrew the lamp until it became level with the wet soil about thirty feet below ground and decided that this would do, there was a large outcrop there which would offer a foothold for him. It was damp down there and the box was iron, it might rust but it would only have to wait for a few years. When the war was over and he had a permanent home he would collect it and take it to somewhere dryer.

He secured the rope to the low wall by placing a rock on it and then dragged the other end to the tall fir tree beside the chapel. Having wound the slack around the thick trunk he tied a knot. He patted the tree, he had played in it when a boy and now it was to support his weight again. Back at the well he removed the rock, drew up the lantern and rested it on the wall while he took the iron chest out from his canvas bag.

For some reason he felt compelled to look over his shoulder. There was no way anyone could see what he was doing but still his spine shivered. Maybe it was because of what was in the chest. He wanted to take it out once more, to say goodbye to it and to apologise to it for confining it to the dank depths. There was no one behind him. Maybe he was sensing his father's presence, watching over him and approving of what he was doing.

'You must protect it, for all people like you. For history,' Christos had said. And that is what Dimitris was doing.

He checked the combination, aligning the dials to a row of three noughts, and wrapped it back in the canvas bag once more. This done he let the box and the lantern back into the well until the rope was taught and then he took a rest.

Only the chapel, the tree and the stars witnessed Dimitris lowering himself into the well, secured by a second rope. And only they saw him climb back out some fifteen minutes later with muddy hands. By the time he lifted the lantern from the depths its light was all but extinguished and the chest was hidden.

It was silent up there that night, even the night animals slept. The slight breeze that had disturbed the trees took itself higher and started moving small clouds about the sky. They covered the stars making black holes in the heavens as Dimitris packed away his ropes and let himself into the chapel. He prayed for his family and for the fate of the treasure that he had just buried. He prayed that his father would understand why he had had to sell everything, why he had given the houses away, why all that was left of the Panandreas empire was a portrait and a hidden chest.

SEVENTEEN
Villa Sargo
9.00 pm

The guests had arrived for their late supper, all except Oliver Simpson. Jason was on his way to find him and ask if he was eating with them that evening. The others had already started on the various plates he had put out in the salon and, having gathered that Oliver was keen on his food, Jason was anxious that he didn't miss out.

He turned right, out of the back door of the villa and walked along to the end of the courtyard to knock on Oliver's door. It was quiet outside that evening as it was on most nights. Only the cicadas scratching out a rhythm in the fruit trees provided an accompaniment to the still, jasmine scented air. He reached the end of the courtyard and raised his knuckles to the door.

He stopped. The door was slightly open and a strange sound was coming from inside.

'Hello, Mister Simpson?' Jason called in, giving the door a slight nudge.

There was a rustling of paper and a clatter of something metallic.

'Yes?' Oliver's small voice piped up from inside the darkened room.

'We are about to do dinner. Are you going to join us?'

More rustlings; more frantic this time. 'Be there in a moment,' Oliver replied, he sounded flustered.

Through the slightly open door and reflected in the dressing table mirror, Jason caught a glimpse of the old man sitting cross-legged in the middle of the bedroom. He was gathering piles of something towards him and covering them with blue carrier bags.

'Everything alright Mister S?' he enquired, squinting into the gloom.

'Yes, just… Tidy, tidy, tidy,' Oliver said more cheerfully but with a hint of panic. 'Like to be organised. Dinner? Yes please. Are we having something fibrous?'

'Er… I'm not sure. There's giant beans, bread, cheese pies and salad.'

'Oh.' Oliver sounded disappointed. 'Then I'll find something in my case. I brought supplies. For the regularity.'

'Okey-doky. See you in a mo.' Jason backed away from the door and headed to the dining area shaking his head. He couldn't be sure but it looked like Oliver had been holding a pair of scissors in his hand. 'Bloody old people,' the young rep muttered to himself.

Back inside the villa he found that his five ladies were happily investigating the local fare that the day cook had prepared for them. He stood and watched as they helped each other to the various dishes, passing the bowls along the line and politely thanking each other for their assistance. His grandmother was dissecting some dolmades, unwrapping the vine leaves to discover what was inside. She seemed amused by the dish, her face displaying a slight smile and a cheery though vacant look.

Maybe this is going to be an easy week after all, Jason thought. His new arrivals seemed to be getting along better now and there hadn't been much fuss, as yet. Apart from Harriet's wrecked newspaper there had been no complaints or incidents. Unless you counted Mrs. Shaw hitching a lift with the army lads rather than taking the complimentary transport, but that was understandable. Jason didn't like riding up on the donkey and he was a healthy twenty three. Some of his guests were well into their sixties and some, like his grandmother, were even older; he often marvelled at how game his guests were for the adventure. But no, this lot didn't look as if they were going to be a problem. They had introduced themselves to each other, were already on first name terms and were now chatting as if they had known each other for years. Even Polly Arnold was being reasonable.

'Are you eating?' Margaret had noticed him and waved him to the table.

'Come and sit lad,' Harriet ordered. 'You'll be needing sustenance if you're going out on the pull tonight.'

'I'm sorry?' Jason said as he approached the table.

Harriet winked at him. 'Secret's safe lad, safe as houses.'

'You have a secret? Do tell,' Lesley enthused. 'I love secrets.'

Jason looked at her as he pulled out a chair at the head of the table. She was now wearing a black evening dress, cut so low on the front that she was practically topless. *No secrets there.*

'No secret.' Jason smiled weakly. He sensed his grandmother staring at him from the other end of the table and tried to ignore her. Even though he was pleased to see her mixing with the other guests, there was something about her presence that unsettled him. He was reminded of a time in his first year at University. It was the time that his German language professor had sat in on his first conversation with a real, non-English speaking, German. He knew he could manage the conversation but felt intimidated by having his teacher with him. He felt the same about having his grandmother watching him at work, as if he was being judged and that points were being awarded somehow. He also felt intimidated because he could not be himself. He didn't know why but he found himself having to keep his personality in check. He sat down.

'Flaming arseholes!'

The ladies around the table stopped what they were doing en masse. Forks hovered before open mouths, napkins remained poised at the lip, eyes opened wide and everyone glared at Jason.

'Oops, me and my mouth,' he said, reaching into his back pocket. 'Just sat on something unexpected.'

'Bet that made your day lad.' Harriet gave a huge wink and laughed. 'Hey up! Pretend I didn't speak.'

'What on earth do you mean Ms Smith?' Margaret asked as she resumed her investigation of the stuffed vine leaf.

'Me lips are sealed,' Harried said. 'Not like yours eh, Jas?' And then she pulled an apologetic face at Jason as if to say *I can't help it.*

'Sealed against what?' Margaret persisted.

Something told Jason that his grandmother, though being easy going and amusingly dotty, was also pretty backwards when it came to forward thinking. There had been a couple of times already today when she had eyed him suspiciously and raised her eyebrows. It had happened when he had said things like 'love' and 'dandy'. He realised why he felt he had to modify his behaviour. It had occurred to him that his grandmother didn't know he was gay and, that if she did, she would not be amused. He thought he should try and butch it up a bit for her. Old folk, he knew, fell into two camps when it came to camp; his previous guests had taught him that, the women in particular. They either found his gayness amusing and acceptable, mothered him and said 'bless' a great deal, or they disapproved about him behind his back, tutted and cut themselves off. He suspected that his grandmother was camped in the latter enclosure and he did not want to distance himself from a relative he had yet to get to know by shocking her.

'Take no notice gran,' he said and pulled the cigarette case from his back pocket.

'Gran?' Lesley turned her head to Margaret in joyful surprise. 'You are related?'

'Grandmother,' Margaret said sternly. 'I wish you would use the correct address.'

'What have you got there?' Lesley looked back to Jason and spied the cigarette case. Like a magpie she was attracted to anything precious, semi-precious or capable of being passed off as expensive.

'I had forgotten it was in there,' Jason said by way of explanation for his previous outburst. He put it on the table before him and sat down at last.

'You got it open yet?' Harriet waved a fork towards it, splashing tomato sauce across the tablecloth.

'Not yet.'

'It was a gift from my late husband,' Margaret said to the group. 'You may as well know, now that it has appeared. And it's all very strange. A bit of a mystery actually… Oh, I shouldn't have told you that.'

Everyone looked at her and tired eyes started to light up at the news.

'Go on grandmother, you can tell them.'

'Well… Stanley did not say that I couldn't talk about it, only that I shouldn't mention the name Panandreas.'

'So that's that cat out of the proverbial bag.' Jason winked at his grandmother.

She realised what she had said, looked shocked momentarily and then sighed. 'Very well.' Her face broke into a smile of childish glee. 'Let's share our news with these nice people.'

'It's an heirloom.' Jason held the cigarette case up to show it off. He'd never had an heirloom before.

Faces turned to look at the artefact.

'And it used to belong to the man who lived on Symi,' Margaret added as if sharing the very latest piece of hot gossip.

'Really?' Cassie was interested.

'*And*,' Jason emphasised to go one better, 'I can't open the blessed thing.'

'*But*,' Margaret did likewise, 'there is something inside.'

'But there *has* to be a way of opening it.' Jason shook it and felt the thing inside rattle about. But the sound it made was too quiet for anyone else to hear.

'We have tried *everything*. It just will not give up its secret.' Margaret announced.

'More secrets?' Lesley looked from one end of the table to the other, from grandmother to grandson to silver box and back again, trying hard to follow the gist of the conversation. Her hair had trouble keeping up with her head and the hairspray began to lose its hold.

'I just know there's something valuable in here,' Jason said half to himself as he felt the thing inside slide from one side to the other.

'My late husband hardly spoke about it but he did intimate that it was important.'

'Probably make me rich.'

All heads were zipping backwards and forwards now like the crowd during a Wimbledon rally at match point.

'But it's useless if we can't open it.' Jason thumped it back onto the table.

'Pollack's!'

Everyone bolted upright and turned to the voice. Oliver had appeared in the doorway and had been listening.

'Have you tried squeezing the hinges?' he asked, his eyes wide and twinkling.

'We've tried everything Mister Simpson,' Margaret explained.

'May I?'

Oliver approached the table and Jason shrugged. 'Sure,' he said and handed the small case to Oliver. *Did he say Pollack's or...*

'Thank you.' Oliver smiled and held the box to his eyes. He closed one and squinted with the other. 'I don't suppose anyone has a magnifying glass, or a stethoscope?'

'Funny you should ask,' Jason replied. 'No.'

'I have some strong reading glasses,' Cassie volunteered and opened her purse.

'You never admitted that before,' Polly said with a mixture of delight and surprise.

'Hey, I'm sixty seven. I'm allowed.'

Cassie passed a pair of large, thick spectacles to Oliver. He took them and the box to a vacant seat at the table and sat down.

Drawing the case back to his eye he examined it carefully through the glasses, holding them away from him and then bringing them closer until he found the correct focus. He turned the case in his fingers, following the minute join between case and lid. Then he examined the hinges, held the box to his ear, tapped it with one finger and then sniffed it.

The other guests were silent as they looked blankly at each other. Only Harriet carried on eating, noisily.

Oliver put the box carefully down on the table and looked across at Jason.

'Just how did you try to open it?' he asked, passing the glasses back to Cassie. 'What have you tried?'

'I pressed where the catch should be, on the front,' Jason explained. 'Pressed each side, two sides together, even fiddled with the hinges but that didn't work.'

'Yes, it's a challenge isn't it?' For the first time Jason saw Oliver smile. 'Margaret, may I call you that?'

'You may.'

'Margaret, did your husband ever open this?'

'Not in my presence,' Margaret admitted. 'I saw it once back in 1944, when Stanley arrived home from the war to be treated, he was very badly injured you see. He lost his legs in a booby trap that also took out his eyes and scarred him both physically and mentally for the rest of his life. The doctors at the hospital said he was lucky to be alive. Shrapnel had embedded itself into parts of his body causing hundreds of lacerations and…

'Do you mind? I'm eating meatballs,' Harriet grumbled. Her voice brought Margaret back to the point of her story.

'When he was released from hospital,' she carried on addressing Oliver, 'he put it away and I did not see it again until two weeks ago when he died.'

'Hon, just two weeks? I'm so sorry.' Cassie laid a hand on hers.

'Thank you Missus… Thank you.'

'Cassandra Devereaux.' Cassie patted Margaret's hand sympathetically. 'But call me Cassie.'

'It's a stage name,' Polly said flatly.

'So you're an actress too!' Lesley exclaimed cheerfully. 'We'll have *such* a fun time.'

Someone kicked her under the table.

'Did I say something wrong?' she asked sweetly but everyone was looking back to Oliver now. He was nodding eagerly and Jason could tell that he was just itching to say or do something.

'Can you open it Mister Simpson?' he asked.

'I can but I won't.'

'Oh now that's not fair.' Lesley was leaning across the table to look more closely, her breasts pressed against her half eaten cheese pie and her dress picked up a nasty grease mark. She didn't notice. 'You must if you can. We are all intrigued now.'

'I won't open it…' Oliver handed the case back to Jason, 'because you should.'

Jason took the case and saw how Oliver was smiling at him. It was kind of fatherly. He shivered.

'But how?' He turned the case in his hands.

'Hold the box in your left hand,' Oliver began and Jason did exactly as instructed. 'No, with the hinges facing upwards. That's it.'

'But it's upside down…' Lesley started but Polly shushed her.

The ladies were all watching intently now, their dinner forgotten. Harriet watched over the rim of her beer glass as Oliver went on.

'Now then, place your right hand thumb on the little hinge that is closest to you. Does it press in?'

'No.'

'Good. It shouldn't. Now then, keep your thumb there and with your index finger try and slide the other hinge towards you. Will it move?'

'No.'

'Good.'

'Good?' Lesley said, exasperated.

'Yes, good.' Oliver looked at her. 'It proves that it was well made. I thought it was a Pollack but couldn't be sure, now I am.'

'Pollack?' Jason shook his head. 'No idea. What do you mean?'

'Benson and Pollack,' Oliver said as if everyone would know who they were. 'Ah, I see. They were a firm of safe makers operating from London's Hatton Garden in the nineteenth century. Famous in certain circles because of their... tactics.'

'Tactics?'

'Yes.' Oliver sounded as though he was choosing his words carefully, trying not to give something away. 'They built safes for banks, jewellers, silversmiths the usual sort of clients who would buy secure containers. But they had other clients er... *on the side* you might say. When they were commissioned to produce a safe, let's say for a rich merchant's shop, they would alert local criminals, burglars and the like. Whoever paid them the best bribe would be given the secret.'

'You're not making much sense Oliver dear,' Lesley insisted.

'It's quite simple pet,' said Harriet. 'They were bent. No offence Jas.'

'Yes, bent indeed.' Oliver chuckled and then checked himself. 'They would build into their safe, chest, box or whatever, a kind of backdoor entry.'

Jason shot a look at Harriet. *Don't you dare.* She bit her lip.

'The new owner of the safe would be shown how to set the combination, or would be given the key, depending on the style, and the highest bidder from the criminal underworld would be given the secret, backdoor information. That is, how to open the thing without a key. Basically they would build some ingenious opening system that was undetectable to the naked, innocent eye. The new safe would be installed and, usually a few months or even years later, so as not to draw suspicion to the safe makers, the shop would be burgled and the safe cleaned out. The police would investigate and find no trace of a forced entry, thereby laying suspicion and often blame, on the employees, or the merchant himself. The thieves got away with it and Benson and Pollack were blameless.'

'That's just dandy,' Jason said. 'But my fingers are starting to ache. What do I do now?'

'What happened to this company?' Polly asked, genuinely interested in the story.

'They went out of business in eighteen ninety five I think,' Oliver told her. 'Basically they died without passing on their secrets. It was only years later, by accident, that their techniques were discovered. A young assistant at Cartier was trying to access one of their safes but had been given the wrong key. Finding that it wouldn't work, he became so frustrated that he kicked the great lump of iron out of annoyance. But he kicked it in exactly the right place you see. To his amazement the door to the safe opened. Simple when you know how.'

'Lovely but...' Jason held up the cigarette case, his fingers still poised for his next instruction. 'Do I have to kick this, or what?'

'Yes do show him how to open it Mister Simpson,' Margaret encouraged eagerly.

Oliver returned his attention to Jason and checked that his fingers were still arranged awkwardly on the hinges.

'If I am not mistaken,' he said examining either side of the upturned case quickly. 'This is what they called a double action spring hinge mechanism. DASH as we... enthusiasts call it. You were trying to open it from the side opposite the hinges?'

'Yes, hello?' Jason's eyes were wide. 'You usually do.'

'Exactly.' Oliver rubbed his hands together and laughed. 'The obvious is usually simple enough to confound. O.k. young man.' He settled down a little but his face still displayed great anticipation, as if he was about to open a sealed tomb after three thousand years. 'The hinge closest to you *will* allow itself to be pressed inwards, but only at exactly the same time as you slide the other hinge towards you, do you follow? Timing is everything. Ready?'

'Chomping at the bit.'

'So,' Oliver said slowly, 'press and slide together.'

Lesley giggled coquettishly, everyone stared at her. She covered it with a cough. Everyone looked back to Jason and there was a communal holding of breath as he pressed and slid the hinges.

Nothing happened.

'Not working,' Jason said and blinked at Oliver.

'Try again.'

He did. Nothing happened.

'Nope.'

Everyone exhaled and sat back.

'Oh well.' Margaret picked up her fork again. 'Thank you anyway Mister Simpson.'

'A lighter touch,' Oliver said. He took Jason's left hand and released his grip on the body of the case. 'You are holding it so tightly that even if it were a normal lock it would not be able to open. Less pressure, more trust.'

Jason saw him wink and relaxed his left hand. The case barely rested in his palm as he positioned his fingers on the two hinges again. Not believing that it would do any good he repeated the action, pressing in one hinge while simultaneously sliding the other towards himself.

The case sprang open.

'Well I'll be…' Cassie gasped.

'The great deception about the DASH,' Oliver explained, beaming, 'is that these hinges are in fact the clasp and the *real* hinges are internal and on the opposite side. Just where you would expect them not to be.'

Jason held the small box flat in his palm and now that it was open he saw how it worked. Simple. His pleasure at seeing the case opened, however, did not last long.

There was no treasure inside, no coin or jewel, nothing valuable at all, not even a last cigarette.

'So what is its secret?' Lesley asked enthusiastically. 'What's inside?'

Jason looked up at the group of guests, all now involved in his inheritance, all now connected to him by their intrigue. They were all looking at him expectantly, eyes round and alert, heads nodding slightly with encouragement. All waiting to hear a great piece of news.

He looked back down into the box and took out what had been hidden in there for so many years.

'What is it?' Margaret was the most excited. She stood to look down the length of the table. Jason held something up between his thumb and forth finger. It looked small and worthless.

'I have absolutely no idea.'

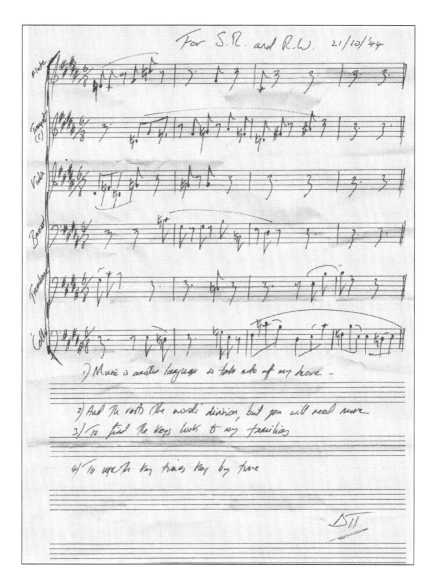

The manuscript

EIGHTEEN
Villa Sargo
9.15 pm

They were all staring at a small piece of paper that now lay unfolded in the centre of the dining table. Harriet was poking at her food and mumbling about meatballs but no one was listening to her. The others were all too intrigued by the strange manuscript that lay before them, the secret that the cigarette case had revealed.

'It's music,' said Cassie.

'We can see that Cass.' Polly tutted.

'It's in English.' Margaret sounded surprised. 'But it is not in Stanley's handwriting.'

'What does it say?' Lesley was dabbing at her dress with the corner of a recently licked napkin.

'Read it out Jason,' Cassie prompted.

'You read it Gran.' Jason pushed it towards Margaret. It felt right, somehow, to involve her.

Margaret seemed to appreciate this gesture, she didn't even correct him for not calling her Grandmother. She smiled at Jason, delved around in her handbag and took out a pair of reading glasses. Having cleaned them on a tissue, she placed them carefully on the end of her nose and draped the safety chain behind her head. She held the paper in one hand, at a distance, and tipped her head back to achieve the best focus.

It was a piece of music manuscript paper with rows of thin black lines that Margaret knew were called staves; Stanley had told her that many years ago, when they were growing up next door to each other and after his accident, he taught her music in the hope that she would learn to play. She never did but she had learned the theory. This page had notes and symbols scribbled across the upper part but also had words written beneath, not lyrics but sentences. Although the handwriting was neat, the words were written between unused staves and their horizontal regularity created an optical effect that seemed to blur them. Margaret concentrated, squinting slightly, and read the title slowly.

'"For SR and RW. 21/10/44". Oh I say.'

'What is it hon?' Cassie said. 'Does that mean something to you?'

'SR?' Margaret appeared to be talking to herself. 'Stanley Reah.'

'A relation?' Lesley asked.

'My late husband,' Margaret explained. 'The cigarette case was given to him back in 1944. The person who gave it to him must have put this paper inside before he passed it on. And the music, according to the title, is written for SR and RW. Stanley Reah and... who?'

'How very strange,' Polly said languidly lighting a cigarette for herself. 'Read the next bit.'

Below the title were six lines of music, joined on the left hand side of the page by one vertical bracket. Beside each line was the name of an instrument. In descending order: Flute, Trumpet, Violin, Bassoon, Trombone and Cello.

'Strange combo,' Cassie pointed out as she shuffled her chair closer to Margaret for a better look.

'Are you musical Mrs...' Margaret looked up at the thin American woman and placed the manuscript on the table. 'Cassandra?'

'And it's Miss,' Polly said pointedly. 'Very much a Miss.'

'Just call me Cassie. And just call her bitch.'

'Miss?' Harriet looked up from her diner plate. 'Are you two dykes?'

'No dear, actresses.' Polly shot Harriet a withering look. 'Heterosexual actresses.'

'More exactly,' Cassie said, 'I am a singer and she was a dancer.'

'Performers? I knew it!' Lesley chipped in gleefully. 'What fun. I am very active in CRAP.'

The other women looked at her and waited for an explanation. It took a while before Lesley realised that she should qualify her remark.

'Cynthia Rawling's Amateur Players,' she laughed. 'We perform out of the church hall in Little Sutton. We call ourselves CRAP for fun.'

Cassie stretched out a graceful hand and dipped it by the wrist. 'I perform out of Carnegie Hall hon, and they just call me.' Lesley accepted the hand shake with a nervous laugh.

'So, Cass,' Harriet poked towards the manuscript with a breadstick, 'you was saying, strange combo?'

'Right.' Cassie drew her chair a little closer to the table and turned the paper towards her. 'A strange mixture of instruments. This bracket down the left side shows that they all play at the same time and in the same time, here's the time signature, six-eight, that's six quavers to a bar. It's a piece of chamber music, kind of, but for two wind, two brass and two strings. Unusual. And what's more,' she looked at the music and appeared to be reading the notes, 'playing together they would make a pretty nasty noise.'

'You can read it all and hear it in your head?' Margaret asked.

She was always impressed and confused as to how someone could read music and have it make sense. She had never been very good with languages and Stanley had always insisted that music was just another language. He had had the ability, from an early age, to read the notes from a piece of music and actually hear that music as if it were being played. When Margaret looked at music she had only ever seen symbols on staves and had heard nothing.

'Not very well,' the American admitted. 'But I can see, for example, that some of the notes that sound together would clash and produce discords. There you have the bassoon playing a G sharp and the violin playing a G natural. Ouch.'

'What's a sharp?' Lesley asked, already finding the conversation a bit over her head.

'An accidental,' Cassie said by way of explanation.

'Oh.' It explained nothing to Lesley. 'And what is an accidental.'

'Musical terms, symbols that you put before notes to change their pitch. A sharp raises the note by half a tone and a flat lowers the tone.'

Harriet belched.

'Right on cue,' said Polly dryly. 'She's a natural that one.'

'And a *natural*, in musical terms, returns the note to its original pitch, got it?' Cassie smiled at Lesley who still looked vacant.

'I am sure I will one day,' she said cheerfully.

'Stanley spoke of sharps and flats and things,' said Margaret. 'He was a very fine musician before his accident.'

'I see,' Cassie went on. She could see Margaret's eyes start to moisten and realised that all this talk of her recently dead husband was starting to affect her 'The point is that the music looks like a mess. It's a weird combination of instruments, there's no discernable melody and the harmony is suspect to say the least.'

'What are those lines underneath?' Lesley asked, pointing to the list of sentences, numbered from one to four.

'Let's see.' Margaret was keen to get back to the mysterious manuscript and turned it back to face her. She read the lines out loud. 'One, *Music is another language so take note of my score.*'

There it was again; music is another language, just as Stanley used to say.

'Sorry hon but that's *off*,' Cassie pointed out. '*Take note* off *my score.*'

'Quite right,' Margaret agreed. 'I was assuming that the man who wrote this was Greek, Dimitris Panandreas. I was assuming that he had made a mistake but I am wrong to assume anything of course.'

She looked down the table to Jason who was following the conversation with interest. The day's coincidences played through her mind; Stanley sending her to find Jason, Jason being on the island Stanley wanted her to scatter his ashes on, the two of them now sitting in the house that used to belong to the man who gave Stanley the cigarette case and who possibly wrote this strange manuscript. The same man who gave it to Stanley who then gave it to Jason, who knew much about the Panandreas family. A cold shiver scuttled across her skin and brought her thoughts back to the paper in her hand.

'So: Line two reads, *And rests the words' division, but you will need more.*'

'This sounds suspiciously like a set of clues to me,' said Polly and Margaret nodded in agreement.

'Or at least a riddle of some sort. Line three, *To find the keys look to my families*.'

'Clues to something that is locked away?' Cassie's voice had quietened. Even Harriet was paying attention now. 'Keys? Musical keys?'

'And four,' Margaret shrugged and read on. '*To use the key times key by time*. And then there are two symbols that look like a signature.'

She showed the manuscript around and the others saw $\Delta\Pi$ at the bottom of the page.

'Pi,' said Polly. 'The second one is Pi, like you use in math's. Triangle and Pi. An equation do you think?'

'It's Greek. Delta and Pi. D.P. in English. Dimitris Panandreas.' Everyone looked at Jason who waved back. 'Not just a pretty face.'

'Does any of it make any sense to you Mags?' Harriet asked. 'Ring any bells?'

'No, nothing,' Margaret admitted. 'Except...'

A thought had occurred to her. Something Stanley had said on his return from the war. Once his injuries had healed enough for him to start remembering what had happened on the island before the accident he had told Margaret about his time on Symi. He had also written letters while he had been away. He had mentioned Dimitris Panandreas, but what exactly had he said? In her mind the years were rolling back in waves to reveal something faint in her memory, but there were nearly sixty years to wade through and whatever memory still existed was hiding in the depths. It would need coaxing out.

'Go on pet,' Harriet was prompting.

Margaret looked up from the manuscript and along the table towards her grandson. She could see him as Stanley might have been at that age. A fresh faced youth, proud of his uniform, his kit bag over his shoulder as he stood at the end of the garden path. He had lived next door, they were childhood sweethearts, Margaret had been sixteen when he went off to the war and she had been eighteen when he returned. When they brought him back, in an ambulance from the hospital, he had been carried up the path to his house, his legs missing, white bandages across his eyes. His face was pale and his hair had turned prematurely grey in places. Margaret had watched from the front room window, tears in her eyes. Stanley had somehow known she was watching and, although he could see nothing, had waved to her. She knew then that they would marry and that she would spend the rest of her life caring for him.

She looked into Jason's eyes, clear and alive and pictured Stanley recovering from his dreadful injuries, regaining his lost spirit and his love for life. The memory that hid in her mind took a tentative step forwards.

She remembered what Stanley had written in the instructions that were read out with the will. *The music will guide you.* She suddenly realised that Stanley had known what was in the cigarette case. He may even have seen it before his accident, or at least had been told about it. It was also clear that he had not understood it. If he had he would simply have told Margaret what the paper meant.

But maybe he had.

'It's to do with music,' she said and there was a far away tone to her voice, as if she was back in the past talking out to the present day. 'The concert. There was a concert here.'

Jason blinked and nodded. The action brought Margaret back to the room and the memories of sixty years ago scattered in all directions like a shoal of frightened fish.

'There was too,' Jason said. 'In 1944 after the English had retaken Symi for the second and final time someone organized a concert for troops and locals, morale boosting.'

'That's right,' Margaret said. 'It was just before Stanley… Oh dear.'

'It's o.k. hon.' Cassie put a reassuring hand on the other woman's arm. 'If it's difficult for you we'll leave it.'

'No, I am fine.' Margaret swallowed hard and sniffed. 'Thank you, I will be fine.'

'You're sure hon?'

Margaret regained her composure.

'Jason dear, tell me if I get this wrong.' She looked at her travelling companions around the table and took a deep breath. 'Stanley spent many hours telling me about his time here on Symi. I remember a few details. After the English had liberated the island from the Germans the man left in charge organized a celebratory concert for the islanders who had endured so much. Stanley wrote to me about it the very next day. I remember it because his letter arrived with me on the same day as the war ministry letter arrived with his parents next door. Their letter told of his accident and his injuries and told them that he would be coming home. My letter told of a late night celebration in the harbour square where Stanley and his new friend Dimitris Panandreas had played a duet. Stanley was an outstanding young musician. He was going to teach after the war, but, well he couldn't. But he wrote about this old Greek man who had played the piano beside him. They improvised some very fast, very technical variation of... what was it? I don't remember but Stanley said that at the end the whole audience was on its feet. That was October the twentieth, 1944. But what is important, what links that concert to this music...'

She fell silent again. The others waited for her to explain, Cassie nudged her gently.

'The date.' Margaret looked down to the manuscript. 'October the twenty-first. This music was written on the day after the concert. Am I right Jason?'

Jason bit his bottom lip and made a clicking noise with his tongue as he thought. As the memory came back to him he started to nod his head. 'You got it babe,' he said and then smiled.

'Babe?' Margaret frowned but only briefly. She looked back at the other guests. 'This music was written on the same day as Stanley wrote his letter to me. Which was the day before Dimitris Panandreas died and Stanley met with his accident.'

'Which means..?' Asked Lesley. Her mind was still stuck on the image of a young soldier in uniform.

'I don't know what it means,' Margaret admitted. 'But don't you think that it is a little strange? That Stanley and Dimitris play music together, they are both of a high standard. Stanley writes about his new friend and then Dimitris gives Stanley this cigarette case. Inside the case is a piece of music, written on the day after they play the duet, and on it are what appear to be clues. It is dedicated to Stanley and it has remained hidden all these years, only coming to light when at the very villa that Dimitris used to own.'

'Get out of here,' Cassie said in disbelief. 'He used to live here?'

'So my grandson tells me.'

Everyone looked at the far end of the table where Jason was now deep in thought. He looked back at them before indicating the portrait behind him with a tilt of his head.

144

'Meet the Panandreas family.'

'Well, I'll be...' Cassie exhaled through her teeth. 'As you say Margaret, strange.'

'Coincidental,' Polly decreed. 'Can I help myself to a drink, young man?'

'Of course,' said Jason. 'Everything at the bar over there is included in your package. If anyone wants to go out before bed the village cafes are not far away.'

No one seemed to have heard him. Polly had gone to the bar and the others were studying the manuscript paper and listening to Margaret.

She explained why she had chosen the SARGO holiday; to pass on the cigarette case to Jason, who happened to be working on Symi where Stanley had wanted his ashes scattered. The others agreed that there were indeed some strange coincidences playing around them.

'Scatter the ashes?' Lesley's lips curled down at the corners.

'Stanley wanted to be laid to rest on the island,' Margaret said. 'I've brought him with me. I hope to find the right resting place before I return to England.'

'Well don't tip him here,' Lesley said with distaste and looked around the well kept salon. 'He would get hoovered up.'

'I will investigate the location tomorrow,' Margaret said. 'I know the name of the place but not where it is. Jason will help me.'

Cassie had been studying the music again. Now she lifted her glasses from her face and placed them on top of her head.

'It's a code,' she said simply and the others turned to look at her.

'I'm sorry dear, did you say something of importance?' Polly smirked from across the room. 'A code?'

'If you ask me,' Cassie said confidently, 'this music is a code. Plain and simple.'

'How do you work that out?' Harriet asked. 'And what's simple about it?'

Cassie stood up and took the paper over to the bar where she accepted a tall glass from Polly. She ran her long fingers across her chin and hummed a short melody.

'Oh lord,' Polly sighed. 'She's going to sing. Stay away from the light fittings girls.'

'Don't be so mean,' Lesley said protectively. 'I'm sure she has a lovely voice.'

'She has a clarity of tone that shatters glass,' Polly warned, remembering a past incident or two. 'We were once in a show that required her to blast this hideously loud note every night. Follow-spots blew regularly and in Carlisle the chandelier nearly crashed to the auditorium. Very Phantom of the Opera.'

'What's she doing now?' Margaret whispered.

Cassie was ignoring everyone else and had started tap dancing, moving her feet delicately and shuffling her toes in a strange rhythm.

'It'll be sunstroke,' Harriet diagnosed. 'Does strange things to the elderly.'

'It looks more like a sand dance,' Margaret observed.

'Cassie, what *are* you doing?' Polly's strident voice cut loudly through the night air and in the distance a donkey started braying.

Cassie stopped dancing, spun on one heel and faced the others.

'It's a musical code. I'm sure of it.'

'Very good dear.' Polly gave her a sneer. 'Can we have your Shakespeare now?'

'Look,' said Cassie returning to the table excitedly.

She kicked aside a chair and turned it with her foot before sliding onto it. She pointed to the numbered sentences as the others gathered around her. All except Polly who stubbed out her cigarette and leant against the bar.

'*Music is another language so take note off my score.*' Cassie pointed to the words with a sharpened but perfectly manicured fingernail. 'Music is another language, we use notes on the score but each note has a name. The name of a letter.'

'Yes?' Margaret did not follow the train of thought.

'Letters make words.' Cassie then pointed to the first line of music. 'Take notes off the score, in *another language*, and you might get words.'

'No idea,' said Polly. 'Explain woman.'

146

'The musical scale starts from A and goes through G,' Cassie was starting to talk more quickly as the ideas poured into her head. 'Or they can be *do, re, me, fa, so* and so on.'

'I know this one!' Lesley exclaimed cheerfully. 'We did it in CRAP. A female deer, drop of golden sun and Marcus Hill dressed as a Nazi storm trooper in tight jodhpurs and a black leather overcoat. I played a nun.'

The others looked at her, mouths open, until Cassie cleared her throat and went on.

'I get The Sound of Music reference doll, but it's not exactly what I mean,' she said flatly. 'What I mean is; if we read the notes as letters maybe then we'll get words.'

'Go on then Miss Devereaux,' Margaret enthused. 'Read us the first line.'

'O.k., give me a second.'

Cassie reached into her handbag to pull out a pen and her SARGO helpful handbook. She opened the book at the blank inside back cover and, pointing to each note in turn from the top line of music, wrote down the English letters that they represented. When she had finished she looked at what she had written and said, 'ah, phooey. Strike out.'

'What does it say pet?' Harriet asked.

'DC FC FC.' Cassie replied, her voice edged with disappointment.

'I don't mean to rain on your parade,' Polly was leaning over her friend's shoulder now, 'but there's a lack of vowels.'

'What if we use the Germanic scale?' Cassie said half to herself. 'Do, re...' and started to write another set of words.

'What does it say now?' Margaret was intrigued by the idea that someone had given a coded musical message to her husband. Even more exciting was the knowledge that it now might fall to her to crack it. She so loved a good mystery.

'If middle C is Do,' Cassie said, 'and we work up from there... then it reads, Re do fa do fa do.'

'Wrong trees and barking up come to mind Cass.'

'Give over Pol.'

'It's all Greek to me.' Harriet laughed. 'Gerrit? All Greek to me?'

'Is it Greek?' Margaret asked Jason quickly.

'Redo fado fado?' Jason replied. 'The only Greek I know that sounds close is stiffado, a meat dish.

'Well then,' said Margaret sadly, removing her glasses. 'Thank you for your interest but I think we are overreacting.'

'I'm with you.' Cassie also sounded deflated as she stood up and started to pack away her guide book. 'Sorry guys.'

'Ah well, it was a nice idea.' Lesley tried to sound sympathetic, she could see that Margaret looked abashed. 'So, who is going to join me in the village for a bit of talent spotting?'

The others looked at her and Margaret thought Polly was about to take a swipe when her mood unexpectedly changed.

'Read the second clue.'

'I don't think there's any need,' Margaret started but the one time dancer had trotted to the head of the table and grabbed the manuscript.

'*And the rests the words' divisions...*'

'What is Poll?' Cassie stopped what she was doing and sat slowly.

'The rests,' Polly replied as if the answer made perfect sense.

'Rests?' Oliver spoke for the first time in ages and the sound of his voice turned heads. Most of the ladies had forgotten he was there. 'Of course, the rests!'

'I don't get it.' Even Jason was being drawn in now. He circled the table and came to look at the manuscript over Polly's shoulder.

'*Rests the words' divisions,*' Polly repeated.

'For god's sake woman, explain.' Cassie huffed.

'It has to be what you said,' Polly went on. 'The music is written in another language and if we take the notes off the score then somehow we will get letters. When we get the letters we will get words. The clue here, number two, clearly says *the words' divisions.*'

'I understand...' Oliver started but was interrupted.

'The rests!' Polly insisted. 'It's so simple.'

'And what's more...' Oliver tried again.

'So that means…?' Margaret asked, not understanding what Polly was getting at.

Oliver could contain himself no longer. 'He's telling us again that there are not only letters represented by the music but whole words,' he blurted out. The others looked at him en masse. 'You were right, Mrs. Devereaux'

'Miss.'

'You were spot on in fact. This manuscript is indeed a code. Clue one tells us there are letters represented by musical notes and clue two tells us how to divide the letters up. By using the rests.'

'What's a rest?' Lesley asked. She had taken out her notebook and was writing some of this down so that she could keep up with what everyone was saying. It was giving her a headache.

'A rest,' Cassie explained slowly, 'is when the instrument, or voice, is not sounded, when there's no music.'

Lesley still didn't understand.

'You've been in shows?' Cassie asked her and Lesley beamed.

'I was a triumph in *The best little whorehouse in Texas*. The reviewer for the Little Sutton Parish News called me *the most natural woman of easy virtue on the stage*. Or was that for Oklahoma?'

'A musical, good, then you know what a rest is,' Cassie said and opened her mouth to ask Oliver something.

'It's that lovely part of the evening when you put your feet up, have a Gin and Tonic and Marcus Hill comes to your dressing room in his costume…'

'Lesley!' Polly thumped her fist on the table and spoke with all the flourish of Dame Edith Evans playing Lady Bracknell. 'A rest is when you have nothing to sing, nothing to perform. There is silence, wonderful and golden, no sound. *Nothing to perform*. Listen to Cassie, she knows. She has spent most of her career resting.'

Lesley just smiled vacantly, her pencil poised to jot down another useful piece of information. But she had still not understood the connections.

'Oklahoma,' Cassie said quietly. 'You sang in Oklahoma?'

'Only the chorus,' Lesley replied modestly, clutching at her pearls. 'But they knew I was there.'

'So when you sang the finale you also came across rests.'

'Finale?'

'Oklahoma where the wind, and all that O.K.L.A.H.O.M.A. business, remember?'

'That was a very tricky song, yes,' Lesley agreed. 'They should have called it Ohio, I could have spelt that.'

'Whatever.' Cassie was losing patience and approached Lesley with simple words. 'When you sang the spelling song, hon, you also had rests.'

'Did I?'

Cassie knew she would have to demonstrate. She rolled her eyes said, 'listen, I'll show you.' She filled her lungs with a deep, controlled in-breath. Her chest swelled outwards straining against her brightly coloured blouse and her shoulders rose. She started to sing.

'O...'

The note was delivered with clarity and precision. Beginning quietly at first, Cassie held it masterfully, filling the room with the sound. She swelled her upper body and drew her hands up towards her chin as the sound increased. The others around the table smiled appreciatively and only Lesley looked confused.

The note continued. The whole room began to fill with the perfect soprano delivery and everyone could tell that Cassie had great command of her voice.

The note continued and increased in volume. Lesley shifted uncomfortably in her chair as the sound became louder.

The note continued. Clear, unwavering, as if someone was pressing on a solitary organ key releasing air to the pipe without interruption or change in pitch, and opening the volume pedal at the same time.

The note continued. Everyone waited for the closure, the 'K' sound that they all knew would come next. It didn't.

The note continued. Cassie now raised her hands up to her chin and turned them outwards as if offering the sound to Lesley who sat before her.

Lesley's face set solid in a forced smile. She recognised the beginning of the song but she had never heard it so close and powerful before. She was sure that the air from the American woman's lungs was blowing her hair out of shape and she felt pinned into her chair.

The note not only continued but got louder. Lesley was holding her own breath, waiting for the end of the word, the 'K' that would bring release. She was desperate to hear it so that she could gasp for breath in the pause that she knew would follow. But the note continued.

And got louder, and louder, and clearer and more powerful.

Until a light bulb in the fitting over the table imploded, showering the remains of their supper with glass. Only Lesley winced, the others were rooted to the spot, willing Cassie to take a breath and put them out of their anticipation.

Finally she did. '…*k*.'

Everyone breathed in during the slight pause that followed.

'…*lahoma where the wind comes whistling down the plain.*' Cassie continued without a breath as the others slumped in their various places.

'Now then,' Cassie said as if nothing had just taken place. Her stare was still fixed on the dumb, dyed-blonde who sat pale and quivering before her. 'That little gap, just as you were about to pass out? *That* was a rest!'

Silence.

A round of applause.

Lesley thought she should pretend to understand, recovered slightly and said a quiet thank you.

'Brava Diva.' Polly clapped once and reluctantly. 'That's going in our new review.'

Oliver was twitching with excitement. He took the manuscript from Polly and pointed to some of the symbols on it.

'These are the musical rests if I'm not mistaken,' he said showing them to Cassie. She nodded. 'Good, and these are the things that will divide the letters into words when we find them.'

'Great,' said Polly. 'But how do we find the letters?'

'We need the key,' Cassie said calmly, seemingly unaffected by her performance. 'All codes have keys. To find out what note is what letter we will need a key.'

'And…' said Jason.

The rest of the sentence hung in the air with the scent of a blown light bulb. Everyone turned to look at their rep. He stood, resting his weight on one leg and examining one of his perfect fingernails. He grinned cheekily back at them.

'I know where it is.'

NINETEEN
The monastery of Stavros
June 16th 1915, 7.30 a.m.

Dimitris had slept the rest of the night outside, curled up beside the well. The lantern burned out just before the dawn leaving the courtyard in total darkness as he dreamed of his parents and their pride in their only son.

Before he left the grounds of the monastery in the morning he checked the courtyard to ensure it was cleared of any ropes, lanterns or other evidence that he had been there. It looked exactly as it had done for years. He closed the iron gates behind him, straightened the framed sign that he had hung there the night before and sealed the gate with a chain and lock. Satisfied that his tasks had been carried out well and in secret he turned to retrieve his donkey.

'What are you doing up here?'

Dimitris froze in shock and felt his face redden in an instant. Even the donkey pricked up an ear and stopped chewing.

A small boy about ten years old dressed in ragged clothes and carrying a shepherd's crook far too tall for him, stood directly in Dimitris' way. Dimitris thought he recognised the child.

'I said, what are you doing up here?' the boy repeated. His tone was aggressive, adult and in a way, menacing.

Dimitris gathered himself. He felt guilty, as if he had been caught doing something wrong. But this was his place, his land and he had nothing to feel guilty about. So why was the boy making him feel uncomfortable? Who was he?

'I am checking on my property,' he said, wondering why he felt the need to justify himself. 'Not that it is your business. What are *you* doing up here?'

They were a morning's hard walk from the village, nowhere near a track or path and a long hard climb from the nearest bay. How had the lad got to Stavros so soon after dawn? Dimitris suddenly felt panicked that maybe the boy had witnessed his secretive activity the previous night.

'Father says I am to find the sheep and bring them down,' the boy explained. Suddenly the menace was gone from his voice and he sounded proud, as if he was carrying out his first grown up chore. 'Do you have any bread? I've run out.'

And then Dimitris placed the boy. Petros Tzankatis, youngest son of Michaelis.

The Tzankatis family had worked for Dimitris' parents and Petros' father had once been a sponge boat captain, his uncle had been Christos' secretary. Several of the other male members of the family had been divers, most had either died or been crippled while working for Christos Panandreas. The remainder had recently left the island in search of better lives. Village talk was that Panandreas had starved the family from Symi and it was well known that for many years the two families had been at war. The Tzankatis dynasty had worked hard for the Panandreas family and all they had received in return was death and poverty.

The feud had been established long before Christos took up the sponge trade however. There was some ancient family dispute over land, the land that Dimitris had just re-established as his. He remembered reading something about it in his mother's paperwork after she had died. But now the Italians had confirmed that Stavros and the surrounding land was his. There could be no dispute about it anymore.

Petros was blinking up at him with huge brown eyes. Dimitris smiled.

'I have some food Petros,' he said, feigning kindness and starting to walk again. 'We'll have breakfast down in the forest shall we? Or would you rather a sweet?'

Dimitris reached into his pocket and opened his cigarette case by springing the false hinges. He had mastered the art of opening the puzzle box and had used it to keep a variety of things safe, anything and everything that would fit in it, apart from cigarettes. He drew it out of his pocket and offered its contents to the boy. Inside were three boiled sweets wrapped in brightly coloured paper. Young Petros' brown eyes grew larger.

'I must go around to the other side to meet papa,' he said. He pointed to somewhere beyond the monastery but his eyes remained fixed on the sweets.

'Then you should take one for your journey.'

The boy reached out his hand tentatively, his fingers taping the air as he decided which colour sweet to take.

'You take that and I will whip you!'

Dimitris looked up and to his right. Michaelis Tzankatis was stumbling down from the mountain with huge, cumbersome strides, using the boulders as stepping stones. What could be seen of his face through his unkempt, black beard was red and taught with rage.

'Get away from him, boy,' he yelled but it was too late. Petros had accepted a sweet and had started unwrapping it.

Before Dimitris could react, Tzankatis was on the boy. He knocked him to the ground with one swipe of his solid dark hand. The sweet flew from the young fingers and the donkey ate it without concern.

'Get off my land and keep away from my family,' Tzankatis spat at Dimitris through clenched teeth.

'Your land?' Dimitris flinched but tried to remain calm. He glanced to the boy who was now lying curled up, trembling and crying with shock.

Tzankatis strode up to the gate and glared at the notice. 'What does this say?' he demanded.

'It reminds people like you that this land belongs to me,' Dimitris replied coolly. He knew he had the advantage; the land was his, the papers proved it and Tzankatis couldn't read.

'This place is ours.' The other man turned back, his anger still visible, his face still screwed up.

'It belongs to the Panandreas family and has done for over three hundred years.' Dimitris smiled. He knew he was right and that the smile would annoy the uneducated man.

'Panandreas stole it from us.' Michaels beat on his chest like a gorilla as he advanced. 'Just like he stole my brothers' lives and the lives of my cousins. Stole our livelihoods and our lives like he stole my dignity turning me from boat captain to pauper overnight.'

He squared up to Dimitris and shoved him in the shoulder. The cigarette case fell to the ground. Tzankatis glared at it, picked it up and squeezed it in his huge fist as if to crush it.

'My family died so he could buy you silver.' But for all his strength he could not crush the case. He stared at it in his hand, turned it over and pretended to read the writing.

'I will have that back,' Dimitris whispered calmly.

Tzankatis looked back at his adversary with black, piercing eyes. They held each other's stare, neither allowing himself to be the first to back down.

Tzankatis let out a growl from the back of his throat, a deep rumbling noise like a lion preparing to pounce. 'For what your family has done to mine,' he said slowly, 'I will have revenge.' He let the case fall to the ground and headed back to the gate.

'What are you doing?'

'This land is all we have left. I will take back what is ours.'

'Take it up with the Italians,' Dimitris called after him. Regaining some of his nerve he pulled the donkey's tethers free from the tree. 'Set foot in there and I will have you thrown into Kalymnos gaol.'

Tzankatis stopped in his tracks.

He could see that Tzankatis knew he could not win. Not this argument and not here. Maybe the Panandreas ancestors had wrongly acquired the land all those years before but the current prefecture had decreed that Stavros now belonged to Dimitris. Even if Tzankatis did break in, there was nothing in there for him. The chapel was empty, the ruined buildings useless and he would never find the hidden chest. And the chest was really the only thing that mattered now. Dimitris could also tell that the larger man feared him. The boat captain turned shepherd may have had physical strength but both men knew that Dimitris had intelligence. The Panandreas family had always been clever and they had always had clout with the authorities, whether through bribes or respect it didn't matter. Having just given the family villa and the summer house to the Italian authorities, Dimitris knew that any dispute over this area would be won by him. Tzankatis had nothing to give apart from a few sheep. If the Italians wanted sheep they would just take them.

As Dimitris put the cigarette case back in his pocket the shepherd pulled his weeping son to his feet and pushed him towards the mountain.

Nothing more was said but Dimitris decided to make regular visits to the monastery in the future to check on his property and what he had hidden in the well.

After all, the only thing that mattered now was the treasure that lay secure within the chest.

TWENTY
Villa Sargo
9.30 pm

'It's in the second part of the clue.'

The guests were still recovering from Cassie's explosive demonstration of a silent musical rest but slowly, as Jason sat down among them, they turned their attention back to the manuscript that he now held. He read the second clue again.

'*And rests the words' divisions, but you will need more.* We've decided that the notes represent letters and that the musical rests will divide the letters up into words,' Jason summarised. 'And Miss Devereaux says that all codes have keys to unlock them. Well, the second part of the clue tells us that we will need *more*.'

'That is plainly obvious,' Polly cut in, lighting another cigarette. She was tiring of this conversation and was put out at having been upstaged by Cassie's recent glass shattering performance.

'Why do you emphasise *more*?' Oliver asked. He had started snacking again, checking the breadsticks and Tzatziki for any signs of broken light bulbs.

'Well.' Jason pulled his chair up to the table and lay the manuscript down in front of him. He rested his elbows on the tablecloth and propped his head up with his hands. 'We have assumed that whatever the notes represent is written in English because the clues are in English, am I right?'

'I guess,' Cassie nodded. 'It kind of makes sense.'

'But,' Jason looked at the portrait across the room. 'Dimitris, who wrote this, also spoke other languages. He was a well educated man.'

'Can you be sure Dimitris wrote it?' Margaret asked.

'It's his initials on the page.' Jason pointed to the ΔΠ. 'Delta, Pi. Dimitris Panandreas. I think we can be certain. Particularly as the cigarette case has his name on it and he gave it to granddad. So, maybe the *you will need more* refers to the mention of language in clue one. *Music is another language but you will need more.* More than one language. English for the clues, the language of music for the code and another language entirely to translate the music into words. What about Greek?'

'What about it?' Margaret was starting to build her enthusiasm again. She was impressed at not only how intelligent her grandson seemed to be but also how keen he was to solve the riddle his heirloom had revealed. He had obviously inherited her love for a good mystery. She watched him as he took Lesley's notepad and pencil from her and wrote some letters on a page.

'Miss D.,' he said across to Cassie, 'tell me again the English letters that these notes represent.'

'Sure hon.' Cassie turned the music to face her. 'Starting with the top line: DC FC FC, second line: CG GBCD, third line: DGE FG AEDF. Want me to go on?'

Jason shook his head. His eyes were fixed on the page and his writing. He sat back and looked up at them.

'Nope. Just a thought.'

'What do you mean?' asked Margaret.

'I thought that maybe the notes represented letters of the Greek alphabet; A for Alpha, B for Vita and so on and that we might get some Greek words. But it's the same issue. Not enough vowels.'

'What if...' Oliver started and then fell silent.

Everyone waited.

'Go on Mister Simpson,' Jason encouraged him. The old guy had been quietly concentrating on his food but Jason had sensed that he had been following everything intently.

'Well,' Oliver said quietly. 'In my opinion, the issue is not only the lack of vowels but the lack of letters. More, it is the fact that there are a lot of notes representing only a small amount of letters, A to G. The first seven letters of any alphabet, I imagine, will have a lack of vowels. It would be very difficult to make up any meaningful words, sentences or even code with only seven letters. Don't you think?'

Cassie nodded. 'I agree.'

'Well then,' Oliver continued. 'I know a little about music and one thing I do remember is that all cows eat grass and every good boy deserves something beginning with F.'

Jason looked up sharply and noticed that Lesley had done the same. His eyes flashed to Harriet who seemed to have missed the chance of a cheap innuendo. She was swilling from a fresh beer bottle with her eyes closed.

'Not sure I follow you Mister S.' said Jason.

'What do cows have to do with anything?' Lesley asked. She was peeved that Jason had taken her notebook without asking. She needed it to keep track of things.

'What I mean, dear Mrs. Shaw,' said Oliver with a shy smile, 'is this. Between the bottom of the bass clef and the top of the treble clef there are ten lines and eight spaces. One puts a note on each line and in every space and gives them a letter. Am I right Miss Devereaux?'

'Nail on the head hon.'

Lesley looked blank. Jason had to admit he was also a bit confused.

'But where are you heading to with this clef thing?' Cassie asked.

Oliver held up a finger to her and looked across at the rep. 'Do you know French Jason?'

'Oui,' Jason replied. 'And German and Greek, but not music.' *Or old duffer language. What's he on about?*

'And what is the Greek word for key?'

'Klethi.'

'And the French?'

Jason's eyes opened wide. 'I see where you're coming from,' he said as something dawned on him.

'The planet loopy if you ask me,' said Polly. 'Would one of you two boys like to explain?'

'The French word for key is clef,' Jason began as he took back the manuscript for another examination.

'Clay?' said Lesley.

'Written C.L.E.F. From which we get the English word clef,' Oliver continued.

'And, in music, the clef shows whether music is in the treble or the bass,' Cassie finished off. 'It shows us the *key* to the stave.'

'Stave,' Polly explained to the others helpfully, 'being derived from the Sanskrit word for; *would someone please talk in English so that I may stand a chance of following this!*'

'Yes please do explain in simple terms,' said Margaret. 'Poor Mrs. Shaw is turning quite pale.'

'Okey-dokey.' Jason sat up straight. 'If I'm following you Mr S. What you're saying is that the key to unlocking the riddle lies in the fact that there are more notes than letters.'

'Absolutely... not.' Oliver shook his head.

Everyone groaned.

'What I was getting at,' Oliver said, 'is that we need more than seven letters. There are more than seven notes on this music. What if each of the lines and spaces from the bass to the treble was a different letter of the alphabet? Start with A on the bottom line and work upwards for example. What would that get us?'

'I'm on it,' Cassie started to scribble in the back of her guide book again.

'I still don't understand about the cows,' Lesley muttered and went to pour a drink at the bar.

All eyes watched as Cassie looked from the music to her book and translated the notes into another set of letters. When she had finished she sat back.

'What have you got?' Jason asked.

'The top line reads: MLOSOLL and the second one reads: LIIKEF. Crap.'

Another group sigh was interrupted by a loud belch from Harriet.

'Beg pardon,' she banged her bosom with a fist.

Everyone looked at her. Margaret in particular seemed offended by her lack of manners. Harriet realised that she was being glared at.

'Well it were an accident,' she protested.

'Accident!' Cassie shouted triumphantly. 'Jesus H Christ, it's staring us in the face!'

TWENTY ONE
The monastery of Stavros
July 14th 1944 – 8.30 a.m.

'What the hell was The Golden Fleece anyway?'

The SS officer sat with his feet up on a table and smoked a cigarette. Ash dropped onto his black tunic and he brushed it off, cursing when it left a grey smudge.

'You should always blow away the ash, Ulrich, that way it leaves no trace.'

'Shut your mouth and keep digging.'

The second officer stood with a crow bar in his hand and glared at his colleague. 'I work and you sit and smoke? How do you figure that one out?'

'I am in charge,' Ulrich said quietly but there was no mistaking the threat in his voice.

'Yeah, yeah, we know.' A third uniformed officer, on his knees by the window, was chipping away at the wall plaster with a hammer. 'We get covered in shit and you smoke your expensive cigarettes.'

'The privilege of my contacts,' Ulrich replied with relish. 'Get a move on.'

The soldier with the crowbar, SS-Oberstormführer Karl Grauber, sneered at Ulrich and bent towards the floor. They were all three of them the same rank, it just so happened that Ulrich had once had dinner with The Führer and so classed himself as a personal friend. It made no difference to Ulrich that there had been three hundred other officers and soldiers in the room at the time and that he had never actually *met* The Führer. It was enough to have been invited to dine with him. Ulrich felt

162

even closer to his leader now that the Fuehrer had charged the garrison on Symi with a 'special' mission. Ulrich saw it as a personal stamp of approval for him, direct from the man himself. Hitler had known that Ulrich was on the island and therefore had entrusted him to find whatever it was they were searching for. The truth, which the lazy Ulrich had overlooked, was that the command had come via a long stream of other, superior officers and that Hitler would have had no idea who was running Symi. He probably didn't even know Ulrich's name and wouldn't recognise him if he sat on his face. His proof of this? Even Ulrich hadn't been told what they were looking for. He only knew its code name.

Grauber smashed the crowbar into the floor and began to rip away. By the window Schmitt hacked at the plaster, sending dust and debris up to cloud the sun that was starting to glow through the broken shutters. Ulrich flicked his ash away from himself and admired his boots.

'To answer your question,' Grauber said as he yanked up a floorboard, 'the Golden Fleece was the skin of the ram that rescued prince Phrixus of Greece from a sacrificial altar. It was given to King Aetes, again of Greece, who hid it away at Colchis at the end of the world. Until Jason, challenged by Pelias who had usurped his throne, came to find it with the Argonauts.' He threw a lump of floorboard to one side. 'No dead sheep under here, only rock.' Grauber became aware that the other two were gawping at him. 'You want more detail?' he smirked. 'I studied many mythologies before…'

'Just rip up the fucking floor.' Ulrich was getting bored. They'd been systematically tearing the outhouses apart for two hours now looking for something that didn't exist in the first place.

'How will we know when we find it?' Schmitt asked for the tenth time.

'We will know,' Ulrich replied.

His orders had been as clear as sludge. *"Operation Golden Fleece. Any property belonging to, or once belonging to, Christos Panandreas, Symi, is to be searched thoroughly. Known property includes: Villa Panandreas, Chorio. Large house at south end of beach at Pedi. Chapel and buildings of monastery 'Stavros', in the area 'Manos' in the hinterland. Previous offices of C. Panandreas Direct Sponge Importers, North side of harbour, Yialos.*

"Complete destruction of internal walls, floors, ceilings etc. is acceptable. Discovery of 'The Golden Fleece' or any letters, records etc. dating from circa 1882, originating from (or to) Venice with signatures R.W. or C.P. to be recovered intact.

"Highest secrecy mission. Urgent."

Ulrich drew in on his cigarette and imagined himself receiving his medal from the Führer in Berlin as he handed over the Golden Fleece.

They had disembowelled the Pedi house, the harbour building and the grand villa from top to bottom, starting in the pitched roofs and finishing with the cellars and grounds. So far they had found nothing but dust and old furniture presumably forgotten by the previous resident. The Italians had left the island and the properties in a hurry two years before and had left everything in a mess. None of the buildings had yielded any secret treasure. There was nothing but stone walls behind the plaster and nothing under the floors except dust and builder's rubble. Nothing in the void above the painted wooden ceilings and beneath the floor joists.

Ulrich had turned over a few rocks in the courtyards, uprooted a few dead plants to show willing but there was nothing buried there either. They had shone torches into the oven recesses, into the dried up water cisterns and in the outhouses before totally smashing down a few walls for good measure.

They thought they were onto something when they discovered an alcove hidden behind wood panelling in the salon of the grand villa, but it had been empty. No Golden Fleece, no plunder. Not even any tapestries hanging on the walls to bundle up and send home. The villa had more or less been stripped bare by the time they had walked into it. If there had been anything of value there it had probably been taken many years before when the Italians first came to the island.

And so, earlier that morning, they had moved on to their final venue. The chapel near the top of the mountain. When they had arrived, just before daybreak, Grauber had requested that they destroy the chapel last.

'What does it matter?' Ulrich had said. 'We're going to tear down the lot anyway.'

'The other buildings are already half ruined. They will make for an easier start.' Grauber reasoned.

They were standing in the small chapel with torches looking at the frescos and icons that adorned the walls. Ulrich had seen what he thought was a tear in the other soldier's eye.

'We don't have time to be sentimental.' Ulrich slammed his crowbar into the wall sending the face of a saint crashing to the ground in pieces.

Grauber glared at him and opened his mouth to protest.

'Yes lieutenant? You have something to say.'

The other soldier clicked his heels and snapped to attention.

'With your permission, Schmitt and I will begin in the buildings across the courtyard.'

Ulrich looked at Schmitt, who just shrugged gormlessly, and then back at Grauber. It didn't matter where they started as long as they found what they were looking for. It had been a long trek up to this god forsaken place and Ulrich was in need of a coffee and a cigarette. He decided to let the other two do what they want and told them so.

He followed them across the courtyard to the first of the outbuildings and stopped to light up.

'Start with than one,' he ordered. 'I will join you.'

As he stood flicking his ash into the black hole of an ancient well and watching it fall into oblivion, he listened to the other two start their work. He took his time over his smoke, letting them get on with the hard work, and enjoyed the view. As the sun rose he could see the Aegean Sea spread all around him and far below. He wondered when he would get a chance to swim again. His mind wandered to thoughts of the lake at Potsdam, picnics on the shore, his wife...

Ulrich was distracted from his reverie by the sound of boots hurrying across the courtyard. He was suddenly back in the outhouse again, his two colleagues were still hacking away at the building and his cigarette had turned to ash in his hands. He looked up from his feet to see two red faced boys, gasping for breath, as they crashed into the room and stood limply to attention.

'What?' he demanded of them.

'Hiel Hitler. Orders from HQ Sir.' The older of the two boys, no more than eighteen, looked straight ahead, his eyes fixed on the wall rather than the officer.

'The General is here?' Ulrich swung his legs from the table and flicked his cigarette butt across the room. Schmitt cursed as it hit him on the back of his neck.

'No Sir. The order came over the radio.'

'Well, what is it?' Ulrich marched to the door and peered out into the now harsh sunlight just in case the boy was lying and the General had arrived. As he looked out he heard the sound of distant gunfire. It seemed out of place. 'What the hell?'

'The British, sir,' the boy said and Ulrich noted the fear in his voice. He also noted his rank and number. 'They landed in the night on three sides and have taken us by…'

'We're coming. Go.'

The two boys bolted from the room without question.

'That is that then,' Ulrich said as he surveyed the debris around him. They had taken apart most of the building and found nothing. They had done the best they could in the time they had had. The Fuehrer would thank him for that. 'Schmitt, Grauber listen to me…'

But the older boy had reappeared in the doorway.

'What now!'

'I am sorry Sir, but the order is to fall back to the Castro. *Now.* The enemy are already in the village…'

'Bloody hell.' Schmitt was on his feet, leaving the hammer and heading for the door.

'Stay where you are Schmitt. You boy, go.' Ulrich's voice was decisive. The boy went. 'Gentlemen we can't just leave this property like this. We haven't finished.'

'You heard him,' Schmitt complained. 'If they get the Castro we're done for.'

Ulrich knew exactly what the consequences were and it struck him that he should have known about an attack well in advance. Obviously someone had screwed up. He now had new orders; to return to base and fight, but he had not found what The Führer had charged him to find. He thought quickly, aware that his colleagues were hovering by the door.

'This is what we do,' he said and saw their faces fall. 'We cannot risk having the English or, god forbid, the bloody Greeks finding The Fuehrer's Golden Fleece. We set booby traps in case they get this far inland and we return to our search when they've gone.'

'Surely not the chapel?' Grauber sounded shocked.

'Only what you have time for. Act quickly. Schmitt you can do this?'

He was pleased to see a smile cross Schmitt's face. 'Oh yes.' The officer grinned menacingly.

'Well do it now, and quickly. Grauber, you help him. Lay them well.'

'And where are you going?' Grauber asked as he began reluctantly unpacking a bag and pulling out explosives.

'Me? I'm getting the hell out of here.'

TWENTY TWO
Villa Sargo
9.45 pm

Cassie was scribbling again, her pen making quick darting movements across the inside cover of her handy SARGO handbook. Already it resembled something like the Rosetta stone. There were neatly crossed out lines of nonsense, capital letters and musical symbols, # and *b* featured prominently. None of what she was writing made sense.

Lesley returned to the table with a drink and retrieved her note book from Jason. She sat and started writing down useful reminders like 'cows', 'good boys', and 'something to do with F..?' The others were waiting for Cassie to finish writing and explain her most recent outburst.

When Harriet had said 'accident', something had jolted the American singer into life and, without explanation, she had started to translate the musical notes from the score to her book. Now everyone was hoping that she would provide the letters that the music possibly represented. She stopped writing and looked up at the group.

'Strike two,' she said defeated and turned her book to show Jason.

He read the latest line of letters: TSW?WS RNNQFH

'What's that got to do with Harriet's accidental burp?' Jason asked. 'Apart from looking like an accident itself?'

'Close.' Cassie gave a short laugh. 'Remember we spoke of accidentals, the symbols that raise and lower musical tones? I just thought that maybe if we put one letter per half tone instead of Mister Simpson's whole tone, we may get something else. We did, we got nowhere. We run out of letters before we get up to the top note, hence the question mark.'

'Still not quite with you Cass,' Polly sang out.

'I started with the letter A as the bottom line in the base and went up letter by letter, note by note using accidentals, a chromatic scale. Note G becomes letter A, G sharp is B, A is C...'

'I see what you're getting at,' Oliver said. 'But the problem surely is where to start.'

'I know this one.' Lesley suddenly cheered up. '*You start at the very beginning! A very good place to start...*'

'Shut your Von Trapp woman,' Polly chided and Jason laughed out loud.

'I'm so sorry love,' he said to Lesley who looked abashed. 'Couldn't help it.'

'You're all being horrible to me.' She pouted. 'And you're all missing something very simple.'

'Something *else* very simple,' Polly muttered under her breath.

'Dear Mrs. Shaw is quite right,' Oliver said chivalrously. 'We do apologise.'

Polly snorted.

'What have we missed dear?' Margaret asked with all the patience of a primary school teacher. She patted Lesley's hand to reassure her. 'All contributions to solving this puzzle are gratefully accepted.'

'You are talking about keys, and codes and,' Lesley consulted her book. 'Cows. But you have not yet looked at clue three. If you spent more time seeing what is in front of you and less time making jibes at me you would have seen it.'

The others crowded in to look at the next handwritten clue on the manuscript.

'*To find the keys look to my families,*' Lesley read aloud. 'Keys, see?'

'Well, I'll be...' Cassie hissed. 'She's right.'

'What keys though?' Jason had noticed the clue before but had got stuck on the previous ones and trying to find a quick answer. The notes are letters, the letters are divided into words but without a key they made no sense. They needed the key to work out how to read the letters.

'This music is in the key of B,' Cassie announced. Jason didn't understand. 'There are five sharps on every line, there.' She pointed to the five # symbols at the start of each line of music. 'That tells the musicians to play in the key of B.'

'So start your chromatic cipher on B and not G you mean Cass?' Even Polly was starting to get interested now. 'What do the letters read then?'

'Give me a minute.' Cassie started writing again.

'That would be fun wouldn't it?' Oliver rubbed his hands together. 'If the key to the code was something to do with the key to the music?'

'It would make sense,' Jason agreed. 'Not that anything else has made sense since we opened the cigarette case.'

'Give it time, I'm sure we'll crack it,' Margaret said and stifled a yawn. 'Though if we don't do so soon I will have to admit defeat and head for bed. It has been a long day.'

'You're telling me,' Cassie agreed. She didn't look up from her writing. 'I've been on the go since dawn. If this doesn't work I'm calling it a night.'

Jason felt wide awake, surprisingly. He had been working since six that morning, He should have been asleep by now but, thanks to Cassie and Oliver's enthusiasm for solving the riddle of his heirloom, his mind felt wide awake. And when his mind was awake his body had no choice but to keep up with it.

'Pot to be job if fog.'

'I'm sorry?'

Jason looked at Cassie, startled. She was studying her notes as if they had just sworn at her. She blinked in surprise and looked up.

'The only words I can discern in this jumble of letters are, *pot to be job if fog*,' she explained. 'But it's not right.'

'It is a start isn't it?' Margaret asked hopefully. 'We must be on the right lines.'

'Not really Margaret,' Cassie said. 'If I break the stream of letters where the rests occur, as instructed in clue two, I actually get, po | tz | to | nj | jmbe | jo | and so on.'

'You started from the B in the bass as being the letter A and worked up?' Oliver checked.

'Yup.' Cassie nodded. 'Up by semitones, chromatically.'

'What if you started at B in the treble and worked down in the same way?' Oliver enthused. 'Is that worth a try?'

Cassie growled, tiring of this game. 'O.k.' she agreed. 'One last try.'

It didn't take her long to realise that this was another dead end. The forth note of the top line of music was above the note B that Oliver had suggested she start working down from. She explained this and everyone slumped in their seats.

'So what now?' Lesley ventured to ask after a moment of dejected silence.

'Now we go to bed,' Margaret suggested and there were murmurs of agreement from around the table.

'But we're close, I can feel it,' Jason said and it sounded like he was sulking. 'What's this about families in clue three?'

No one seemed that interested any more except for Oliver who politely read the clue again.

'*To find the keys look to my families,*' he read. 'It says *keys*, plural.'

'Ah, who gives a big rat's arse?' Harriet yawned loudly displaying to everyone the contents of her throat.

'Family?'

At the back of Jason's mind a little voice started to whisper. Not his usual, inner voice that told him what he really wanted to say and often got him into trouble, but another voice. Someone in the glittery cavern that was his memory had picked up a tiny bell and was starting to ring it. And as they rang it they whispered the word *family*.

'What more can you tell us about the family?' Oliver was asking. 'The family of the man who wrote this?'

Jason dismissed the tinkling bell from his mind and looked over at the painting.

'That's Dimitris there,' he said pointing. 'The boy. And his father Christos with his wife, very wealthy merchants in the late nineteenth century. Dimitris studied music in Paris before returning here at the start of World War One. Which was odd.'

'World War One was odd?' Lesley said. 'I'd call it many things but not odd.'

'I'm sure you did your bit for King and country darling,' Polly said sarcastically.

'I wasn't in it silly,' Lesley laughed. 'But one of my grandfathers and an uncle died, so I would call it tragic rather than odd. Odd is how people look when wearing a polyester shell suit. Or when they use unnatural foundation colours...'

'What I mean,' Jason interrupted her. 'Is that it was odd for someone to return to Symi at that time. Most families were leaving, going to fight, or getting out of the Italians' way and avoiding poverty and starvation. Polyester shell suits? Does anyone still wear those?'

'Apparently in Essex,' Lesley said knowingly and both she and Jason shuddered.

'Anyway...' The rep pulled himself together. 'Dimitris returned from a concert tour when war broke out and came back because his father was dying. After his father's death he stayed here. Even after his mother's death, which came quickly once his father went, he chose to stay. He had money and talent, he could have gone anywhere. But he decided to stay on the island. He gave this villa away to the Italians and chose to live in poverty. That's what I call odd.'

'And how does that knowledge help us with our little riddle?' Cassie asked.

'What else can you tell us?' Oliver was keen to learn more. 'Were there any other members of the family, or just the three people we see in this painting?'

'Yes and no,' Jason said. He stood and walked around the table to the painting, the bell had started ringing at the back of his mind again.

'Well that's as clear as mud,' Polly grumbled. 'Explain child!'

'Apparently,' Jason said to the people in the painting rather than those in the room. 'At some point Dimitris fathered a child.'

'Stanley never spoke about that,' Margaret put in. 'He never mentioned that Dimitris was married.'

'He wasn't,' Jason said. 'It was an illegitimate child.'

'Well really.' Margaret pulled her shawl about her shoulders disapprovingly. 'Free sex and lack of responsibilities. And I was just getting to like him. It was in the sixties I suppose?'

'No gran, between the wars. And that's all I know. Somewhere there is, or was, a Panandreas heir.'

'Do you think we could find him? Perhaps he, or she, will know how to solve these clues?' Oliver asked. 'Perhaps that's what is meant by *look to my families*?'

'Doubt it,' Jason said. 'For one, I don't know who it might be or if he or she is even still alive. And two, I only heard this as a rumour. Back in those days, the war days, there were a lot of illegitimate children being popped out but no one ever spoke about them. Not around here, it was all covered up. There was great shame attached to that kind of thing. Even now we'd never get anyone to talk.'

'And this little piece of bastard history leaves us where, exactly?' Polly had finished her drink and was debating whether to have another. She hovered between bar and table.

'Up another blind alley.' Cassie moaned. 'And with a headache. I'm hitting the sack.'

She stood and started to gather her things.

'So if the clue doesn't refer to living family, maybe it refers to those in the picture.'

Jason turned to look at Lesley. She smiled and shrugged. 'Just a thought,' she said.

Jason turned back to the painting. Suddenly the campanologist in his head was thrashing the bell so hard that he could feel the clapper banging against his temples. It was obvious. The key was there for everyone to see.

TWENTY THREE
Villa Sargo
10.00 pm

The guests were now gathered behind Jason, studying the portrait.

'You remember what you said earlier, gran, about how this had been signed twice?'

'Yes.' Margaret nodded. 'But by two different people.'

Jason raised his hand and lightly touched the artist's signature in the bottom right hand corner. Then he trailed his finger across the painting to where Dimitris was holding his manuscript paper.

'More music,' Lesley groaned.

'Precisely not,' said Jason. Aware that what he had just said made little sense he moved his finger down the page of scribbled, symbolised music until it rested on the second signature, the second letter M that had been crossed out. 'What are we doing right now,' he asked the group behind him.

'Thinking about bed,' Polly replied flatly.

'Concentrate woman.' Cassie nudged her. 'We're looking at a piece of music in a picture.'

'The same piece of music as we have over there on the table.' Jason pointed to the list of instruments that had been added to the manuscript in the painting. They were the only legible things on it, the notes were no more than scribbles but the instruments were the same and in the same order. 'This is a connection for sure. But there's more. What is the picture of?'

'It's the view from the front terrace,' Lesley pointed out. 'There's the sea.'

'And...'

'And it's a picture of a family,' said Oliver.

'Exactly! The Panandreas family, painted in 1882 by a local artist, Masarakis. There's his signature there, the M.' Jason pointed back to it. 'Doesn't clue three say *look to my family*?'

'*Families*, plural,' Oliver corrected.

'O.k. well we've got one of them right here,' Jason said. 'They've been watching us for the past hour and I think that the key we need to translate the music into letters is right here.'

'Where? Oh don't keep a secret,' Lesley said impatiently.

Jason's mobile phone rang. *We're all going on a…* He answered it.

'Yes boss?'

Margaret took a step back to let Jason move around her and away from the group. Once he had crossed the room she returned her gaze to the painting. Although she was interested to know what Jason was going to say to them next, she couldn't help but listen in to his conversation.

'We are all fine… Yes, I have…' His voice dropped to almost a whisper but Margaret strained to hear. 'Tomorrow… I've sold all the places.' She knew he had not sold anything. 'What?' She knew that her grandson's boss was the same horrible man who had been so rude to her earlier in the day. 'When?' And she knew that Jason was getting another telling off.

Her heart went out to him. It seemed so unfair. As far as she could see Jason did his job well. He spoke authoritatively about the island and he knew his history. He could speak the language, he had made all the guests feel at ease, he had been polite except for a few slips but that was just how modern boys were. So why was that horrible Mister… what was his name, Slope? Slop? Slipe, that was it. Why was he hounding Jason now? She looked at her watch. It was gone ten o'clock, he should leave the boy alone.

She felt herself starting to anger when she heard Jason finally get a word in.

'I will see you the day after tomorrow and you can ask them yourself,' he said curtly before switching off his phone.

When Margaret felt Jason return to the group and stand behind her she could sense that he was upset. And she knew that she had to do whatever she could to make things better.

Jason tried to get his thoughts back onto the painting and the clue he had recently discovered. But the only voice he could hear in his head now was Slipe's. *'I will be coming to Symi, the day after tomorrow, and I want to ask the guests how they enjoyed your new excursion.'* The one that Jason had said he had invented and sold. The one that didn't exist. He would have to think of something tomorrow, for now there were far more interesting things to think about than Slipe and getting the sack in front of his grandmother. He tried to pull himself together and became aware that everyone was waiting for him to continue his explanation.

'Is everything alright?' his grandmother asked him.

'Just dandy love,' he lied. 'Where was I? Oh yes. Excuse me can I mince by?'

He squeezed his way through the little group and stood in front of the painting again. 'The Panandreas family, 1882,' he said, sounding like the curator of an art gallery showing his exhibits. 'Christos, Maria and young Dimitris. In his hand Dimitris holds a piece of music paper. He was ten when this was painted, already studying music and languages at the island's school and already, as far as I know, an accomplished harpsichord player. But that's just background. Please look more closely at the family, as the clue tells us to. What do you see?'

Everyone stared, no one spoke.

'Miss D.?'

'I'm looking hon,' Cassie replied, 'but I don't see diddly… Oh my god! That is so in your face.'

'Will you try it and see what we get?' Jason asked her without taking his eyes from the painting.

'Right away,' Cassie replied and hurried back to the table.

'What am I missing?' Lesley asked, searching the portrait for whatever Cassie had just seen.

'Quite a lot I imagine,' Polly said. 'But sadly, so am I.'

'Have you seen it grandmother?' Jason asked. He was enjoying keeping them all waiting. He was sure he had just cracked the riddle of the coded music and wanted to make the moment last.

'I'm sorry dear?' Margaret said. 'I was miles away.'

'Have you seen the clue in the painting?'

'Oh yes dear,' Margaret replied. 'I saw it straight away but I didn't want to rain on your parade, as Miss Cassie might say.'

Jason turned to look at her and could tell she was telling the truth. She winked at him. 'Shall we go and see what Miss Cassie has come up with?'

Back at the table Cassie had torn a page from Lesley's notebook and written a table with each row of the table representing an instrument's musical line. As the others sat once more she checked what she had written against the music and then sat back in her chair.

'We're close,' she announced and turned the page to face the others.

Flute	O N S Y	S	N	
Trumpet	O U R	S T V R	O S W	
Violin	P R O T	T T		
Bassoon	M	I I L A	D	
Trombone	I N	S	E L	L
Cello	E C	H E	G O L D E N	F L E E C E

They stared at the strange collection of letters and all eyes fell to the bottom right corner of the table.

'Golden fleece?' said Lesley excitedly. 'I should like one of those for the winter. I have the perfect chemise to match with...'

'How on earth did you get all that?' Polly asked dumfounded. 'There's vowels and everything.'

'Even words,' Cassie admitted proudly.

'The painting,' Margaret said. 'The key is in the painting.'

'Absolutely,' Jason agreed.

He looked back up to the portrait and the others followed his gaze. It seemed that Dimitris was now smiling at them. 'You saw the second M? It looks like another artist has signed, or the same artist has signed twice. As grandmother pointed out to me earlier, it's a different handwriting. Different to the M in the bottom corner.'

'I noticed that too,' Oliver said. 'My first thought was of forgery.'

'It's the same handwriting as on this manuscript,' Jason said and pointed to the beginning of clue one. *Music is another language.* The capital M at the start of the clue was in the same hand as the M written on young Dimitris' music paper. 'It even looks like it might have been written by the same pen.'

'So Dimitris wrote the letter on the painting at some point?' Lesley was trying to work things out.

'Uh hu,' Jason said. 'And he added the list of instruments so that we would know to connect our manuscript with the painting. And that answers the question of who added the writing.' He shared a look with his grandmother who beamed proudly back at him and nodded.

'But why did he cross it out later? The M on the painting has a line through it,' Lesley persisted.

'Precisely! It's a ledger line,' Cassie said and immediately knew she would have to explain further. 'When notes don't fit on the five lines of the stave, or in the spaces, you have to write them above or below the five lines and add an extra line to accommodate them. Those added lines are called ledger lines.'

'Yes?' Lesley was no more enlightened and prompted further clarification.

'The M on the painting has a line through it because it is where middle C would be if it were music,' Cassie said.

'Yes?'

'When you write middle C in music you write it on a ledger line, between the treble and bass staves, so that you know it's middle C.'

'Yes?'

'Without the line through it, it would unclear as to whether it was the middle D or the B below that should be played.'

'D and B, yes.' Lesley nodded enthusiastically.

'Because the note D sits over middle C and under the bottom line in the treble stave and the note B sits below middle C and above the top line in the bass stave. Get it?'

'Yes?'

'You do?'

'No.'

'Give me strength,' Polly said, exasperated. 'Just tell us how you got some legible words from that music by looking at that painting and then we can all go to bed.'

Jason took the manuscript paper and took Lesley's pencil. Between two of the empty staves at the bottom of the page he wrote a capital M, just like the one on the music in the painting. Then he drew a line through it.

M

Beside it he copied one of the notes from the music and drew a line through that too.

0

'In music,' Cassie explained, 'the note that Jason just drew would be middle C.

'Yes?' Lesley said.

'Oh don't start her off again,' Polly grumbled. 'Just get to the point.'

'Well if I'm right,' Jason said and glanced at his grandmother. She smiled at him and nodded encouragingly, the gesture reassured him. He looked back to the page and wrote another symbol between the letter and the note:

M = 0

'The letter M equals middle C,' Cassie said. 'So instead of starting our cipher from the top and working down, or the bottom and working up like we did before, we start at the middle of the music, middle C and the middle of the alphabet, M. Working chromatically in *both* directions we substitute the notes for letters and we get what I wrote in the table there. ONSYSN, MIILAD, OUR STVROS and so on.'

'Which still makes no sense to me,' Polly interrupted. 'Apart from the words On, A, In, Our and He. Apart from Golden Fleece I see no coherent combination.'

'But we're close,' Jason enthused. 'We must be on the right lines.'

'Maybe,' Polly sighed. 'The right *ledger* lines. Which is exactly where you can keep your notes that don't make up words.' She looked at the table of letters. '*Ilad ell prott.* That's Polly Arnold code for I'm going to bed.'

With that she stood and took her glass back to the bar.

'Good idea,' Oliver agreed. 'I have an early start in the morning. As intriguing as this all is I really must rest.'

'What are you getting up early for?' Harriet asked. 'You're on your jollies.'

'Early bird catches worms and all that,' Oliver said cryptically.

He stood up and looked down at the remaining supper that littered the table. 'I'll just take some supplies if I may.' He started gathering breadsticks and Doritos and stuffing them into his pocket.

'Well,' said Lesley collecting her notebook and reaching for her pencil. 'If we are done here I am going to investigate the local bars, it's still early.'

The group started to disintegrate around him and Jason just watched. He was keen to carry on with the puzzle, he knew there was a message in there and they were close to finding it. There was no way he could get to sleep before he did so. But if his guests wanted to go to bed, or go out, he couldn't prevent them.

'Do you want me to show you where the bars are?' he asked Lesley.

'The army boys told me earlier where to find them,' Lesley replied looking at her watch. 'Good lord, I will be late.'

Margaret had been quietly studying the table of letters. Now Jason noticed her move very close to the portrait. She held the table of jumbled letters up to it. She was blinking fast and chewing on her bottom lip, apparently thinking hard about something. As the other guests filtered away to their various rooms Margaret took the paper and slipped out to the terrace leaving Jason to clear the table and prepare it for breakfast.

A few minutes later, when Jason was alone in the room, Margaret popped her head around the door. She was smiling.

'Jason dear,' she said in a whisper. 'Come out here.'

'What is it gran?'

'I think I've found a solution.'

'You've solved the puzzle?'

'Better than that, dear. I have also solved Mister Slipe.'

TWENTY FOUR
The ruined village
October 19th 1944
20.30 hours

'Hello, anyone in here?'

Stanley shone his torch into the pile of rubble that had once been a house; he was sure that he had heard a noise. There was no reply. He called again trying Greek this time, still no reply. He moved on along the narrow lane, picking his way carefully among the debris.

Around him the night had darkened to blackness. Apart from the stars the only light came from torches as other soldiers searched the ruined village for signs of life. In all probability its inhabitants were either dead or hiding up in the mountains. It was possible that some of them wouldn't even know that the island had once again been taken by the British.

Stanley called out again. Again no reply. The night was a warm one and he cursed his heavy uniform that now stank of stale sweat. Oh for a long bath and a clean pair of socks. He sat and swigged water from his can, warm water, but fresh at least. Something stirred in the shell of a house behind him and he was on his feet in seconds.

'Who's there?' he called. No answer. 'I am a British solider, you are safe, who is there?'

Nothing but a scratching sound, a rat probably. Above him he could see that his mates had reached the ruins of the Castro, their torch beams flashed around the night sky like miniature anti-aircraft searchlights. The straight lines of light reaching off into space until they faded, consumed by the night sky, lost in the million stars that burned overhead. Stanley continued his search, checking his watch; another two hours to go until he was to return to the camp. Not for a long bath maybe but at least he would be able to rest his feet and catch a minute to wash his socks.

To his right he could see a few lights in the harbour. A couple of buildings were still intact and in their windows he could make out lamplight as officers and the island's new officials discussed the future. Word was that, of the many families who had been on the island when the British were last there in June, only a few had come back to the village from their hideouts in the mountains. There were many people still unaccounted for. Some of them might still be alive. Hence this final sweep of the island, hence his late night trawl through the village. Some of his mates were out in the hills, away in the woods seeking out any pockets of islanders who might still be in hiding there.

Stanley stopped in his tracks and looked behind him. Nothing there but the dark street and the fronts of cracked houses, their windows blown out. Blinded buildings. Ahead of him the lane disappeared into blackness long before he could see the end of it. But a sound was coming from within that blackness and that was where Stanley knew he had to investigate.

He shone his torch ahead. Piles of rocks that had tumbled down from the Castro above blocked his path and he clambered over them carefully. On either side of him the empty houses barely stood, their doors hanging off, glass crunched under foot. Destruction all around. Nothing here but ruins and rats.

And the sound of a harmonica. A tune he didn't recognise.

'Billy?' he called out.

What was Billy doing up here at this time of night and playing his mouthorgan?

'Bill, that you?'

Of course it wasn't. Billy was up the mountain with the others. No one else played the harmonica, only Billy and Stanley. So who was that playing now?

'Hello? Who's there?' Stanley called into the night.

The music stopped. Stanley waited. The music started again and he approached carefully.

'British soldier, who's there?' he called as the sound grew louder.

The music stopped again but not before Stanley had pinpointed its location. He shone his torch towards the fallen wall of a grand house. One of its roofs had fallen in under the weight of the Castro rubble that had landed there and then piled up inside half of the building. The other roof and most of that part of the house was still standing, but barely.

And on the step, where a once grand iron gate hung from one hinge like a broken limb, sat an old man, ghostly thin, nearly bald and squinting against Stanley's torchlight. In his hands he clutched a silver harmonica, his lips were still moist from blowing it.

'Good evening British soldier.' The man spoke with a rasp in his voice but even so Stanley was surprised at the clarity of the accent. He could have been British himself.

'You play well.' Stanley, now that he had found someone, was not too sure what to say next.

'Many things,' the man replied. 'Come, sit.'

'We should get you down to the harbour,' Stanley said as he stood over the man, his hand moving to his rifle just in case.

'I think not.' The old man put his harmonica to his lips once more.

'We're rounding up the islanders and giving out rations,' Stanley told him. 'If you come with me we will find you something.'

'I need nothing but this.' The man blew a few notes on the instrument.

'You live here?'

'Not any longer. But once.'

'Where have you been staying?'

The old man looked upwards, towards the torches around the Castro and beyond. 'In the forests. Tell me soldier, is it really over?'

'For the moment yes sir,' Stanley replied. 'The Germans have left, we're back in command again.'

'Like you were in June? You took them by surprise then but then they came back with their bombs.'

'This time we are staying.'

Stanley let go of his rifle, this man was not the enemy. He sat beside him and searched for cigarettes, offering one when he found the packet. The man declined.

'I have no time for that,' he said and Stanley knew that this man was ill. Starved, weak and realising that he might not live to see the island returned to normality if and when the war ended. There was a feeling of death about the skeleton of a body that he now sat beside. Stanley lit his cigarette.

'We heard that there were still people living out in the mountains and the village who didn't know we were here. I have been sent up to gather the islanders and take them to the harbour...'

'You said. I know what is going on,' the old man interrupted. Obviously he didn't have time for explanations either. 'There are no more people out in the mountains. Once the Fascists surrendered they trickled back. One or two families might have stayed up there but only because that is where they live. But I meant is it all over throughout Europe?'

'No,' said Stanley feeling redundant now. 'It will take time.'

'And you, young soldier, what for you after the war?'

'I'm going back to England to get married,' Stanley said proudly. One day he would be sailing home, demobbed and looking for a job. One day he and Margaret would be walking down the aisle.

'Well, good for you.' The old man's face cracked into a smile and he held out a hand. 'Dimitris Panandreas,' he said by way of introduction.

'Stanley Reah. You are Greek?'

'Or Italian, or Turkish. We have been called many things on this island but I myself have always called myself a Symiot.'

'And your island will be yours again one day soon.'

'Who knows who will claim it this time? Anyway, I shall not be here to see it.'

Again Stanley felt death waiting in the ruins behind him.

Dimitris offered the mouthorgan. 'You play?'

Stanley played very well, as he played many instruments very well, but he was reluctant to accept the instrument. It was damp with spittle and was in the hands of a man who looked as though he was about to die.

'Yes, but not now,' he said apologetically. 'I should be getting you down to the harbour.'

'Ah,' Dimitris shook his head. 'There's no point, I would only have to climb up again.' He almost laughed. 'I know you play. I heard you two nights ago. You play well.'

'You heard me?'

'I was passing your barracks. Your music stopped me. I looked in. I saw you. Play for me?'

Reluctantly Stanley took the mouthorgan. He wiped it on his trousers, threw away his cigarette and held the instrument to his lips. He could smell the old man's breath still lingering on the metal. He swallowed hard. He had seen and done worse things in his few months in the army.

The tune was a plaintive one. A single strain of an old English folk song. A minor key. The sound drifted away from him and wound its way among the wreckage of the village, floated up towards the stumps of the Castro and off into the night. When he had finished he handed it back to Dimitris who took it from him with a sigh.

'You understand music,' the old man said. It was a statement and a compliment.

'I try.'

'No, you do not need to try. It is an instinct, I can tell.'

'Thank you.'

'I will play no more.'

Dimitris put the harmonica away in the pocket of his jacket. Stanley noticed how the material hung from the body. This man had once been broad, strong. Now he was reduced to bones and his frame was nothing more than a coat hanger.

'Come on.' Stanley made to stand up. 'You will play again. Tomorrow night there is to be a concert in the town square. You should play, lift people's spirits.'

A surprisingly strong hand stopped him from standing.

'No thank you.' Dimitris coughed deeply and Stanley could feel the man's pain as he gasped for breath.

He waited for the attack to die down. Dimitris composed himself and took a few long breaths. His eyes were wet, maybe from the coughing, maybe from sadness. Stanley shone his torch onto the ground so that only their feet were illuminated and he didn't have to look at the face.

'You understand music,' the old man said again once he was fully recovered. 'I could tell from the moment you made the instrument sound.'

'Yes, well it's always been a passion.' Stanley was aware of the time. He should be moving on, there were more buildings to check.

'Please,' Dimitris said, himself sensing that the soldier would soon be leaving. 'I want you to do something for me.'

'Certainly. That's why I'm here.'

Dimitris tried to laugh but was unsuccessful. 'No,' he said and his voice was drier than before. 'This is different. You understand music?' This time Dimitris asked it as a question.

'Yes.' Stanley did not tell him that he had played a concerto in front of Churchill a few years ago, it sounded like showing off. 'Well I read it and think I have a pretty good grasp of interpreting what the composer…'

'Good. And you can be trusted?' Dimitris interrupted him. No time for long explanations.

'I like to think so.'

'I must be certain my friend.'

Stanley had no idea what the man was coming to. 'Yes, you can trust me. Now shall we get you down to…'

'No. I have something to pass to you, there is no one else. I must trust *you*.'

'With what?'

'With your understanding of music and your love for its history. I am assuming that you dislike the Germans?'

'Of course.'

'But I need to be sure.'

'That I don't like Germans or that I can understand music?'

'Music, history, everything.'

'Then play with me at the concert tomorrow night,' Stanley said. 'Together we can show everyone that the Symiots and the English are united against the Nazis. We will play a duet. Do you know Rimsky-Korsakov?'

Dimitris suddenly seemed distracted. He thought for a moment before a thin smile broke across his lips. He looked at Stanley.

'Bumble bee?'

'You know it?'

'What instrument? Flute? Violin?'

'Piano duet,' Stanley said, smiling back.

The old man seemed to have gained back some of his life, he was more animated now. 'In front of the whole island?' he asked. Starlight caught in his eyes and they were sparkling.

'Everyone.' Stanley nudged him with his shoulder, carefully. 'I'll take the right hand if you can play the left?'

'But my music is all destroyed.' Dimitris said with a sigh.

'Oh, well if you need the notes...' Stanley began and then realised that the old man was pulling his leg. They both laughed.

'Very well then, I am persuaded,' Dimitris said. His voice was suddenly clearer as if the thought of playing music to his island had given him a new lease of life. 'Tomorrow we shall play for the island and then, when they have seen how we understand music I have a favour to ask of you. It's a deal?'

'Deal,' said Stanley and they shook on it.

TWENTY FIVE
Villa Sargo
10.50 pm

Jason crossed the room and went out onto the front terrace following his grandmother. He held the cigarette case in his hand. The feel of the cool, smooth metal seemed to give him some reassurance, as if old Dimitris was patting him on the back, or standing behind him and saying that everything was going to work out fine.

Margaret was now sat at the round iron table with the table of letters in her hand. She was staring at it by the light of the terrace lantern.

'*Look to my families*,' she mused and then invited Jason to sit with her. 'I think…'

'Dimitris had no family,' Jason interrupted as he sat, 'apart from possibly one illegitimate child born between the wars. She, or he, would be over sixty by now, if still alive.'

'Yes, but that's not…'

Jason had another thought and interrupted again. 'Perhaps Dimitris' child later married and had a family? Maybe this is what he meant in the clues, families plural?'

'Possibly dear, but…'

'But who and where this half-family is, is a mystery. Who would know of them now? Besides, when the coded music was written, Dimitris would only have known that he had a son or daughter, not that this person would go on to produce a family who would still be on the island sixty or so years later.'

'Quite, but I think that is…'

'No,' Jason decided, 'that's not the second family reference.'

His mind teamed with thoughts until his head started to ache. He longed to feel tired but thoughts of strange music, secrets and history galloped through his brain like racehorses. They approached the first hurdle in Jason's mind, the riddle of the music, and leaped over it. There were no fallers as they quickly approached the second hurdle, the spurious excursion he had to organise and execute. *Tomorrow.* It was a big fence, there was no way Jason could leap over it and beyond it was an even higher one, Slipe's impending visit on Friday. With his thoughts refusing and stumbling, throwing riders and generally falling apart, Jason saw that he was not going to cross the finishing line. He would not win the trophy; his dream of an idyllic life on Symi. He was hardly even in the race. Slipe was coming up fast behind him and was odds on favourite to win.

He stared at the glittering sea in the harbour beneath him and let his eyes fall out of focus until all that he saw were blurry lights and shimmering colours set against the pitch black, deep ocean. He was starting to cry.

'Jason dear, I have had something of an epiphany.'

A faint whiff of lily of the valley came to him on the gentle night breeze and the touch of his grandmother's hand on his brought him from his thoughts. He looked at her.

'Your grandfather spoke of musical families.'

Jason took in a deep calming breath, wiped his eyes and told himself to stop being such a drama queen.

'What's wrong dear?' his grandmother asked kindly.

'Nothing gran, sorry. Just tired.'

But she looked at him in such a way that he knew she was not convinced.

'What's this about musical families?' he asked and cleared his throat.

'Present families first.' Margaret tilted her head down and looked up at him from under her brow. 'What is the matter?'

And Jason felt, for the first time in many years, that he had found a member of family that he could actually trust and talk to.

'Just work problems,' he said.

'The weasel in Rhodes?'

'Yup.'

'And?'

'I've got a problem with him.'

'Yes, I know that. And you also lied to him so you are in more trouble.'

'Gran! How do you know that? Were you listening in?'

'I am your grandmother dear. It is my job. What exactly did you tell him when he telephoned you earlier?'

'In a nutshell: I told him I had organised an excursion tomorrow and sold all the places to the guests. He is coming over in two days to find out how it went.'

'I thought so. But there is no excursion tomorrow?'

'No.'

'And when he finds out…?'

'He wants me sacked gran.' Jason's voice rose higher in pitch. There was something about the old woman's presence that was freeing him. He felt able to confide in her like he'd never confided in anyone before. 'He's looking for one last excuse to get rid of me.'

'Why?'

'Because he knows I want his job. Rather, he knows that I should have had his job and with me around there's always a chance I'll get it from him. If the company knew what he was really like he'd be out and I'd be in, where I should be.'

'And why don't you tell them?'

'They wouldn't believe me. They think the sun shines out of his arse and he tells them that nothing shines out of mine.'

'Yes, well…'

'He's put in false reports about me so they wouldn't believe me anyway.'

'And you want his job do you?' Margaret asked once she'd removed the thoughts of Slipe's backside from her mind.

'No. Well yes and no. All I want…' Jason faltered.

Margaret took his other hand and held both, looking at him kindly. 'Tell me.'

'All I want is to stay here. To live on this island and be happy.'

'Could you take another job?'

'Not now. It's September, businesses will be winding down soon, I will need my last two month's pay to see me through while I find a job back in England and this job comes with a room. I can't afford to rent anywhere or to stay here…'

'It's alright dear.' She squeezed his hands. 'We will think of something.'

Jason looked at her and realised that she was out of focus. His eyes had been watering again and suddenly he felt stupid.

'Sorry.' He sniffed. 'It's been a long summer, I'm knackered.'

'You have been treated unfairly.' Margaret let go of his hands and sat back. 'But you have also been selfish.'

'Eh?'

'So you have a dream, to live in this place and be happy. Why should you? What have you done to deserve it?'

'Gran?' Jason was taken aback. She now sounded like she was having a go at him.

'We would all love to live out our dreams dear. I used to dream of travelling with your grandfather. That Stanley and I would take cruises, see the pyramids and the Sphinx. We would explore India and discover the secrets of Tibet. I used to imagine us taking long holidays on exotic islands, visiting temples and ancient sites in Asia, crossing Europe in an open topped car. I even had a very silly dream once that Stanley would carry me over the threshold on our wedding day. But… Well, sometimes we have to forget our dreams and live in the real world.'

'Why?'

'Because.'

'Why can't I live here? Why do I have to go back to England at the end of the year and get some crappy office job?'

'Why? Because you do not deserve to stay here. Why have you not saved any money for your future here, for example?'

Visions of late night drinking, eating out, buying clothes and CDs flashed through Jason's mind.

'It's difficult to save money here,' he said and shrugged.

'So.' Margaret reached into her bag for her glasses. 'There we have it. You have told a lie to the man in charge and done nothing about your dream. Now you must live with the consequences. So, back to this music.'

Jason knew she was right. As his heart sank, as thoughts of Slipe crept back into his mind, he knew that he was, as he would have put it, "stuffed". His grandmother was right. He could have saved, he could have looked for another job earlier and he could have stood up to Slipe. But he had not done any of these things. Why? Who cared why? It was done now.

'As I said,' his grandmother was saying, 'I had something of an epiphany.'

Jason had all but lost interest in the music now. He felt too low to worry about it. But his grandmother seemed intent on finishing what they and his guests had started earlier. She spread the page of letters and the music side by side on the table and adjusted her glasses. Then she looked around, checking that they would not be overheard.

A light came on in the far, downstairs bedroom and Margaret shuffled her chair closer to the table.

'I remembered something Stanley had said,' she whispered conspiratorially. 'About musical families and it struck me that there was... is... something missing. The musical families are the last piece of the puzzle. I am sure of it.'

'I don't understand,' Jason admitted, shaking his head to clear his thoughts.

'Here is the table of letters that Miss Cassie drew.' Margaret studied the paper as best she could in the gloom and then fetched out a small torch from her hand bag. 'And here I think we have it! Bear with me.'

Again she delved into her bag and this time produced a pen. Jason wondered if her bag was bottomless but the thought vanished as she started to scribble on the paper. She explained as she wrote:

'Something was not right about the arrangement of instruments,' she began. 'Flute on top, then Trumpet beneath it and Violin beneath that. Stanley talked a lot about music as you know and I am sure that I remember him saying that, on a score, even one with a small combination of instruments like this, there are rules as to layout. If our Dimitris Panandreas was as trained in music as you say then he would have known those rules, surely. Basically one groups all the woodwind together in a certain order, and then the brass, strings and so on. Flutes

193

are at the top, so that's right, and low strings like Cellos are near the bottom so that's right. But Bassoons are wind. Do you see what I am getting at?'

'Er… no.'

'Flutes are wind and Bassoons are wind. They are in the same musical family.' His grandmother beamed at him. He knew that she was waiting for some kind of joyous response. None came.

'And your point is…?'

'My point, dear,' the old lady rolled her eyes, 'is that the instruments are not grouped correctly on this music. It took me a while to work out why this should be but, when I looked at the portrait again, it came to me. The list of instruments that appears in the painting is the same list of instruments as appear here. But if you look closely you see that they are written in the *wrong* order.'

'Why?'

'Protection,' Margaret said. 'In case someone, like us, worked out how to exchange the notes for letters. By putting the musical families in the wrong order he has further jumbled up the words that the notes represent. Our old Symi friend did not want anyone but a musician finding the message he had written here, that's for sure.'

'I still don't understand gran.'

'But what is he hiding… no, what is he *protecting*? Look!' Margaret had drawn out a new table putting the instruments in the correct descending order, as they would appear on a score:

FLUTE	O N S Y	S	N	
BASSOON	M	I I L A	D	
TRUMPET	O U R	S T V R	O S W	
TROMBONE	I N	A	E L	L
VIOLIN	P R O T	T T		
CELLO	E C	H E	G O L D E N	F L E E C E

Jason looked at the second table, it made as little sense to him as the first.

'I know I'm a bit dim,' he said, 'but…?'

'Very well.' Margaret smiled. 'I will explain. How are you reading this?'

'Left to right.'

'How do you read music?'

'I don't know. The same?'

'Yes.' Margaret continued to smile.

Considering the fact that she had endured a long journey, flown for the first time and was over seventy years old, Jason admired her energy. He could see that she was of tough stock and wondered if any of that resilience had found its way to him. If it had he had not noticed it before. He suddenly felt proud of her.

'But when you have a musical score,' his grandmother went on, 'it is read from left to right but also from top to bottom, at the same time. If one was conducting an orchestra, as your grandfather did before the war, one would read the whole set of instruments at once, bar by bar. So, now read it across and downwards simultaneously.'

Jason looked at the page and read, 'Onsy, mour, in prot ec,' and then looked back up blankly.

'Now we need to read it by family. We must look to its *musical* families, just like the clues instruct,' Margaret enthused. 'Remember Flutes and Bassoons are the same family. Read just their two lines together, down and left to right simultaneously. What would you read then?'

Jason took a quick glance. 'Fuck knows!' he said and then blushed. 'Sorry gran.'

Margaret drew in a long breath, fixed him with disappointed stare and shook her head.

'Are we really the same family?' she said quietly.

'I just don't understand gran.'

'Very well.' She removed her glasses and rubbed her eyes before continuing. 'Basically, in this music there are three sentences with two instruments of the same musical family sharing the words of each sentence. The rests on their lines indicate the breaks between words in the sentences as Miss Arnold pointed out. You will notice that the two instruments in the same family never sound together? That is because each of their notes is a different letter in their sentence. This music was written to be read, not played. Now do you understand? No? Never mind, just trust me. Read the first sentence aloud, the top two lines as you see them.'

'Onsy mii sland,' Jason said, pronouncing the strange combination of letters and sounding like a tape running slowly in reverse. But his grandmother was shaking her head, still disappointed in him.

'What you are doing,' she explained kindly, 'is reading them block by block. The rests, remember, show where the breaks are. Put a break after the "N". Then read the first word.'

Jason looked at the table and did as he was told. 'On,' he said.

'And the second break comes after the first "I", so we get...?'

'Sy...mi.' It took a moment. 'Symi!' Jason looked up at her, his eyes wide. 'On Symi...' He studied the paper again and the code started to fall into place. 'On Symi island! Flaming arseholes you're a genius gran.'

'We must have some kind of English language lesson together before I leave,' Margaret said dryly. 'So, now read the brass instruments, the Trumpet and Trombone, in the same way.'

'In...Our... Stavro swell...Stavros well. I get it! On Symi island in our Stavros well...'

'Protect the Golden Fleece!' Margaret finished the translation triumphantly.

Jason took a folded Sargo form from his back pocket and wrote out the sentences so that he could read them more easily.

'But what does it mean?' he asked as his grandmother sat back in her chair looking very pleased with herself.

'Well, that's where your expertise will come in I think,' she replied.

'Mine?'

'On Symi island.' She pointed to the first sentence of the three. 'You know all about the island so tell me what is a Stavros?'

'Not a what, where. Oh my god!' Jason finished writing the lines and read the whole message as one sentence. 'Well that makes sense!'

'What does?'

'This coded message suggests that there is something called the Golden Fleece.'

'Yes. And...' Margaret leaned in closer to him.

'It is on this island, presumably hidden in the well up at Stavros, and should be protected...'

'Yes...?'

'And it's gold.'

'And if you can find it...' Margaret let the sentence hanging.

'If *I* can find it?'

'It is your inheritance. It came from your cigarette case.' She smiled. 'Do you see what this means?'

'Not entirely,' Jason admitted. 'I mean I know about the Golden Fleece, the myth, but it is just a myth. Isn't it?'

'Do you want to find out?' Margaret was smiling impishly now.

'You mean... go and look?'

'Of course! Why not?'

'But gran....'

'Mother, *grandmother* for pity's sake boy. But what?'

'The monastery of Stavros, which belonged to the Panandreas family, is the highest and most inaccessible monastery on the island.'

'And?'

'It would take half a day to get there.'

'So?'

'In fact I am not even sure that you can get to it anymore. It's private land, beyond an army base...'

'You must try.'

'But...'

'But what!'

'But I've got that arsehole Slipe coming in two days and a bunch of old wrinklies to take out tomorrow...'

Margaret threw back her head and laughed loudly. She stopped herself and covered her mouth, looking around in case she had woken anyone. The light in the end bedroom went off.

'I am sorry,' she whispered through her fingers, her eyes dancing with laughter.

'What is so funny?' Jason hissed back.

She shook her head as she regained control and put her hand on her chest. 'You have inherited your mother's brains. Or lack of them.'

'Gran!'

Margaret waved him to silence as she lent forward. Then she signalled for him to lean in closer.

'Listen to me Jason,' she said. 'And listen carefully.'

Her whispers carried through the stillness of the late night as if they were coming from somewhere high above. Jason lent towards her so that their faces were close.

'Your grandfather left you that cigarette case for a reason. Ever since your mother cut us from your life he wanted to do right by you. He left nothing in his will but this case and the secret within. He said that the music would guide you. You now know the secret of the music and you have a chance to act on it. Seize it. Forget the obstacles. I will help you with them as best I can. Don't you see what you have to do?'

Jason shook his head.

'You must find the Golden Fleece Jason. Find it and do what is right for it. Whatever it is.'

'But how?'

'Don't think how, think why.'

'Why? I don't understand.'

'This opportunity has come to you from far back in history.' Margaret's voice was less hushed now and seemed to float away from the table; across the terrace and out over the harbour where the dark sea lay calm and the harbour lights were dimming. 'The secret was given to Stanley by Dimitris. Who knows how or why it came to him or how old this story is. But now it has come to *you* and together we have unlocked the secret. Now it is your duty to take it forward. You must find the Golden Fleece. And don't ask why again. The answer is simply because it is your duty. That is all.'

Jason shook his head and dropped his shoulders. He knew she was asking the impossible.

'Look at it this way,' Margaret said and cleared her throat. 'What if you organised an excursion, tomorrow, to Stavros? We will all come with you. We will have a lovely day out and you can find what is hidden up there in the well.'

'But that's...'

'Simply killing four birds with one stone. You have your excursion, Slipe will be kept off your back and, more importantly, you will fulfil Dimitris Panandreas' wish.'

'That's only three birds.'

'The fourth is mine,' Margaret said and Jason noted that a hint of sadness had crept in to her voice. 'You don't remember where your mother said that Grandfather Stanley had lost his legs do you?'

'I was very young.'

'You still are dear but do the words Stavros Symi ring any bells?'

'Stavros... You don't mean...'

'Yes dear I do. Your grandfather met with his accident at the same place. While you are finding the Golden Fleece and carrying out Dimitris Panandreas' last wish I will be scattering Stanley's ashes and carrying out his. So you see, we have to go.'

The more Jason thought about it the more impossible it all sounded and yet he knew his grandmother was right. It would provide the last minute excursion Slipe demanded, it would allow her to say goodbye to his grandfather and perhaps, just perhaps, they would find something in the well that was valuable. Perhaps he would be able to stay on the island after all.

All he had to do was organise it.

Overnight.

He shook his head.

'I can't take you all on a wild goose chase just because some dead Greek guy wrote a piece of music,' he said. 'I'd have to organise a boat, get supplies. I'd have to ask you to hike through the forest and up the side of a mountain. Not to mention the army base we'd have to get through undetected and trespassing on someone's private land. I can't expect a group of old... of guests to help me clamber down a well to search for something that may not even exist, and then do the whole thing in reverse to get home again! No gran, I can't do it.'

Margaret gripped his hand again. 'You must if you want to realise your dream.'

TWENTY SIX
Stavros, Symi, 1944
October 20th, 13.00 hours

Dimitris sat among the ruins that had once been his family churchyard and controlled his breathing. It had been a long arduous trek up the mountain, even with a borrowed mule for transport. His chest burned and his mouth was dry. He knew that he did not have many days left to live. So few days, so many decisions.

He propped himself up against the tree and stared at the well. Beyond its low stone wall the opening gapped like the entrance to Hades, black and uninviting. There was no way he could lower himself down there again. But he knew that the Golden Fleece was safe. Since war had broken out he had spent much of his time visiting the land, ensuring that what was left of his property remained safe and as undisturbed as possible by invaders, foreign and domestic alike. Many local families had moved to their mountain homes to escape the occupation as best they could, some to hide supplies, others to engage in espionage work and others simply to try and carry on a normal life. Dimitri had shared his time between his village room and the crumbling walls that now surrounded him, his life driven by the need to protect the piece of history that the well contained. He had had cause to fear for its safety only once; last June when three German soldiers had destroyed the rest of his family property.

He had watched them early one morning at the monastery, ready to kill them by whatever means he could muster if they started investigating the well. He had known what they were looking for but had not worked out how they knew that the Golden Fleece was on Symi. As far as he had ever understood no one but him, his father and his father's friend who originally sent the chest knew of its existence. But Dimitris knew that Hitler had been desperate in his quest for mythological artefacts and had ways of discovering secrets. Who knew what he had learned from the libraries of Venice, Paris or even Bayreuth? He had sent troops on quests for the Holy Grail so why not the Golden Fleece?

Dimitris allowed himself a smile. How disappointed Hitler would have been had he found it. And how disgusted.

But his smile faded as his mind returned to the jumble of decisions he now had to make.

Would his plan work? Could he really trust the young soldier? Would even he be able to unlock the clue that would lead to the Fleece? Should he have retrieved the chest and fled the island when he had the chance, between the wars when the days had not been so turbulent? Probably. So why didn't he?

Anna.

He had stayed for Anna. Secretly doing what he could for his illegitimate daughter for the last sixteen years. The thoughts of her illicit conception warmed him. He put his decision making to one side again as he remembered her mother. And then his thoughts chilled him. The one off 'fling' born out of late night revelry and revenge on his name day back in 1928 came back to both cheer and haunt him.

It had been at the church of Saint Dimitris, outside of the village. The night had been a warm one for October, cloudy with no moon and seductively dark. He had sat on one side of the courtyard, alone, staring at the Tzankatis family on the other. The boy Petros, by then twenty three, sat with his young wife, Sophia. She was beautiful; dark eyed with flowing brown hair that was cut short in the latest style. Michaelis Tzankatis, the ignorant shepherd who had tried to claim the Panandreas land a few years before, had been dead and buried for three years leaving Petros as the head of the rival family. Handsome, cocky and evil, anger glowed permanently behind his black eyes. He had taken after his bullish father; his fists too were always clenched, ready for a fight. He sat with his arm around the back of Sophia's chair not to hold her or touch her in some affectionate way but to ensure that she remained beside him; subservient, behaved, under his control. He shielded her from the assembled villagers, challenging them to deny that she was his. He could not possess the Panandreas land at Stavros but he could posses the most beautiful woman on the island.

Or so he thought.

As the night wore on and the dancing and music became more uncontrolled, Petros could not resist showing off more. He took to the courtyard floor in a long, agonising dance, kicking, swirling, showing his prowess and his strength. He danced the Mihanikos, the sponge diver's dance that portrayed the life of the divers. Proud, invincible, agile and strong to start with, the dancer glorified the ancient traditions of the diver in his movements as the other men circled around him. He danced for a long time before suddenly falling to the ground, apparently writhing in agony, desperate, struck down. As he did this, Petros glared across accusingly towards Dimitris. He was the son of the hated Christos Panandreas, the man who introduced the suit and forced them to use the deadly skafandro that claimed lives and livelihoods alike. The master behind the monster that the dance described.

Petros saw that Dimitris was no longer in his chair.

But everyone was watching Petros and he could not stop dancing now. He was as transfixed in his dancing as those who were watching him, hypnotised by the story and the lengthy, complicated dance. The villagers were engrossed in the tragic story that he played out; the diver once proud and manly suddenly struck down in crippling agony as the diver's disease hit him. Petros slowly and painfully staggered to his feet as the band played out a mournful, plaintive melody. Slowly he rose, his face as contorted as his body, his mind now on only his dance and the admiration he would get from the crowd around him when he finished. He rose to his feet, every movement showing the pain and desperation of a young man unexpectedly afflicted, his youth destroyed. And, as he rose, the crowd started to move forward waiting for the final act, the triumph over adversity. The other men moved to Petros, aided him, until he was once again swirling and leaping with bravado, the determination of men triumphing over the evils of the skafandro.

When, after fifteen minutes, the dance came to an end the crowd applauded wildly. Amid shouts of 'bravo' and the smashing of glasses the men crowded in on Petros to slap him on the back. They begged him to dance another story and offered half full glasses of ouzo and wine.

Petros parted them with one sweep of his powerful arms, his mind now back on the empty chair. He took two mighty steps towards where Panandreas had been sitting and stopped, breathing quickly and sweating with his exertions and with rage. Someone else was missing. He spun and forced his way back through the crowd as people pressed him to dance some more. Emerging on the other side of the throng he glared to where he had left his wife… and saw her sitting, her hands on her lap, smiling demurely back at him. Again he pushed back through the crowd, growling and swearing, only to find Panandreas once more in his chair, a full glass of wine now in his hand.

Dimitris raised the glass to him, bowed his head slightly and drank.

And now Dimitris laughed at the memory. Quick, full of passion and revenge. He had not loved Sophia, merely been infatuated with her. She was barely twenty, he was in his early fifties, it was a blasphemous and illegal thing that they did but, in those times, these things happened. But it had been a triumph for Dimitris, to know that he had made love with the wife of his family's enemy.

Triumph turned to mild panic and then to elation when the following summer Anna had been born. Sophia was discrete in the way she got messages to Dimitris. Petros assumed the girl was his, Sophia knew better. 'She is yours. She is a Panandreas. We women know,' she had whispered to Dimitris one night as they passed each other on the dark Kali Strata. Dimitris was allowed a brief, furtive glimpse of his daughter before Sophia passed by. He held the image in his mind for as long as he could, until the next time he saw the child, being carried to the baptism by a godfather.

He watched her grow up from a distance. Although she carried the name of his rivals, the Tzankatis family, she carried the blood of Panandreas. Dimitris prayed that one day she would learn her true background and would realise that she was more than just another village girl. She was the bond that could reunite two families, could end the feud between them and could carry the name of Panandreas on Symi for the future.

But he would never know if it would happen. Anna was fifteen now, unaware who her true father was. She was part of the Tzankatis family and, with death fast approaching him, there was no way Dimitris could protect her any more. Undoubtedly she would have children of her own, but who would she marry? Who would continue the Panandreas bloodline? The name would die with Dimitris but the spirit would live on in someone.

He had thought long and hard about this over the past few years and, at the outbreak of the war, had decided that one day someone should know the truth. A few years ago, before he had become ill, he had written a message and placed it in the chest in the well. When the chest was opened the truth would come out. Not only the truth about the Golden Fleece but about his family line. He was already old by then and

204

knew that he would not live to see his daughter marry, would not know who the next Panandreas heir was. But somehow, at some point in time, the world would know. The note had been written in Greek, Italian and English and had been precise:

To whoever finds this letter.

I am Dimitris Panandreas, the only son and heir of Christos Panandreas (1844 – 1914) and Maria Panandreas (1848 – 1914), Symi.

The object in this box belongs to history. Whoever finds it must do what is right for it and must ensure that it is kept for mankind. As the letter (signed by the author and dated 1882) explains, this is a genuine article. My father and I have protected it for as many years as we can. I only hope that, when it is found, the world will be a safer place for it and that the world will understand, will forgive us for keeping it hidden for so many years. When you think of the times we have lived through you will understand why.

But this chest contains more treasure than the Golden Fleece. I must also leave you information. Please ensure that this news reaches the appropriate parties:

In 1928 Sophia Tzankatis (wife of Petros Tzankatis) and I conceived a daughter. Anna Tzankatis (as she had to be known for her own protection) was born in July 1929. She will, I hope, one day marry. Any children born of Anna, or Anna herself if she is still living, must know that she was the daughter of Dimitris Panandreas. Her children will be of my family. Our name will live on through them.

Dimitris Panandreas - 1939

That was why he had stayed on the island, through two wars, four governing countries, poverty and strife. To protect the Fleece and, later, to watch over his daughter.

But now the end was fast approaching. He suspected the typhoid would let him live a few more days at best. After that the Fleece and his daughter would have to survive on their own.

At least he had believed that until a few nights ago.

He had found someone who would, he felt sure, carry the secret for him. Not a local person, not even his daughter – she did not know she was his daughter and even if she did she was too young to understand. Petros Tzankatis must never know about the fleece. He would sell it straight to the authorities, Nazi or British it didn't matter.

The war had warped men's minds and not even the British could be trusted with it.

At least not all of them.

The young private who understood music was the only hope for the secret now. He would understand what must be done. But not yet. He could not be told outright what the Golden Fleece was or where it lay hidden. He would be in an impossible situation if he knew. Stanley would find it impossible to keep the chest with him, return it to England and find a safe place for it there. He was a soldier, a private, he would have to hand it over to his commanding officers and they would not appreciate its worth.

And so Dimitris had decided to write some music. Something that only a musician would understand.

He took the piece of manuscript from his pocket and checked it over once more. It seemed easy enough to decode, a little too easy maybe? He decided not, in fact he now thought it too complicated. It was only because he knew where the strange clues and the badly written tunes led that it appeared easy to him. It was obscure enough to make sense only to musicians. And, as his father had said, only a musician would understand the importance of the contents of the chest. He hoped his new friend would understand well enough as he dedicated the piece of paper to him absentmindedly writing *For S.R. and R.W. 21/10/'44.*

He dated it for tomorrow as that would be when he would pass on the Panandreas secret to Stanley, it seemed appropriate.

But there was still one last thing to do before passing on the secret.

Having recovered now from his journey up the mountain, Dimitris rose and slowly approached the chapel. Taking the iron key from his pocket he rattled it in the great lock before pushing as hard as he could on the door. It opened a fraction, complaining at its years of neglect, but allowed him just enough room to manoeuvre his skeletal form inside.

The chapel smelled of damp, lingering death and the stale air made Dimitris gag. He crossed himself, drew out a candle and some matches and approached the ancient carved screen. Asking for forgiveness, as he had last done back in 1915, he slipped behind the screen and lifted the alter cloth. It fell to pieces in his hands like dusty cobwebs.

Dimitris knelt at the altar as if in prayer; but his only prayer was that the portrait was still there and preserved. He reached under the stone slab and felt the frame. The thin rope that held it in place seemed intact and he searched with his fingers for the knot. With some difficulty he pulled at the tangle of rope and freed the heavy painting. The portrait started to fall but he caught it and lowered it gently to the floor. Shuffling back on his knees he drew the painting out from under the altar and unwrapped the blanket that shrouded it.

In the flickering light of the candle he gazed down at his history. He had tears in his eyes as he looked on the faces of his parents for the first time in nearly thirty years, still clear and undamaged by their years of incarceration.

'I hope I am doing the right thing, papa,' he whispered as he took a pen from his pocket.

He positioned his hand over the blank music paper the young Dimitris held out on show and remembered what his father had said on the day that he set off for Paris. 'You said to paint it blank as one day you would write some fine music on it. You said it was to represent your achievements yet to come.'

Achievements? Dimitris laughed scornfully at himself. Nothing achieved. And then he thought of Anna and the way that he had protected both her and the chest. Maybe he had achieved something. But the music he was about to write on the painting would not be fine at all.

The coded music was a fine piece of code but a dreadful piece of music. All he needed now was to add one final clue, and this would be added on the painting itself. Another level of protection for the Fleece; if young Stanley could not solve the riddle from the music alone he would have the portrait to show him the key.

Dimitris scribbled some thin, wavy lines on the staves, to represent the coded music and then, in unsteady, but legible writing he wrote the names of the instruments. Finally he wrote a letter M between two empty staves, a treble and a base, and drew a line through it. Then he rewrapped the painting, put it back into place with the rope and pocketed his pen.

There, it was done. The secret was now secured. One day someone, hopefully Stanley, would figure this all out. By then the world might be at peace. Stanley would return to the island, discover the clues, maybe even the portrait and would descend into the well. There he would find the chest, rescue the contents, pass the news to Dimitris' daughter or her family and put two pieces of history right back where they belonged.

As he stood up he had no idea how many lives his last few actions would affect.

'I've got it all arranged folks, the excursion of a lifetime.' Jason put on his most disarming smile and beamed at the group of slightly mystified guests who sat in the wicker chairs before him.

That morning, once he had roused them early from their rooms, he had broken the news that he and Margaret had solved the riddle of the music. Everyone was interested to know how and what the consequences were and everything had been explained over a quick breakfast. Jason had also told them that they should dress for a boat trip and countryside walk. He was pleased that some had listened to his advice and dressed appropriately. Most were wearing flat shoes and light clothing with hats and sunglasses. Harriet however looked like she was prepared for a day's logging in the Canadian Rockies, in heavy boots, shorts and a checked shirt. Lesley's footwear looked totally inappropriate but she had brought a large shoulder bag with her that no doubt contained spare clothing. Harriet had carried it down the Kali Strata for her and the group now sat in a harbour café where Jason was explaining the day ahead.

'During the night I made some plans,' he went on as the café's waiter placed an assortment of coffee cups on the glass topped tables. 'And early this morning I made some calls and have arranged a boat and supplies for our SARGO mystery trip.'

'We're going to find the Golden Fleece,' Harriet said flatly. 'Aint no mystery.'

'I would rather just go and find a beach and a sun bed,' Polly moaned. 'I need a day to recover from yesterday's journey. Must we go traipsing off around the island today? Can't it wait until tomorrow?'

'Come along Missus Arnold, it will be an adventure. And we are the first SARGO guests to be taken on this excursion. We should feel honoured.' Margaret sipped her coffee and smiled up and her grandson.

'Yes, an adventure.' Jason smiled back at her. He was determined not to let her down today and determined that his impromptu day out would be a success. It would keep Slipe happy, thrill his guests and secure his job.

Jason had been awake for most of the night, planning, plotting and preparing what he could for the excursion. He had grabbed a short sleep in the very early hours but had woken before dawn so as to catch Yiannis, a fisherman, on his way to work. He knew Yiannis vaguely from the few times they had chatted at his favourite bar. Jason had originally been attracted to The Rainbow Bar in the village square because he thought the owner understood the significance of the name. He had been sadly mistaken, it had been called Rainbow for some mysterious reason now lost to time and had nothing to do with gay politics or Judy Garland. Happily though it turned out to be a place where the local fishermen met for ouzo, beer and a damn serious chat about the state of their boats, their women and the country. And, by sitting there when off duty, Jason had come to know quite a few, if only superficially.

He had learned the habits and work routines of some of the fishermen and thus, at four that morning, Jason had managed to secure a boat and a captain for the day.

At six he had gone back into the village, had a coffee at Jean's all night cocktail bar, fought off a couple of forty-something divorcees who were under the influence of too many G and Ts and too much HRT for their own good and had escaped to the bakery next door as soon as it opened. He bought bread hot out of the wood fired oven, dashed back to the villa, prepared packed lunches and assembled any other things he thought he would need for the day ahead. Even his mobile phone battery had been charged; no doubt Slipe would be calling before long to check up on him. When he did Jason could floor him with the news that all the guests had signed up for the new excursion. The fact that none of them had been asked to pay for the trip was something he would worry about later.

He had thought about his grandmother's words during the early hours as he assembled his maps, first aid kit, ropes and provisions. She was right of course; he should have saved some of his wages to see him through the winter. He was annoyed at himself now for being so hedonistic and not planning ahead, but it was too late. At least with Slipe's challenge about to be met he knew that he would have a few more weeks of work on his idyllic island. After that? Well, a winter back in England wouldn't be so bad, particularly if he worked hard and saved up so that he could return to Symi next year. His thoughts started to wander and he knew that that was a luxury he could not afford today. He had to put his plan into action with a clear mind. He was on a mission now and would need all his resources to make the trip a success. It was time to concentrate.

He sat at the round table with his guests and showed them the route they would be taking.

'Detailed maps of Symi are few and far between,' he explained to the small group as he spread an un-detailed one out before them. The best map he could find for today's purpose was 'Editions Kamiros, Symi,' which proudly boasted on its cover that "It includes historical text and photos". On one side, under the promised photographs, was a short history of the island, in Greek, English, Italian, French and German and Jason couldn't help feeling a little smug that he could read the text in four out of those five languages.

'We have a boat that will take us around to the West coast...'

'Does the boat have a toilet?'

'I am not sure Mrs. Shaw but we shall not be on it for long.'

'Should I buy some snacks for everyone?'

'Not necessary Mister Simpson, I have made lunch for eight of us.'

'Eight?' Margaret gave him a quizzical look.

'Captain Yiannis,' Jason explained. 'The man whose boat we are using.'

'Oh,' Lesley's ears pricked up. 'A captain? My third husband was a naval man and taught me all about sailing.'

'Well, he's not actually a captain,' Jason said. 'But it is his boat so I suppose...'

'Go on pet,' Harriet encouraged. 'I want to go and buy me daily paper, chop-chop.'

Jason showed them the route. The map, in 1:34.000 scale, was basic. It showed the road snaking across the island in red and the various tracks and ancient paths in dashes. He looked closely at the area of 'Manos' where the monastery of Stavros was marked with key reference number 62. A long, dashed line headed towards it from the road but stopped well short of the actual site. No easy path that way.

What it didn't show, and what Jason knew from his walks in the mountains, was that to one side of Stavros was an almost vertical drop to the uninhabited, rugged area of Kourkouniotis. Even less apparent was the army installation which lay to the north and the jagged cliffs to the west. Totally missing from the map were any signs of what land was public and what was private but Jason knew that the whole area surrounding Stavros was now private land. He did not know whose but he did know that, to reach the monastery and the well, they would have to trespass.

He would cross that bridge when they came to it.

If they got that far.

'Well it all looks very exciting.' Margaret drew her handbag to her in her lap and studied the route. 'Is this the monastery of Stavros here?

'That's it grandmother. And here is the bay where we will come ashore.'

'You're surely not expecting us to walk up that hill are you?' Polly was outraged.

'It's a gentle climb.' Jason tried to appease her. 'Through the woods, we will stop for lunch along the way. And we may even see some wild tortoises.'

'Oh whoopee!' Polly sat back in her seat and scowled at her coffee.

'Oh get over it,' Cassie chided her. 'You've done nothing but whine since we got here. It'll be good for you. Character building and all that. Well, o.k. Character *restoration* in your case.'

'See, I've drawn the route on the map,' Jason went on, 'the path of least resistance if you like, starting from here in the harbour.' His pen mark began at Yialos and headed north across the sea. 'We will sail around the island to the west as this will be the quickest and safest way to reach the bay of Apiana, the nearest practical shoreline to Stavros. It lies on the more accessible side of the mountain.' There was another bay, due south, which would have been closer but Jason couldn't think of a way to easily transport six O.A.Ps. up the sheer cliff face behind it, so he had decided on Apiana as the place to come ashore. 'From there we will enjoy a short ramble across open fields to the church of Nikolas Kefalis where we could stop for lunch.'

He watched their faces closely. Most of the guests seemed interested and a little excited at the journey ahead. Jason noted this and relaxed. As they took their coffee and studied the map he kept the details of the second part of the journey to himself. After the easy walk across the fields they would have to ascend the west slopes of the mountain to the army encampment. If they could get around that without problems then Stavros would be only an hour up and to the left.

'*Up and to the left. Up and to the left...*' What film was that from? Kevin Kostner describing how the Kennedy assignation had to have been a conspiracy. JFK. Sudden death. Jason shivered.

'Well, we ready for the off then?'

Jason was roused from his vision of Slipe aiming a rifle at his head from behind a grassy knoll by the sound of Harriet's chair scraping as she stood up. 'Just go fetch me paper...'

'Yes, right. If you've finished your coffee...' Jason gathered his map and folded it back into his flight bag. 'Toilets inside if you need to go.'

'The boy is obsessed with toilets,' Polly mumbled as she reluctantly stood up.

Ten minutes later and the small party stood on the quay waiting for Harriet. The harbour was full that morning. Charter yachts and luxury cruisers lined both north and south sides while the rank of taxi boats crowded along the west wall. Some boats were moored two or even three abreast and the only empty space was reserved for the day-trip ferries that would soon be arriving from Rhodes. Jason checked the sky, blue and clear but with a small gathering of cloud behind the mountain far off to the south. That shouldn't be a problem. There was no wind to speak of and the sea was flat. It was one of those days when the only thing disturbing the calm lie of the water were the warm and cold currents showing on the surface as different shades of blue, like veins in marble.

Jason saw Harriet thundering towards them waving a newspaper and his heart sank.

'It's been done again,' she bellowed as she finally joined them, panting, flushed and spraying them with sweat. 'Same great bloody hole cut out of every single one. Woman in the shop said it weren't her but I reckon these Greeks are keeping all the coupons for themselves. What the hell do they want bloody English coupons for, and I had to get the ruddy Daily Mail, no Mirrors to be had.'

'Well, I'm very sorry about it love.' Jason tried to appease her but knew it would be useless. She would calm down eventually and of her own accord. 'We will look into it when we get back. But now we should be moving. Follow me.'

He led them over the bridge and around to the north side of the harbour where the morning sun was already beating down ferociously. 'I've arranged for everything to be on board so we just need to find the boat and we're off.'

He felt his grandmother trot up beside him as Harriet's mumbling and cursing faded into the background.

'Are you excited?' she whispered to him.

'A bit nervous gran.'

'Well don't be.' She smiled and tapped his arm. 'I will help you.'

'You already helped me.' He nudged her back. 'You were right last night when you said I'd been selfish and all that. I'm going to show everyone a great time today. We're going to unravel this mystery and put granddad Stan where he belongs. Did you bring him?'

'He's in the bag,' Margaret replied and tapped her handbag. 'Literally. He would be very proud of you.'

'I haven't done anything yet.'

'You have dear, you've made a decision. A good one I think.'

Jason stopped and the party drew up around him. He winked again at his grandmother and addressed the group. 'Our boat is…'

'Oh my god! I will have to run back and change.' Lesley's eyes were open almost as wide as her mouth. She stood looking up at a sleek white yacht that towered beside them and rummaged in her shoulder bag. 'I can't go aboard a boat like that without jewellery.'

'We shan't be on it for long,' Jason explained. 'And you look just fine. Follow me everyone.'

'I'm starting to get interested,' Polly said as she admired the luxury craft. 'Can't we just stay on this for the day?'

A man in uniform waved down at Jason and welcomed him aboard as the others climbed the rutted gangplank up to the lower stern deck.

'Good morning, Captain Yiannis I assume?' Lesley pushed forward and held out one hand to be kissed while she attached some sapphire earrings with the other. 'I do apologise for my dress...'

'About time,' Polly mumbled.

'Come along Mister Simpson, Miss Devereaux.' Jason herded them into a group as each guest gazed in disbelief at the polished wood floor, the gleaming steel railings and brass fittings. He could see Oliver peering through the smoked glass doors into the cabin where a table was set for a sumptuous breakfast and was aware of Lesley advancing on another member of the crew. 'Follow me please.'

He led them along the port side walkway until they came to the bow, some fifty feet out into the harbour. The guests, all now mumbling approval, lined up along the rail waiting delightedly for their next surprise. Polly ran a finger over the rail and checked for salt dust. Even she looked pleased when she found none.

'Well done lad,' Harriet said, her vandalised newspaper already forgotten. 'I'll be writing to SARGO about this, ten out of ten.'

'Yes, well...' Jason coughed slightly. 'I am glad you like it but our boat is down there.'

He pointed beneath the bows and everyone looked down.

A tired old fishing boat sat in the water, tethered to the anchor chain of the yacht by a fraying rope. The open boat had once been blue but layers of paint peeled from it like dead skin revealing a dull red beneath. The windows of the tiny wheelhouse were almost opaque with encrusted salt. Around the stern seating area some concession to comfort had once been attempted as several cushions were strewn about, their orange and brown patterns only partially disguising some dubious looking stains.

'We are going on that?' Lesley said, crushed. 'But I am wearing fuchsia.'

'Down the rope ladder everyone.' Jason remained cheery and opened a small gate in the railings. 'Who's first?'

He looked back at six stony faces glaring back at him. It was going to be a long day.

'Come along,' Margaret barked after shaking her head and tutting at her grandson. 'We may not be young any more but we are all capable of climbing down a rope ladder, surely?'

'I rather had my eye on the breakfast,' Oliver said sadly. 'I only had time for a boiled egg at the villa.'

'You first mister Simpson then you can help us ladies down.' Margaret manoeuvred the small man to the rope ladder and kindly held his cagoule while he climbed unsteadily down. 'Jolly good. Who's next?'

A few minutes later and Harriet was the last to step into the small boat. It dipped dangerously low in the water as she did so and everyone else grabbed the grubby side for support. The boat seemed to emit a strange noise, somewhere between a sigh and cough as it righted itself. The sound brought a tense silence to the group. Cassie looked at her friend and Polly shrugged her shoulders. The others made themselves as comfortable as they could in the crowded stern seating area and Lesley started applying copious amounts of sun tan lotion to her bare arms.

'I don't want to singe,' she explained. 'If I am careful I avoid the embarrassing pink of sunburn and turn immediately to that deep golden colour that men find so attractive. Harriet dear, would you like some Ambre Solaire? Your nose is already glowing a little fiercely.'

'No thanks pet, I prefer to go the colour of boiled lobster if it's all the same to you. Puts the men off, avoids confusion.'

Jason had been checking that everything had been placed in the wheelhouse as instructed. Yiannis had arranged and stowed the supplies he had been asked to provide and everything seemed to be in order. Apart from the packed lunches, canned drinks and some beers there was a duffle bag containing a small first aid kit, a few torches and a long length of nylon rope. He had the SARGO form in his back pocket with the translated message written on it and the cigarette case with the original manuscript in his flight bag, just in case it was needed. He was all set. The only thing missing now was the boat owner himself.

'We're just waiting for our captain,' Jason explained as he reached for his mobile phone.

'Would he be a slightly rounded gentleman with a great deal of facial topiary?' Margaret asked, looking up at the yacht.

'Yasou Yianni!' Jason waved and everyone else turned to look.

A middle aged Greek man with a large untidy beard, small black eyes and curly hair was staring down at them. Although he was red faced and panting, as if he had been running, a lit cigarette hung from his turned down mouth and he chewed it, as he blinked impassively.

'Maybe the sapphires were a bit premature,' said Lesley sadly.

'I don't believe I am entrusting my life to him,' Polly said. 'Is it too late to change my mind?'

'Yes,' Margaret shot back harshly. 'Now pull yourself together and do try and have fun.'

Polly glared at her through narrow eyes as she placed a cigarette into her mouth and lit it silently.

'Hey up folks.' Harriet intervened by offering out some cans of Ice Tea. 'I got these for us all, pass them round. Very important to keep your fluid levels up.'

The boat dipped once more as Captain Yiannis boarded.

'Kalimera,' said Jason, cheerfully offering his hand to be shaken. Yiannis just looked at it and spat his cigarette overboard. 'Yes, well. To Apiana then please, as quick as you like.'

Yiannis grunted something unintelligible and reached up to untie the rope. He threw it forward into a heap and ducked into the wheelhouse.

'Here we go then, cheers.' Jason beamed at his guests as he opened a can of Ice Tea and raised it for a toast. 'Is everyone ready?'

'As we'll ever be pet. Come and sit lad, there's room for a small one up here. Hey up! I've started already.' Harriet laughed and then shuffled along the seat, squeezing Oliver into a corner.

Jason was just about to sit when the boat spluttered into life and jolted forward. His can went flying from his hand as he reached to steady himself and Ice Tea spilled over into the harbour. Harriet caught his arm and he fell into his place.

'There we go pet, nice and cosy like.'

As the small boat nudged its way out into the harbour Margaret lent forward and put a hand on Jason's knee. 'I just had a thought,' she said and chuckled. 'You are Jason and we are your SARGO-nauts!'

Jason smiled back at her weakly and wondered if being fired might not have been a better option after all.

* * *

Two ancient Greek men sat on the bench beside the clock tower and gazed silently over the water. They had sat there every day since long before the war and knew the sea as well as they knew each other; which was almost as well as they knew every boat on the island. One smoked a pipe, the other played with his worry beads, working each one slowly between his fingers as though they were a rosary.

As they watched the mirror flat sea before them they saw a small, overloaded fishing boat chug across their line of vision. Their eyes did not follow it however, but remained fixed on the water. But as the boat passed them they noted the strange collection of English people sitting in the stern drinking from cans and gripping the sides of the craft. They heard the engine straining with the weight and noticed how it misfired.

And they continued to stare ahead, out across the years and the memories as they smoked and worried silently until the little boat was out of sight, heading for the narrow channel between Symi and Nimos. They heard the sound of the engine fade until all around was restored to calm again.

Only then did they speak.

'What do you think Panioti?' asked the smoker.

'What do I think?' the worrier replied. 'I think that was Yiannis' boat.'

'Ah yes. I think you are right.'

'And I know something too Georgos.' The worry beads started to move faster.

'What do you know, Panioti?'

'I know that I last serviced that engine in nineteen fifty three.'

'Ah yes, I remember nineteen fifty three.'

The first of the day trip ferries appeared around the far off headland and made its cumbersome way towards them. The two old men stared ahead and ignored it as they had done every day for over thirty years.

'So, what do you think Panioti?' the smoker asked again.

'What do I think?' The worry beads were slapping into his palm now in a quick, anxious rhythm. 'I think it will sink.'

'Ah yes,' the smoker said sadly. 'I think you are right.'

TWENTY EIGHT

Aboard the boat
10.15 a.m.

'I am not sure about the health of this boat,' Lesley declared as she opened another button on her blouse.

'And you know a lot about boats do you?' Polly asked curtly. The lurching movement of the boat (to say nothing of the sight of Lesley's wrinkled cleavage) was starting to turn her stomach. Every time the boat dipped over a wave something wobbled beneath Lesley's sleeveless dress.

'A little. Do you?'

'We've done The Pirates of Penzance and HMS Pinafore so we know the theory,' Cassie put in.

'And we have also done The Tempest, Cassie, and remember how that starts?'

'Well. Husband number three was a sailing man and so I think I know a little more than you.' Lesley settled back and lifted her chin to the sun.

'What did he sail?' Polly asked. 'Pedalos?'

Harriet was searching the way ahead, trying to see where they were going. She turned to Jason looking worried.

'Is he on the right course pet?' She pointed to the rocky coastline that they were approaching. 'Looks like he's heading straight for them there rocks.'

'It's alright Ms Smith,' Jason reassured her. 'In a moment you will see that that island of Nimos there and the land here are separated by a small channel. From here it looks like one land mass but it's actually two.'

'Well, if you're sure. Hey,' another thought struck her and she reached into a carrier bag for a can, 'shall I see if our driver wants a drink?'

Jason realised that she was nervous. He'd not seen this large confident woman nervous before and assumed she had some kind of fear of boats, or water. 'Go ahead,' he said and immediately regretted it.

Harriet leapt to her feet causing the boat to tip to one side. The rocking became more intense as she headed forward, stumbling towards the cabin.

'I say,' Lesley piped up once she saw how the motion was being caused. 'I do so admire your leggings Ms Smith. What colour is that? Mauve, Cerise?'

'I'm not wearing leggings pet, them's me legs.'

'Oh.'

Polly waved her drink in the general direction of Harriet's backside. 'Gives a whole new meaning to the expression *Avast behind.*'

'Hush your mouth woman,' Cassie kicked her friend as she tried to repress a smile. 'And do try and be pleasant.'

'I'm not that good an actor.'

'You said it hon.'

Harriet had handed the can to Yiannis and was making her way back. She stopped in the centre of the boat and looked over everyone's heads. 'Will you look at that!' she said and everyone turned to follow her gaze.

Behind them the harbour had grown smaller, distant in their vision. The jumble of houses, they could now see, spread out up to the crest of the hill where the church at the Castro caught the morning sun, dazzling white and gleaming. The village clambered on behind until it petered out at the base of a mountain.

'Where's me camera?' Harriet made a lunge for her bag and the boat tipped. Yiannis shouted something angrily and Harriet stumbled towards her seat with a yell.

'Please sit down Ms Smith,' Jason said as he pulled her. 'Sit down!'

'Sit down, you're rocking the boat,' Cassie sang out.

'What a fabulous idea!'

Everyone turned to Oliver who had suddenly perked up.

'We should sing,' he explained. 'It will take our minds off… everything.'

'I'll have to speak to my agent,' said Cassie.

'You have a stunning voice Miss Devereaux,' Margaret encouraged. 'Perhaps you could give us something.'

'A headache most likely,' Polly said flatly. 'But there's no glass to shatter so we might be safe.'

'Honestly Margaret,' Cassie protested. 'I couldn't.'

'Let's sing a round.' Oliver was sitting up straight and beaming. 'I could conduct.'

'Conduct hon?'

'I was choirmaster at Plymouth before…' He stopped suddenly and everyone waited for him to finish the sentence. He didn't; he just fell silent and looked sheepish.

'Before the war maybe?'

'Polly Arnold! If you don't hush your mouth…'

'I think it's a lovely idea,' Margaret piped up. 'Please Miss Devereaux, would you sing for us?'

Cassie sighed deeply and nodded. 'Very well, but you're joining in Arnold.'

'I am a dancer,' Polly protested.

'But you're fully trained hon.'

'Yeah, trained to handle Alsatians,' Harriet mumbled.

Only Jason heard her, he sniggered, recovered himself and said, 'we are going to be at sea for an hour or so, it would pass the time.'

'Oh my, look!' Lesley suddenly exclaimed and everyone's attention was drawn to where she was pointing.

The boat was facing a narrow channel of rough water. On one side sharp and jagged rocks clambered up the side of the small island of Nimos and on the other side water broke around equally dangerous looking outcrops on the edge of the main island. The boat pitched and dipped in the water which had suddenly turned from clam flat to boiling turbulence beneath them.

'It is just the little straight of Diapori,' Jason announced as if it would mean anything to anyone.

'Just a little straight pet?' Harriet laughed. 'And what would you know about that?'

'Please Ms Smith.' Jason nodded his head sharply towards his grandmother who now sat with a hand over her mouth, she had turned pale. Harriet looked from Jason to Margaret and the penny dropped.'

'She don't know?' she whispered.

'No. And I don't want her to either.'

'Secret's safe with me lad, secret's safe.'

Jason doubted it.

'Are we going to get through this alright?' Oliver had already started to turn green. 'Only I think my breakfast egg will be making a comeback if this bouncing up and down continues for much longer.'

'It's quite safe Mister Simpson.' Jason tried to smile. 'I am sure Yiannis knows what he is doing. It's not a long channel and it's always a bit choppy, we'll be through it soon.'

'Those rocks don't look too safe,' said Lesley, pulling her blouse shut against a breeze which had blown up. 'Perhaps I should put my sapphires in the purser's safe in case we capsize?'

'Yes do,' Polly said encouragingly. 'After all, sapphire earrings with a fuchsia frock? Your rocks are clashing darling. And while you're about it will you ask the purser to send some coffee up to me? I will be in the first class smoking room.'

'Just hold tight everyone,' Jason called out, 'and Miss Devereaux will lead us in a sing-a-long to take our minds off it.'

He looked at Cassie imploringly. She looked at Polly. Polly flicked her cigarette overboard, blew out the last of her smoke and nodded reluctantly. Cassie started to hum the introduction to a show tune. A sombre, deep melody that showed she could produce low booming notes as well as high ones that shattered glass. It didn't take Polly long to catch on. It was a song from a show they had both been in many years ago. Cassie started:

'*A sailor's life is supposed to be a hell of a lot of fun.*'

Polly continued:

'*Yes but when you're a sailor take it from me, you work like the son of a gun.*'

'I recognise this!' Lesley chirped excitedly. 'CRAP did it – I was...'

Polly cut her off: '*They give us jobs of every kind and chores of every sort. But sweat away sailor you don't mind...*'

Both Lesley and Oliver joined in the final line of the introduction:

'*'Cos you know when we reach port...*

There'll always be a lady fair, a Jenny fair or a Sadie fair, there'll always be a lady fair who's waiting there for...'

'Hold it, hold it!' Harriet held up her huge arms and waved the singers into silence. 'None of this sexist crap if you don't mind.'

The boat lurched in the water and bounced over a few rogue waves as silence settled in the stern.

'It's art darling,' Polly said, 'just a song.'

'That's as maybe but I guess it's men sailors singing about women ashore as though they was some kind of object for sex only and it don't empower them with self respect or the like. Am I right?'

'I have no idea what you just said so I can't possibly comment.'

'What's wrong with being a sailor's sex object anyway?' Lesley asked. 'It works for me.'

Jason had been paying attention to the direction that Yiannis was steering the boat and hoped, prayed rather, that he would soon be making a turn to the right else they wouldn't be reaching any kind of port. A huge lump of rock projected from the surface of the water a few metres ahead and they were heading straight for it.

'Maybe you could choose something else from the same show?' Margaret offered. 'What was the show anyway?'

'Anything Goes, hon. Cole Porter.'

'How about "Public enemy number one"?' Polly suggested glaring directly at Harriet.

'Or Blow Gabriel blow,' Lesley said with a salacious wink.

'You'd like that Jason wouldn't you?' Harriet bellowed with a raucous laugh but then caught Jason's glare. 'Blow Gabriel? No you wouldn't, scrub that. Secret's safe.'

Yiannis had steered them away from the rock and they were once again in safe, though slightly choppy, waters. Jason relaxed a little. 'What are we singing?'

'Do you think about anything other than sex Mrs. Shaw?' Polly was gunning for someone and her voice was rising in pitch.

'Yes,' Lesley said defensively. 'Clothes, fashion...'

'I mean anything of value?'

'Of course. All the starving and poor of the world who can't afford Couture...'

Jason could sense tension rising among the guests. It might have been nerves brought on by the rough water or simply tiredness following their long journey the previous day but whatever it was he knew he could not allow dissent in the group. They had a longer, harder day ahead of them and any in-fighting could jeopardise his mission. 'Calm down folks...' he started to say but Cassie had now joined the fray.

'If you ask me, Ms Smith's mind is on the same wavelength.'

'How d'you mean?'

'Absolutely Cassie,' Polly agreed. 'A mind like a Welsh railway.'

'You what? I'm from Bolton.'

'One track and dirty. Darling, all you've come out with since you stepped off the aeroplane are innuendoes and smut. Most of them aimed at young Jason here.'

'I'm having a laugh pet, I'm on me jollies.'

'Please, people...'

But Jason's words went unheard as insults started flying freely between the actresses and the other two women.

'You're no better than that blue rinse bimbo.' Polly re: Lesley.

'My hair is naturally blonde actually.' Lesley's riposte.

'Sure and I'm a monkey's uncle.' Cassie to Lesley.

'Well that wouldn't surprise me.' Lesley going into a sulk.

'I can talk about smut if I like. As a working class feminist lesbian I've got the right to laugh at sex.' Harriet, of course.

Neither Jason nor Margaret could get a word in edgeways as the jibes and complaints continued until another voice joined the mêlée. Joined it, cut through it and slowly brought it to a stunned silence.

Oliver had stood and started to sing quietly, sweetly and with a clarity that seemed to calm even the waves. The boat left the narrow channel and turned left, following the coastline where the water was once again peaceful.

'*Times have changed. And we've often rewound the clock, since the Puritans got a shock when they landed on Plymouth Rock.*'

'What a charming voice Mister Simpson.' Margaret rearranged her handbag on her lap and sat up to listen, pleased that the other women had stopped their bickering.

'Well, who'd have thought it?' For once Polly actually looked impressed with something.

'*If today any shock they should try to stem,*' Oliver sang on, his voice rising in volume now that he had distracted them from their squabbling. '*'stead of landing on Plymouth Rock...*' But he looked at the women pointedly so that there would be no confusion as to his meaning: '*Plymouth Rock would land on them.*'

It worked. Cassie and Polly winked at each other and grinned before joining in.

'*In olden days a glimpse of stocking was looked on as something shocking but now god knows, anything goes!*'

'Bravo Mister Simpson!' Lesley clapped her hands together, jangling her bracelets and sang along.

'I hope this doesn't offend you Harriet dear,' Margaret called across. Harriet listened to the next line before replying.

'*Good authors too who once knew better words now only use four letter words writing prose...*'

'Oh no pet. *Anything goes!*'

Jason sat back in his seat and relaxed as his guests forgot their differences and sang. Mister Simpson did indeed conduct, using a ham and cheese baguette from his cagoule pocket as a baton. Even grandmother Margaret joined in, her voice high and brittle as if she had never used it for anything so frivolous before and, by the time they passed Cape Toli, a party atmosphere had descended on the small craft. Jason smiled to himself, they were half way to their landing place already and nothing had gone seriously wrong.

But then his phone rang and all singing stopped.

'Yeah hello? Morning boss...'

'Is that the horrible Slope person?' Margaret lent forwards and asked. Jason nodded. 'Give him here.'

Jason put his hand over the phone and hissed, 'no!'

But Margaret insisted and reached for it. Jason pulled away, leaning back out over the edge of the boat as he tried to speak.

'It's going really well boss, yes honestly. We're on the trip now... Chartered a boat. No it wasn't expensive...'

'Give me the phone Jason.'

'Shh gran. Sorry boss, what? Of course everyone's paid up.'

'Paid?' Polly said. Her voice was perfectly clear and loud enough for Slipe to hear over in Rhodes. 'Are we supposed to be paying for this?'

'She's talking about the... bar,' Jason covered. 'I'm charging extra for the drinks. I thought you would approve.'

'He wants us to pay extra?' Margaret had heard enough. She scowled and grabbed for the phone. Jason pulled it away from her but she grasped his wrist with surprising strength and jerked it towards herself. Jason lost his grip and the phone shot up into the air, heading overboard.

His career flashed before his eyes as Slipe's voice headed towards a watery grave. But Margaret was quick and caught the phone in time. She pressed it to her ear, upside down, and flapped Jason away when he tried to get it back.

'Hello? Slope? I can't hear you...' She noticed Harriet making a gesture and turned the phone up the other way. 'There you are, that's better. Now listen here... What do you mean who am I? I am Margaret Reah, nee De Lacey, thirty-two the Pines, Crowdley Green... What? I am one of your guests! No you listen to me. I just want to inform you that on my return to England I shall be putting in a formal complaint about you to your superiors. You are rude, arrogant and... What? No, you may think you are superior Mister Slime but you most certainly are not in my... I beg your pardon!'

'Give me the phone gran,' Jason hissed at her but she just turned away, her face flushed with anger.

'How dare you talk to... No you listen to... I said... Oh you insufferable man. I will not... No, *you* fuck off!'

And with that uncharacteristic use of a four letter word Margaret threw the Motorola into the sea. Jason thought he could just hear Slipe's outraged voice gurgling through the waves for a second before his beloved mobile sank to the depths.

'Oh dear,' Margaret said suddenly quiet and composed. She sat back looking embarrassed. 'I must apologise for my language. I don't know how you put up with him Jason, you must have the patience of a saint.

He may have had but he had no patience with anyone who threw his phone into the sea.

'Do you know what you've done!' he yelled looking over the edge in the vain hope that the thing would float to the surface.

'Sorry dear.' Margaret, having told Slipe what she thought of him, now felt her old self again. Was it important?'

Jason stared at her in shock. 'Important?'

'I expect the driver will have one you can use,' Margaret said, shuffling her handbag and trying to appear nonchalant.

'Gran, do you realise what you've just done? This is great. It's just fucking great!'

'Jason, don't swear!' Margaret said hypocritically.

'I'm dead, do you realise? Dead. If he rings and I don't answer I'm sacked. End of story.'

'Calm down dear, it was just a phone.'

'Just a....'

'Yes, just a phone,' Cassie said trying to be helpful. 'You can ring him when we get home later and explain can't you? Yes, so calm down and hush up.'

'But...'

'But nothing,' the singer went on. 'We were having a lovely time, you lost your cell phone and it's gone. *That's* the end of the story. So, who's for another show-stopper?'

'Miss Cassie is right dear,' Margaret said, placing a hand on Jason's knee. He brushed it off, folded his arms and sulked. 'Well if you are going to be a baby about it.'

But Jason was not just concerned for his job right then. It was true he could call Slipe back later and explain what had happened and why he had been out of touch all day. Slipe wasn't the real problem. The real concern for him was that, without his phone, there was no way of calling for help should they run into trouble during the rest of the day. And, as they rounded the next headland, he could see nothing ahead but trouble.

TWENTY NINE
In the boat
11.25

'So, Oliver,' Lesley said as she shifted herself along the bench towards him, 'tell me more about yourself.'

The singing had petered out and everyone else seemed lost in their own thoughts as the boat neared a group of small islands. Polly had stood to stretch her legs leaving a space beside Oliver, a space that Lesley was keen to fill.

'What more can I tell you dear lady?' Oliver replied.

'But you have told us nothing so far, except that you were a choirmaster in Plymouth. Was that at the cathedral?'

'Er, no, not exactly.' Oliver had removed his cagoule a while ago. The day was hot and, even with a slight sea breeze, it was too warm to wear the garment. He had spread it on his lap to catch the crumbs from the last of his baguette and now brushed it off before folding it away beneath the seat.

'A parish church perhaps?'

'No.'

'Oh.' Lesley couldn't think of where else a man might master a choir and decided to change the subject. 'Well. Have you ever been married?'

'Married?'

'I hope you don't object you me asking you such direct questions.' Lesley smiled as she batted her false eyelashes and placed a manicured finger on his arm. 'But I think, at our time of life, there is little time to waste.'

'At my time of life maybe,' Oliver said graciously. 'But surely not at yours?'

'Flatterer. You are quite right of course. So, have you been married?'

'Actually…'

But Lesley interrupted. 'You may have gathered that I have had a few husbands.'

'And not all your own I dare say.'

'Polly!'

Lesley was aware that the others were listening and let go of Oliver's arm.

'Actually I was faithful to all of my husbands,' she announced to anyone who was rude enough to be listening in. 'It was they who were unfaithful to me. Well, some of them. Clive, the Colonel who taught me to shoot had an affair; Lionel who taught me to sail, had two; Simon the tailor was faithful but died during a hemming accident and William…'

'A what accident?' Cassie lifted her sunglasses and peered across the boat.

'A hemming accident,' Lesley replied. 'And William…'

'What is a hemming accident and how does one die from it?' asked Polly trying to suppress a laugh.

'It is an accident one has while hemming,' Lesley said as if it were a common enough occurrence. 'He was working on an industrial sewing machine when his sleeve caught in the mechanism and he was dragged head first into a blanket stitch. Happy now?'

'Please go on Mrs. Shaw.' Oliver patted her arm. 'I am fascinated. William?'

'Ah yes, William.' Lesley glared momentarily at Polly and then smiled sweetly back to Oliver. 'He was a bit of a cad and had two affairs while we were married. One with a married lady from Sutton and one with her husband the butcher. As far as I know they are still together.'

'Poor Mrs. Shaw,' Oliver said quietly. 'What a rough ride you have had. You were married four times?'

'No, dear Mister Simpson, six times. But only four of them had affairs; Clive, Lionel, William and Abdul. In fact I am not totally sure that the last two did not have an affair with each other, it's quite possible. Simon and Troy were faithful but both died. It is from Troy that I get my current surname.'

'What an exciting life you have led Mrs. Shaw,' said Margaret. 'Quite different from my own.'

'You wear a wedding ring I notice.' Lesley pointed across at it. 'Are you married?'

'I lost my husband.' Margaret linked her fingers, placed them in her lap and looked away. She was still not used to telling people and was slightly annoyed at Lesley for asking. She had told the group about Stanley's recent death only last night. Lesley had obviously been too intent on her notebook and had not been paying attention.

'I do sympathise,' Oliver said gently. 'I lost my wife.'

'I knew you had been married,' Lesley said triumphantly 'Was it a long illness?'

'Oh no, nothing like that.'

'A sudden bereavement then? They can often be the most difficult to recover from.'

'She's not dead,' Oliver explained with a smile. 'I just lost her.'

Everyone was listening in now.

'You mean as in, she'll turn up someday?' Polly asked as she sat down in the vacant space.

'I doubt it. I get messages from her via our daughter only occasionally now.'

'It all sounds a bit strange,' said Polly. 'How exactly does one lose a wife?'

Oliver looked at the group of expectant faces and knew he had to tell his story.

'We had been to the opera. I am a great opera fan, we both were. At least I was until a rather disturbing event at Glyndebourne involving Mozart and some horse manure. I think they called it progressive or experimental. I called it sacrilege. There was a dead horse hanging up and all this dung on the stage, people booed. Nothing to do with Don Giovanni at all. But there you are. When I was heavily keen on opera, however, I would go regularly to Covent Garden with my wife. We were friends. Of the Opera, that is. Well also of each other, or so I thought.

The last thing we saw together was Lohengrin, Alicia Belgranno singing the role of Elsa. I thought Elsa was supposed to be beautiful. Well her voice was nice but she looked far too much like Jabba the Hut for my disbelief to be suspended. Anyway the performance was fine, lovely voices.

'After the performance we headed straight home, my ex-wife and I, as it was late. We went by way of Covent Garden underground where you either have to descend an endless flight of smelly steps or use one of the lifts. It was while pressed in the lift that my wife struck up a conversation with a man carrying a tuba. Being somewhat musical myself I recognised the instrument by its case. As we left the lift and headed for the train I was explaining to my wife about the Wagner tubas, instruments Wagner used in the Ring cycle. Bruckner also made use of them incidentally. They really are a fascinating instrument did you know...' Oliver looked up to see a couple of glazed looks and heard an impatient cough from Ms Arnold. He decided to move the story along.

'As I got onto the train, which was luckily just pulling in, I asked my wife beside me for her thoughts on the use of the tuba in that evening's performance. Her answer was, "don't know what the hell you're on about mate." I turned and realised that she was no longer beside me and I was, instead, holding the hand of a burley middle aged man in blue overalls. And then, after a brief apology and as the carriage doors closed, I saw her. She was standing amid a sea of people in the tunnel leading to the exit. Behind her the young man with the tuba appeared to be waiting. I couldn't open the doors nor stop the train and my last glimpse of her was as she stood, open mouthed as if she'd just made a terrible, life changing decision. The train pulled away and I lost sight of her. I have not seen her since. Solicitors dealt with the divorce. So you see I literally and figuratively lost my wife in the underground.'

During the pause that followed Jason stood and carefully made his way to the cabin to consult with Yiannis on their progress. By the time he returned the conversation had changed.

'Something you just said has rung a bell,' Margaret was saying to Oliver. 'But I am not sure exactly what.'

'Are you alright Mister Simpson?' Jason asked as he sat again.

'Yes, fine thank you Jason. But... Would you call me Oliver? All this Mister Simpson is making me feel rather old whereas being out on this boat and singing and having fun is making me feel very young. Let's use first names shall we?'

'I know exactly what you mean, Oliver,' Lesley agreed. 'Maybe it's the sea air, maybe it's the freedom but I feel like a twenty year old today.'

'You'd have to pay for one like everybody else dear,' Polly quipped but no one laughed.

'Okeydokey boy and girls,' Jason said, slapping his hands together. 'That's' the SARGO attitude we like to see.'

'Oh hi-di-bloody-hi!'

'Oh for the love of... Polly Arnold lighten up or I'll crack your other hip,' Cassie complained and splashed seawater over her friend.

'Careful pet, she'll melt.' Harriet laughed and slapped her thigh.

The others chuckled too which only helped to darken Polly's mood. To distract their attention from her she said, 'right then. Golden Fleece. Maybe we should talk about what we are expecting to find, eh?'

'Now that's probably the most sensible thing you've said all day Pol,' Cassie said. 'Jason, what exactly do you think the Golden Fleece is?'

'I know what it *was*,' Jason replied. 'It was probably a real sheep's fleece that they used to pan for gold. No, honestly. In Georgia, where the land of Colchis was, they still pan for gold in the mountain streams using fleeces to filter the crap from the water. It's probable that, in real life, a trader called Jason brought back one of these panning fleeces encrusted with gold.'

'So you think we might actually find real gold up there?' Lesley said wide eyed and looking across at the island. She shielded her eyes from the sun with her hand and then said, 'what was that?'

'What was what?' Jason turned to look.

'I thought I saw something catch the sunlight. Like binoculars do in bad westerns,' she said and pointed towards the hills. 'Up there on top of that cliff.'

'I can't see anything,' Jason said, turning back. 'Maybe a window or something.'

'But there are no buildings up there and I am sure I saw it.'

'Whatever,' Cassie dismissed her. 'So, it's possible that this Greek chap from the past... Dimitris? Possible he inherited some gold and hid it up there, you think?'

'To be honest,' Jason said, 'I don't know what to think.' He reached into his pocket and drew out the piece of SARGO paper on which he had written the clues the previous evening. 'It says here to *protect* the Golden Fleece.'

'Which suggests that it's valuable or at least important,' Oliver noted.

'I don't understand something,' Lesley said and ignored the loud sigh that Polly gave. 'Why all the musical clues and notes and things?'

'Because Dimitris Panandreas was a musician I guess,' Jason reasoned. 'I mean, if he had been a mathematician maybe he would have left a mathematical code for us to crack.'

'That makes sense hon.' Cassie nodded. 'And something else has been bugging me. May I?'

Jason handed her the sheet of paper and she read the clues again.

'What is it Cassie dear?' Margaret asked. She had been deep in thought about Stanley but now tuned in to the conversation.

'Panandreas...' Cassie removed her glasses and started to chew on one of the arms as she repeated the name. 'Polly babe, do you remember The Student Prince?'

'Never met him darling.'

'Nineteen eighty four?'

'Never read the book.'

'The year?'

'I remember the year certainly. Why?'

'The tour?'

'Now *you* are talking in riddles Cassie,' Margaret chided gently. 'Can you translate?'

'Well,' the singer explained, 'in nineteen eighty four - the year, not the book - Polly and I were touring Europe with The Student Prince – the operetta not an actual person – and we did a performance or two in Venice – Italy not America. I remember, one afternoon on a day off, I went to a concert hall. I can't remember the name now but I remember the performance. It was some kind of experimental chamber music so dull and difficult to listen to that I slipped out and took a Highball in the bar. Well, the walls of the bar were covered in old bills – play bills Lesley not dollar bills or men called Bill before you ask.'

'Thank you, I was wondering.' Lesley was taking notes again as if she were a student at a lecture. Cassie continued:

'So there I was, just sipping my drink and looking over the old play bills and I'm sure I remember one from way back when... I don't know the year but it was old, pre World War One I should think, and I remember trying to read the names. It was a concert of piano music and I recognised all the names, Rachmaninov was one and Delius another. I recognised them all apart from one. I'm pretty sure that the name was Panandreas. Dimitris Panandreas.'

'Why would you remember his name?' Polly asked sceptically. 'I've never heard of him in musical circles.'

'I remembered,' Cassie replied defensively, 'because there is a Panandreas theatre in L.A. and I wondered if there might be a connection.'

'Doubtful,' Jason said. 'As far as I know none of the Panandreas family had anything to do with the States. But Dimitris was a concert pianist as well as a composer. It's quite likely he performed in Venice at the turn of the century. It was not until nineteen fourteen that he returned here and stayed here. Well, over there.'

He pointed across the water to where the island stood, half of the mountain in shadow the other half bathed in glorious sunlight.

'I remember now!' Polly exclaimed. 'The death tour.'

'Of course! I'd forgotten,' Cassie said and laughed.

'Death tour?' Lesley scribbled it in her book. 'Why death tour?'

'Oh my god.' Polly finally cracked a smile. 'Do you remember Cass? Herbert Hill and...'

'...Hilary Hump.'

'Hump and Hill and Death in Venice!' they both roared with laughter sharing a joke that completely sailed over the heads of everyone else and splash-landed in the sea some way off.

'Now you've lost me entirely,' Lesley moaned. 'And I *was* trying to keep up, honestly.'

'Sorry hon,' Cassie said. 'Let me explain.'

'Please do dear.' Margaret was watching the singer intently while tapping her fingers on her handbag. 'I think something is ringing that bell again.'

'Herbert Hill and Hilary Hump, their real names I swear to god, took the leads at the Venice performances of The Student Prince. They were dreadful, I mean real crap and the whole show bombed, died. We all died. Someone made a joke about our Death in Venice and it stuck, so we called it the Death Tour after that. That's all.'

'I see,' said Lesley quietly.

'You do hon?'

'Yes, all apart from what has that got anything to do with the Golden Fleece?'

Cassie sighed. 'Not much you're right. Only that Dimitris Panandreas played in Venice in nineteen something and we died in Venice in eighty four and...'

'Benjamin Britten.'

Everyone looked at Oliver.

'He wrote an opera, *Death in Venice*, he explained.

'Opera!'

Everyone looked at Margaret.

'And death in Venice...'

'Come on gran what's on your mind?' Jason had been watching her intently. She had been trying hard to remember something during Cassie's long-winded story. She had been biting her lip, concentrating and her face had been twitching as she tried to recall something from deep inside her memory.

'Someone died in Venice,' she said. Her voice was soft, as if she was talking to herself and not to the other guests.

'Yes, we did.' Polly laughed.

'Someone else...'

'Who?' Jason prompted. He edged forward on his seat. For some reason he knew that whatever his grandmother was trying to recall was relevant somehow.

'Not who.' Margaret looked up at him. 'When.'

'O.K. When?'

'Maybe there is a connection.' The old lady reached for Lesley's notebook. 'May I dear? You may have jotted down something that will remind me.'

Lesley let her take the book and Margaret immediately started skimming through the pages. She read out some notes as she went.

'*No toilet paper, Andrex included. Gingham...* Honestly Mrs. Shaw, how your mind works.... *Soldier number two: 6946734556 Saturday night...* No there's nothing in here that... One moment. *Painting, portrait....* Oh well done Mrs. Shaw!'

Margaret handed the notebook back to Lesley and sat back in her seat with a look of absolute triumph on her face.

'Well?' Several guests lent towards her, keen to hear what she had discovered.

'Eighteen eighty two,' said Margaret and folded her arms.

'Yes gran, what about it?'

'The Panandreas family portrait was painted in eighteen eighty two.'

'So?'

'So... someone died in Venice the next year. Someone important.'

'Several people I expect,' Polly mumbled.

'Someone musical though.' Margaret was straining to remember again. 'Stanley mentioned it... him. But who was it... who?'

'And why is it relevant?' Jason asked.

Margaret looked at him blankly and then her enthusiasm waned. 'I have no idea,' she said. 'It's probably not relevant at all. Just an old woman trying to exercise her fading memory.'

'After all that,' Lesley exclaimed as she crossed out the notes she had just made and closed her book.

'It's all too much for me in this heat,' Harriet complained. She had been trying to keep up. 'But at least it passed some time.'

'Well, if you remember who this important musical person was gran,' Jason said, sounding deflated, 'let me know.'

'One final thing.' Cassie handed the set of clues back to Jason. 'We've still a clue to solve. The last one. I'll leave that with you.'

'*To use the key times the key by time.*' Jason read it and put the paper roughly in his back pocket. They'd found the key, the key to decoding the music and they knew where they were heading. He'd suddenly had enough of clues and coincidences and decided it was time he broke out the beer.

Having made his way forward to the tiny cabin he rummaged in a box and pulled out some warm cans of Mythos. He offered one to Yiannis who took it without saying a word. As Jason bent down to pick up a couple more cans, to save himself the return trip, he didn't feel the piece of SARGO headed paper with his clues on it being gently pulled from his back pocket.

Nor, as he headed to the stern with the drinks, did he see Yiannis read the clues, screw up the paper and smile wickedly.

THIRTY
Symi Harbour
October 20th 1944, 20.00 hours

Stanley stood nervously behind the last row of wooden benches that had been placed to face the makeshift stage and straightened his uniform. In front of him his fellow soldiers sat patiently as the Lance Corporal made a speech in English. The officer paused after every few words to allow his interpreter time to translate his words into Greek and the interpreter spoke very slowly.

'If they don't hurry I will die right here.'

Stanley felt a hand on his shoulder and turned to Dimitris who had shuffled up behind him.

'Where have you been?' Stanley started but then saw the colour of his friend's face; it was near white. The arc lights that had been set up for the concert blanched it further and made deep black shadows out of the old man's features. 'Dimitris?'

Dimitris was gasping, his lungs clawing for breath as he struggled to control himself.

'I will tell you later my friend,' he said. 'For now let me concentrate on what we must do. I need what little strength I have for our performance.'

'They will understand if you are not up to it...'

'Asta re!' Dimitris gripped Stanley's shoulder tighter with his fingers and tutted. 'Once I am at the piano I will no longer be in pain.'

'If you are sure?'

'I am sure.'

While the Lance Corporal prattled on about freedom and friendship Dimitris pulled Stanley down to a bench where they sat and rested. A few of the older Greeks, skeletal thin and grey themselves from hunger, pulled blankets over their knees and looked to the skies. Above them a clear night had settled in, the stars only slightly dimmed by the glow of the electric lights around the town square. The island had suffered blackouts for so long recently it was almost as much a treat to have electric light as it was to have a concert. Children, driven nearly mad with boredom by the Englishman's speech, had started to play in the rubble of fallen buildings. Stanley watched as they aimed twigs and sprayed each other with imaginary machine gun fire. He felt a chill himself then and his thoughts wandered to home as a way to warm his heart if not his body.

He pictured Margaret; her deep grey eyes always so warm and inviting, her soft hair and lips that were permanently curled into an innocent smile. Would she still be as innocent when he returned or would the war in England show her as many horrors as Stanley had recently witnessed? Would she have become older too quickly as he had done? She would be eighteen now, she would be waiting for him to return so that he could fulfil the promise of marriage he had made to her on the night before he left for the war. He pictured her in her garden next door to his, planting the spring bulbs and cutting back the roses she tended daily for her parents. He imagined her working with her mother; preparing the house for winter, bringing in the wood for the fire, walking to the factory each day to help with the war effort and returning home via the allotments, gathering what food they could grow themselves. He pictured her bathing and preparing for bed where, as she said in her letters, she prayed for Stanley each night before kissing his photograph.

'I have an idea.'

He was brought back to the here and now by the sound of Dimitris' voice rasping in his ear.

'An idea?' Stanley looked up to the stage. Lance Corporal Roberts had finished his speech and a priest had appeared. He stood far taller and more regal than the English commanding officer and his voice was more confident and powerful. Stanley assumed he was blessing the stage or the audience and noticed that everyone else was listening intently. Everyone else except Dimitris that is; he appeared to be chuckling but in his failing health it was hard to tell if he was laughing or suppressing a chest ripping cough.

'Yes, a brilliant idea!' Dimitris was definitely laughing although the apparent pain of it had drained the last traces of colour from his face. 'We shall play something German tonight and not Rimsky Korsakov.'

'German?' Stanley could hardly believe what the old man had said. 'Are you mad?'

'Yes and no,' the old Greek laughed again but this time it did descend into a coughing fit and it took until the priest had finished his blessing before the coughing subsided. 'Listen quickly, we shall be called to perform in a moment,' Dimitris said when he had recovered. His voice was suddenly strong and intent again. 'Tonight, after the concert, I have something to give you, something to pass on. Its secret came to this island sixty two years ago to the day.'

'Fine, but you want German music?' Stanley said impatiently.

The priest had left the stage and he could now hear Roberts announcing the programme for the concert. He and Dimitris were to be on first and his heart had started pounding with the pre-performance nerves he had suffered since he was a boy. Why was Dimitris suggesting that they change the piece that Stanley had prepared all day to play?

'Although it is only six days away I shall not see my next name day,' Dimitris went on apparently oblivious to their impending performance. 'Let's mark it tonight. Let's bring all the events together, they are connected vaguely...'

'They are calling our names Dimitris.'

On stage Roberts had announced the first act. As he called Stanley's name the other soldiers cheered and whistled. When he called Dimitris Panandreas there was a noticeable silence from the Symiots.

'Let them wait. Tonight we play music by the great man himself. My father knew him; he was a patron of his music.'

'Who?'

'The Germans have brought us here, to this state, to this condition but they do not know where their treasure is. Only I know that...'

'We must go,' Stanley stood up. 'And we will play Rimsky Korsakov like we planned to.'

Dimitris griped him by the elbow and pulled himself to his feet. The English soldiers were turning and clapping for Stanley and he waved them down with his free hand, trying hard to smile as he helped Dimitris upright. But the old man was still rattling on with a new found vigour.

'It all fits,' Dimitris hissed as they started towards the stage. 'German music, you, me, death… it all fits! We must play German music. His German music. As a tribute to him yes, but in such a way that it will show what he always wanted to say.'

'Dimitris I don't know what you are talking about.' Stanley approached the edge of the stage where the lights were brighter and hot.

'What German music do you know by heart?' Dimitris clawed at Stanley's arm as the two mounted the stairs slowly.

Stanley thought quickly. He knew lots of music by German composers; piano music by Schumann and Beethoven. He tried to concentrate. 'Moonlight Sonata?' Stanley offered as they made their way to the piano stool.

'No, no, no.' Dimitris dismissed it. 'Do you know Jazz?'

'What?'

'You can play in the jazz style yes? Of course you can, I have heard you. Then this is what we will do.'

Once they saw the two men sit at the piano stool the audience settled with anticipation. They waited patiently while Dimitris whispered something to the young English soldier. But after a while they started to shuffle in their seats as a great discussion appeared to be taking place at the piano and still no music had been played. Whispering had just broken out when finally the young soldier turned to face the audience and cleared his throat. He sounded nervous as he addressed the crowd.

'Tonight,' Stanley started, hardly believing what he had just agreed to do, 'we were to play you a duet of "flight of the bumble bee"…' The audience sat up and paid attention. Stanley noted their eager expressions and his heart pounded faster. 'But, after discussion, we have decided to play something more… appropriate to tonight's celebration.'

He turned and looked at Dimitris. His fingers were poised over the keyboard, stroking the keys lightly as if he was gently waking a lover from sleep. Colour had returned to his face and, when he looked back at Stanley and winked, there was mischievousness there too. Stanley swallowed hard and addressed the audience again.

'So tonight, ladies and gentlemen we would like to give you our tribute to a great German composer.'

All Stanley heard as he took his seat was the sound of the sea in the background and even that seemed disturbed by what he had just said. He looked to the sky, remembering a melody and reminding himself that he was only the right hand of this duet. Then he looked out across the audience. Lance Corporal Roberts now stood at the back, scowling and shaking his head. But Stanley ignored him, knowing that everyone would understand in time. He glanced at Dimitris who just laughed.

And then they started to play.

If the audience had been mystified by the soldier's announcement they were now dumbfounded by the tune that they heard. The German national anthem played out solemn and proud from the slightly out of tune piano. A few Greeks started to mumble and the English prepared to show their displeasure with silence.

Petros Tzankatis sat at the back with his arms folded, a dark grimace on his face, and watched his old enemy make a fool of himself. He lent over to his wife and daughter and made a disparaging remark about Dimitris. His wife pretended to agree but, unseen by her husband, she put her arm around her daughter's shoulders and gave her a protective squeeze.

'Why are you crying mama?' the daughter, Anna, asked quietly as people shuffled and grumbled around her.

Sophia Tzankatis looked at the man playing the piano. He was old and frail now, close to death, no longer the handsome, brilliant father figure who had stolen her heart sixteen years ago. She was aware of her husband on her left, cursing the Panandreas name under his breath and scoffing at Dimitris for playing German music. And she felt the warmth of her daughter on the other side, her daughter who would one day have to learn who her real father was. The man now dying, in more ways than one, up on the stage.

She said nothing, just squeezed Anna tight and put her finger to her lips.

Anna listened. She recognised the tune as the national anthem of the people who had fought over her island and been sent away by the English. But there was something different about it now. The music had grown louder, to drown out the grumblings from the unhappy audience she supposed, but it was also growing faster and more rhythmic. It was not what she remembered from the radio broadcasts she had heard in the last few years. It reminded her of another kind of music. Dance music, fast and jazzy.

And then the music changed again. Now the Germans' song was no longer discernable to anyone in the audience. The two men at the piano had changed it. They were building to something else, something unrecognisable but still in the same jazz style. Anna's eyes opened wider as she concentrated on the two pairs of hands she could see dancing over the white and black keys. The young Englishman was now smiling and even old Panandreas was having fun. The two men looked at each other as they nodded their heads in time with the music and the tempo slowed slightly. The audience had fallen silent again and all Anna could hear was the music, building, slowing and getting louder until it changed into a tune she did recognise from somewhere.

The audience suddenly roared with laughter and Anna realised that the Germans' song had been just a build up to a joke, a musical joke. And, without knowing exactly why, she laughed too and then started clapping with everyone else, in time to the jazzy, silly music.

She looked at her mother and assumed that the tears were tears of joy. Up on the stage an Englishman and a Symiot were poking fun at the Germans through their music and the islanders of Symi were happily joining in.

THIRTY ONE
Aboard the boat
12.15

The drone of the engine and the effects of two cans of Mythos had sent Jason into a doze. He was vaguely aware, through half closed eyes and ears, of his guests chatting around him. Since the earlier argument between the actresses and Lesley the three women seemed to have settled into a vague kind of friendship and he listened to them discussing previous holidays and their lives in general. But he was not really paying attention. He daydreamed of the handsome soldier, played his film script in his mind and saw long days and nights ahead with his perfect love on their perfect island.

But someone kept getting in the way. At first it was the evil looking old man who had dragged Michaelis away and then shouted at Jason from inside his truck. A twisted grey face that Jason recognised from somewhere he couldn't place. But then that face morphed into another twisted, evil visage set on a wiry body; Slipe. Each time Jason tried to allow thoughts of the soldier to drift into a dream where anything was permitted, Slipe would appear. Each time Jason and Michaelis opened the door of their romantic cottage in the Symi hinterland, Slipe would be there. Whenever the fire had burned low and they were heading for the bedroom, Slipe would be waiting for them with clipboards, checklists and excursion targets. Jason even heard his voice and the sound of it brought him right back to the real world.

His guests were looking at him and they were looking worried. He realised that he had slumped in his seat, his legs were stretched out before him and he had been drooling.

'What?' he said quickly wiping his mouth. 'Was I snoring?'

Then he realised what the problem was. The continuous background chug and hum of the boat had stopped and there was nothing to be heard apart from the lapping of waves against the wooden hull. It was very peaceful and calming and Jason would have been happy to nod off again had he not heard Yiannis swear loudly from inside the cabin. The deep grunt was accompanied by the sound of an engine struggling to wake up.

'What is it?' Jason called forward to Yiannis but the boat owner did not reply. He just tried to start the engine once more with no success.

'We've stopped,' Margaret said. 'The boat has broken down.'

'We think we might have to swim for shore,' Oliver said and he sounded quite serious.

Suddenly Slipe was in Jason's head again. But this time he was giving evidence in a Greek court and Jason was defending the charges.

Jason looked behind him at the rocky shoreline. It was not so far away and would be an easy swim for those who were able. The problem would be getting ashore as the rocks were numerous and sharp, water broke around the ones he could see and bubbled over the razor edges of the ones just below the surface. He looked the other way, out to sea and was surprised to discover that they had reached the small chain of islands off Symi's eastern most headland, Cape Kouri. That was good; there was land on either side of them and close too.

Actually that was bad. They were navigating through a small archipelago and dangerously sharp, half concealed rocks were all about them. Without power they were in immediate danger of running aground.

And then it all made sense to him. Why Slipe had given him the seemingly impossible challenge. He had told Jason to come up with, and execute, an excursion today, giving him less than twenty four hours to make the arrangements. That part had not been difficult with his grandmother's encouragement. It would have been fairly straightforward without any help; he could have come up with any number of trips if he had put his mind to it. What was not as easy, given the limited amount of time he had been allowed, was to ensure that the trip was properly organised and, more importantly considering the age of his clients, insured.

The boat would run aground, possessions and maybe people would be lost and Jason would be totally to blame and uninsured. Slipe would not only fire him but, assuming that he escaped gaol (unlikely) no other tour company would employ him. Worse; he would have to leave the island. Slipe had it all sewn up. Not only was the little boat doomed now but so was Jason. He made a mental note to prepare a list of words to be learned before he was arrested. Drowning was one, quickly followed by guilty.

'And we're off!'

Lesley's voice jolted him out of his sudden despair. The engine had started and they were underway again. Lesley was squirming her way back into her place between Oliver and Harriet and looking very pleased with herself.

'It was the fuel line,' she explained to the other, open mouthed, guests. 'I could see it from here. That silly man must have knocked the switch without realising it.'

'Well done Mrs. Shaw.' Oliver applauded. 'Would you like a marmite sandwich?'

Lesley declined but Oliver ate heartily while Jason went into the cabin on shaky legs to check with Yiannis.

'Is everything alright?' he asked, once he had squeezed himself in beside the boat owner.

'All o.k.' Yiannis said and there was a hint of annoyance in his voice. 'But keep the women out of my cabin.'

'I was asleep.'

'There is a problem.'

Yiannis looked up through the salt encrusted windscreen and squinted. Jason followed his gaze and drew in a breath. He could see the next cape ahead of them and leading up from it the mountain on which stood Stavros, their destination. On its seaward side, the mountain fell steeply towards the coast but to the east the hill fell gradually down towards the bay of Apiana where they were to come ashore. Between the boat and the bay the water, though a little choppy, looked passable. Everything below and around the mountain looked exactly as he had imagined it from his map. What made him draw breath however was above the mountain.

Above and behind it and heading their way on a high southerly wind were large black and white clouds. Jason could tell at a glance that the dark ones contained rain and that the high stacked white ones probably held thunder and lightening. He knew that if his guests were caught outside in a thunderstorm he could add exposure to his list of Greek words to learn before being charged by the police.

'Should we turn back?' he asked Yiannis.

'Why?'

'That looks like a storm.'

'That is not the problem,' Yiannis said and pointed to his dashboard. 'That is the problem.'

Jason looked at the two levers, one wheel and three dials none of which meant anything to him. He shrugged and Yiannis tapped one of the dials.

'Fuel,' he said. 'Problem with the fuel.'

'We don't have enough?'

'Yes we have enough.' Yiannis sounded annoyed.

'So what is the problem?'

'We have enough to get to Vassilios. Not enough for Apiana.'

'What?' Jason was outraged. 'But you knew where we wanted to go, I told you this morning.'

'And I told you that you were stupid.' Yiannis turned the wheel slightly and the boat started to head shoreward.

Jason reached into his flight bag that was stashed beside the box of beer and pulled out his map. He opened it and unfolded it across the dashboard. 'Look,' he said pointing to Apiana, 'that's where we want to go.'

'I know. I am not stupid, you are stupid,' Yiannis growled.

'And there is Vassilios.' Jason pointed to the bay opposite Apiana. 'It's the same distance, so what's the problem?'

Yiannis laughed, which made Jason feel very small, and tapped the dial again.

'We can go to Apiana,' he said as if he was talking to a three year old. 'But then we cannot get back. If we go to Vassilios I can walk up to Xisos and arrange more fuel. Then when you get back from Stavros I can bring you back to harbour. If we go to Apiana we stay at Apiana.'

'But my guests can't walk…' Jason stopped. Something was not right.

'I know,' Yiannis said and nodded. 'But it is the best I can do. Take it or... or swim it.' He laughed again and headed the boat further shoreward towards the bay at Vassilios.

Jason put his hand on his head and drummed his fingers while he thought. If they landed at Vassilios, as they were now destined to do, his party would have a longer walk. Glancing between the map and the island he could see that it would not be an easy one. From Apiana there was a vague path for at least some of the way; from Vassilios there was none, just bolder fields and slopes until they reached the woods below Stavros. The climb from there actually looked easier and they would reach the monastery at some point but it would take them longer to get up the mountain. And longer to get down.

He looked at Yiannis and shook his head. What could he do?

'Very well,' he said reluctantly. 'Take us to Vassilios, fetch more fuel and wait for us to return.'

Yiannis just nodded.

Jason folded his map away and headed back to his place in the stern. Something new was playing on his mind now. Something Yiannis had said.

'Everything alright pet?' Harriet asked as Jason sat.

'Slight change of plan, that's all,' he replied.

He didn't mention the approaching storm or the extra walk. He thought it best to keep those things quiet. Particularly while he tried to put his finger on the something else that had started to bug him.

'Shall we sing again?' Oliver piped up but everyone else groaned.

'To be honest darling I am getting a little arse sore here and my hip is playing up.' Polly tried to stretch her legs.

'Are we nearly there?'

Jason looked at his grandmother and saw her smiling back encouragingly. 'About another half an hour,' he said and tried to return the smile.

'And what will we find when we get there?' Margaret asked looking up at the mountain.

'Your guess is as good as mine gran.'

'I don't mean the Golden Fleece, dear. I mean the monastery.'

'I haven't actually seen it,' Jason admitted. 'As I mentioned…' He lowered his voice, remembering that not all of the guests knew exactly what the land part of their journey had in store for them. 'It's private land so no one apart from whoever owns it has seen it for a long time.'

'I see,' Margaret whispered. 'Anything else?'

'I heard that it was ransacked by the Nazis in the Second World War.'

'Yes I know that.'

Jason was taken aback. He didn't remember telling his grandmother this information.

'I have been thinking Jason,' Margaret said quietly, 'about conversations Stanley and I had after the war, and I would like your help to put some pieces of a puzzle together. So please, humour me and tell me what you know.'

'O.k.' Jason conceded. 'Well Stavros was taken apart just like the villa was. There were orders, sent from Hitler himself apparently, that all Panandreas property was to be searched. He was looking for something but no one is sure what.'

'Well, that's interesting,' Margaret said and shivered. The wind was rising and the boat was moving unsteadily over the increasingly choppy water. 'And rather obvious.'

'Obvious?'

'Yes dear,' she said. 'Sometimes I am sad to see that you have inherited your mother's stupidity.'

That stung Jason and he sat back. Margaret beckoned him forward again and he lent to her reluctantly.

'It is also rather encouraging,' she went on. 'Stanley told me that when he was at Stavros, on the morning after the concert, the buildings were derelict, near ruined. All but the chapel. He said more or less what you have just said. That the area had been raided by the Nazis looking for something important. He was told that Hitler had got wind that something dangerous to the Germans was to be found on Symi.'

'I don't get you gran.'

'Grandmother,' Margaret said wearily. 'Can't you see Jason? The two things are connected. Dimitris Panandreas knew what they were looking for, he had it in his possession and so he hid it up at Stavros. He then entrusted your grandfather with the clues to its whereabouts because he knew he would not live long enough to guard it until after the war.'

'Maybe the Nazis already found it and we're on a wild goose chase.'

'Think boy!' Margaret hissed. 'Dimitris gave Stanley the clues *after* the Germans had left. Therefore the thing that was dangerous to them was still there. Is still there.'

Jason worked through his grandmother's train of thought, concentrating hard now. He had forgotten his concerns about the altered landing place and the extra walk that would be involved. 'If it is still there then it is obviously something very valuable?'

'Obviously.'

'Once dangerous to the Nazis…'

'Yes.'

'Something they wanted kept secret.'

'Go on Jason.'

'Something that would these days be of historic interest?'

'Undoubtedly.'

'And something, therefore, now very valuable.'

'Indeed. Good boy.'

'But…'

'But what?'

'But what is it?'

'The Golden Fleece,' Margaret reminded him.

'Yes, but what is the Golden Fleece grandmother?'

'I still have no idea,' Margaret admitted and Jason's heart sank yet again. 'But something came back to me earlier when the girls were talking about Venice and I want you to listen to this. Stanley once told me everything about his time on Symi and his conversations with Dimitris and yet I am sure he had no idea what was in the cigarette case that Dimitris gave to him. He can't have, else he would have mentioned it to me. Instead he put the case away and forgot about it until he made his will. But what he did tell me was this: It was the night of the concert and, at the last minute, Dimitris changed the music they were to play. He rambled on about all manner of strange things. Things like the date, Germans and death. Now then, what date was the concert?'

'Er, October twentieth, nineteen forty four.'

'Dimitris also told Stanley that something had come to the island sixty two years previously, to the very day. What year would that have been?'

'Eighteen eighty two,' Jason said without hesitation. Margaret blinked at him. 'Not quite as stupid as mum am I?' he winked.

Margaret looked doubtful. 'Earlier Cassie talked about their dreadful experiences in Venice,' Margaret went on, 'and mentioned death, just as Dimitris did on the night of the concert. Well, all these thoughts have been churning in my head and I am sure I should now know what the Golden Fleece actually is.'

'You know?' Jason exclaimed.

'No dear, I said I *should* know. I need to think some more.' Margaret sat back and sighed.

Jason waited for the conversation to continue. It didn't.

'So..?' he prompted after a while.

Margaret put her finger to her lips and closed her eyes. 'It'll come,' she said.

THIRTY TWO
Vassilios bay
12.45 pm

The small fishing boat finally spluttered into silence just a few metres away from shore. The waves were higher by then, driven landwards by the wind which seemed intent on attacking that part of the island. This was helping the craft in the right direction but without the engine it was difficult for Yiannis to steer. He waded through the legs of the guests, into the stern, and started searching beneath the bench seats.

'Watch what you're doing pal,' Harriet said as the scruffy fisherman fished around beneath her seat. She heaved her legs up to one side but Lesley was in the way. 'Can you shift or what Lesley?'

Lesley managed to stand up, clinging hold of Oliver for support and manoeuvred herself towards the bow.

The boat tipped dangerously low in the water as it started to turn side on to the breaking waves and the guests clung to the gunwales for safety. After a few moments of grunting, Yiannis stood upright and dragged two large oars out from under the bench. He looked around and thrust one towards Jason.

'You have got to be joking,' Jason said slowly. Yiannis added a grunt to his thrust and Jason took it.

He nearly dropped it immediately, surprised at the weight, but managed to lift it over into the thole pins on his side. Meanwhile Yiannis looked around at the other guests trying to decide who else might be capable of rowing.

'Oh give us it here.'

Harriet took the oar as if it were made from balsa wood and fitted it to place on her side easily. Yiannis actually cracked a smile of admiration before heading back into the cabin and grabbing the wheel.

The boat turned slowly to face land again and Jason looked across at Harriet.

'Now what?'

'Pull pet,' she barked back. 'Ready?'

Sitting side saddle on the gunwale Jason lowered his oar into the water and prepared to heave, waiting for Harriet's command.

'And pull!'

Jason pulled but nothing happened, it was like the oar was set in concrete. He swore loudly.

'Jason please!' Margaret barked. She was looking very pale now, her handbag clutched to her bosom.

'And again, pull!' Harriet yelled just as a wave pitched them forwards.

Again Jason heaved, trying to pull himself backwards and his oar forwards at the same time. Still nothing happened on his side of the boat but Harriet executed a grand stroke and the boat turned to port. Oliver swapped places with Cassie and came to Jason's side. Between the two of them they managed to pull a stroke of the oar and the boat inched closer to land.

'A couple more should do it,' Harriet bellowed as she crashed her oar into the sea. 'Heave!'

The three rowers heaved and the boat crested a wave, dipping at the prow as it landed back in the water.

'And another!'

There was a great crack, the sound of wood splintering and then a deep, northern groan followed by a splash.

Jason looked across to see only half of Harriet's oar still in place. There was no sign of the other half until suddenly it broke through the water with Harriet's hand attached to the other end. She rose up from the sea like Poseidon with half a trident, gasping for breath and laughing.

'Are you alright Harriet?' Cassie called to her,

'I'm fine pet. Oops!' She laughed louder. 'Hey, you can stand up, look.'

Sure enough they were so close to shore that Harriet was able to wade to the beach. Within a few more waves the bottom of the boat scraped the seabed and Harriet dragged it as far in as she could. A couple more pushes from the sea and the boat was stationary.

'If you don't want to get wet I'll carry you ashore,' Harriet called along the length of the boat. 'Form a line.'

'I'd rather drown,' Polly mumbled and collected her bag.

'I'll have a lift please,' Lesley volunteered. 'The shoes are Prada.'

Within a few minutes everyone and their belongings were ashore and dry thanks to Harriet carrying those who couldn't jump and Yiannis who simply threw everything else.

On dry land the day appeared rescued. The wind, though blustery, was warm and the sun still shone. There was no sign of the storm clouds Jason had noticed earlier but he knew they were there, on the other side of the mountain, with luck they would skirt the island and vanish. The last few minutes had put everyone back into an adventurous mood and, now they were not confined to the boat, they seemed more relaxed. Oliver insisted that it was time to eat but no one else was interested as their stomachs were still a little disturbed by the voyage, and so he sat alone picking at some pickled onions and cheese while Jason spoke to Yiannis.

'We will be back in five hours,' he said. 'Be here at six this evening, o.k.?'

'No problem.' Yiannis nodded and headed back to the boat to fetch a fuel can or two.

'Any chance of a toilet break for old Poll before we head off?' Cassie asked as she approached. Behind her Polly was hopping from one foot to the other and Jason realised why she had been so quiet during the last part of the voyage.

'There aren't any facilities here, I am afraid,' he replied and rolled his eyes at the thought of more toilet discussions.

'No sweat hon,' Cassie said. 'I spy some boulders, she'll manage.' She must have seen the look of surprise on his face because she added quietly, 'when you've played certain out of own venues like we have, a rock is a piece of... is a luxury, believe me.'

'Are you coming Cass?' Polly called across, hopping faster.

'Right with you Poll.'

'We should be getting ready to press on.' Jason was studying his watch and recalculating the time they would now need to walk up to Stavros and back. If they didn't leave immediately they would not be back by dark and he would have to learn the Greek for "May my grandmother sleep with your goat?" After thinking about that for a moment he realised that he could manage that sentence after all; he just hoped he wouldn't need to.

'I'll go on my own then,' Polly called back and set off towards the large boulders. 'No peeking.'

'I have some Andrex if you need it,' Oliver called after her but Polly just circled her wrist in the air and carried on up the beach.

Margaret turned to her grandson. 'Jason dear, I think I...' But she stopped short.

Jason was staring over her shoulder out to sea, his mouth wide open and his face pale. Margaret followed his gaze, aware that a commotion had started on the beach.

Oliver was standing, Lesley was waving and Harriet was running into the sea and hollering like a mad woman.

Margaret turned to see what the commotion was about and saw that their boat, although apparently out of fuel, was now heading back out to sea, its engines running at full speed.

'What's going on Jason?' Margaret asked but Jason was rooted to the spot.

'Oi!' Harriet yelled as she splashed in up to her waist. 'Get your arse back here now!'

'I thought he said he was going to walk inland to... He said there was no more fuel on the boat,' Jason spluttered. 'What's he...'

And then, like a deck of cards in the hands of a master magician, everything was shuffled neatly into place and put down face up in front of him.

He stood there, one hand over his mouth and the other tucked into his back pocket, until all the guests had come up to him. They stood around him waiting for an explanation as the boat grew smaller in the distance.

'Jason,' his grandmother said quietly as she pulled at his sleeve. 'Jason dear, we should start walking.'

'What?' He looked down at her, noticed all the others waiting for an explanation and pulled himself together. 'Walk? Yes.' He turned away to face inland. 'If we walk up this path we will get to the road in an hour or so. It's quite far to the village but…'

'Not to the road,' Margaret insisted. 'To Stavros.'

'We can't get to Stavros now,' Jason said. 'We will have no way of getting back.'

'He's not coming back to get us later then pet?' Harriet asked. 'Thought as much. What's his problem?'

'His ancestors,' Jason replied carelessly.

'You what?'

Jason took his hand from his empty back pocket.

'So where is he going?' Polly asked. She had returned after the commotion had died down but felt much more comfortable now.

'Stavros,' said Jason.

'Then we can get the boat from there.'

'Lesley dear,' Margaret said as kindly as she could. 'Stavros is at the top of that mountain. We won't find him and his boat there, he isn't Noah.'

Jason sighed and looked at his grandmother. 'We're too late,' he said. 'We may as well go home.'

'Jason please explain,' Margaret said, now sounding like a very tired primary school teacher.

'He is the cousin of the man that led us to the villa on the donkeys yesterday,' Jason said but could instantly tell that no one but him knew what he was getting at. 'O.k. I'll put it in a nutshell. The donkey man is related to the Tzankatis family…'

'The what?' said Harriet.

'Is that a kind of nut?' Oliver asked, keenly interested.

'The Tzankatis family, Harriet, owned the area of Stavros hundreds of years ago. There was a dispute between them and the Panandreas family. Dimitris Panandreas…'

'Him with the music and the house, like?'

'Him with the... exactly. Dimitris reclaimed the church and land at Stavros, where we were heading. The family feud went on, would still be going on if there was a Panandreas left on the island. Yesterday donkey man saw that I had Panandreas' cigarette case. Today his cousin offers me his boat to take us to Apiana bay and to wait there while we take a two hour walk...'

'Hang on hon,' Cassie butted in. 'He knew you wanted a boat?'

'No,' Jason admitted. 'I went to find him this morning, early, knowing that he would be preparing to go fishing. I persuaded him to take us to Apiana. His ancestry didn't occur to me at the time.'

'Do I need my notebook?' Lesley asked. 'Only it's over there in my bag.'

Jason ignored her, as did everyone else. 'Well, on the boat,' he explained, 'when we first had the fuel line problem, he told me we would have to land here so he could refuel.'

'Yes?' Margaret encouraged.

'He told me that if we went to Apiana we would not have enough fuel to get back to the harbour when we got back from Stavros.'

'Yes, which is why we came here.' Polly put in. 'But it doesn't explain why he's gone and abandoned us, does it?'

'How,' Jason said very slowly. 'Did he know we were going to Stavros? I didn't tell him. When Donkey man saw the cigarette case even I didn't know what was in it.'

'This donkey man,' Lesley asked keenly. 'Why do you call him donkey...'

'Because he works with donkeys!' Polly cut her down. 'For god's sake woman!'

'I reckon,' Jason went on almost to himself, 'that donkey man told his cousin, Yiannis, about the cigarette case. That something belonging to Panandreas was in my possession. When I walked up to Yiannis and asked to go to Apiana he agreed to take us because he wanted to see what we were up to.'

'And he tricked us into being marooned here...' Margaret was following her grandson's train of thought.

'...while he sails around to the other side of Stavros, scoots up the hill and finds the Golden Fleece before we do.'

There was silence for a moment until Harriet spoke up.

'So what are we waiting for? Let's shift.'

'We will never get there before him,' Jason said.

'So? He don't know what he's looking for or where to look do he?'

Another silence followed as everyone waited for Jason to reply.

'Do he Jas?'

Jason felt tears at the back of his eyes and saliva in his mouth. He swallowed and nodded. 'He does now.'

'How's that pet?'

'Did he steal the clues?' Margaret asked. Her face became animated as she thought the situation through. 'It would take him some time to work them out if he did, that gives us the advantage.'

'No Gran.' Jason took the cigarette case from his flight bag. 'The original manuscript is still in here.'

'Well then...'

'He stole the answers. I wrote them down on a piece of paper. Put it in my pocket. It's gone. He must have found it, or taken it... I don't know. All I do know is that he's on his way there now and we're stuck here, two or three hour's hard walk away and...'

'All right lad, calm down,' Harriet slapped a heavy hand on his shoulder. 'There's only one of him, there's seven of us. He won't get away with it. Come on.'

'We can't,' Jason sighed. 'We must go back by road.'

All of the guests broke into cries of disagreement and started talking at once. Even Polly had decided that now she had come this far there was no way she was turning back. It was still early enough in the day to get up the mountain and back again. At this point Oliver started asking about provisions and what they could have for breakfast if they had to camp out and the group was in danger of turning into a rabble. Margaret held up her hand for silence and one by one the voices fell quiet.

'Jason, this is simple,' she said when she had everyone's attention. 'We have to go on. He may know where the Golden Fleece is but he doesn't know *what* it is.'

'And I suppose you do gran, eh?'

'As a matter of fact,' Margaret said and smiled sweetly. 'I believe I might.'

THIRTY THREE

Stavros

October 21st 1944, dawn

Stanley was stunned.

The principal reason for his disbelief of the situation he found himself in was that Dimitris was still alive. The second thing he could not believe was where they both were. Dawn was approaching with streaks of grey light under low storm clouds across to the east; he could see them beyond the forest. He and the dying man had been struggling uphill for most of the night but now they were almost at their destination.

After their triumphant performance the previous night Dimitris had slipped away saying he had one last thing to do before they set off. He had not told Stanley where they were going, only that they had something of historic importance to do. While he waited for the old man Stanley wrote a letter to Margaret back home. He told her of the concert, the liberation of the island and of his love for her. It was well after midnight when Dimitris returned wearing a long shabby coat and carrying two canteens of water. Stanley dated the letter, put it in an envelope and gave it to his friend Bill to take back to barracks for him. He told Bill that his Symi friend wanted to take him somewhere and that he didn't know what time he would be back. Although discipline for the small garrison of soldiers was fairly informal, now that the islands were liberated and the war was all but over in the area, Stanley was still expected to be on duty the next morning. Bill reminded him of this with a wink, assuming that Stanley was off to meet some local girl, or to take advantage of the brothel at the back of the harbour.

But Dimitris had nothing of the sort in mind. Without saying anything about their destination he told Stanley to expect a long hike and not to question anything.

The journey had actually taken about six hours, Stanley guessed, and it was dawn when they reached their destination. Finally he saw the black iron gates that Dimitris had long promised would mark the end of their hike.

Stanley's legs were aching, his eyes sore with lack of sleep and his chest raw from the walk. Yet Dimitris seemed unstoppable. Even when he had coughed and stumbled he had continued moving forwards. Sometimes in apparently effortless strides and sometimes in short bursts of staggering and lurching, but at no time on the trek had he stopped. He was being driven by some desperate need and Stanley still had no idea what.

It was not until they were both inside the gates of the monastery that the old man stopped and half collapsed onto a low wall. Stanley gratefully sat beside him and wiped sweat from his brow. Somewhere at the back of his mind was the thought that he was going to be in serious trouble, he was away from barracks, without permission and would soon be missed. But there was also something else nagging at him. The thing that Dimitris had said he needed to pass on, the thing that only another musician could understand.

Well, Stanley had surely passed the test, the musical test. They had improvised and ridiculed German music for ten minutes back on that stage, bringing the house down and receiving a standing ovation that lasted almost as long as the performance. Stanley smiled to himself as he recalled his moment of triumph. The faces of the crowd when they started playing 'Deutschland, Deutschland, uber alles' was something he would never forget. Horror, disbelief and then slowly, understanding. They took the solid melody and started to twist it, started to up the tempo, roll the bass and began slipping into a comedic, ragtime style. Then the audience got the joke and were suddenly on their side. And then, when they started on the 'Ride of the Valkyries', Stanley trilling the right hand and adding the swooping string part, Dimitris thumping out the melody, the crowd really sat up and took notice. The heavy Wagnerian theme soon descended into fast and witty jazz, somehow poking fun at the great Teutonic mythology and reducing the music of Hitler's favourite composer to an object of ridicule.

For those few minutes Dimitris had been alive again, but now as Stanley watched him recover his breath as best he could, he looked closer to death than ever before. The grey light of dawn turned everything around him to silver, the cool morning breeze dried the sweat on the back of his neck and the skeleton of a man gasping for the last moments of his life sat beside him. What had been driving him on? Why was Dimitris so determined to get up to this churchyard before he died?

'Come,' Dimitris said and his voice was a cross between a whisper and gasp. 'There is something I must tell you.'

He pushed himself from the wall with a great sigh, grasped at Stanley's shoulder to steady himself and then very slowly the two of them walked around the edge of the chapel to the ruined outbuildings. To his right Stanley could see the black mass of hills and trees that was the island. Beyond it and invisible was the sea and Turkey. No lights shone now, the dull ache of morning light was the only thing that lit their way. Dimitris stopped in the small courtyard that separated the chapel from the outbuildings and turned his back on the island.

Stanley followed his gaze and saw nothing head of them apart from the dawn.

'Over there,' Dimitris said, 'is the island of Rhodes, there is Tilos...' He stopped and fought for his breath.

'I know.' Stanley gripped his elbow to keep him upright.

He had no idea what Dimitris wanted to say or do but wished he would hurry it along. He was aware that not only would he not make it back to barracks in time but also that the man would probably die on him there and then, leaving him with a body to transport back down the mountain. He glanced over his shoulder at the dark hinterland and saw a tiny light flickering on the other side of the valley. Some of the islanders who lived out in the forest no doubt, he thought, starting to wake.

'What are we doing here?' he asked in the hope that Dimitris would now explain his intentions so that they could leave.

'My friend,' the old man said. 'I have a story to tell you and something to give you.'

Dimitris moved across to the wall of the outhouse and lent against it, Stanley stood close beside him. The building behind them was derelict, the windows just gaping dark holes in the growing light.

Dimitris reached into his coat and pulled from a deep pocket something small and flat. He turned it in the palm of his hand and then held it out.

'My father gave this to me when I was eighteen,' he began. 'Life was so different then. Before the wars and the...' He broke down in a fit of coughing and Stanley saw sprays of blood and spittle fall from his near white lips.

'Let me help you inside,' he began but Dimitris stopped him.

'In a minute… I am alright. Here, take this.'

Stanley took the thing that was offered. It was metallic and cold and he thought it was a cigarette case.

'Protect this,' Dimitris croaked before another bout of coughing scraped his lungs. 'What is inside is valuable. Open it and the music will guide you.'

'Come on.'

Stanley put the case in his inside breast pocket and took the man firmly by the arm. He pulled them both away from the wall and walked towards the outhouse door. Tiny speckles of rain had started to fall, the clouds overhead were low and in the distance he could see flashes of lightening approaching across the sea.

'There!'

Dimitris would not move. His feet were rooted to the ground and Stanley could not budge him. Dimitris was pointing ahead.

At first Stanley thought he was pointing to the approaching storm. It was impossible to tell where the black clouds ended and the black sea began, even when distant explosions of lightening lit up the clouds from behind. But then the young soldier noticed that he was not pointing out to sea or sky but across the courtyard to a round, low wall.

'What is it?' Stanley asked.

'History.'

'Come inside Dimitris…'

'You must protect it, with your life. The music will guide you.'

Fearing that these were going to be Dimitris' last ramblings, that he was on the verge of his final collapse, Stanley pressed him with more effort to enter the building. But still the man would not move.

'Wait,' Stanley said, 'I will open the door.'

He left Dimitris propped up against the wall and moved along to the outhouse door. Its recess was deep, the door was low and it was also locked. He squinted into the gloom and saw the key in the lock. He turned it gently and nothing happened. He applied more force and felt the lock begin to give. It complained against his intrusion with the sound of grating metal. He encountered resistance and applied more pressure until finally he felt something click into place.

'Come inside and we will talk,' he said as he turned back to Dimitris, his hand still on the key.

But the old man was not where he had left him. He was at the chapel door now. He had managed to push it open and was supporting himself with a hand on either side of the door frame. His upper body leant into the black interior of the building, his head on his chest. To Stanley he looked like a diver about to take a freefall.

And then lit by fast flashes of approaching lightening, Dimitris fell forwards in short, jagged bursts, as if caught in the light of a stroboscope. He vanished into the chapel and Stanley heard him hit the floor.

He called out the old man's name and let go of the door key.

A sound inside the outhouse made him spin back around. He heard the clunk of a metal object falling. Someone was in there.

'Hey!' he called out and pushed open the door.

THIRTY FOUR
Apiana bay
2.30 pm

'The booby trap had been set just on the other side of the door,' Margaret continued relating Stanley's story to her silent audience. 'The Germans set it for some reason. Apparently others were later found around the monastery. As soon as Stanley unlocked the door he was doomed. The blast caught him from low down, taking off his lower legs and throwing him backwards into the courtyard. His eyes were seared by the explosion. His life was saved by the cigarette case. It stopped shrapnel from piercing his chest. A family across the valley heard and saw the explosion and reached him about half an hour later. Just in time.'

The other guests had listened to the story in silence. Even Oliver stopped eating his prawn and mayonnaise baguette as the tragedy unfolded. Jason sat holding his grandmother's hand, enthralled at the detail and her lack of emotion as she recounted the horror.

They had walked with determination and surprising speed from Vassilios bay to Apiana, where they should originally have come ashore. Everyone was aware that the fishing boat captain was ahead of them and that time was of the essence. After his initial doubt at the sense of their mission Jason had allowed his grandmother to take charge. She showed great resilience to the uneven rocks, the harsh scrub that clawed at her skirt and the blazing midday sun and he warmed to her further. Oliver had offered to carry the large bag that Lesley had been struggling with and they had spent much of the walk in quiet conversation together. The actresses on the other hand had been more vocal. Cassie sang and Polly complained about her aching hip. Harriet had carried most of the supplies and equipment with the stoicism of a pack horse, leaving Jason only to carry his flight bag and bring up the rear. He had longed to ask his grandmother to explain what she had meant when she said that she knew what the Golden Fleece was but she insisted they wait.

'We will press on until lunch time,' she had commanded to everyone like a Girl Guide leader. 'When we stop to eat I will explain everything that I have been thinking about.'

That had been over an hour ago and, by the time they did stop to rest, everyone was too excited to discover what she knew to complain about their aching feet. Only Lesley asked Margaret to wait before telling her story. Her Prada shoes were being ruined by the lack of a path. As Oliver organised the picnic she disappeared behind some rocks with her bag, returning five minutes later in khaki shorts, a linen shirt, safari jacket, ankle boots, a pink scarf and a pith helmet.

No one was surprised.

Finally, when everyone was settled and she had got her breath back, Margaret started to explain. She began by telling what she knew of Dimitris' last night, the concert, the walk to Stavros and Stanley's injuries. As she spoke she held her handbag close to her, protecting the urn that it contained. She did not falter in her story, she did not breakdown or cry even when she told them about Stanley's injuries and how the accident had happened.

'So,' Cassie said after a suitable pause had been left. 'Your Stan knew nothing about what was in the cigarette case? Only that it was valuable and that "the music will guide you"?'

'No, Dimitris never got a chance to explain. If he had, then maybe this mystery would have come to light sooner.'

Margaret examined the inside of a sandwich and tutted. She put it down and chose another one. 'Ah, chicken will do. I have trouble digesting tomatoes, Jason, for future reference.'

'I can see why he forgot about it for all those years,' Polly said. 'Didn't want to be reminded of that morning. Actually I am surprised he remembered so much.'

'Aye,' Harriet agreed. 'That kind of trauma does strange things to your mind. I know from my days on the farm. Young lad got crushed by a charging bull and was gaga for years.'

'Yeah, thanks Harriet,' Jason said quickly. 'But grandmother, about what you were saying on the beach? The Golden Fleece?'

'In good time dear.'

'We don't have good time Gran. Yiannis is ahead of us, he'll get to the well first and...'

'Then so be it,' Margaret said. 'We can only do what we can do.' She looked at her watch and then over her shoulder to the steep climb behind her. 'I calculate that that hill will take us an hour or so. What awaits us on the other side?'

'There's a valley,' Jason replied after checking his map. 'It dips down across a... flat bit, then leads up sharply to Stavros. We could head around the east of the valley and through the forest. It's not such a sheer climb that way but would take longer.' He didn't think the time was yet right to mention the army encampment that lay over the hill or the inevitable trespassing beyond. It would only have made his Grandmother more determined to press on.

'Then we will see how we are when we reach the top. Oliver may I trouble you for the salt? Oliver what is the matter?'

Oliver was fighting off a variety of flying insects that were intent on sharing the contents of the picnic basket, flapping his arms around in frustration.

'These damn flies and bugs and... bloody harpies!' he yelled out as if insulting the things would send them away.

Jason pulled a can of mosquito repellent from his flight bag and calmly doused Oliver with it while avoiding as much of the food as possible.

'There, they won't trouble you again,' he said. 'Now can you pass the salt to my gran and chill out, per-lease!'

When Margaret had adjusted the taste of her sandwich and taken a bite, she dabbed her lips and continued with her story. The others, perched on rocks around her, listened intently.

'Firstly,' Margaret began, 'what do we know? That there is something called the Golden Fleece hidden on this island, in the well at Stavros, the old Panandreas family monastery. The clues tell us that much. But what is it and why has it been kept hidden all these years? I have a theory. Listen to this:

'Everything is connected to music. The clues were written in the language of music and the music on the portrait helped us unlock those clues. Dimitris Panandreas was a musician. He told Stanley that the music would guide him. Music is the key. This knowledge led me to wonder about the nature of the Golden Fleece. I thought that perhaps it might be somehow connected to music as Stanley clearly remembered Dimitris telling him that only a musician would understand what this was all about. But what musical thing could be so important that it had to be protected? More importantly what musical thing was so dangerous that it had to be hidden from the likes of Hitler who we know was searching for it during the German occupation in the 1940's? Dimitris told Stanley that it was history, something historic.'

'An instrument maybe?' Cassie offered picking up on Margaret's mounting enthusiasm. 'You know some Stradivarius violins have specific names.'

'Possibly,' the older lady replied. 'To be honest, earlier this morning I had thought of that but then later on the boat other possibilities occurred to me. Let me continue.'

'Sorry hon.'

'Not at all. Now then let's think about the concert, the one the British organised to rally the islanders after the liberation. On that night Dimitris and Stanley were to play "The flight of the bumble bee", but at the last minute he told Stanley to change the programme. He rambled on about German composers that his father knew and death and how it all fitted. Stanley of course thought it was the fever he was suffering from in the final stages of his illness. But what if it was not, what if he was giving him further clues? What if he was preparing him for what he found when he received and opened the cigarette case?' She paused briefly for a sip of water before continuing. 'He told Stanley he had a secret to pass on after the concert. A secret that arrived on the island sixty two years previously.'

'And how does that fit with anything?' Jason asked as he brushed crumbs from his Sargo shorts.

'It was the same year that the family portrait was painted,' Margaret shot back quickly.

'I still don't see where this is heading,' Jason complained and opened a can of beer. He offered one to Harriet.

'Let your nan go on Jas.' Harriet accepted the can, drained it and wiped her mouth with the back of her hand.

'Nan? Where was I? Oh yes, on the boat. When Oliver told us his sad story and mentioned the opera he had been to see on the night he misplaced his wife…'

'Poor Mister Simpson,' Lesley sighed.

'When he told us that story something else occurred to me but I did not make the connection until Cassie happened to mention her dreadful experienced in Venice.'

'Hello? I was there too?'

'I apologise Polly, when Cassie mentioned your *collective* Venetian trauma. Words started to ring bells from my memory, from a long time ago when Stanley and I would listen to the radio and he would explain to me all he knew about music. I started thinking about Death in Venice, opera. Tubas and then the date. And then suddenly, for no reason, it all fell into place.'

She looked at their blank faces and took another bite of her sandwich.

'Is anyone else having the same trouble as me?' Lesley asked timidly.

'You're alright pet,' Harriet said, 'it's as clear as mud to me and all.'

'So tell me hon.' Cassie lent forward and lifted her huge sunglasses from her face. 'How do eighteen eighty two, Venice and Tubas connect with the Golden Fleece?'

'Well, to cut a long story short…'

'Too late.'

'Zip it Poll.'

'To cut it short...' Margaret paused and her face lit up with enthusiasm. 'The connection is Wagner.'

'Wagner?' Jason's face was as blank as everyone else's.

Everyone apart from Cassie.

'I think I see the light Margaret. Yes! It's coming at me.'

'Cassie, I knew you'd follow me.'

'Margaret dear we will all follow you willingly,' Oliver said kindly. 'If we only knew what you were talking about.'

Margaret spoke more quickly now, trying to get the jumble of thoughts from her head before she forgot them.

'It is as you said, Oliver. Wagner used special Tubas for his operas, Wagner Tubas as they became known. His operas were heavily Teutonic and nationalistic in theme and it was known that he held anti-Semitic views. Hitler adored Wagner's music and his views and held them up as a light to show off fascist beliefs.'

'So?' Jason grunted.

'And Wagner died in Venice,' Margaret ignored him. 'I remembered that fact not long after you mentioned your death in Venice tour Cassie. I learned a lot from Stanley. I also learned that Richard Wagner died in eighteen eighty three, a year after Dimitris' secret came to Symi…'

'Holly cow Margaret…' Cassie's eyes were wide, her mouth covered by a long fingered hand.

'Yes, yes and…'

'The manuscript?'

'Yes, exactly!'

'What about it Gran?'

'Think boy!' Margaret practically exploded at her grandson so intense was her excitement. 'Leave your hair alone and think. The clues that Dimitris left were dedicated to S.R. Stanley Reah and R.W., Richard Wagner.'

She sat back and looked triumphant.

'But…' Jason seemed uncertain as to whether he should ask his next question. His grandmother glared down at him but indicated with a nod that he could.

'But what has this got to do with what we are looking for?' A thought occurred to the young rep. 'You don't mean…'

Margaret's eyes lit up. He had finally understood.

'You mean we've got a dead German composer up there?'

Obviously he had not.

'Oh dear,' she sighed. 'All I am saying Jason is that I believe the Golden Fleece has something to do with Richard Wagner. That it came from him in Venice to the Panandreas family in Symi, in eighteen eighty three. That Dimitris knew this and wanted to pass on its location to your grandfather.'

'And do you have any thoughts on what it actually is?' Polly lit a cigarette and shifted uncomfortably on her rock.

'Ah, now this is the second part,' Margaret replied. 'What we can suppose. And the following is only supposition. Mostly.'

'Do go on Margaret,' Oliver enthused. 'I am quite intrigued and something is coming to me too. Or as Cassie would say, coming *at* me.'

'Well, let's suppose that Wagner owed money to Christos Panandreas…'

'Now hang on,' Jason interrupted. 'That's a bit dodgy. We don't know for certain that they knew each other.'

'You said yourself Jason that the Panandreas family had business all over Europe including Paris, where Wagner lived for many years and Venice, where he died. Dimitris told your grandfather that Christos Panandreas was a patron of the composer whose music they played at the concert. They played music by *Wagner*. Maybe he owed Panandreas money. It is quite possible. So let us just suppose he did and let us also suppose that he had nothing to give in repayment of his debt. He knew he was coming to the end of his life and so he sent Panandreas the only valuable thing he had. The Golden Fleece. It arrived here the year before Wagner died and has been hidden away ever since.'

'But why has it been kept hidden?' Jason reasoned. 'Why didn't Dimitris just sell it, or publish it or whatever you do with dead people's writing to make some money out of them?'

'It's my belief,' Margaret said calmly, 'that Dimitris didn't know anything about it until after his father died. Dimitris didn't know Wagner like his father Christos had done.'

'And so why didn't Christos bring it to light or sell it before he died?

'He didn't need to,' Margaret replied simply. 'He had his business, he was wealthy, you said so yourself.'

'Wealthy only for a time.'

'Ah yes. Until the sponge businesses started to die out. Until the Turks cut back on fishing rights, until Panandreas became hated by the islanders. Not a good time to suddenly say you have a priceless artefact in your house. Also, and you won't understand this yet Jason, maybe he wanted to leave something for his son. Like Stanley left you the cigarette case. Adults think that way.'

Jason looked slightly abashed for a moment. It was a fleeting pout but Margaret saw it and was pleased to see that he might be learning a little about family responsibility.

'I still don't see why Dimitris hid it for so long. He could have done with the money in later life,' Jason said sulkily.

'When did Christos Panandreas die, Jason?'

'Nineteen fourteen.'

'What was happening in the world in nineteen fourteen?'

'First World War starting?'

'Exactly. Not a time to bring an unknown Wagner… thing to light. People had other things on their minds.'

'So after the war?'

'And who was occupying Symi during that time?'

'Italians.'

'Quite. Who you said commandeered land and property and would have simply taken the thing if they had known about it along with everything else.'

'So after the…' Jason stopped.

'You see? After the war Dimitris was dead, Stanley had the clues to the whereabouts of the Golden Fleece but didn't know it. That's why it has never come to light.' Margaret left a pause while the logic worked into Jason's brain. 'So the only question left to answer now,' she said with a twinkle in her eye, 'is: what exactly *is* The Golden Fleece?'

THIRTY FIVE
Meanwhile

The man watched through his rusting binoculars as the small party of foreigners picked their slow way around from the bay of Vassilios. He had been watching them from his vantage point high above the valley since they first came into view. His original intention of the morning was to spy on the army encampment, to carry out his daily check on activity down there on the edge of his land. In recent months the army had started to encroach on his property and he would soon need to take some drastic action to stop them. So far they had only moved their boundary a little way onto the useless boulder field at the base of his mountain but a little further and they would be encroaching on useful grazing land. Each morning he checked their progress and formed his plan. Another few metres and he would need to act.

Today he had been distracted from his spy work by the sight of a small fishing boat, far off and overloaded, appearing from around the headland at Kouri. As it approached Vassilios and grew larger in his sights he recognised the craft as belonging to Yiannis, one of the part-time fishermen on the island. He knew Yiannis to be unscrupulous, he would do anything to make money including taking tourists on his unlicensed fishing boat, he had done it before. But one thing he had not done before was fish on that side of the island and this put the watcher's suspicious mind into gear. When later he saw Yiannis apparently abandon his group of tourists and head further along the west coast towards the his land, his mind started to go into overdrive.

Now he trained his binoculars on the sea away to the west. The boat had vanished from his sight, it had come ashore somewhere on the west side of the mountain and that could only mean one thing.

The watcher grunted to himself and looked back to the north. The small party of foreigners had also vanished, but they had also been heading towards him. His view of them was now blocked by the hill on the other side of the valley. Between him and them was the army, lazing about in the hollow below. If the tourists were coming towards him they would not get past the military. That was a good thing; it would give him time to turn his attention to Yiannis and the west.

He put the binoculars away, shouldered his shotgun and started off across the rocks to the northerly summit. From there he would get a clear view of the fisherman and would be able to work out what he was up to.

* * *

Yiannis stood at the base of the cliff and looked up. It was not that sheer, a few difficult places where he would have to be careful but mostly they way comprised of juts of large boulders that would offer plenty of hand holds. He judged that it would take him half an hour or so to climb to the top. He looked over to the south at the approaching storm clouds, judged their progress and looked at his watch. If he was quick and found what he was looking for without problems he would be back down and heading for home when the storm rolled in across the south end of the island. He shoved the piece of paper with the strange instructions into his pocket and started up the mountain.

"In our Stavros well" the note had said and then "protect the Golden Fleece". He had known exactly where the well was, how to get there and that the SARGO rep was intent on taking his party of foreigners to the summit of the mountain and the monastery. To search for something made of gold.

The legendary Panandreas treasure.

Tassos, his cousin who the SARGO boy hired weekly to transport his guests to the villa, had called him yesterday in an agitated state. He reported seeing a silver box with the name Panandreas on it. The SARGO boy had it in his possession. This could only mean one thing – that some of the legendary fortune had come to light. At last.

Yiannis thought back to the stories he had heard as a child in the lean years after the war. Christos Panandreas had been the wealthiest merchant on Symi, he had built the new villa, a house in Pedi and he had owned all the land around the area of Manos, including the monastery at Stavros. The story went that, when Christos died, his son remained on the island despite having plenty of opportunity to leave it when times got really hard. Why did he stay? To protect the family treasure of course. The family owned too many valuable things for Dimitris to be able to take them away, no one on the island had enough money to buy them from him so he hid them, guarded them and planned to cash in on his fortune when the war ended. But he died before he could achieve this. So the treasure therefore remained hidden on the island.

When the silver case appeared with the SARGO rep, and Yiannis learned the news, he immediately started thinking things through and came up with the idea that if there was one piece of treasure at the SARGO Villa, there could also be others.

That morning, rising earlier than usual, he had headed down to the villa with the intention of having a look around inside while the tourists were sleeping. He did not count on meeting the SARGO boy in the lane leading from the villa but disguised his intent saying that he was heading out early for fishing.

Things just got better after that. The boy asked him if he would be interested in taking his group on a trip to Apiana, leaving from the harbour at ten that morning. Yiannis asked how many guests, the boy said all six of them and Yiannis immediately agreed. He watched from the ruin above as the party left at nine fifteen, waited for them to disappear from view and then let himself into the open courtyard.

The villa had been left in a mess. Obviously the boy had hurried his guests out before they were completely ready. Plates and cutlery stood unwashed in the kitchen, the breakfast table in the salon had not been cleared and some of the rooms were unlocked. He searched the villa from room to room looking for further clues and signs of the Panandreas treasure.

The first bedroom on the ground floor yielded nothing but clothes. A straw hat hung on the peg behind the door, the dressing table was cluttered with bottles and make up and the wardrobe was full of costly looking clothes; but no treasure. The other room downstairs was much neater apart from a large amount of foreign language newspapers scattered about and cuttings stuffed in the bin. Upstairs he found three of the rooms locked and there was nothing he could do about that but in one he found something which caught his attention.

He was in the rep's room there was no doubt about that. A clipboard lay on the untidy bed, the list of guests clearly visible. A uniform was thrown across a chair, the bedside tables were cluttered with hundreds of CDs, music machines, pop magazines and hair products.

The wardrobe revealed very little other than clothes, a pair of old sandals one of which had a strap missing and swimming trunks. But the dressing table was a different story.

He carefully moved a pile of report forms and more CDs to check what lay beneath and came across a letter. He could read English reasonably well; he had been in the merchant navy in the nineteen sixties and seventies like most of the island men and had been to Liverpool and London in his youth. And so his eye was drawn to some of the words in the neatly handwritten letter. The words "Symi", "heirloom" and "will" leapt out at him and he read the paragraph:

And finally the intrigue. Your grandfather left a will. In it he mentioned only two beneficiaries, me and you. And through it he left only two things: a list of instructions for me and an heirloom for you. I will be bringing your bequest with me. Quite simply put: We both have duties to perform while I am on Symi. I will explain this in much more detail when we meet but in the meantime Stanley left one last cryptic set of instructions for us both. I quote them here:

"Margaret and Jason: Tell no one of the contents of my will. When you get to Symi do not mention my name or the name on the case to anyone on the island. The music will guide you. And, above all, trust each other."

To Yiannis it was clear: The case was the silver case his cousin reported seeing and the name not to be mentioned was Panandreas. What was less clear just then was why the rep wanted to take his guests to Apiana bay. There was nothing there. Unless it had something to do with the "duties" that had to be performed.

He was jolted from his thoughts by the sound of the bell up at Triada striking ten. Having put the letter and other papers back as he remembered seeing them he dashed from the villa and scooted down the Kali Strata to find the tourists waiting for him on his boat.

As he sailed them towards Apiana he was still moodily pondering what was going on when he noticed the paper poking from the rep's back pocket. As the boy helped himself to beers in the wheelhouse Yiannis had simply lifted the paper from his pocket. He read it once the boy was back with his guests in the stern, discussing Panandreas and saying interesting things about "The Golden Fleece". It was then that things fell into place. They were heading for Apiana so as to be able to climb up to Stavros, the old Panandreas monastery. Well, Yiannis was damned if he was going to lead them right to the treasure and not get any of it for himself. He acted quickly and marooned them at Vassilios, raced across the bay of Vassilios and now here he was a few hundred feet up the cliff and preparing to discover what the Panandreas family had hidden in their monastic well.

He paused on the rock face, lent against a reasonably flat outcrop and lit a cigarette. A chill wind blew at him and he looked up half expecting to see the ghost of Dimitris or Christos Panandreas glaring down at him. All he saw were more rocks and, on top of them, the spikes of the iron railings that surrounded the monastery. Not far to go now.

Across to his left he saw one of the tourist boats pull out of the harbour at Panormitis and he apologised to the saint for what he was doing. He also prayed to Saint Michael to protect him from the evil man who now lived in the monastery above. He prayed that he would be out seeing to his land and not lying in wait for Yiannis when he got up there. He reminded the Saint that this man was a killer, that he did not deserve the Panandreas fortune that lay beneath his feet. He added, for good measure and because he still felt a little guilty at breaking into villa SARGO, that Saint Michael should not forget that the current owner of Stavros had not used the chapel for many years, that he had turned the sacred place into little more than a farm and that Yiannis was only doing what he thought was right. The Panandreas treasure, whatever it was, had to be found for the good of the island, it was part of the island's history and he would donate it all to the museum.

When he thought the Saint had heard enough he flicked away his cigarette and prayed to the Virgin Mary to forgive him for lying to Saint Michael.

Whatever he found he was keeping for himself.

THIRTY SIX
Climbing the hill
3.30 p.m.

'After this little exercise,' Polly said as she hoisted her right leg up onto another boulder, 'we should seriously consider the Pirates of Penzance.'

'I don't follow you Poll,' Cassie said. She reached down, took her friend's hand and helped her up another step.

Polly sang breathlessly, '*Climbing over rocky mountains.*'

'Yeah, sure. Got ya.'

'Barry didn't specify that it had to be a revue, did he?'

'Don't think so, but a revue would give us more scope.' Cassie hopped up onto the next boulder and offered her hand again.

'Scope! I'm not going to be capable of anything after today. Apart from perhaps playing the corpse in "The real inspector Hound." Oh what I wouldn't give for ninety minutes flat on my face.'

'Watch your step or that's exactly where you will be. And heave!' Cassie pulled her up another step.

'You don't have to make me sound like rigging, Cassie dear.'

'Now there's an idea.'

'What?'

'Boats, rigging... something's coming at me...'

'Perhaps we should wait until we're on flat ground before you start having ideas.' Polly panted as she pulled herself up onto yet another piece of grey rock. 'You might start singing and cause an avalanche.'

'Don't be silly.' Lesley overtook with an agility that Polly found scary. 'Avalanches happen in snow, even I know that.'

'All right then, a landslide.'

'Whatever,' Cassie said. 'I have this idea. Jees that woman's got some stamina.

'She probably gets a lot of physical exercise.'

Polly stopped to get her breath back. Below her she could see the shore was now at some distance. Harriet was helping Oliver up the hillside with the various bags. They weaved in and out of the larger rocks as they climbed, sensibly avoiding the thistles that had scraped Polly's legs. Above her the others were making good progress, with Jason leading, and she guessed that she was over half way.

'You know Cass, I think for once I am grateful to my ballet mistress. I'm not in as bad shape as I thought.'

'You'd be better if you didn't smoke, listen to those lungs. Come on hon.'

Polly took a deep breath and lifted her leg onto the next stable rock. 'So tell me this idea of yours,' she said. 'Anything to take my mind off my hip!'

'Well,' Cassie started. She was having no trouble with the climb. She controlled her breathing and took it slowly. 'Everything today so far has been about boats, so I was wondering about a nautical theme? Maybe call it "Two dames at sea" and have us as sailors who get shipwrecked on a magical island. Lots of scope there for sea-shanties and jigs.'

'If you think I will be able to dance a hornpipe after this little farce you are very much mistaken.'

'We'll oil you up before we wheel you on.'

'Ha bloody ha.'

'I'm sure the provincial theatres would take it, especially in the summer. And places like Brighton and Southampton would love it, being by the sea. Hey! What about the numbers from "Anything Goes"?'

Polly looked up, about to complain again. She looked hurriedly away.

'Cass, I can see your bloomers.'

'Eh?'

'From down here everything's showing darling. Tuck your skirt between your knees when you stop, will you?'

'O.k. hon. Hey, "Everything Shows!" A brilliant title. Shows as in Theatre shows and everything as in…'

'I am not getting my kit off!'

'As in everything. We can do what we like, with a Cole Porter connection maybe.'

'Oh just curb your enthusiasm woman and get me up this bloody hill. We'll have plenty of time to talk about the show when we get this blasted day over with. Now heave!'

Up ahead Jason was talking to Margaret.

'Grandmother,' he said tentatively, 'there's something I have been meaning to ask you.'

'Yes dear?'

'Well, two things actually. First off, how come you're so fit?'

Margaret laughed and pulled herself up another notch.

'I am just pretending to be,' she said. 'You can overcome anything with a little determination.'

Jason could feel his shirt clinging to his back with sweat, his mouth was dry and his legs felt like lead. Yet below him his guests seemed to be taking the hill within their stride. *Never knew oldies could be so determined*, he thought as he rubbed at his sore chest.

'What's the other thing?' his Grandmother was asking.

Jason walked beside her and concentrated on the ground rather than look at her.

'When I was young I remember my mother went into hospital. I thought she was going to have a baby but she didn't. Did I remember that right or am I wrong?'

His Grandmother stopped for a moment, took a deep breath and then carried on. It looked to Jason as if she had just summoned up even more determination.

'Did you ask your parents about that?' Margaret asked.

'Only at the time and I can't remember what they said, I was young.'

'You still are dear, but I suppose that you're old enough now.'

'For what?'

'To know. But I shouldn't have be the one to tell you. Your mother should do that.'

'We don't talk much,' Jason admitted sadly. 'Since I…'

He was about to say since he came out to them, but he still did not feel comfortable talking about being gay with his Gran. One of his gay university friends had once told a story about coming out. He had called his entire family together one Sunday afternoon, grandparents included, and announced to them en masse that he was 'queer'. His mother nearly fainted, his brother said he always suspected and one grandmother suggested Milk of Magnesia. When he spelled it out for his older relatives the other grandmother took it badly and had an angina attack. She died three days later in hospital.

Jason didn't want any of his elderly guests going the same way, particularly not his Grandmother and particularly not half way up a remote hillside on a small Greek island.

'Since you what?' Margaret enquired.

'Since I came to work out here,' Jason said quickly.

'I see. And you would like me to tell you?'

'If you would.'

They had reached the top and Margaret immediately took shelter from the sun under a lone pine tree, with her back to the valley on the other side. She sat and faced the sea. Jason checked that the other guests were still moving towards the summit and then joined her. He took a bottle of now warm water from his flight bag and they both drank before Margaret spoke.

'You were three at the time,' she began and her breathing was remarkably controlled considering the climb she had just made. 'And yes, your mother fell pregnant. Your father called us one morning saying that the baby was on the way and we raced over to babysit you while your parents went to the hospital. I spent the night reading to you and your Grandfather while we waited for news. After I had put you to bed I made up the crib in your parent's room. It was to be a surprise for them, they had made very little preparation for your sibling's arrival. I assumed, at the time, that they either knew or hoped it was to be a boy and they would simply reuse all your baby things. They had bought nothing new that I could see and nothing had been laid out ready for the baby.

'The following day was a warm day I recall, Stanley was outside in his chair and you were playing on the lawn. I was giving the house a final clean when your parents returned from the hospital.'

She stopped and took some more water. It did not help; her throat was still dry when she went on.

'But there was no baby. They came back empty handed. Your mother went straight to bed, still recovering from the birth, and your father… Well he announced he was going straight to the pub but when I found out… But Stanley and I left, so he had to stay with you and your mother.'

'What happened Gran? Was the baby stillborn?'

Beside him he heard Margaret take a very long, deep breath. He looked down at the sea and the archipelago of small islands they had passed through previously. They diminished in size the further they went out to sea. Jason saw them as a line of brothers and sisters.

'No dear,' Margaret said and her voice was now quiet. 'I am afraid not. You mother gave birth to a healthy baby girl. It was one of the few coherent things she said to me that day. "It was a girl."'

Jason felt uncomfortable now. Not only because he was learning something about his past that he had never known before but also because he sensed that his grandmother was crying. He was never any good with upset old people at the best of times, but when that person was family he was even more at a loss as to what to do. He just stared at the water breaking around the chain of small islands and waited for her to say something else.

Finally Margaret wiped her nose on a handkerchief and tucked it back up her sleeve. She coughed slightly.

'They gave your sister away,' she said.

'Gave her away? Why?'

'Your mother insisted that they could not afford another child. They did not ask us for help, they were too proud. Instead she made a decision as soon as she knew she was pregnant and arranged to have your sister adopted the moment she was born. By the time I knew about it your sister was already gone.'

Jason didn't know what to say, or how to react. He swallowed hard.

284

'Do you know where she is now?' he asked, his voice too had dropped to almost a whisper.

'No dear. I did not speak to your parents again until a few weeks ago. As you know I had not seen you since you were three. That I regret. I also regret that your father never confided in me about their financial troubles, or the trouble he had with your mother. It was she who insisted that baby be adopted. And so...' Her voice became stronger and she lifted her shoulders. 'Your grandfather and I did what we could for you, from a distance. Which was little more than keep in touch with your life by way of news from friends and neighbours. But you should know that your grandfather Stanley always spoke of you and promised he would see you right one day. And so here we are. And that is that.'

Jason let out a long sigh. It was a lot of information to take in, especially with half his mind on the other guests who he could now hear approaching.

'Thanks for telling me,' he said.

Margaret did not reply.

She had been so open with him, so honest, that Jason wondered if this was the right time for him to get his secret out in the open after all. She could hardly throw a fit or storm off when she heard the news and besides, he doubted she would have an angina attack after climbing that hill. If she could do what she had done today and tell him all that stuff she was probably o.k. to hear his news.

He felt slightly sick, not with nerves but because he was not used to having discussions about his family with his family. He had never shared an emotional or difficult conversation with his parents and the thought of doing so with his grandmother turned his stomach. But if she could be that determined at seventy something, then surely he could be at twenty three. He took a very deep breath and swallowed hard.

'Can I tell you something now?' he asked, his eyes still on the sea shimmering far below.

'Of course dear, anything.'

But, before he had a chance to open his mouth and shock the old woman, a gunshot rang out across the mountains. Its retort cracked into echoes that bounced from rock to rock until they faded into silence.

THIRTY SEVEN

Stavros

3.20 pm

Yiannis crouched on the cliff side of the iron railings and listened hard. All he could hear was the sound of the wind as it blew up from the sea far below. As far as he could make out there was no one moving about inside the grounds of the monastery. He lifted his head slowly until he could see over the low wall and between the railings. The place was run down and untidy. The outbuildings looked like they had been badly repaired following dereliction and the chapel itself was grey and in need of a new roof. The trees were wild and untended and the ground a mess of dead branches, litter and stones. He could see the well. The circle of stones, once painted white but now green with weed cover, was no more than a metre high. It looked to be uncovered and that was a blessing but it also stood in the dead centre of the courtyard, in the open. He would have to be on his guard if he was to investigate it.

He knew the buildings were occupied. And he knew who lived there.

Evil lived there.

Very carefully he made his way along the outside wall, constantly checking for any signs of life inside, until he reached the iron gates on the landward side. Still no signs of occupation, no one was at home. The gate creaked slightly as he pushed it open and he paused. Already his heart was thumping in his chest and his hands felt clammy. He checked behind once more before slipping in through the gate. Crouching, he sidled up to a large tree. Looking around its trunk he could see the well and the outhouse opposite. He listened.

Just the wind in the forest sounding like the sea in the distance. He suddenly longed to be out at sea casting his net, throwing his bait, dropping his dynamite. But then again, a few minutes investigating the well for the Panandreas' treasure, the 'Golden Fleece', would be time well spent when he cashed in on his find. It would undoubtedly be worth a great deal more that he would ever make from fishing, even with dynamite. A bird twittered somewhere nearby, a goat-bell clanged in the valley below and he shuddered; he was not a land animal and these sounds were alien to him. He would swap soil and trees for water and the chance of drowning any day. He threw a small rock across the courtyard and it hit the door of the outbuilding. He ducked behind the tree and waited. No one came to investigate.

Feeling a little more confident now that he was certain he was alone, he left the cover of the tree and crept up along the side of the chapel. When he reached the far end he peeked around the corner. Although he could see no one he felt certain that someone was watching him, somewhere. At least at sea, with the huge expanse of the Aegean spread out all around, you could see someone creep up on you. Here on land there were too many things for someone else to hide behind, too many shadows.

'Ella malaka,' he said to himself. 'Only God is watching and he approves. You are doing this for the island. Aris is not here. Quick.'

Talking to himself gave him enough of a boost to cross the open space to the well. He crouched beside it and took a torch from his pocket. Checking that he was still alone he lent over the wall and looked down into the blackness below.

It was deep, deeper than Hades, deeper than the sea and so much blacker. As he lent further over he could smell the air within the shaft, it was cold and smelled of damp, mouldy earth. *The smell of the dead*, he thought, *the land dead*.

The beam from the torch only allowed him to see a little way down but he could see enough to realise that the wall of the well was made of rock. He would be able to find handholds and places for his feet so climbing down should not pose a problem. Getting back up with whatever he found down there would be another matter, but he would have a look and then decide what to do. If there was too much for him to carry he would find some way of getting Aris away from his property for a few hours and then return with ropes and transport of some sort. If the treasure was large, and he was praying that is was, he would have to involve cousin Tassos and his donkeys, but that would be o.k. he would pay him off. The rest of the loot would be his.

His mind flashed to what he would buy once he had sold the Panandreas treasure. A new boat for fishing was the first thing that came to mind but then he dismissed that idea. He would not need to work. A few nights at a brothel in Rhodes, a few days in the Casino, a trip to see his family in Australia, a new house…

He checked himself and concentrated on the matter in hand.

He rose and lifted one leg over into the shaft. Well aware of the bottomless pit beneath he searched carefully for somewhere to put his foot and found a solid outcrop of rock. Certain that this would hold his weight he slid his other leg over, gripping the wall with both hands for support. When both feet were firmly placed he started to lower himself until only his head was visible above the rim of the well.

It was enough of a target.

Aris had come down from where he had been watching the soldiers and the tourists. As soon as he saw the small group appear over the brow of the hill on the opposite side of the valley he had known for certain where they were heading. Unless they were going to have tea with the lazy army boys there was only one place they could be going; his land. He hurried back to his home in a state of agitation. If they were coming to pay him a visit then he needed to prepare for the special occasion. His hunting rifle only had two cartridges in it, the others were back in his house and he would need more than two shots to welcome them.

He stopped when he reached the gates. He had not left one of them open. He never did. Someone else was trespassing on his land today; he had never been so popular.

Aris' memory was older than his fifty years. He remembered his grandfather Michaelis telling him the story of the old family feud. Grandfather Tzankatis often mumbled on about a certain day, when Aris' father was about ten, when they had actually encountered Dimitris Panandreas face to face. The old man had been caught laying claim to the monastery on Tzankatis land. Aris remembered his father, Petros, telling how the Italians had been bribed into granting the Panandreas family permanent rights to Stavros. Old Panandreas had even offered Petros a sweet as a bribe to keep quiet about it and sweets were not easy to come by in those days. He remembered his father telling him, moments before he died that, as there was not a single Panandreas left alive, the land should return to the Tzankatis family. His father had never wanted the land, the run down chapel or the crumbling outhouses but Aris had decided that even if they were not valuable they should be his, if only to put right the injustice committed by the Panandreas lot all those years ago. They had stolen the land from the Tzankatis line and Aris Tzankatis would take it back. There was no one left around to complain.

But that had not stopped other interested parties in the past. He had often fired off warning shots to trespassers and didn't care if he did one day hit one of them. Tourists who had somehow wandered around the valley, avoiding detection by the army and found their way up to this idyllic looking church, or locals trying to graze their animals on his land, even the military themselves had not been exempt. Twice Aris had had a showdown with youthful soldiers on national service who had gone exploring up his mountain. Anyone who trespassed on his land was fair game.

And someone had trespassed since he had been out, or was still trespassing. The gate had been left open.

He stealthily crept up the last few steps to the monastery grounds and listened. Nothing. He crept along the north side of the chapel wall until he reached the end. He poked his head around the corner and his face immediately flushed red with rage. He took a great stride out into the centre of the courtyard.

'Ella!' he yelled as he lifted the rifle. The sight was up to his eye in a flash with the fisherman's face dead centre in it.

Aris fired off one shot and hit Yiannis directly between the eyes. The fisherman's final grunt of surprise echoed in the well and faded with the sound of his body bouncing down the rocky shaft. By the time Aris came to the well and looked in, the sounds had stopped and the man was certainly dead. All Aris saw was the light of the torch as it ricocheted its way into oblivion.

Reminding himself to throw some quicklime down the dried up well sometime he went into the outbuilding that served as his house.

He poured himself a large glass of Metaxa, took it outside and sat on the wall looking down into the valley below. He drank while he calmly watched the group of tourists approach from the north while the storm gathered behind him in the south.

THIRTY EIGHT
South side of the valley
3.31 pm

'I don't think they were shooting at us,' Lesley said as she lay flat on her stomach beside Jason.

As soon as they had heard the shot ring out they had instinctively thrown themselves on the ground for cover. Actually only Jason had thrown himself down, the others had lowered themselves gracefully on Lesley's instruction and Polly was glad for the chance of a lie down.

Jason had been on the verge of coming out to his grandmother when he had heard the shot and decided it was someone's way of telling him to keep his mouth shut. He would bring the subject up later if the opportunity arose. Similarly he would ask more about the sister he never knew. For now, though, his head was suddenly full of insurance claims, dead guests and long prison sentences. But even these disturbing thoughts had to be pushed to one side, Lesley was nudging him.

'Do you have any thermo-imaging binoculars?' she asked in a whisper.

'No, why? Do you?'

'What is going on?' Margaret asked. She was on Jason's right hand side, close to the tree and squinting into the valley below.

'I say we carry on,' Harriet grunted down the line from her place at the far end. 'Probably just target practice going on, or some such.'

'Leave it to me.'

Before Jason could stop her Lesley had slid backwards on her belly, got up and was off, running at a crouch.

'Mrs. Shaw come back…' he began but she had disappeared down the hill towards the valley pausing only to collect her bag from Harriet.

'She suddenly seems to have woken up,' Oliver hissed. 'Do you think it's too much sun?'

'Let her go,' said Polly. 'With any luck she'll get taken prisoner and won't have to listen to her rabbit on about husbands and sewing accidents.'

'Oh Mrs. Arnold you can be so cruel.' Oliver threw her a stern look.

'I want everyone to stay calm and stop talking,' Jason hissed. 'I need to think what's best to do.'

'I am having so much fun.'

Margaret laughed but Jason didn't see the funny side. He assumed his grandmother was displaying the first signs of hysteria.

'This is not fun,' he protested.

'It is certainly a great deal more exciting than sitting on a beach with a Dick Francis, or whatever other people do on holiday.'

'Say Jas,' Harriet called. 'You should market this trip a bit more. Outward bound for the housebound, or orienteering for the terminally disorientated.' She laughed loudly and Cassie elbowed her in the ribs.

'Those soldiers are not so far away damn it!'

'And,' Jason added, 'we are trespassing. We should not be here.'

'Do you mean you knew we would come across this?' Oliver said. 'And you didn't think to mention it.'

'I was going to…'

'You knowingly brought us and dear Mrs. Shaw into danger? You knew we would…'

'Hush Mister Simpson, it'll be o.k.'

'I doubt that very much young man.'

Jason doubted it too. From their position on the brow of the hill they could see the army encampment a few hundred metres below them. They were close enough to see two separate groups of soldiers. One was gathered around a table outside a small hut, they appeared to be drinking coffee and playing a game, possibly cards. Their rifles rested up against a wall and most had their backs to Jason. They seemed undisturbed by the recent gun shot.

The other group of three soldiers was pacing the perimeter of a high wire fence that ran around the encampment. They held their rifles and appeared to be actively guarding the place. The fence itself ran from the edge of the forest on Jason's left, up to the top of the cliffs on his right, across the bottom of the hill opposite on which stood the grey and white buildings of Stavros and back around the edge of the forest once more. It encircled the entire valley and formed an impenetrable defence against the direction in which they needed to go.

There was no way through, they would have to go around. That would mean a long hike across the top of the hill they were now on until they reached the trees. Then they would have a steep climb on the east side of the mountain to approach Stavros from the side. And all that without being seen by the soldiers below. *At least*, Jason thought, *the monastery is deserted so there will be no one there to stop us if we get there.*

But thoughts of what they would find at Stavros when and if they got there would have to wait; his first priority now was to get his guests safely away from the army camp and into the woods. But how?

'Lesley's back!'

'Oh my god it's Rambo in drag,' Cassie said under her breath.

Jason looked along the line and saw Lesley crawling her way back towards him. Although she still wore her Safari outfit she had scored her face with eye shadow, presumably for camouflage, and appeared now as a cross between Meryl Streep in Out of Africa and a zebra. Jason couldn't think of anything to say and so just gawped as she squeezed back into place beside him, throwing her bag down at her feet.

'Here's how it is,' she said quickly. 'Three boys guarding the perimeter, the others are distracted. For how long I can't say. Our safest way through this is to scoot along to the woods and go up and around to the east.'

'Our safest way around this is to go back,' Jason replied.

'Negative. These old girls would never make the return trip. We have to go on.'

'Old girls?' Polly exclaimed, getting to her knees. Cassie pulled her down sharply.

'Trust me,' Lesley said. 'Ex-husband Clive was a Colonel. Taught me everything I need to know for this kind of situation.'

Suddenly this blue rinse bimbo had turned into a twin set and pearls commando and Jason didn't know whether to laugh or cry. He just stared at her, open mouthed.

'Here's the plan, team,' she went on and there was no questioning the authority in her voice. 'We split into two parties. I will lead a diversionary advance to the west, along the coastal cliff line. Jason will lead Red Team across to the woods. They may spot one team but I doubt they will be able to track both. Stay low and if you are captured give nothing away even when they torture you. Whichever team gets to the monastery first, find what we're looking for and get back to base. Survivors rendezvous at twenty-hundred hours to debrief. Leave casualties behind. If a team member gets wounded shoot her...'

'Hang on love.' Jason finally found words. 'This isn't some adventure movie. This is for real. They won't torture anyone, they'll just take you down to the police station where you'll get told off for trespassing and be given a cup of tea.'

Lesley almost looked disappointed. 'And what would they do with you?' she said pointedly. 'You're a SARGO rep, you should know better.'

'Here here!' Oliver exclaimed.

'Yes, well I'd rather not think about that.'

'It seems to me,' Margaret said, 'that Mrs. Shaw knows more than the rest of us of what she is talking about. She certainly has the parlance. I vote we do as she says until we are on the other side of the valley.'

'I'll go along with that,' said Harriet and the others agreed.

'I would follow dear Mrs. Shaw anywhere,' said Oliver and blushed.

'Settled then,' Lesley said decisively. 'Jason, you take Margaret, Oliver, Cassie and Polly. Harriet you come with me. Bring only what we need to get down the well, dump any unnecessary supplies. We're travelling light.'

'Shouldn't I go with you?' Oliver asked. 'One man per... team?'

'Sorry Oliver dear but I don't need wit, charm and a disarming smile.' Lesley winked at him and Oliver blushed further. 'Each team needs someone with lots of brawn, a little speed and no brain whatsoever. I will take Harriet. The girls can have Jason.'

Harriet and Jason turned red.

'I am really not sure about this Mrs. Shaw...' Jason began but she cut him off.

'Stay low, stay quiet and if you get caught just feign the early stages of Alzheimer's.'

'Too late for some,' Polly quipped glancing sideways at Cassie who was tucking sage twigs into her hair.

'Camouflage hon.'

'On my mark... Red Team away.'

Jason slid back and crouched on his haunches. Cassie, Polly and Margaret fell in behind him, staying as low as their aching legs would allow.

'Good luck Mrs. Shaw,' Oliver said as he fell in line. 'You're my heroine.'

'Remember,' Lesley whispered back. 'Tell them *nothing*.'

Jason watched as Harriet and Lesley set of in the direction of the cliffs. With his heart in his mouth and his flight bag over his shoulder he headed nervously across the top of the hill towards the woods.

Below him he could see the group of soldiers playing cards and could hear the occasional laugh. Sound travelled up from the valley, carried on the slight breeze that had drifted in from the south. He looked to the sky and noticed the same threatening clouds that he had seen from the boat. They were closer and larger now, the storm was definitely heading their way.

'Well this just gets better and better,' he mumbled to himself.

They had only gone about a hundred metres when Oliver, at the back of the line, exclaimed, 'oh no! Look!'

Everyone stopped and Jason signalled for them to take cover. Getting as low as they could among the boulders and shrubs without snagging tights or straining backs the SARGO guests turned to see what Oliver was pointing at.

Jason saw his career in tourism crumble before his eyes. He saw three years behind bars in a Greek prison, he saw law suits and tabloid headlines and he saw Lesley approaching the soldiers with her hands above her head. There was no sign of Harriet.

'She's in the shit,' Cassie said unnecessarily. 'And she don't look pretty.'

Sure enough the usually well poised Mrs. Shaw was now being ordered down the hill and was stumbling towards the three soldiers with her bag like an escapee from Tenko. The soldiers opened a gate in the fence and waited for her to arrive. One soldier kept his rifle trained on her while another lifted a walkie-talkie to his mouth. Jason could hear Lesley calling a faint but friendly greeting as she neared the enclosure waving what looked, at that distance, like white lacy underwear. He prayed that she would not say anything more stupid than normal.

He watched as she reached the gate and lowered her surrender flag. He pondered for a moment on the irony of Lesley lowering her underwear in the presence of the military but snapped to when the soldier raised his gun at her. He heard her familiar coquettish laugh, saw her offer out a hand to be shaken and knew she could handle herself, if not the entire platoon. The three arresting soldiers looked at each other. One shook her hand but another brushed him away and shouted. Lesley was marched brusquely at gun point towards the group who had been playing cards. Jason could now see there were five of them and they were all standing, some were laughing while others reached for their weapons.

'Down!' Margaret's voice snapped and everyone fell flat.

Peeking over the top of the rock, Jason could see why his grandmother had sounded so urgent. One of the soldiers now had binoculars pressed to his eyes and was scouring the hillside. Jason ducked as the solider scanned their part of the hill. He signalled for everyone to stay down. No one moved.

'I don't wish to trouble anyone,' Polly whispered after a long silence. 'But may I ask if there is wild boar on this island?'

'Hush!' Jason ordered. 'Don't be...'

But then he heard it too: the rasping, low breathing of some wild animal. The rhythm was steady, as if the animal were concentrating, stalking its prey maybe.

'It must be a sniffer dog,' Oliver said and began to stand up.

'Stay down!' Jason couldn't make out where the sound was coming from but it was getting nearer. 'Nobody move.'

'That would be an appropriate way to go,' Polly whispered to Cassie. 'Mauled to death by a wild animal half way up a Greek mountain. Very classical.'

'Put a sock in it woman.'

'Hush!'

Jason carefully glanced out from behind his rock. The heavily breathing animal was nearly on them and he needed to see whether they could get away from it without being seen. The solders were leading Lesley into their guard hut, all eight of them following her, nudging and pushing each other with youthful excitement like they were about to get on a white knuckle ride at Disneyland.

Maybe they were.

A rock tumbled down the hill behind him and he flipped onto his back. He heard a low growl, a grunt, the breaking of twigs and...

'Hey up pet, we're in the clear.'

Harriet scrambled up to them, her knees grazed, her breathing shallow. She was red in the face and sweating heavily.

'Wild boar indeed.' Margaret tutted.

'What happened?' Jason asked quickly checking the situation below. The door to the hut was now shut and the compound was deserted.

'What will they do to her?' Oliver looked very concerned.

'It's what she will do to them what worries me,' Harriet replied. 'Poor lads. Any road, no time for chat. Here's the plan...'

'The plan is that we must go and rescue Mrs. Shaw.' Oliver protested. 'We can't just leave her.'

'She said you'd say that,' Harriet said. 'A bit clever after all is our Lesley.'

'What do you mean?'

'Her instructions were clear Ollie. She distracts them and we cut straight through the enclosure. She reckons we got about fifteen minutes before they come out of that hut.'

'But what are they doing to the poor woman?' Oliver was now sounding quite distraught.

'I know what you are thinking Mr S.,' Jason said. 'But I am sure they would not do anything… untoward. They are probably checking her passport and then they will take her home to the villa.'

'They should get off so lightly,' said Polly.

'You're right Poll. She has other ideas,' Harriet said.

'Oh lord.'

'No Ollie, nowt like that. She's distracting them with musical highlights from the Sound of Music. She reckons it will be a good ten minutes before they get bored and then she's got five minutes of Oklahoma in her repertoire before they have enough and ship her out. We best run.'

Without saying another word Harriet got to her feet, picked up the duffle bag and started off directly down the hill.

'Well come on,' she called back and the others, too surprised to object, followed.

THIRTY NINE
Crossing the valley
3.50 pm

The gate, when they reached it, was unlocked. Across the enclosure Jason could see an identical gate some two hundred metres away. The group was completely exposed now and if anyone stepped out of the hut to his left they would be seen instantly. Harriet opened the gate and hurried the small group inside.

'Quick as you like,' she ordered. 'Keep to the right, there's some trees ahead will do as cover, run if you can.'

The ground in the valley was mercifully flat. The soft cushion of dry grass and soil beneath their feet was a welcome change from the rocks and harsh scrub they had been walking on since they left the boat. Jason ushered his guests ahead towards the opposite side.

'Once we get through the other gate,' Harriet whispered to him as they headed for the shelter of the trees, 'it looks like a quick dash to the bottom of the hill. We'll still be exposed, mind.'

'At least we will be on the right side,' Jason replied. 'And it's not far to those woods over there.'

'Good lad, keep going. Want me to carry you Mags?'

'Certainly not.'

'I can't believe we're doing this.'

'We're doing it for you Jason,' Margaret said to him. 'And for history!'

'I feel a song coming on.'

'Not now Cassie.'

They reached the trees and had cover for a hundred metres. But they did not slow their pace until the trees ran out and they were once again faced with open ground; about fifty metres between them and the far gate.

'I hope it's unlocked.'

Jason poked his head out from behind the last tree. The hut was now far off in the distance and several other small sheds stood between it and him. It had taken them five minutes so far and he hoped that Lesley's selections from Rogers and Hammerstein would hold out until they were through the gate and in the woods. He could hear faint sounds of laughter coming from the hut and he calmed a little.

Looking back at the group of guests behind him he felt a strange sensation; a mixture of panic and pride. They were all looking back at him expectantly, Harriet grinning, Polly frowning. Had they really done all this for him? His grandmother winked at him and nodded towards the far gate.

'Look...' he began.

'Later pet,' Harriet said pushing past. 'You bring up the rear, so to speak. Let's shift arse.'

She thundered off across the enclosure and the others followed. Jason came last, constantly checking the distant hut. No one came out and by the time they reached the gate he was sure they were home safe. But when he arrived there was a confab going on.

'What is it?' he asked, slightly breathless.

'Bloody locked.' Harriet kicked it. It rattled but remained shut.

The gate was made up of wire strung inside an eight foot high metal frame and the frame was padlocked to a steel post concreted into the ground. The wire fence on either side was the same height and topped with razor wire, similar steel posts kept it taut and there were no signs of any gaps or crawl spaces.

'Now we're done for,' Polly said and everyone looked.

Two solders were coming out of the hut, rifles over their shoulders. They were talking, laughing about something and heading towards the group of guests mustered at the gate.

'They've not seen us yet,' Harriet said as she tried to wrench the padlock from the gate. The padlock was sound but she noticed that the wire inside the frame had rusted in places. 'But it's only a matter of time.'

There was no time to race back to the trees, besides the movement would have attracted too much attention. The nearest possible cover was an old oil drum between them and the soldiers, but even if they could get there undetected it would not conceal all of them. Jason decided it was time to give themselves up.

'Come on folks,' he said quietly. 'It's time to go.'

He took a step towards the soldiers and opened his mouth to call out.

'Oi, Alex!'

The soldiers stopped in their tracks. Jason stopped too, his mouth still wide open. Harriet yanked on the gate.

'Here, Alex! George!'

The soldiers spun on their heels, turning their backs to the group at the gate. Harriet yanked harder on the rusty wire.

On the other side of the enclosure a tall young man stood with his face pressed up against the wire fence. He was waving at the soldiers and they waved back as they approached him.

'Who the...?'

'I got it!'

With a final pull from Harriet part of the wire came away from the frame. She bent it back as far as it would go allowing just enough space for the first of the escaping guests to squeeze though.

'Do mind the sharp edges.' Margaret fussed around as Oliver climbed through. 'It looks lethal and I am worried about your shirt.'

'I was more concerned about tetanus,' Oliver said as he passed successfully through the opening. Once on the other side he stopped to assist the ladies through the gap one by one.

Jason stared across at the group of three young men now chatting amiably to each other through the fence. He thanked someone up there for their luck as Harriet encouraged him through the gate.

Once on the other side however he realised that there was still one more obstacle to overcome. The hole Harriet had created for everyone to clamber through was not big enough for the big woman from Bolton herself and she became wedged.

'Flaming arseholes,' she swore as she tried in vain to manoeuvre through.

The soldiers were inviting their friend into the camp, heading along the fence to meet him at the other gate. The tall man on the outside was keeping pace with them and Jason was sure he would look across and see them at any moment. Harriet's bright Bermuda shirt stood out like a Turkish flag at a Greek wedding.

'Can you hurry Harriet?' he begged. 'We're not free yet.'

'Too bloody right lad,' she replied and grunted as she tried to push through. Wire snagged her shorts, ripping them across her upper thighs and she swore.

'Everyone else make a dash for those trees,' Jason instructed pointing across to the safety of the woods. 'Go.'

Margaret herded the others towards the woods as Jason started to pull on Harriet's arm.

'Aint gunna help pet,' she gasped back. 'I think I'm right caught by the short and curlies.'

'Oh gross!' Jason didn't want to picture what that looked like. He just tugged harder.

Across the enclosure the soldiers had admitted their friend and the three of them were now heading back towards the hut. All they had to do was glance across to their right and they would see a young SARGO rep dragging a fat woman through a gate backwards. But Harriet's bulk was still wedged in the torn-back wire.

'Breathe in Harriet.'

'I am lad!'

'Well breathe in more.'

'I can't.'

An idea struck Jason like a bullet.

'Breathe out,' he ordered.

'Well I will have to eventually.'

'I mean push yourself out, push your beer gut out.'

'Oi, it's relaxed muscle is that.'

'Well push that then.'

'I can't.'

'Remember your newspapers?' Jason was thinking fast on his feet. He had to get this woman out of the wire and under cover before they were seen. The soldiers had stopped to smoke cigarettes. The tall man who had come to visit them now stood facing Jason, his head bowed as he accepted a light. As soon as he looked up...

'What about me newspaper?'

'Remember how you were when you found someone had cut bits out? Picture your beloved Daily Mirror with half the page missing.'

'Aye, and when I find who ever did that...'

'That's it, get angry girl. Remember your paper with great big holes in it. Tabloid vandalism...'

It worked.

Harriet growled, pushed her stomach out as far as it would go and the wire bent under the force. The gap widened and she broke free like the Incredible Hulk bursting through a wall.

But as Harriet stumbled away to the safety of the trees the young man opposite lifted his head and stared straight into Jason's eyes.

FORTY
The last climb
4.00 pm

'Thank heaven's you are safe Ms Smith.' Margaret was fussing around Harriet's bloodied legs when Jason scrambled into the cover of the trees.

'I think he saw me,' he gasped as he reached the others. 'We have to keep moving.'

'Who saw you?' Cassie asked.

'Some guy, couldn't see his face, probably an off duty soldier. Mates with the others. Let's go.'

'Slow down Jason dear.' Margaret looked up at him from where she was kneeling behind Harriet. 'Ms Smith is injured.'

'I'll be right pet. Let's keep moving.'

'If you are sure? I have some iodine somewhere…'

'Later Mags. Come on folks.'

And with that Harriet grabbed the duffle bag and started off through the trees towards Stavros and the final climb to the summit.

The others followed silently and they quickly reached what looked like a rough track, suggesting that other people had used this path before. The ground was trodden underfoot and, a little further on, the natural formation of the rocks turned into rough steps.

Jason overtook Harriet and started climbing. Although he was very grateful to Harriet for carrying the bag of equipment he felt it was his duty to lead the party. After pulling himself up a few of the uneven steps he paused to look back. He wanted to check that they were not being followed. Through the trees he could just make out parts of the army enclosure but could see no sign of life. Nor could he hear anyone shouting or anything that suggested the soldiers were running towards them; the whole place seemed eerily quiet. He looked up and caught sight of clouds gathering across the top of the mountain. *The calm before the storm*, he thought and suddenly felt a chill run through him.

Below he could see his guests helping each other up the steps. His grandmother still seemed to be taking the trek in her stride and showed no signs of flagging. Polly was limping a little and clutching at her hip but her friend was lending a helping hand. Harriet's scratched legs seemed to be giving her no trouble at all and it was only Oliver who was lagging behind. He, too, was stopping to look back, looking concerned. Probably for the fate of Lesley; the two of them had stayed close to each other all day.

Jason allowed himself a smile. It wouldn't be the first time two of his elderly guests had 'bonded' during a SARGO holiday.

'It can't be much further,' Margaret said as she stepped up behind Jason.

'I don't think so. We should be careful from now on but we must move quickly.' He indicated the clouds that were quickly gathering above.

'It looks like it may rain.' Margaret touched his arm. 'So we will get a little wet, who cares?'

Jason did. If the storm hit them head on it would make the walk back virtually impossible. But then it was not going to be an easy return journey in any case. He had no idea how they were going to get back to the village, he hadn't thought about it at all. There was a road marked on his map but this was a couple of miles away and on the other side of the mountain. Even if they could reach it his only hope was to flag down a passing car or truck and beg for a lift; he had no phone to call for assistance. And what if they found the Golden Fleece and it turned out to be something huge or heavy? How would they carry it?

The others had bunched up behind him and were now waiting for him to move on. They had stopped at a place with the rock face on one side and a sheer drop of about twenty feet on the other. Below was nothing but sharp rock and spiky bushes of an indeterminate species.

'I do hope Mrs. Shaw will be safe,' Oliver grumbled. 'Are we stopping for tea?'

'Sorry Mr S.,' Jason replied. 'I think we should push on. We are almost there.'

'What are these?' Oliver asked kicking a pile of small, round black things at his feet. 'Are they olives or goat droppings?'

'Why don't you try one and find out,' said Harriet.

'Oh I couldn't possibly.' Oliver screwed up his nose. 'I can't stand olives.'

'It's all been very exciting, if a little tiring,' said Margaret. 'I for one am looking forward to a good sit down. My feet are quite done in.'

'How are you doing Polly?'

'Oh just wonderful thanks Cass. My hip is throbbing, I'm sweating like a rapist and I shall never dance again.'

'I reckon another ten minutes and we will be at Stavros,' Jason said to try and encourage them all. 'We should get there before it rains so we can take shelter. Then we can have something to eat before we search for the treasure. Come on folks, one last push.'

Jason bounded up the rough steps ahead with renewed enthusiasm. Now that he was close to their destination he could practically smell success and the treasure that was waiting for them. He banished all thoughts of the return journey, Lesley's fate and the trouble he was in with Slipe. The only thing he thought of now was finding the Golden Fleece and cashing it in to finance his dream.

'It's all so thrilling,' Margaret enthused as they set off again.

'I can hardly contain my indifference,' said Polly and took a step forward.

A rock moved suddenly beneath her foot. The foot that was connected to the leg that was connected to the weak knee that was connected to the thigh that was connected to the replacement hip.

'Oh my god!'

Jason stopped dead in his tracks when he heard Cassie call out.

'Hold on!'

'Grab her.'

He spun around when he heard someone scream and he turned white when he realised that Polly had disappeared. Those warm, fuzzy thoughts of his dream come true evaporated in an instant to be replaced by flash visions of a public enquiry and Polly in a body bag.

'Hold on pet.' Harriet appeared to be calling down to the trees below. 'I'll throw you a rope.'

Jason was back down with the others, manoeuvring them aside so that he could see what was going on. He tentatively approached the edge and peered over while Harriet began feeding the nylon rope over the side of the cliff.

About five feet below he saw Polly, sixty-something, trim and dressed in a light summer dress, clinging by her fingertips to a small outcrop of rock. Beneath her was a fifteen foot drop to the rocky ground. She was struggling to find a foothold.

'Hold on Ms Arnold,' Jason called down. It was the first thing that came to mind.

'Ya think?' said Cassie sarcastically.

'Grab the rope pet.'

'Don't let go Ms Arnold,' Margaret chipped in. 'Hold tight.'

Polly looked up at them as her legs thrashed about beneath her. 'Any more sensible advice?' she growled.

'Just grab the rope,' Harriet commanded and the tone of her voice left no room for debate. 'One hand at a time.'

'Really Jason,' Oliver sounded annoyed. 'I shall be writing to SARGO about this excursion. One lady incarcerated by the militia, another dangling over a cliff...'

'Put a sock in it Mr Simpson and give us a hand.' Harriet ignored Oliver's contemptuous glare. 'Take the rope with me and pull.'

At the other end Polly had managed to grab the rope and wrap it around her wrist a couple of times. Finally finding a foothold she dared let go of the rock and clutched the rope with both hands.

'Heave away,' she called up. 'But slowly, I don't want to tear my dress.'

Harriet pulled and Polly shot a few feet towards safety.

'Ouch!'

'Sorry pet. A bit slower Mr Simpson.'

'It wasn't me.'

Jason knelt down at the edge and offered a hand down to Polly as she appeared from below, red faced and panting. With Cassie on the other side the two of them managed to lift her back onto the relative safety of the steps.

'You o.k. hon?' Cassie sounded genuinely concerned.

'Yes, I'll be fine, don't fuss.' Polly stood shakily, feeling more embarrassed then scared. 'Just a little slip.'

'Thought we'd lost you there,' Cassie went on. 'I was already recasting for the revue.'

'You're not getting rid of me that easily,' Polly replied dusting down her dress and touching up her hair.

Harriet packed the rope back into the bag as Margaret checked Polly over for injuries.

'I am fine, honestly,' Polly protested. 'Just a couple of scratches.'

'You were very lucky,' Margaret said. 'A fall of only a few feet can kill people of our generation. I saw a documentary about it on the BBC. If you hadn't managed to grab that rock you could have crushed your spine, or twisted your neck to such an extent that…'

'Yes, thank you Margaret.' Polly silenced her by grabbing her shoulders and looking directly into her eyes. 'I am fine. Now let's get moving.'

Jason ignored Oliver's disapproving stare and turned to carry on up the mountain. The group followed him silently with Polly grimacing at the pain she felt in her legs and picking grit out of the scratches on her hands.

After a couple of minutes the steps levelled out and they passed through some more trees before doubling back on themselves at a higher level. Jason stopped and looked up. Ahead he saw the end of their climb. A set of man-made steps leading up to an iron gate. To his right, rising above him was a stone wall. It was higher than the trees and at the right hand end of it he saw a metal cross.

'Nearly there,' he whispered as the others clambered up behind him.'

'Well about time,' Oliver said loudly.

'Shh, Mr S.' Jason waved a finger in front of his lips. 'We can't be certain that the place is deserted.'

'I sure hope it is hon. How else are we going to get down the well?'

'We will cross that bridge when we get there,' Jason replied. 'Let's just pretend we are a group of tourists who got lost in the woods.'

'Which is exactly what we are.' Harriet agreed and gave Jason a reassuring nod.

Jason went on and outlined his plan. 'If there is anyone there you lot just leave the talking to me. Now stay close and act innocent.'

He started off again, slowly mounting the final steps to the gate. When he reached it he was pleased and yet concerned to see that it was not locked. He had understood the monastery to be disused, if so, why was the gate not locked? He put his hand on it and gave a gentle push. It opened easily with only a slight squeak. If it had not been used why were the hinges not rusty?

He stepped inside, into a small enclosure with a few more steps ahead. Above him stood a large tree and the grounds of the small churchyard. But something was not right. If the place was uncared for how come the floor had been swept, a plastic dustpan lent against a wall in the corner. He mounted the steps and found himself at the back of the chapel; a path ran along the right hand side following the wall he had seen from below, to his left was the tree and beyond it an iron railing running around the far wall of the grounds. Beyond this was the sea, stretching dark grey and speckled with white until it melted into low, thunderous clouds. Further off to his left the clouds were lower still, the top of the mountains lost in their stormy depths.

A cool wind had picked up and, just as his guests gathered around him, bedraggled and puffing, the clouds finally obliterated the sun. The temperature fell dramatically and Jason shivered in the sudden cold.

'Well Jason,' his grandmother whispered into his ear. 'We are here.' She clutched her handbag to her, cradling it in her arms. 'This is the last place your grandfather ever saw.'

'Are you going to scatter him now?' Jason asked nervously. He had forgotten all about granddad Stan, even though Margaret had been carrying him with her all day and he was not looking forward to seeing what was in her bag. 'Only he'd get swept away in this wind.'

'Not yet dear,' Margaret replied softly. 'First things first. Let's find the well and take a look inside shall we?'

Jason swallowed hard. He looked at his group of guests and felt a small sense of pride. These five old folk had shown considerable resolve and bravery during the day. Something he would not have expected of them when he met them on the coach yesterday. Was it only yesterday? He remembered the coach trip, the toilet discussions, Mr Simpson fussing about carbohydrates, Mrs. Shaw fussing about quilted Andrex. He could hardly believe that that was only yesterday and he could hardly believe these were the same finicky oldies who'd booked a SARGO holiday expecting a 'Sensational and Relaxing Getaway Overseas'. They had come a long way. And there was only a short way left to go.

'Go ahead lad,' Harriet prompted. She nodded towards the way forward.

Jason nodded back and walked slowly onwards. He moved to the back wall of the chapel and then to the far corner. He poked his head around it, had a quick look and then ducked back again. Behind him the others had sidled up to him like cartoon characters, he could almost hear the xylophone rattling out in time with their hurried tip-toe footsteps. He smiled. His sense of adventure was taking over, his nervousness forgotten.

'Looks deserted,' he said. 'And I think I saw the well.'

Everyone exchanged excited glances. Even Oliver seemed less grumpy now. He was munching on a Rich Tea biscuit and catching the crumbs in the palm of his hand.

'I'm going to take a closer look,' Jason whispered. 'Stay here.'

'Hell as like I will,' Harriet hissed back. 'I'm sticking with you lad.'

'Quite right Ms Smith,' Margaret agreed. 'We're all in this together now.'

'O.k.,' Jason acquiesced, 'but stay close.'

He led his small group of intrepid tourists out into the open and followed the wall of the chapel towards its far end. Directly ahead he could see a circle of stones, the well. Behind this was a row of buildings, outhouses with shuttered windows and low doors. The walls had once been painted white and any renovation work that had been done had been done pretty badly.

They reached the end of the chapel where the courtyard opened out. To his right Jason could see the far off hills beyond the wood. Down there in the valley was the army encampment and poor Mrs. Shaw. He would go back for her when they had found the Fleece. They were finally at the well, it shouldn't take them long now.

The group gathered around the low stone wall, crouched and peered in.

'Hang on pet, I've a torch somewhere.'

Harriet rummaged in the duffle bag and pulled out a torch. She switched it on and shone it down into the well. At the top the walls were rock but after a few feet gave way to what looked like slimy earth or mud. Beyond this they could see more rock and then the torch beam gave way to dark shapes and blackness.

Cassie picked up a stone and dropped it into the void. They all listened silently as it bounced from wall to wall, echoed, bounced and then just kept falling until they could hear it bouncing no more.

'It's a long way down,' Polly whispered. 'How are you supposed to get water out of it?'

'It was probably an underground spring,' Jason whispered back. 'Dried up many years ago. It's a natural formation I should think, you couldn't tunnel that far down through these rocks.'

'So who's going down?' Harriet said, fishing in the bag for the rope. 'Hey up, I've started again. Going down Jason?'

'What?'

'Sorry pet, secret's safe.'

'What are you talking about Harriet?' Margaret asked. 'What secret Jason?'

'Not now gran.' He shot Harriet a withering look but she just shrugged her shoulders and started uncoiling the rope.

'I thought family didn't keep secrets.' His grandmother was not letting this one go.

'So,' Jason clapped his hands together and changed the subject. Now was not the time to come out to his elderly relative. 'Somewhere down there is the Golden Fleece. The question is, who is going to go down and find it?'

'You are of course,' Margaret replied as if it had been a daft question.

'Me?'

'Who else dear? You can't expect any of us surely? You're the youngest.'

'Yes, but...' Jason hadn't thought about actually going into the well. He'd assumed... What? He'd kind of assumed that someone else would go and find whatever they were looking for. Not him.

'But what dear?' Margaret was giving him that disapproving look, as if she were telling him not to be such a nancy boy. He'd seen his father give him that look practically every day of his childhood.

'But...'

Thunder rolled in suddenly, tumbling down from the mountain top, crashing around the monastery and falling down the hillside into the valley.

'I felt rain,' Oliver said when peace had returned.

'I'll go down if you like,' Harriet volunteered.

'Don't be daft woman,' Polly said. 'We'd never be able to hold you.'

'Aye, that's true.'

'I would offer,' Oliver said, 'only I suffer from claustrophobia. I once had an episode in a lift that left me, and the other passengers, scarred for life.'

'If I hadn't taken that fall and if my hip wasn't so sore...'

'I'm the thinnest,' Cassie said as she started to stand up. 'I'll go.'

'No.' Jason also stood. 'It's my responsibility. I will go. Pass me the rope Harriet.' He handed his flight bag to Margaret. 'Look after this for me.'

'Good boy.' Margaret smiled at Jason and hoisted the flight bag over her shoulder.

Harriet handed over one end of the rope to Jason who tied it around his waist. While he was fumbling with a knot that he hoped would not come undone Harriet dragged the other end of the rope back to the tree. She fastened it around the wide trunk and gave a tug.

'I'm not happy with this,' she mumbled to herself. 'This tree don't look strong enough.'

So she untied the knot, fed the rope around the trunk again but this time she tied it to herself. She would act as anchor man and take Jason's weight should he fall. She came back to the well and let the rest of the rope out, laying it in a rough coil at her feet. She checked Jason's knot, decided it was secure enough and then gripped the rope. There was plenty of slack on the ground to allow him to descend a fair distance.

'Off you go son.'

Jason stood up onto the rim of the well.

'Torch hon.' Cassie handed it over.

'Good luck,' Margaret said.

'I have no idea what I am looking for.'

'You'll know when you see it. But do be quick dear, the rain is getting heavier.'

In fact it had started to pour. Oliver pulled out his cagoule and offered it to the ladies but no one was bothered by some rain. It was actually quite refreshing after the heat of the day and was washing sweat and dirt from arms and faces.

'Can you abseil pet?' Harriet asked and Jason shot her a horrified look.

'What?'

'If you lean back, I'll take your weight and you can just bounce down the shaft on your feet. That'd be the best way I reckon.'

'You must be mad!'

'Do as she says Jason.' His grandmother tutted. 'I am getting wet here.'

'You'll be right lad, stand on the edge, just lean back and drop in. I've got you. I done it loads of times when I worked on the outward bound farm and eco-project in Barnsley. Piece of piss.'

'There is no need to overdo the vernacular Ms Smith.' Margaret chided.

'Move it along hon.' Cassie had to speak up over the sound of the wind and ever nearing thunder. 'Polly's hip will rust up if we're not careful.'

'And she will melt if she gets too wet,' Polly shot back.

Jason reluctantly did as he was told and stood with his back to the well.

'I've got you lad, lean back so as you're horizontal, I'll take your weight and then you just step down the shaft.'

Jason started to lean back and felt the rope creak as it became taught between him and Harriet. He was very aware of the gaping black hole beneath him. He was a little bit aware that should he slip even a little way he could do himself an injury.

But he was not aware of the stranger who had appeared behind his guests with a shotgun.

'What you doing?'

Everyone turned in surprise at the sound of the voice. They instantly saw the gun pointing towards them and raised their hands.

Including Harriet. Who let go of the rope.

As he fell backwards Jason was acutely aware that he was about to crash into a bottomless pit and die.

FORTY ONE
Down in the valley - 4.15 pm

Michaelis heard the gunshots ring out just as he stepped out of the hut and into the rain. He knew instinctively where they had come from and he cursed. He had come to recognise the sound of gunfire during his childhood, and he could tell the difference between the sound of his uncle's shotgun and any other firearm, even from that distance. What was his deranged uncle up to now?

He pulled his jacket tighter around himself and headed off into the rain. Reaching the side of the hut he looked out and up towards the monastery above him. He could see the black clouds sweeping down the mountainside, their innards lit by savage bolts of lightening. As the sky was ripped apart by bursts that looked like mortar explosions, the walls of the monastery were lit up. But he was too far away and too low down to see if there was anyone up there. But his uncle was firing at something. Two more gun shots rang out close on the heels of the thunder cutting through the sound of the rain.

He headed off across the army encampment towards the far gate and the path up to the hell hole he was forced to call home. Aris would be angry enough that Michaelis had not been home all day. He would be even angrier when he discovered that he had been having coffee with the soldiers who, so his uncle thought, were living on his land. He could already feel the back of Aris' hand across his head, he could practically smell the whisky on his breath as his uncle bellowed and ranted at him. He knew what to expect when he got up to the monastery.

But then he stopped in his tracks and an even colder fear overcame him.

Fear mixed with excitement.

The Englishman. The stupid, handsome young man who he had seen on the boat and later on that ridiculous donkey. The same

Englishman he had seen pulling a fat woman through the gate backwards. The one he had let escape by distracting the guards.

What had he been doing trespassing on military land on a Thursday afternoon with a group of old people? And where had they been running to?

The answers all fell into place for him in a flash of lightening as he hurried across the enclosure and neared the gate. And, as it became horrifically clear, so he felt fearful for them and excited for himself.

There was only one place they could have been headed. Stavros. Why they should be going there was a mystery that would have to wait until later. Now he had to concentrate on getting to them to see if they were still alive. And, judging from the shots from his uncle's gun, that was unlikely.

What was most likely was that they had wandered into the grounds, been seen by Aris and promptly fired upon. Aris always shot first and asked questions later. Michaelis feared for the lives of not only the handsome young Englishman but the old people that had been with him.

But why feel so excited?

At first he thought it was because, if his uncle had killed again then he was sure to be put away for life, leaving Michaelis free to live peacefully at Stavros. Free from the man who had made his life hell since Michaelis' parents had died. Free from the man who had given Michaelis his family name, the one that the island despised. Uncle Aris was his guardian, his godfather and now his gaoler, and the only way he could be free of the man who ruled his life would be if Aris had his own gaolers and that would only happen if he was caught and sentenced. And, if he had just shot at least one of the tourists then Michaelis would see to it that he was put away. The other tourists would see to it, the handsome Englishman would see to it...

The Englishman. That was why Michaelis had a sudden rush of adrenaline through his chest. He had been feeling it since he spied the lad on the boat the previous day. He'd never felt so hopeless about anyone before. But he was probably dead by now. And, even if he had not been shot by Michaelis' deranged uncle and was still alive... well there was nothing that Michaelis could say or do to explain how he felt, not in front of Aris. Aris must never know what his nephew was.

All these thoughts crashed and bounced around inside Michaelis' head as the storm did the same around the valley. But the thoughts melted into just one as he pushed through the broken gate and into the forest.

He had to get up to Stavros and see what the hell the shooting was about.

FORTY TWO
Stavros - 4.15 pm

Cassie saw Jason's arms flapping in circles as if he was trying to take off. She instinctively grabbed Polly by the shoulders and pulled her down. They sat heavily on the rope and felt it slide beneath them.

'Ouch!'

A gunshot rang out and Harriet fell flat on her face. She saw the rope sliding towards the well and grabbed it, looked sideways, saw Cassie and Polly sitting on it with pained expressions and clung on for dear life. Jason's dear life. Out of the corner of her eye she saw him hovering over the well at a forty-five degree angle, his face pale.

Another gunshot.

'Will you stop firing that silly gun!'

Margaret had already had enough. She was wet, shocked and frightened, she felt compelled to act. She saw the ugly, filthy looking man start to reload his shotgun and took a step forward. He looked up at her in surprise.

'Welcome to Stavros!' he shouted as he forced two more cartages into the barrel.

'I said no more shots,' Margaret replied fiercely. It was only fear that was making her so bold.

'This is my land. I do what I want.' The gun was loaded again, snapped shut and pointed carelessly towards Margaret's face.

She pushed it to one side.

'Now listen here…'

'What you doing?' Aris had never had his gun pushed away from its target by anyone before, let alone a woman. He didn't know how to react. He fired off two rounds harmlessly over the chapel roof, as if to assert his masculinity and make a point.

Margaret was aware that there was a commotion going on behind her and turned to look.

Jason had been saved from his backwards fall into oblivion by the combined efforts of some of the others. Harriet was now untying him and herself from the rope.

'Welcome to Stavros. What you doing here?' Aris repeated as he loaded more cartridges. The rain was running off his large forehead, over his hairy protruding eyebrows and dripping into his black eyes. He wiped them with the back of a huge, hairy hand.

'We are on a climbing holiday,' Margaret improvised. 'Our guide was about to show us how to abstain when you rudely interrupted us.'

'That'll be *abseil* hon,' Cassie pointed out helpfully, standing and rubbing the rope burn on her backside.

'Holiday! Guide!' Aris looked at each trespasser in turn as he reloaded his gun menacingly. 'On my land. Yes, yes!'

Jason thought it was high time he took charge. He didn't like his gran being so close to the gun and, although still very weak at the knees from his near death experience, he stepped down from the well and approached the Greek man. He recognised him as the idiot with the truck he had seen yesterday in the harbour. The one who had been so cruel to the handsome hunk in the tight fitting uniform who had since been in Jason's daydreams slipping out of his uniform and...

'Yes, sorry about that,' Jason said, pulling himself back together. 'We didn't mean to trespass but we got lost...'

Suddenly Aris took a huge step forward and brought his face close up to Jason's. He grabbed the pale rep by the arm with one hand and let the shotgun droop in the other.

'I know you!' he bellowed.

Jason almost threw up from the stench of stale alcohol that blasted at him. The guests exchanged uneasy glances, not sure what was coming next.

'You holiday rep.'

'Yes I am...'

'You take these people on... trip?'

'Yes I do.'

'And you bring them to Stavros? To my private place?'

'Well, yes but…'

'You no phone me.'

'What?'

'You no write.'

'No, but…'

'You no call me!'

'He sounds like my mother,' Cassie mussed in the background.

'Why you no tell me you coming?'

Jason's complexion was fast turning from white to green. 'I don't get you.' he said, trying not to choke.

Aris suddenly pushed him away, raised the gun over his head and fired off another shot. Everyone ducked.

Then, for no apparent reason, Aris started laughing and hopping from one foot to the other. He held the shotgun over his head as if he was taking part in some tribal war dance.

'I wait years for this,' he bellowed out. 'You from SARGO. I write SARGO and say why not make a trip to my monastery. I put on party. But I no hear back. Now you here, now we have party. I was waiting for you, I see you coming.'

He was beaming all over, his smile showing yellow teeth and gaps through which poked an equally yellow tongue. He grabbed Margaret by the arm and pushed her towards the outhouse. Jason stepped up to him as threateningly as he could. But Aris just pushed him in the same direction.

'Quickly, inside from the rain! I light fire, we drink ouzo and we dance. I make food, I have killed goat today. We party. Inside, inside.'

'Best we do as he says,' Jason instructed and helped Margaret duck through the low doorway and into the building.

The others had no choice but to obey and everyone headed for the outhouse to get out of the rain. They actually welcomed this sudden turn of fate, they were already soaked through and the afternoon was turning to evening and they had started to feel the cold.

'Yes, yes,' Aris encouraged. 'Inside and we make party. Only fifty euros each.'

'How much?' Jason was outraged.

'It's better than being shot,' Polly whispered to him as she ducked into the small building.

'I left the ropes out lad,' Harriet said furtively as she passed Jason. 'We'll find a way to sneak out and pick up where we left off. Let me think about... Oi!'

She rounded on the large Greek man who had just pinched her large, rounded English bottom and pointed a large threatening finger in his face.

'I'm a dyke so keep your frigging mitts off me jacksie, gerrit?'

Aris looked blank.

'Lovely lady.' He winked salaciously. 'We make special party together.'

'Just try it mate and I'll have your calamari off,' Harriet growled and squeezed her way through the door.

'Will we be having pies?' Oliver asked as he passed Jason, heading inside.

'Not the faintest idea what's going to happen Mr S.'

Jason was the last to enter the small building but before he did he looked back to the well. He had to find a way to get down there. He looked up into the pouring rain and flinched as another bolt of lightening cracked to earth. How the hell was he going to find the Golden Fleece without being found out and how was he going to get it and his guests safely away?

FORTY THREE

Stavros - 4. 25 pm

As she stepped over the threshold and entered the dark, low room, Margaret was acutely aware that this was the exact spot where Stanley had met with his accident all those years before. She remembered him telling her how, just as Dimitris Panandreas had stumbled dying into the chapel behind her, he had opened the door and set off the booby trap.

She felt tears behind her eyes and her heart turned to rock. She had that strange feeling again, that she was not alone, that Stanley was in the room with her breathing down her neck and giving her strength.

'Come along Margaret, let us in we're drenched.' Polly limped her way past giving Margaret a gentle shove.

'Sorry dear,' Margaret replied quietly stepping to one side.

The room was small, claustrophobic and dim. A couple of candles standing on a small table against the furthest wall gave out some weak light. A single light bulb glowed faintly from where it hung from some very ancient looking wires in the centre of the ceiling. This seemed to be the only sign that the building had electricity. To her left was a fire place, large enough to fill the length of the wall but with only a small grate in the centre. A fire had been set in it but was not yet alight. Around the fireplace were various pots and pans, all dented and black and in the corner was a small sink, a pile of dirty crockery stacked up within.

The other guests ducked their way through the low door, shaking off the rain water and looking relieved to be inside. Until they saw the room they were in, then they each looked concerned.

'Some party venue,' Cassie said as she flapped her blouse around in an attempt to dry it.

'Stinks of damp,' Harriet observed as she sat on a bench beneath the only window in the room.

'Do you think that dreadful man actually lives in here?' asked Polly.

'Either him or his pet goats pet'.

Jason was the last to enter the room and Margaret sensed that he was not at all happy. His keen eyes scanned their surroundings, his mouth wrinkled up in a sneer and then he bit his bottom lip. He looked back over his shoulder as if judging which was worse, the storm or the shelter. He shook his head and then went to sit beside Harriet where the two of them fell into a whispered conversation. Margaret found a place to sit, at the far end of the room on the edge of a raised platform that she assumed was a sleeping area. A motley collection of old rugs and sheepskins were thrown across the boarded platform. She was sure she saw one of them move of its own accord and immediately started itching. She put Jason's flight bag down on the floor beside her but kept her handbag close to her chest, as if Stanley's ashes inside would give her some protection from the ghastly surroundings. She was opposite the fireplace and could see the whole room, Harriet and Jason to her left beneath the window, the other guests on chairs along the right hand wall. And the big Greek man now closing the door firmly behind him.

For some reason Margaret sensed that she, they, were now trapped.

'I light fire so I cook,' Aris declared and everyone exchanged uneasy glances.

'Will we be having cheese pies?' Everyone that is except Oliver.

'Goat,' was all that Aris said in reply as he heaved a large pot onto a hook above the grate.

A few minutes of uneasy silence followed as he wrestled with the wood in the fire but before too long a warm orange glow was filling the room, brightening it somewhat. The crackling flames seemed to help calm everyone and, when Aris found a large bottle of ouzo there were even some murmurs of approval.

'This is all very rustic,' Polly said as she looked around. 'People would pay a fortune for this look in Hove you know.'

'I am guessing,' Cassie said, 'that that door there leads to the powder room?'

She indicated another low door in the wall beside her.

'I sincerely hope so,' Polly replied.

Aris handed round some plastic cups, much to Margaret's relief as the ones in the sink didn't bear thinking about, which he promptly filled with neat ouzo. When everyone had a drink he raised his own and announced, 'yamas!'

'Cheers,' said Jason and took a large swig.

Aris downed his in one gulp and immediately poured himself another.

'Music and dancing while goat cooks,' Aris declared.

'May I use the bathroom?' Polly piped up raising her hand.

'No bathroom.'

'No bathroom!'

'Only toilet. There.'

'Thank the lord.' Polly opened the small door, said 'oh my god,' and then exited with a resigned sigh.

Margaret's thoughts were drifting again as she scanned the inside of the room. This is where the Nazis had been looking for the Golden Fleece. Why? How could it have been so important to them? They had been close, only a few feet away from it, but they had missed it. She hoped. And how did they know about it? She had been thinking about this on the walk up, how Hitler had caught the scent of the story that Wagner had a secret. How he had suspected that it would be hidden on Symi of all places was a mystery. She could only suppose that he had found some record somewhere, perhaps Wagner himself had left a clue before he died; something that tied him to Panandreas, Symi and the mysterious 'Golden Fleece'. Whatever had happened to lead Hitler to search on Symi it had also led him, indirectly, to permanently maim her future husband. This was the room where they had set the booby traps. This room was part of Stanley's history. She clutched her handbag to her more firmly. This may have been the place where Stanley wanted his ashes scattered but she was not going to do it here. When the storm abated she would find a suitable place outside.

Her thoughts were interrupted by the sound of music and she looked up sharply.

Their host had opened up an ancient gramophone which had been hiding under a pile of clothes on the table. He wound it up and placed a record on the turntable. Suddenly strains of some Greek folk song were filling the room. The music seemed out of place and surreal but their host was enjoying it; he immediately started dancing, swinging the ouzo bottle in one hand and his plastic cup in the other.

He danced suggestively over to Harriet who looked decidedly uncomfortable.

'Lovely lady what your name?' he leered down at her.

'The name's Harriet and I'm a…'

'My name Aris, you know, like Aries… the ram,' he said with a thrust of his hips.

'Oh please.' Harriet turned away from him but he continued to gyrate at eye level. 'Could somebody not get this old git off of me, please!'

Polly had reappeared from the toilet looking decidedly pale.

'I advise emergency use only,' she said as she closed the door behind her and sat. 'But I shouldn't worry about what you put down it. Man made or otherwise.'

Margaret watched as Jason stood and crept over to Cassie and Polly. He kept one eye on Aris as if he were afraid of being caught. But Aris was too intent on trying to turn Harriet on to notice. Jason sat with the two actresses and another whispered conversation started. All three of them looked at Aris, then at each other. Polly rubbed her hip and shook her head, Cassie seemed to be encouraging her until, finally, Polly shrugged her shoulders and nodded.

Jason slinked back to his place and whispered something to Harriet who was still trying to avoid eye contact with the Greek man's groin. After a couple of sentences Harriet nodded and looked across at Margaret.

Margaret shrugged. Something was being organised but she didn't understand. She caught Jason's eye and he winked, mouthing the words 'trust me'. Margaret nodded back.

Polly stood up and started on some stretching exercises, as if she was warming up for a track and field event. Margaret noticed she had quite a nasty scrape on her leg, probably from the slip earlier. Cassie stood too and went to the gramophone table where she sifted through a pile of records.

'Oh gerra move on,' Harriet called out from behind Aris' legs. 'I can't put up with this for much longer.'

Aris was swigging from the ouzo bottle, taking great gulps and spilling some down his shirt as he danced.

But his dancing was interrupted by the scratch of the needle across the record as the Greek music came to an abrupt end. He span around to where Cassie was fiddling with his gramophone.

'What you do skinny lady?'

'The word is trim,' Cassie called back over her shoulder.

'Mister Aris,' Polly waved at him to get his attention even though he was only three feet away. 'We will dance for you now, would you like that?' She spoke very clearly and very loudly, nodding her head as if encouraging a small child.

'You dance for me?' Aris sounded delighted. 'Wait, I sit with this big lovely lady.'

'Oh buggering hell.'

He squeezed in between Harriet and Jason.

Margaret looked at her grandson. He seemed to have developed a nervous twitch. Hardly surprising after all they had been through that day. But then... no, he was signalling something to her behind Aris' back. What was going on?

'Over here gran,' Jason finally called out. 'Come and sit with our host.'

'I am quite comfortable here thank you.'

'No gran, you *must* come and sit here, you will see the show better.'

Jason stood up and moved a couple of chairs so that they faced across the room, their backs to the door. And then Margaret understood what he was up to. She looked at Polly who was nodding with wide eyes and then at Cassie who winked.

Margaret, pleased to be doing her bit for the cause, came and sat in one of the chairs, Oliver sat on another and Harriet, grimacing but putting an otherwise brave face on it, led Aris to the centre chair.

'You sit there pet,' she encouraged. 'I'll stand right behind you.'

With everybody in place Cassie dropped the needle onto a different record.

'You aint gunna believe what I dug up,' she said to Polly who was standing centre stage waiting.

'I'm ready for anything Cass.'

'Here goes.'

The record began with a rhythmic scratching sound as the needle rode the slightly warped seventy-eight. Aris beamed with childish excitement, placing the bottle and cup between his legs and clapping his hands with glee.

'Dance lady!' he called out.

'No heckling from the cheap seats,' Polly ordered as Cassie came and stood next to her.

'Just improvise,' she whispered. 'Pretend we're opening our new revue.'

The music started and Oliver's face lit up. 'I can't believe he has this recording,' he said.

'Dance ladies!'

The song started and the performers started singing along and dancing: *"In olden days a glimpse of stocking was looked on as something shocking but now God knows…"*

Everyone else joined in, 'Anything goes!'

By the time Cassie and Polly had reached the end of the second verse even Aris was singing along, kind of. He was clapping his hands, bellowing out 'anything yoes' and drooling over Polly's rather jerky leg movements. Her face displayed no sign of the pain she must have been feeling and Margaret admired her for her gusto. When the first number finished Cassie made a great fuss of Aris for some reason while everyone waited for the next number to start. 'I get a kick out of you,' was going down extremely well with their host when Margaret felt a cold draft on the back of her neck. Stanley's ghost wandering the room maybe? She instinctively looked over her shoulder.

Harriet and Jason had vanished.

* * *

The sky was darker, the thunder louder, the wind whipped the rain into Jason's face and stung him as he hurried across the courtyard to the well. Both he and Harriet knew that they would soon be missed, time was of the essence. Without a word they both went directly to their posts. Jason climbed up onto the edge of the well where he tied the rope around his waist while Harriet passed him the torch and then took up the slack. She simply nodded at him to show that she was taking his weight before wiping her eyes on the back of her hand.

Jason's heart was in his mouth as he peered over his shoulder and shone the torch down. The rain was hurrying down the shaft. Lit by the torch the individual drops looked like a time lapse film of a motorway at night, tiny lights whizzing off into oblivion. And then his thumping heart missed a beat.

There was something down there, glinting wet in the torchlight. He hadn't noticed it when he had shone the torch into the well earlier. It had probably been dry then and was only showing up now because the light was reflecting from its wet surface. Whatever *it* was. But seeing something down there, and not too far down either, encouraged him and he checked his knot one last time. It seemed tight enough.

He looked to his feet. The walls of the well were now soaked and he wondered if he would be able to keep his footing.

Only one way to find out.

With a thumbs up to Harriet he started to lean back and crouch at the same time. He imagined the rope breaking, imagined falling, cracking his head on the rocks. His heart leapt again when he heard the rope creak around his waist, the knot tightening.

One hundred and one things not to do, his inner voice piped up. *Number seventy six; do not go backwards down a shaft in a thunderstorm…* 'shut up!'

He was dangling over nothing now, one hand on the rope, the other holding the torch. Both his feet were planted against the wall all he had to do was move one down and then the other. Harriet had him, she wouldn't let him fall.

He took a step down. Then a second.

See, you didn't fall, you'll be fine babe.

Another two steps and his head was level with the rim of the well.

A couple more and he was well and truly inside, the rope taut, his footing secure. Encouraged by the fact that he hadn't yet fallen to his death he made slow, steady progress downwards, all the time scanning the wall around him for any sign of anything hidden. He had no idea what he was looking for or how far down it would be. Maybe all the way?

How far was that? Would they have enough rope? What was it he had seen from above? Was he getting near it?

Stop asking so many questions and get on with it.

The clues and message from the music raced through his head. 'In our Stavros well, protect the Golden Fleece.' Well, he was well and truly in the well now. Surely the Golden Fleece would reveal itself to him. Whatever had been hidden there had been hidden by another man; another man could therefore find it.

'To use the key times the key by time.'

'What?' he answered his inner voice with his outer one.

'That's the last remaining clue, maybe it can help you now.'

'I don't think so...'

His foot dislodged a small rock and he slipped slightly. He heard the rock bounce from the wall, hit the other side and then land with a dull thud. There was something below him.

Wiping the rain from his face as best he could he twisted his body and pointed the torch downwards. The beam lit up the mud and rocks around him, slimy and wet. He followed the wall down until he saw an outcrop of rock about five feet below, a ledge that reached out into the centre of the well. He twisted the other way to see if this was in fact the bottom, or just a ledge. He aimed the torch and shone it down. Directly onto the twisted body of Yiannis the fisherman, wedged firmly between the ledge and the far wall.

Jason screamed. His legs slipped from the wall. He grabbed at the rope. He dropped the torch and clung to the rope with both hands swinging like a pendulum in the shaft. The torch landed on the body, rolled and finally dropped over the edge. Jason watched it fall until it vanished from sight. He never heard it hit the ground. He guessed that there was about thirty feet of shaft above him and god knows how many hundred below. If the rope should break there was nothing between him and the bottom apart from a dead fisherman with half his head blown off.

He opened his mouth to call to Harriet to pull him out.

And found himself falling.

Harriet had let go of the rope.

FORTY FOUR
5.00 pm

'I get a kick out of I get a kick out of I get a kick out of...'

It had been when the ancient record had got stuck that Aris had realised some of his guests were missing. He had jumped up, spilling his drink, and spun around to see that two of the foreigners were gone. Cassie and Polly stopped their impromptu routine and just stared as he grunted and stomped to the door. He swung it open letting in a blast of wet air and stormed outside.

Nobody else moved, or knew what to say or do.

Until Margaret stood up and lifted the gramophone needle from the record. That action prompted the others back to life.

'Oh dear,' said Oliver quietly.

'Oh dear indeed,' Polly agreed. 'Now we're in trouble. I don't trust his temperament.'

'Do you think they had enough time to find anything?' Cassie asked as she sat, slightly out of breath from the dancing.

'I doubt it Cass, they've only been gone a few minutes.'

'What are we going to do?' Margaret asked as she moved back to her chair.

Thunder rolled around the mountains outside and the rain lashed at the windows. A small pool of water had collected on the sill.

'Not much we can do,' Oliver replied. 'But wait and see what happens. I am sure Jason will figure something out.'

They were suddenly aware that the door had been thrown open, the wind gusted into the room and they turned to see who it was.

Harriet appeared first looking very wet, pale and fed up. She was closely followed by Aris who was also wet but a great deal redder in the face and even more fed up.

'Why you try to run away lovely lady?' he was protesting.

'I told you I weren't running away.'

'Then what you doing outside in rain? Go and dry by fire.'

'Oh my god!' Margaret's hand flew to her mouth. 'Where's Jason?'

'The boy ran away,' Aris answered her. 'Don't give him a tip. He brings you for party, only fifty euro each, you pay later, and then he run away. Pah!'

Harriet turned slowly to face Margaret, steam rising from her clothes as she stood with her back to the fire.

'Harriet dear, what is it?' Margaret could see from the look on the large woman's face that something was dreadfully wrong.

'He were down the well Mags, I had him on the rope when suddenly this twat,' she cocked a thumb towards Aris who was attacking the ouzo bottle again, 'he comes up behind me and grabs me. Grabs me by the arm and pulls me away. Nothing I could do, I had to let go of the rope.'

'What you doing with rope in my well?' Aris was listening in, trying to grasp what he could of the English conversation.

'Weren't doing nothing mate,' Harriet shot back.

'You up to no good.'

'Me no up to anything pet. Just need to get warm and...'

Margaret's legs went from under her. She grabbed for the chair and stumbled over it feeling faint.

'Now look what you've done.' Harriet pointed an accusing finger to Aris who just shrugged and drank some more.

Polly and Cassie raced to Margaret's aid and helped her onto the bench. A little sniff from a cup of neat ouzo brought her round.

'Where's Jason?' she asked as soon as she remembered where she was. 'Is he...'

'We don't know Margaret,' Cassie said, her voice calm but authoritative. 'But we shall find out. You stay there and recover. Head between the knees. Good girl.'

Cassie made for the door but Aris blocked her path.

'You go nowhere.'

'I damn well am, I'm going to look for Jason.'

'You stay here. Let the boy run away and leave you. Me and you four lovely ladies, we have party without him.'

From the corner of her eye Cassie could see Oliver inching towards the door behind Aris' back. 'I demand that you let me out,' she said and stepped to the right.

Aris stepped to his left. 'Why you want to go?'

'Aint none of your business.'

'You stay to the morning with me and we make lovely party.'

'Over my dead body.' Cassie stepped to the left. Oliver was at the door.

'Why you not want to stay with me?' Aris stepped to his right.

And crashed into Oliver was had just got his hand on the door handle.

He twisted around and grabbed the small man by the arm.

'And where you going?'

'I was just… I thought I left some biscuits…'

'Sit down!'

Aris' voice boomed around the room louder than the crash of thunder that accompanied it. Everyone was stunned into silence, frozen by the sound of his menacing tone. As the thunder rumbled away he pushed Oliver to the bench, herded Harriet and Cassie to the far end of the room and stood in the centre, his hands on his hips.

'You play games,' he said angrily. 'I give you party for only fifty euros and you want to leave. You no leave, you all stay here.'

'I absolutely insist we go now,' Polly said but Aris raised his hand.

'Silence dancing woman. You can not go, it rains. Is dangerous. You leave in the morning.'

'Morning!' Everyone said it at once and then broke into a quintet of 'don't be ridiculous,' 'that's absurd,' 'where is my grandson?' 'no effing way pal,' and 'what will breakfast be?'

Aris silenced the cacophony with another yell. 'Oi!' Everyone stared at him. 'I cook goat now, you sit and have party.' He turned to the fire and unhooked the pot of whatever it was that was now boiling.

'What are we going to do?' Margaret whispered to the others as she sat up.

'We'll think of something,' Harriet whispered back. 'And I'm sorry I dropped your grandson down the well Mags.'

* * *

Michaelis came striding up the steps, the summer sun lighting him from behind, a halo around his head of dark hair. Jason stood in the courtyard with his arms outstretched, ready and waiting for him. Somewhere far away an orchestra played a deeply romantic tune accompanying a bird that was singing a late afternoon aria. Everything was perfect as the dashing soldier approached with a loving smile on his chiselled face.

Jason was aware of water running down his own face. His eyes snapped open but it made no difference if they were open or shut. All around him was blackness. An all consuming blackness that disorientated him. He was lying on something soft, cold and wet. It felt like material of some sort. He squeezed some between his fingers and confirmed that it was clothing. But not his. Someone's belt was digging into his stomach; he could feel a metal buckle pressing in through his sodden shirt. He moved a foot and felt someone's boot scrape his ankle. He moved his foot a little further and felt nothing but empty space. He reached out his arm and touched wet rock. He moved his other arm and again felt nothing but empty space.

His head hurt. He touched it carefully as an image of Harriet and a rope flashed through his mind. He felt a bump on his forehead and thought of Tom and Jerry. He felt hair on his cheek. Where the hell was he?

A sudden flash of bright light answered his question. Lightening lit up everything around him for a split second. He saw the walls of the well, his hand resting on a small outcrop and, between his eyes and his hand he saw the hairy chest of the body he was lying on.

Everything went dark again as thunder shook the walls around him.

He grabbed at the outcrop of rock and the body beneath him slipped. His feet scrambled for a foothold but found only mud. He reached with his other hand and wedged himself between the walls on either side just as he felt his support give way.

Suddenly he was no longer resting on the body and, although he was grateful for that, he also realised that the only thing holding him in place now was himself. His arms were taking his weight as he lay suspended, spread-eagled across the shaft, his feet pressing into the mud.

His legs started to slip, pulled downward by gravity and he kicked out. Gripping tightly to the rock with one hand he let go with the other, swung across the void and grappled for another handhold just as his legs slipped from the muddy wall.

He heard Yiannis' body fall further down the shaft but tried not to picture it. He was clinging on for dear life with no idea what was going on above. What had happened to Harriet? Why had she let him fall?

But there was no time to think. He had to get to the top before his strength gave out. His feet finally found purchase on the rough wall below and he rested his arms for a second. Rain water got into his eyes and would have blinded him if he wasn't already blinded by the pitch black around him.

Carefully, with his heart beating wildly and trying not to picture what lay beneath, he reached out for another handhold. He found one a few inches above, grabbed it and lifted a foot into another crevice. His foot slipped, the mud on the sole of his deck shoe offering no grip on the wall. He held on tighter with his hand feeling his forearm muscles start to burn with the effort as his foot searched out another rock. He found one and wedged his toe into a tiny crack above it.

'I hate to think what this is doing to the leather,' he muttered as he pushed himself up. He found another handhold and paused, panting, his face pressed against the muddy wall. 'not to mention my nails.'

Slowly he raised his other hand and fingered around for something to hold onto. He grabbed something soft, moss maybe, and pulled.

Whatever he was holding slid from the wall and he slid with it. He instinctively grabbed at whatever he could with his other hand but it was no good. He was falling again.

It was true what they said about the moment of death. Everything flashed before his eyes. Grandma Margaret storming out of the house. His mother crying, father drinking. The school darkroom, alone with Paul Sullivan in a dim red light, a photograph developing, holding hands. Kissing Darren Williams under the stage while The Mikado was being performed above. A night on a beach. His university halls. The word for goodbye in various languages. Slipe's hideous face, laughing. His grandma holding his hand. The cigarette case…

And then suddenly everything stopped. He felt like he had been punched in the stomach, he was winded and in pain but at least he was no longer falling.

He was dangling in the middle of the well once more, the rope taught, someone had hold of him. And he had hold of something.

It felt like a sack. The thing he had inadvertently dragged from the muddy walls was still in his hand. It was heavy. And it was slipping.

This has got to be it! He said to himself as he tried to secure his grip on the material. But he didn't have time to think of anything else. He was suddenly rising, being pulled towards the surface in short, hard jerks. Each one tightened the rope around his waist and added another scrape to his flesh. But he didn't care. Harriet was back and was hauling him out of danger. Away from the dead body, away from the abyss and back up to safety. He looked directly upwards but could still see nothing. The rain pelted down onto his face and washed mud into his eyes.

But the thing in his hand was slipping away from him. Barely a corner remained in his grip. He tried to lift it to his other hand but it slipped further. He tried to reach across with his left hand but each time it got near another jerk on the rope threatened to yank the heavy thing from him. He couldn't risk changing hands in mid jerk. He scrunched his right leg up so that his thigh supported the weight and that allowed him a couple of seconds to adjust his grip. But his hand was aching now, his muscles failing.

And then the air smelled different and the wind was stronger. He was almost at the top. He reached up with his left hand feeling around for the rim of the well.

And felt someone grab his wrist.

With a final, powerful heave he was out and over the edge. The thing he had been clinging on to banged onto the ground beside him as he rolled onto his back. He was exhausted but gladder to be alive and lying out in a thunderstorm than he had ever been before.

'Harriet what happened?' he called out as he cleared the last of the mud from around his eyes. She was untying the rope from his waist with clumsy hands.

'Who?'

Jason's eyes snapped open and he stared directly into the beam of a torch. He shielded his eyes and stood up. All around him the clouds where still thick and heavy, blocking out what remained of the afternoon sun. It was nearly dark already. Rain landed with great splashes on the stone courtyard and water was running off in streams towards the wall. At his feet he saw a filthy canvas bag, tied with rope. He felt elated.

'We found it Harriet...' he began and turned to the person behind him.

It was not a large lesbian from Bolton.

FORTY FIVE

Apart from felling extremely concerned for the wellbeing of her grandson, Margaret also felt embarrassed.

'I have never fainted before,' she explained to Harriet who was holding her hand.

'It weren't a proper faint Mags, you didn't go all the way under. But it's to be expected, not every day a relative gets dropped down a bottomless pit.'

'I don't think you are helping Harriet,' Polly said as she sat on the other side of Margaret. 'Are you sure you're alright?'

'I don't know, to be honest.' Margaret was numb with shock. She could not believe what Harriet had told her. That she had had a tight hold of Jason who was somewhere down inside the well, when suddenly Aris had run up to her, grabbed her hand and yanked her back towards the outhouse. She had to let go of the rope and had no idea whether Jason was dangling or holding on to something at the time. He could still be down there, dead at the bottom, clinging on, or climbing back up.

She tried to reassure herself with the thought that Jason was probably climbing out and thanked the others for their concern.

'I am more worried about what happens next,' Harriet was saying. She nodded across the room.

Aris was spooning out goat in thin gravy, filling each dented metal bowl with one slop from a large ladle. He had the bowls lined up along the floor in front of the fire and only Oliver seemed to be taking any interest. Each of the guests had tried to get Aris to understand that they wanted to leave but he was having none of it. As far as he was concerned they were staying where they were until the storm passed and, Margaret had to admit, he did have a point. To try and walk back down the mountain in this weather would not be a good idea. Besides, without Jason they had no idea where they were supposed to go.

Aris finished doling out the last of his slop and turned to the room.

'Eat,' he said waving an arm across the line of bowls.

'We may as well folks,' Cassie said as she rose from her chair. 'We don't know how long we're gunna be…'

Suddenly the door burst open and rain swept in on the howling wind. Along with it came Jason, his face and clothes spattered with mud. He had a cut on his forehead, scrapes on his knees and he looked to be at his wits end.

'Thank God,' Margaret exclaimed. 'We were so…'

Aris shouted something in Greek and reached out towards Jason who flinched. But he was not aiming at the muddy rep. His great hand landed on the shoulder of someone behind Jason and dragged him into the room.

'Hey up pet,' Harriet blurted out recognising the young soldier from the day before, 'don't tell me you found *him* down there?'

'No,' Jason replied and smiled as best he could. 'Michaelis pulled me out. But I did find this.'

He held up a grubby canvas bag that appeared to contain something solid. Margaret could see the corner of something metal poking through the material and her heart started to beat faster. Excitement took over from anxiety now that she knew Jason was safe.

'Is it…?'

'Who knows gran, but if it aint I'm not going down for another look.'

Aris had dragged Michaelis over to the table in the corner and an argument was taking place. Margaret tried to ignore the noise and beckoned Jason closer. The other guests huddled around as Jason put the bag on the bench.

'Well untie it,' Polly encouraged. 'Then maybe we can get out of this quaint little hell hole.'

Jason fumbled with the cord that was knotted around the bag but his fingers were still slippery and wet.

'Here you are.' Oliver passed him a cheese knife.

It cut the cord easily and the bag was opened. Slowly Jason revealed its contents.

'It's a box,' said Harriet.

'I'd call it a chest,' said Cassie. 'What is it, is it iron?'

'I would say so, it's rusting a bit on the corners.' Oliver retrieved his knife and, having wiped it on his sleeve, used it to cut up an apple he had found in his pocket.

'Should we open it here,' Margaret said, her voice falling to a whisper. 'Or wait until we are somewhere a little less… frenetic.'

But they did not have time to debate the matter. Aris had finished berating his nephew and had come to see what the huddle was about. He pushed his way into the group, knocking Oliver aside like a skittle.

'What is this?' he said gruffly. 'What you find.'

'Just a box.' Jason started to cover it over again.

'You found this here?' Aris pushed Jason's hands away from the chest and grabbed it. 'It is mine.'

'It certainly is not,' Margaret tried to protest but Aris now had the chest in his hands.

He took it back to his chair by the fire and sat it on his lap. The others crowded around him, complaining.

'Quiet,' Aris bellowed with such force that even the wind died down for a second. 'This belongs to me. You sit and eat goat.'

'You should do what he says.'

The new voice drew everyone's attention to Michaelis. Except for Jason who was admiring a completely different chest entirely, it was far more interesting than the metal one but both looked as solid and strong as each other. Michaelis was changing his shirt, unashamedly pulling the wet one over his head and displaying a naked torso that Action Man would have killed for.

'It's a good job Lesley isn't here,' Polly said, 'the poor boy wouldn't stand a chance.'

'Dear Mrs. Shaw,' Oliver said with a sigh. 'I do hope she is safe.'

'Hey up pet, bet that sight has made your day.' Harriet elbowed Jason in the ribs.

The sudden pain snapped Jason back to attention. 'What do you mean, we should do what he says?'

Michaelis beckoned Jason over. They stood a few inches apart as he pulled a dry shirt out from a pile of clothes and started to unfold it. Jason had already broken out into a cold sweat by the time Michaelis raised his arms and slipped the buttoned up shirt over his head. As he pulled it down and arranged it he nodded towards Aris and said, 'he has been drinking, he is drunk. When he is drunk he is dangerous. Be careful.'

'But we have to leave,' Jason replied. His voice was a whisper and he couldn't help but lean a little closer to Michaelis. He smelt of sweat with a hint of some fading aftershave. 'I have to get my guests back to Chorio, with that box, before it gets dark.'

'Look outside,' Michaelis also whispered. 'It is already too dark. This storm is here for the night, and so are you my friend. You can not leave.'

'But it's only just gone five,' Jason complained. 'I know it's cloudy and raining but we are already wet and it can't be far…'

'Just do what uncle tells you to do and we will find a way to get you out of here safely,' Michaelis said and went to sit in the far corner.

Jason returned to the group who were now back at the bench. Only Oliver was eating the goat stew. Aris sat by the fire turning the chest over in his hands and trying to find a way to open it.

'What are we going to do Jason?' Margaret asked once Jason was beside her.

'No idea gran.'

'This is not right,' she went on. 'That box belongs to you. Stanley left us the clues to find it, you found it. There, it belongs to you. I say!' She stood up and took a step towards Aris. 'You there! I demand that you give that box back.'

But Aris was not paying attention. He had discovered the numbers on the front of the chest and was trying combinations.

'You,' Margaret persisted. 'Look at me when I speak to you.'

'Shut up!' Aris growled back.

'How rude. Now listen here, that chest belongs to my grandson.'

'It is mine. Be quiet.'

'I will not be quiet…'

'Gran…'

'Hush Jason, leave this to me. My grandson found that chest as he was meant to do. His grandfather left him… well never mind about that. I demand you hand it over.'

'It is mine. You found it on my land.'

'He found it beneath your land to be precise so therefore it is not yours.'

'It is not his. He did not put it there.'

'Well, yes I concede that. By rights it should belong to the Panandreas family but…'

And that was when all hell broke loose.

Aris threw the chest onto the floor as if it had just turned red hot and burned him. He shot out of his chair, beat his hands against his head and started a rant in Greek that went on for several minutes with no let up and hardly a pause for breath. The SARGO guests retreated to the far end of the room and huddled together on the edge of the sleeping platform for safety, completely unsure of what this madman was going to do next. The only word that was easily discernable was 'Panandreas' and it was obvious that Margaret had said the wrong thing. He threw himself around the room, kicking the door and splintering it, slamming his fists against the walls and shoving the chest from one side to the other with his booted feet. He even picked up a bowl of goat stew and hurled it down at the chest. It missed and pieces of grey meat slid across the flag stones as gravy splattered the walls.

Throughout the performance Michaelis sat calmly in his corner lifting a pair of dumbbells and watching disinterestedly. He had seen it all before.

Suddenly Aris seemed to be aware that the group of English people were still there. He stopped dead in his tracks and stared at them.

'Panandreas.' He spat. 'He killed my family. He owes me this.'

He kicked the chest towards the door, grabbed his chair and the ouzo bottle and slammed them down by the chest. He ordered Michaelis to do something in Greek and then he sat, his feet resting on the chest while he took three great gulps from the bottle.

Michaelis put down his weights, glanced uneasily at the guests and then picked up Aris' shotgun.

'Oh my god, we're done for,' said Polly.

'I shall certainly be writing to your head office about this,' Oliver mumbled. 'Assuming we survive.'

'Everyone calm down,' said Jason and was surprised at how in control he sounded.

'Yes Mister Simpson,' Margaret put in, 'we must band together now. Any negative things you have to say must wait until later. Please.'

Michaelis handed Aris the shotgun and returned to his seat. He looked across at Jason and shrugged.

Aris checked that the gun was loaded and laid it across his lap. He lifted the chest up and placed it on his knees, rested one foot on the door jam, effectively blocking the exit and drank from his bottle.

'What do you intend to do?' Jason asked, his voice as authoritative as he could make it.

'I sit here and think,' Aris said quite calmly. 'In the morning I decide.'

'The morning! We can't stay here all night.'

The other guests agreed with Jason and started to protest.

Aris calmly shifted the gun so that it pointed towards the group.

They got the message and fell silent.

Having taken a couple more unhealthy swigs of neat ouzo Aris burped loudly and turned his attention once more to the chest. He started changing the numbers on the dial, trying to lift the lid with each new combination.

'Why was he so upset when I mentioned Panandreas?' Margaret whispered.

'I don't know,' Jason replied.

Michaelis put down his weights, checked that Aris was distracted and came over to them.

'Don't mention the name again,' he said quietly. 'My uncle believes that our ancestors worked for that family, they fought over this land. Pan... that family stole it from us and made widows and orphans of my past relatives. My uncle does not let history die.'

'I am not sure I understand,' Margaret said.

'Maybe that is for the best.' Michaelis tried to smile but it was a faint one and soon evaporated. 'Just do what uncle says and you will be safe. Now, I know that it is early but I suggest you try and rest.'

He returned to his corner and continued with his exercises as Aris tried another combination on the chest.

'If he gets that open,' Jason said to no one in particular, 'we will lose whatever is inside.'

'There are three numbers on the combination, am I right?' Oliver asked.

'Yes, as far as I can see.'

'Oh dear. Then he could quite quickly hit on the right one by chance. And if it is a Benson and Pollack as I suspect, then there is always the possibility that he may just hit the secret lock and get it open that way.'

'How many possible combinations would there be from three numbers?' Jason asked anxiously keeping an eye on the chest.

'One thousand,' Oliver replied immediately.

'How on earth do you know that?' Cassie, sitting on the other side of Oliver, asked incredulously.

'Oh... well.' Oliver started fiddling with his fingernails. 'Simple arithmetic and... Never mind.'

'Go on Mister S.' Jason encouraged. 'If you know something now's the time to tell us.'

'I would rather not.'

'I would rather you did.' Margaret's voice was flat and to the point.

Oliver looked along the line of faces that stared back at him. 'It was a... hobby I had. More of a business actually.'

'Hobby?'

'Oh dear.' Oliver shifted uncomfortably and looked at the shotgun that was still aimed directly at them. 'I suppose I should confess. I may not get another chance.'

'Confess what?' Jason had followed his gaze. He did not like being held at gunpoint, which is effectively what was happening, any

342

more than anyone else but he also suspected that the quiet little man beside him knew something that might be helpful. He remembered how Oliver had known how to open the cigarette case and how he had known about those people from London who made it. Perhaps the chest had been made by the same people and also had a… what had he called it? A back door entry. 'Go on Mister S.,' he prompted.

'Well,' Oliver started, 'considering our present predicament I expect you will have other things to worry about than my past so… You remember I told you about Benson and Pollack of Hatton Garden, the dodgy safe makers?'

'Yes.'

'I researched them as part of my business. You see, I used to be what the popular press would call a cat burglar.'

There was a sharp intake of breath along the line.

'But I retired from that line of work many years ago. It started to get too… impersonal. One used to take pride in housebreaking; you pitted your wits against the owners and that was it. These days it's all surveillance cameras and laser lights and not very burglar friendly at all. There was no more fun involved so I gave it up.'

'Stealing is not supposed to be fun,' Margaret chided him.

'But I did not steal.' Oliver sounded hurt.

'But you were a burglar hon, you just admitted it.' Cassie too sounded irritated. She had been burgled twice while living in Los Angeles and had no time for people who stole.

'So you broke into people's houses and did what exactly?' Jason asked.

'Left them notes.'

'Oh yes, like that is so believable.'

'Yes, I left them notes. I would see a house that was vulnerable to a break in, would break into it, usually at night, and leave the householder a note explaining that if I could do it then so could someone with a more evil intent. I gave them tips on how to better secure their homes. I saw it as a kind of community service.'

There was a stunned pause before Oliver went on.

'But it went wrong only a few weeks ago. I was living in Plymouth, my daughter had arranged a lovely little retirement home for me, or so she said. It was in fact a dump. A horrid place that I did not want to, nor need to, be in at all. But it did have one thing about it that attracted me. An antique Benson and Pollack safe in the warden's office.'

'Warden? Sounds like a prison.'

'It was Jason, it was. At least to me. Lock down at nine every evening, having to get permission to go out or stay out late. Intercoms and electronic locks on the doors. Ghastly. The other old folk were o.k., the ones who were compos mentis, but the regime! Anyway, I stuck it out because my daughter was happier knowing that I had twenty-four hour on-call help and a bingo club on Thursdays.' He shuddered. 'And I quite enjoyed running their little choir. But I stuck it out mainly because I was intrigued by the Benson and Pollack safe. I had to see what was inside it. So, to cut a long story short…'

'Too late.'

'Hush Polly.'

'To cut it short, I broke into the warden's office one night and found the secret, back door entry to the safe. A similar device to the cigarette case, the trick was in the hinges. Well, inside I found all kinds of dreadful evidence about the way the place was being run. The money my daughter, and everyone else's daughters and families, were paying was not going on our "care" but being flittered away into some offshore bank account by the people who ran the place. I was outraged of course.'

'So what did you do?' Harriet had crawled around onto the sleeping platform and squatted down behind Oliver. Everyone else had leant towards him to hear the juicy details.

'I came on this SARGO holiday. Well, first I anonymously leaked the information to the local and then national papers and then I came on this holiday.'

'Did your actions help the other… inmates?' Margaret asked.

'I am pleased to say that they did,' Oliver said proudly. 'The home is to be closed down and everyone moved to a much better place. Apparently compensation is due. But…'

'But?' everyone asked in unison.

'But there was an almost immediate repercussion for me. The home counter attacked a few days ago when they discovered who'd done it. At first they had no idea who had broken in, because I did not damage or even crack the safe, such was the genius of Benson and Pollack! But I left incriminating evidence, apparently. No one else in the home had teeth that could cope with Peanut Brittle and no one was known to like Pringles as much as I. I carelessly left behind some crumbs from both irresistible snacks. The Pringles were the final clue that led them to me. They started claiming that I *burgled* them, which I suppose was almost true, and the papers have made quite a fuss about it. Particularly the Mirror for some reason.'

'Hang on a minute...' Harriet began but Oliver turned to her and smiled weakly.

'I'm very sorry about your papers Harriet dear, but I had to try and keep my identity secret. The last thing I wanted was to be sent back to Britain by the Greek authorities. I came here to get away from all that and give myself a chance to think what I would do next. I fear I can never return to England again.'

'I'm sure it will die down,' Margaret said kindly. 'I think you did a very brave thing.'

'Hear hear,' Cassie agreed.

'I think you should keep your mitts off me papers in future.'

'I promise I shall Harriet. If we ever get out of here I shall never doctor another tabloid. I never knew it could upset someone so.'

'And talking of getting out of here,' Polly said and nodded towards Aris. 'He shows no signs of letting us go.'

'As Michaelis said,' Jason said to the group in general, 'we should probably make ourselves comfortable for the evening, well for the night, and see what happens. We can't leave during this storm anyhow.'

'He's got to shift at some point.' Harriet dropped her voice to a whisper. 'We could overpower him.'

'He's got a gun, hon.'

'Yes, it's far too dangerous,' Jason agreed. 'We'll just sit it out and see what happens. I suggest you eat, try and keep comfortable and sleep if you can. Maybe later when it's stopped raining and he's asleep...'

Although some of the guests wanted to make a run for it and the others wanted to stay, Jason did not listen to the debate that started around him. He slipped away to the other end of the sleeping platform and started chewing on a fingernail.

Something that Oliver had just said had struck a chord. His guests were tired, exhausted more like, and they were stuck here for the night. O.k. so it wasn't an ideal situation but he would have to work with it and it could work to his advantage.

Something that Oliver has just said…?

He watched as his group made themselves as comfortable as best they could. They passed out what provisions they had, choosing not to have any goat even though Oliver highly recommended it, and settled in for a long night.

Oi! Queer-boy! Stop biting your nails.

Jason looked at his fingers, realised what he was doing and forced himself to concentrate.

It was time for him to start making plans.

FORTY SIX
Friday
1.30 a.m.

Jason's eyes felt heavy but he was awake. He was lying on his back staring at the cobwebbed ceiling that was lit by the dim light from the single light bulb. He could hear his guests sleeping around him, their breathing deep and heavy, Harriet's snoring deeper and heavier. Outside the wind was still moaning around the building but the thunder had stopped a few hours ago. Stray downpours of rain occasionally whipped against the window but the storm was slowly blowing itself out.

He turned his head to survey the room. Aris was still in his chair, the gun now in his hands and the chest on the floor under one foot. The other foot was propped up against the door, the exit still well and truly blocked. At least he was asleep. He had finally succumbed to the alcohol at around ten, by which time all of Jason's guests were sleeping, exhausted from their long walk. There had been no opportunity for an escape. Aris had even taken the chest with him when he had gone, rather noisily, to the toilet, leaving the door open so that he could still train his gun on the room. Jason had dozed around that time too, but his mind had kept working while he slept and a dream had developed into an idea which had developed into a solution. And this is what had woken him up. He squinted through the gloom to the other corner, to the right of the now dead fire, where Michaelis was sprawled out in his chair, his groin thrust provocatively forwards. His dumbbells were at his feet, his eyes were closed and he, like everyone else apart from Jason, was sleeping soundly.

Jason looked back to the chest. In it lay whatever Dimitris Panandreas and his father before him had been charged with protecting. Possibly something to do with Richard Wagner, possibly only information but equally possibly something actually made of gold. The Golden Fleece sat only a few metres away, so near and yet, with the volatile and clearly insane Aris guarding it, so far. At least Aris had not stumbled on the combination or a back-door entry mechanism; the chest was still locked. All Jason had to do now was get the chest away from him. He had until Aris woke up to try as many combinations as he could. If he could take out whatever was in there, hide it somewhere and then reset the combination to whatever number Aris had been on when he fell asleep, then maybe he would get away with the treasure without being discovered. Assuming Aris let them go in the morning.

To the right of the fireplace, close to where his vision of the perfect man now slept, he could make out a rectangular footstool. If he could swap it for the chest without waking Aris his plan might work. He let his arm dangle over the edge of the sleeping platform and checked that his flight bag was still where his gran had left it. It was.

Slowly and carefully so as not to make any noise, he swung his legs over the edge of the platform and sat up. He waited. No one stirred. He had taken his shoes off before lying down to sleep and the flagstones were cold beneath his feet, but at least he would make less noise. He stood up, glad that he had not worn his polyester SARGO shirt, it would have rustled. Instead his cotton polo shirt made no sound as he reached down for his bag. He stopped in mid lean and changed his mind. He would leave the bag there. If he got the chest safely away he would bring it back to the bag to try the combination. That way he would be as far away from Aris as he could be and, if he succeeded in finding the right numbers, any sound that opening the chest might make was less likely to wake the sleeping ogre.

Satisfied with his plan he started out towards the fireplace. His feet made no sound but the legs of his shorts rustled together so he spread his legs apart. Walking like someone who had just spent far too much time on a very wide horse he swaggered across the room. As he passed under the light bulb his shadow overtook him and then grew up the fireplace wall ahead. It and he were the only things moving as he approached the footstool. Michaelis was only a foot away and the temptation to reach out and touch him was almost unbearable. But Jason had more important things on his mind than his dream man personified. Or at least that is what he kept telling himself as he concentrated on bending down silently and raising the stool in his hands.

He took it carefully over to where Aris slept, carrying it before him as if it were a sacred offering going to the altar for sacrifice. He stopped short when he caught a whiff of the alcoholic fumes Aris was breathing out. A tickle developed in the back of his throat and he almost coughed. But he could not afford to make a sound, if he was caught now he'd probably be shot. He swallowed hard, washing away the cough with the last of the saliva from his dry mouth, and crouched down.

His knee cracked like a gunshot and Aris grunted. Jason froze, his eyes level with the barrel of the gun, the stool only an inch away from Aris' foot. He held his breath and waited.

When his heart rate had returned to as normal as it could manage in the circumstances he placed the stool on the floor as close to Aris' foot as he could. Now came the tricky part. He squeezed some of Aris' trouser leg between his fingers and lifted the leg, just above the ankle. Glancing continuously from the sleeping man's face to his foot he slid the stool towards the chest with his left hand, felt the two things connect and started to push.

The chest scraped on the ground, a piece of grit caught underneath it. Jason swore silently to himself and wondered how it would look if anyone woke up and saw him. He had his face too close to the old man's crotch for comfort, he was lifting another man's leg like he wanted to sniff his sock and he was squatting like he was using a French toilet. He'd been in some daft situations in his time but this was surely the worst of them.

Time.

Why was that word suddenly rattling around his brain? What had Oliver said earlier? What had been his dream that became the idea that was the…

Aris grunted again and his head fell towards Jason. Jason looked up. The man was looking straight at him. But he was still asleep. Jason swallowed. The leg was getting heavy in his hands. He brought his attention back to the chest and another idea occurred to him.

He didn't need to swap the stool with the chest. He simply lifted the leg towards himself slightly and rested the foot on the edge of the stool. Dur! How simple was that? He lent across and, with both hands, lifted the chest clear.

He finally had it in his grip. All he had to do now was open it and discover what all the years of mystery, and secret history had been about.

To use the key times the key by time.

And that was when the final clue finally made sense to him.

Oliver had reminded him of it when he was telling how he had left clues and been found out as the mysterious old folks home burglar. 'The final clue...' he had said and Jason had remembered it word for word just as he had done when he was in the well. They had all ignored it, once they had solved the riddle and were on their way to find the Golden Fleece. But the final clue was the final answer, somewhere within its nine words was the key to opening the chest, Jason was sure of it. Otherwise what purpose did the clue serve?

The answer was in the manuscript. The manuscript was in his pocket. To check his theory he would have to put the chest down again and look at the music. He took a step back.

And trod on someone's foot.

He turned around slowly and looked up at Michaelis who now stood behind him. He had one arm raised. His fist was clenched around a dumbbell and he looked as if he was about to bring it crashing down on Jason's head.

FORTY SEVEN
Stavros 5.35 a.m.

All hell broke loose again at dawn.

Whatever dreams Margaret had been having were blown away by the gunshot. Her heart was pounding and she was shaking before she opened her eyes. Instinctively she turned to face the wall and screamed as small pieces of plaster and pellets rained down on her.

She waited. No further shots rang out. She opened her eyes and looked around.

The other guests and Jason had had a similar reaction. Everyone was suddenly wide awake and cowering, looking across the room with white faces and disorientated expressions. Margaret followed their eyes to see Aris standing over the metal chest, his shotgun aiming directly at it. He had obviously just shot it but, judging from the angry look on his face, to no avail.

'For god's sake man don't do that again,' Polly shouted, seriously annoyed.

Aris looked over at her and then back at the chest. He lifted his gun again and everyone covered their ears.

The second shot sent pieces of splintered metal and pellets flying around the room. The only person who got hit by any was Aris but he seemed not to care. He took a huge in breath, his chest swelled out and his face turned purple, and then he bellowed down at the chest. If two blasts from the shotgun couldn't open it, it was unlikely that his shouting at it would help, but he didn't care. He kicked the chest across to the chair by the door and sat while he reloaded his gun.

'We have to get out of here now,' Jason said as he slid across the sleeping platform to Margaret.

It was taking Margaret a few minutes to wake up and put the events of the previous day into order. Her legs were stiff from the walking and her face felt hot, that would have been from the sun. Her bones ached from sleeping in damp clothes on bare wood. She remembered dozing off early, not long after Oliver had revealed his little secret. She guessed that she had been asleep for around twelve hours; she must have been worn out.

'Gran? It's getting light outside, the storm has passed. We can get out of here now and we have to.'

She was wide awake now. The sight of Aris pushing cartridges into his gun had completely brought her to.

'Yes indeed,' she replied checking around the room. 'But how?'

Cassie crawled over to where they were. Her hair had come undone during the night and now fell in long tresses over her shoulders. It was a startling sight for Margaret who had only seen it up and neat before. Across the platform Polly was tidying herself up and Harriet and Oliver were cautiously eating some dried biscuits with one eye on the Greek man with the gun. Aris had loaded his weapon again but was once more turning the numbers on the combination lock. As for the young Michaelis, he was no where to be seen.

'I have a plan,' Cassie whispered. 'We have to distract him and get the gun away from him.'

'Yes but how?' Margaret repeated. She had assessed the room but could see no easy way of escape. They were in the same position as the previous evening except now Aris had a hangover, so he would probably be feeling even more aggressive.

'What you talking about?' Aris turned on them, lurched from his chair and took two huge strides forwards. 'You Panandreas people, you talking about me?' He spat.

'How very unattractive,' Margaret mumbled.

'Eh?'

'I said how very unattractive,' she repeated more boldly.

'What you mean?'

'Distract him Margaret,' Cassie hissed. 'Polly, get yourself oiled up. I have an idea.'

'It's not nice to spit.' Margaret was aware that Cassie was sliding back across to Polly and the others.

'Careful gran,' Jason started but Margaret ignored him.

'You are a frightful man and as soon as I am away from here I will report you to the police.'

'Bah! Police. They can't touch me. I am Aris Tzankatis, this is my land.'

'They will have you for keeping us prisoner all night.'

'Gran...'

'You go when this is open.'

'That belongs to my grandson. Give it to him.'

From the corner of her eye Margaret saw Cassie doing something with her hair. As she tied it up around the back she made a gesture with her hand. Margaret was doing the right thing in distracting Aris but Cassie wanted him somewhere else.

'That chest is mine,' Aris said and went back to it. He picked it up and threw it down on the ground with a crash.

'I hope it's not breakable,' Oliver said as he inched his way to the end of the sleeping platform. Harriet was already there, her legs dangling over the edge and her toes just touching the floor.

Margaret noticed that the shotgun had been discarded by the chair. She judged the situation safe to stand up. Aris glared at her.

'Where you going?'

'Home.'

'You stay here.'

'I go home!'

'You not pay for the party.'

'No I not pay for the party. Some party! You hold five old age pensioners and my grandson hostage...'

'Hey up pet, I'm only fifty nine.'

'My apologies Harriet.' Margaret made a slight bow to Harriet and then turned back to Aris and continued. 'Hold us hostage and then expect us to pay for the privilege. Come here.'

Aris looked a bit stunned at being given an order.

'I said come here,' Margaret barked and everyone flinched.

'Gran, I had no idea…'

'Shut up Jason.'

Aris shrugged and edged a little closer to her inquisitively.

'A bit nearer, Margaret,' Cassie said and Margaret nodded by way of reply without taking her hands of the bullish Greek man.

'I said here man, stand here.'

'Why?' Aris was in the centre of the room now, a few inches away from Margaret. 'What you want?'

Margaret was about to slap him around the face when Cassie inexplicably started singing.

'Good God not now Cass,' Polly grumbled. 'We're trying to get out of here.'

'*I get no kick in a plane…*' Cassie sang on, starting quietly and getting louder.

'Party was last night,' Aris said with a sneer. 'No singing now. You owe me money.'

'*Flying too high with some guy…*'

'For heaven's sake Cass what are you playing at?'

'I know this is a completely different musical,' said Margaret looking towards Jason. 'But do you happen to know …'

And then Margaret found herself singing '*oh yes, oh yes, oh yes they both reached for the, oh yes they both reached for the…*'

Aris scratched his head, knocking the light bulb above him. It swung, casting his shadow up and down the wall.

'*Is my idea of nothing to do…*' Cassie was really loud now, but getting louder still. And the pitch was rising, she was changing key.

'Gran what's going on?'

'I get you pet.' Harriet nodded at Margaret and glanced towards the door.

Cassie was making great nodding gestures herself, towards Polly. Everyone was standing now, Polly to Margaret's right, Jason to her left. Harriet whispered something to Oliver.

'What all this noise?' Aris said but he seemed to be less angry now; more confused and possibly even a little impressed.

'Music soothes the savage boobs,' Harriet said and thrust out her great bosom with her wrists.

He actually smiled then and licked his lips. But then his smile faded, something was not quite right.

'*Oh yes they both reached for the, they both reached for the gun.*' Margaret looked at Jason and opened her eyes as wide as they would go.

He took a deep breath in and looked just as wide eyed. He glanced across to the door and slowly bent down to pick up his flight bag, checking that Aris did not notice.

'What that noise?' Aris was saying now, looking over at Cassie. 'Why you make that noise?'

Cassie had got to '*but I get a…*' and stopped. To be more accurate she hadn't actually stopped; she was holding the note and projecting it, louder and higher until she settled on an impossibly piercing note that was guaranteed to…

'What she doing?' Aris' anger had returned.

'Everyone ready?' Margaret called above the note that vibrated around the room.

'On your cue Cassie.' Polly, having finally worked out what was going on, took a step back.

Jason had his flight bag on his shoulder and his eye on the gun. Harriet had her eye on the door. Cassie had her eye on Aris who was now grimacing and screwing up his eyes against the cacophony. He looked suddenly frightened, maybe it was the animalistic screech that Cassie was producing or maybe it was because he realised that he was surrounded by a group of mad English people all singing and nodding and behaving very strangely. He was just about to open his mouth to bark a threat when the light bulb above his head imploded. He was showered with hot glass and bits of glowing filament and immediately ducked.

Cassie finished her song: '…*kick*…'

Right on cue Polly executed a high kick that Dora Bryan would have been envious of, catching Aris under the chin with the toe of her shoe and sending his head snapping backwards.

'…*out of you.*'

'Run!' Margaret yelled and pushed Jason towards the exit.

Harriet made a dash for the door shouldering Aris to the floor like a prop forward as she went. She pulled Oliver behind her.

'My hip!' Polly screamed clutching at her leg in pain and falling to the floor.

'Get the chest,' Margaret ordered and Oliver picked it up.

He threw the door open, shouted 'hurry!' and stood back to help the other guests out.

Aris started to rise from the floor growling like a mythological creature about to wreak devastation on a small civilisation.

Harriet pushed Jason to Oliver who practically threw him outside and then went back to help Polly. As she passed Aris she kicked him out of the way and he fell towards Margaret who had just remembered to collect her handbag. The two collided and the bag flew from her hands. The urn containing Stanley's ashes rolled out and across the room.

She was just about to retrieve it when she felt Cassie grab her arm and pull her towards the door.

'Stanley!' she called out. Everything was happening too fast.

'No time hon, sorry.'

Harriet had hoisted Polly into her arms and was stomping back to the door, kneeing Aris between the legs for good measure as she passed him a third time.

'That's for touching me jacksie,' she said, tempted to come back for a fourth swipe at him.

Margaret was at the door, she looked back to the urn that had rolled across to the fireplace. The lid was still on, Stanley was still inside. But there was no time to think about it, Oliver ushered her outside where the air was suddenly clear and the rising sun blinded her.

She felt someone take her arm and then she was running.

Her eyes adjusted quickly but by the time she could see clearly she had stopped moving.

'The gun! We forgot the gun.' She heard someone call out. She thought it was Polly but everything, even the sounds around her, was distorted.

'Stay where you are!' Another voice, masculine and close.

'Out of the way lad.' Harriet.

'Stay where you are or I shoot.' Aris.

She heard the gun being cocked.

'Oh shit.'

Now that she had stopped moving Margaret could take stock. People had stopped shouting. All she could hear now was a breeze in the tree and her own breathing. Jason stood beside her, his flight bag over his shoulder. Harriet had put Polly down on the low boundary wall where she lent against the railings rubbing her hip and wincing in pain. Oliver stood with Cassie, both were panting and pale. Aris stood in the doorway of the outhouse, the shotgun once more trained on them and the tall, strapping lad Michaelis stood behind her and Jason, barring the courtyard exit.

And then Margaret saw the urn in Aris' hands.

'Stanley!' she called out and made to run towards it but Jason held her back.

'No gran.'

'Everyone keep still,' Cassie instructed. 'We have to think carefully.'

'I've had enough of this,' Jason spoke up. 'You want this chest? Then you give me that urn.' He took the chest from Oliver.

Aris looked at the jar in his hands. 'Why? What special about this?'

'I'll swap with you,' Jason went on, his voice calm yet authoritative. No one was more surprised than he. 'The urn for the chest.'

'No you can't Jason,' Margaret said. 'We came for the chest.'

'No gran, that urn is important to you. I am not leaving without it.'

'Give me my chest,' Aris shouted and lifted the shotgun. He tucked it under one arm, aiming across the courtyard at Jason's stomach.

'Put down the urn and I will swap.'

'No Jason.' This was Michaelis speaking. Jason started at the use of his name. 'Uncle let these people go.'

Everyone turned to Michaelis who took a step forward. Aris glared at him.

'You take sides with these people?'

'Let them go uncle or there will be trouble.'

'Get back to the goats boy.'

'The urn.' Jason took a step forward and held the chest out before him.

'For the last time no,' Margaret insisted. 'The chest is yours. Your future is more important than my past.'

'Trust me gran.' Jason took another step towards Aris, closer to the gun.

Aris put the urn down and lifted the weapon to his shoulder, his finger hovered over the trigger. He now aimed it directly at Jason's head.

'Uncle put the gun down and let these people go.' Michaelis had also stepped forward; he was a few inches to Jason's left, his hands held up in a gesture of surrender.

'You keep quiet.' Aris' eyes darted to his nephew and then back to Jason. 'Or are you on the side of Panandreas?'

'This is not about Panandreas,' Michaelis tried to reason. 'The feud is dead. There is no more Panandreas.'

'That chest. The Panandreas treasure. It was on my land. It is mine.'

'But you cannot kill to get it uncle.'

'I will.'

'But uncle...'

Aris turned purple in the face in an instant. 'Are you my family?' he bellowed at his nephew aiming the gun at him. 'Or do you take sides with these Panandreas people?'

'If you do this then I am not your family.' Michaelis replied with equal passion.

Aris pointed the gun back at Jason's head. Jason stood stock still, all colour draining from him.

'You are Tzankatis...'

'I am *not* Tzankatis,' Michaelis shouted, cutting his uncle off in mid sentence. 'I never have been. And neither have you.'

Aris' black eyes flicked from Jason to Michaelis as his nephew's words sank in. His expression darkened until, with a huge roar, a great outpouring of anger and frustration, he swung the gun around and pulled the trigger.

Michaelis flew backwards and landed on his side on the ground. Margaret screamed and covered her eyes. By the time she dared look Aris had grabbed Michaelis and had dragged him to the edge of the well, the gun pointed at his head. The boy was bleeding from a wound in the upper arm. The urn was still across by the door. Jason was rooted to the spot in the middle of the courtyard.

'Now,' Aris said to Jason and his calm tone alarmed Margaret. How could someone who had just shot his own nephew be so calm? 'Give me the chest or I finish him off.'

Margaret looked at Jason. He was starting to walk towards Aris with the chest in his hands. But he was looking only at Michaelis and he had tears in his eyes. Michaelis was looking back at him and shaking his head. His lips were drawn tight, he was fighting back pain, but there was a look that Margaret recognised as... As what?

She remembered Stanley as a teenager watching her across the garden fence. He had had the same look.

She remembered everything she had given up in order to care for him. Why had she done that?

For the same reason that Jason was willing to give away the Golden Fleece in order to save Michaelis.

Margaret had her second epiphany in two days.

'Stop.' She heard herself speak before she realised what she was doing. 'Keep the damn urn, have the chest but not until you hand the boys safely over to me.'

'Gran... But granddad, the ashes... You'd give them up for me?'

'For both of you Jason. I can't have any more time with Stanley but I can have more time with you.'

'But gran…'

'*Grandmother!*' Margaret was exasperated. 'For the last bloody time. I'm sick of all this to-ing and fro-ing. He wants the urn so let him have it, and the chest. Let him keep the damn lot. What is more important? The Golden Fleece or love?'

'You what?'

'Love Jason. Which would you rather survive this? The chest or Michaelis?'

She saw Jason stare at her, his face a mixture of embarrassment and shock. His mouth opened and closed a few times but no real words came out, just some splutters. He swallowed, turned bright red and then looked across at Harriet.

'It weren't me pet,' she said with her hands in the air. 'Told you, secret's safe with me.'

Aris appeared to have understood too. He kicked Michaelis and took a step back from him.

'You…' he yelled. 'You…' But he could think of nothing that would describe his absolute horror and disgust at discovering that his nephew was in love with another man. All he could think of to do was to raise his gun back to the lad's head and wrap his finger around the trigger.

'Take the bloody thing!'

Margaret had taken advantage of Jason's shock and wrenched the chest from his arms. She dumped it down in front of Aris. He swung the gun around to her but she didn't flinch. If she died now at least she would die with Stanley nearby.

'Now give me the boy,' she demanded and pointed down to Michaelis.

'Take him. He is no good to me.'

But as Margaret stepped over to help Michaelis up from the floor she felt a strong grip on her other arm.

'Oh my god!' she heard Polly call out and then heard some expletives from the rest of the party.

Suddenly she was on the floor, the chest in front of her and something hard and cold was pressed against the back of her head. Jason stood a few feet in front of her looking down in horror. She saw

Michaelis stagger across to the far side of the courtyard where Cassie sat him on the low wall and started to tend to his wound. She was happy that the boys would be together and not as shocked as she thought she would have been. She looked over to the urn, a few feet away by the outhouse.

'Be with you soon dear,' she said to Stanley and closed her eyes.

'Give me back my grandmother at once.'

Now it was Jason's turn to start making demands. Margaret wondered what he had left to trade. Aris had it all now.

'You have her back alive if she opens the box,' Aris said, seemingly calm once more.

'What?' Margaret had no idea how to open the chest.

'Open the box,' Aris repeated.

'I don't know how.'

'Open the box!'

'Oh it's just like Take your pick,' Polly quipped but no one found it remotely amusing.

'I count to three.'

Margaret felt the gun nudge the back of her head.

'But I don't know the combination.'

'One.'

'*I don't know the combination,*' she screamed. It did no good.

'Two.'

'I can't do this…'

'Two hundred and forty.'

Margaret looked up at Jason. He simply looked down at her and repeated the number.

'Be sure.' Aris grunted. 'I kill her if you are wrong.'

'Two hundred and forty.'

'Are you sure Jason?'

Jason crouched down to her and whispered. 'Trust me. Grandmother.'

'Open it.' Aris demanded.

Jason nodded reassuringly to his grandmother, stood up and started to back towards the others. Margaret saw his hands behind his back making some gesture, presumably telling them to get ready to run. Her mouth was dry, her hands trembling as she turned the first number on the dial.

Two.

Cassie helped Michaelis to his feet. Margaret was pleased to see that he was not badly hurt. She turned the next dial.

Four.

The chest gave no indication that the combination was working. Nothing clicked or moved within it. She looked across at the urn standing alone in the doorway of the outbuilding. She looked at Jason now standing next to Michaelis. They made a handsome pair. Whatever happened after this last number she hoped they would be happy.

Zero.

Something clicked and the lid sprung open a fraction.

'Oh my god! How did you know?' Margaret started to speak but Aris pushed her roughly aside.

'Margaret, here!'

She heard Harriet's voice and ran towards it, ducking and fearing the sound of the gun at any moment.

Reaching the others she turned to look behind her. Aris had lent his gun against the well and was on his knees in front of the chest, the lid was open and he was lifting something out from within.

'Everybody...' Jason started but he was too late.

Aris let out the loudest roar of frustration that Margaret had ever heard and kicked the chest across the ground. He rose to his feet, a shiny steel dumbbell in his hand. He glared across at Michaelis, pulled back his arm and, like an Olympian javelin thrower, he threw the weight towards them.

Margaret watched in horror as Michaelis pushed Jason out of its path and ran towards the well. He dived on the shotgun just as Aris realised what he was doing. Together they grappled for the gun. Margaret knew there was one shot left in it. The two men wrestled with it and each other, until both had hold of it. But Aris was stronger. He threw his nephew against the wall of the well, smashing him into the rocks on his injured arm. Michaelis shouted out in pain but did not stop struggling even as Aris forced him upwards until his upper body was over the lip of the well. In a few more seconds he would be plunging down it.

Something with blonde highlights darted across Margaret's vision as Jason flew through the air and landed on Aris' back.

'Oh my god no,' she called and started to move forwards. Harriet held her back, away from the danger.

Aris stood up abruptly, throwing Jason from his back with ease. He wrenched the gun from Michaelis, whacked him across the chin with the butt and turned the barrels on his new attacker. Jason had fallen to the ground and was now backing away with one hand held up to the gun.

Aris stopped and grinned showing his rotten teeth. He raised the gun to his shoulder and aimed it at Jason's head.

Margaret heard the shot as she fell to the floor in a proper, dead faint.

FORTY EIGHT

Jason had often wondered what his last thought was going to be. Although his inner voice was screaming in panic and he was looking down the barrel of a gun that was about to blow his head off, the only thing he could think if was, 'did I leave the iron on?'

He saw Aris move his finger around the trigger and instinctively turned his head away, throwing himself onto the ground, flat on his front.

He heard the shot.

He felt no pain, he was thankful for that. Although he wanted to he hadn't wet himself either, he was thankful for that too.

In a doorway stood granddad Stan, legs and all, ready to welcome him to his new beginning.

But it wasn't granddad Stan. It was a small urn.

He felt large hands on his shoulders as someone lifted him up and plonked him down on his feet. He turned to see Michaelis with tears in his eyes. He felt his strong arms wrap around him and he was pulled close in a reassuring hug.

Over Michaelis' shoulder he saw Aris staggering, clutching at his chest. Blood spurted from between his fingers. The man staggered backwards as blood bubbled from his lips. And then he fell over the rim of the well and vanished into the abyss.

Suddenly everyone was around Jason. His grandmother spun him around and was hugging him. Cassie was pulling Michaelis away, fussing over his wounded arm. Polly was limping to collect the urn. Harriet was slapping him on the back and Oliver...

Oliver was applauding someone wildly.

Jason looked up to the monastery wall. Three uniformed soldiers stood there. Two were looking rather surprised at the third, the one who stood between them blowing the end of a smoking pistol.

Lesley, dressed in full military camouflage, spun the pistol in her fingers and slipped it expertly back into its holster.

'I hope I won't get into trouble,' she said cheerfully as she jumped down from the wall. 'But I couldn't think of what else to do.'

The soldiers approached Jason with her.

'No trouble,' one of them said. 'I will say I shot him in this man's defence.'

'How can I ever repay you?' Lesley said with a coquettish giggle.

'Just don't sing,' the soldier replied flatly.

A little while later and most outstanding matters of the day were resolved. The soldiers had first attended to Michaelis, checked the old folk for injuries or signs of delayed shock and then provided them with cups of tea, because that is what Margaret said everyone needed. Oliver fussed around Lesley and she fussed around him, telling him of her apparently innocent antics at the barracks the night before.

'We did so want to come and find you,' she explained. 'But the storm was just too bad and the boys too interested in my life story. We set off at first light to make sure you were o.k.'

'*Dear* Mrs. Shaw,' was all that Oliver could say as he patted her hand and gazed into her eyes in awe.

The soldiers then investigated the well. Michaelis had given them the full story of how his uncle had held everyone prisoner at gunpoint over night, but he did not mention the chest. The soldiers found Aris' body about forty feet down the well, wedged against the body of Yiannis the fisherman. It was clear to them that Aris had shot Yiannis, they recognised the damage only his kind of rifle could do. They called for assistance and, by the time they had covered the dead men in blankets and lifted them clear of the well, more soldiers had arrived to take the bodies away.

They assured Lesley that they would be back in a little while to escort the other guests down the mountain and back to the village. They also assured her and the others, that they would give a full account to the police of the events they had seen and heard. The SARGO guests would undoubtedly have to provide statements at the police station over the next few days but the authorities knew Aris well and would not be sorry to hear of his death. There would be nothing to worry about.

Once the soldiers had left them alone the group sat under the shade of the tall tree, slightly stunned but very relieved that they were all still in one piece. Only Polly seemed to be suffering; she grumbled about probably needing another new hip. The sun was up now and the day was going to be a hot one. The storm had refreshed the atmosphere and the air was clear, the light breeze cooled it and the earth smelt clean and alive.

'What I don't understand,' said Margaret as she cradled the urn in her lap, 'is how you knew the combination.'

'*To use the key times the key by time,*' Jason replied. 'The last clue. I'd forgotten about it in all the goings on until Oliver made his confession last night and mentioned cream crackers were the last clue that led to his discovery.'

'Pringles dear boy.'

'Whatever. It suddenly made sense to me while I was trying to get the chest away from Aris when he was asleep. I remembered that there had been another clue and worked out that to find the key to the chest you had to times the *key* of the music by the *time* of the music. The time signature I think you called it Cassie.'

'Five sharps multiplied by six-eight time,' Cassie said with a smile. 'Now how simple is that!'

'That was it Cassie. Five times six times eight. Two hundred and forty.' Jason looked quite pleased with himself. 'But what *I* don't understand grandmother is how you knew about...' He looked at Michaelis who was beaming at him with an inane grin that simply suggested lust and love combined. Jason felt himself turn red in the face again. 'About, you know.'

'About you and this handsome young man?' Margaret asked with a twinkle in her eye. 'It took a while I must admit but I am your grandmother Jason and it's my job to notice these things. Besides, not all old people are thick you know. I am sorry Mrs. Shaw I didn't mean to look at you when I said that.'

Lesley hadn't noticed. She was adjusting her epaulets, comparing them to her nail varnish and looking uncertain about the combination.

'But all we got for our trouble,' Polly said nursing her very sore hip, 'was a dumbbell.'

'Well not quite.'

Jason looked around to double check that they were alone. They were. As everyone, even Lesley, watched him intently he wedged his flight bag between his feet and reached in with both hands. The others huddled closer as he produced a package about the size of a large book, wrapped in material. Two envelopes were tied to it with string.

'I waited for everyone to be asleep and then sneaked the chest away from Aris intending to try as many combinations as I could before morning,' he explained. 'Then the final clue hit me. Aris was dead to the world... oh bad taste, sorry. He was in a drunken stupor and didn't wake up.'

'I did,' Michaelis chipped in. 'It was my idea to put the dumbbell in the box so he wouldn't suspect.'

'Yes well done love.' Jason didn't like being interrupted in his moment of glory. 'I opened the box...'

'We made the change...'

'And I slipped the chest back under Aris' foot.'

'But I was there in case he woke up...'

'Yes, thank you Michaeli.'

'Now don't fight boys,' Margaret intervened. 'Let's see what this is and then we can lay the mystery of the Golden Fleece to rest once and for all.'

Jason untied the letters and opened the first one. It was written in Greek, Italian and English. He read it out to the guests.

To whoever finds this letter.

I am Dimitris Panandreas, the only son and heir of Christos Panandreas (1844 – 1914) and Maria Panandreas (1848 – 1914), Symi.

The object in this box belongs to history. Whoever finds it must do what is right for it and must ensure that it is kept for mankind. As the letter (signed by the author and dated 1882) explains, this is a genuine article. My father and I have protected it for as many years as we can. I only hope that, when it is found, the world will be a safer place for it and that the world will understand, will forgive us for keeping it hidden for so many years. When you think of the times we have lived through you will understand why.

But this chest contains more treasure than the Golden Fleece. I must also leave you information. Please ensure that this news reaches the appropriate parties:

In 1928 Sophia Tzankatis (wife of Petros Tzankatis) and I conceived a daughter. Anna Tzankatis (as she had to be known for her own protection) was born in July 1929. She will, I hope, one day marry. Any children born of Anna, or Anna herself if she is still living, must know that she was the daughter of Dimitris Panandreas. Her children will be of my family. Our name will live on through them.

Dimitris Panandreas - 1939

'The Panandreas heir?' Cassie asked.

'It would appear so.' Margaret took the letter and read it again.

'What name?' Michaelis looked over her shoulder to read the letter for himself. 'Sophia Tzankatis… Anna Tzankatis… Petros… Oh.' He added simply.

'Does this mean something to you dear?'

'It's me,' Michaelis said. He was working something out. 'Anna Tzankatis was my grandmother so Sophia was my great grandmother.' He scratched his head.

'So how come you're also called Tzankatis,' Jason asked. He'd quickly worked out the family tree and was confused by something.

'When my parents died, soon after I was born,' Michaelis explained, 'I came to live here with uncle. We were the only family left. He started to use my grandmother's maiden name because, he said, we should not forget that we were of the Tzankatis family, as if that counted for anything. He was obsessed with the feud over this land and the history.'

'Poor thing,' said Polly and patted the lad's knee. 'But why is all this important?'

'It's simple,' said Oliver, tearing his eyes away from Lesley. 'It doesn't matter who his grandparents were if Michaelis has no other brothers or sisters and with his uncle dead, then he is the last remaining Panandreas. Albeit by a child born out of wedlock, Anna, he still carries the Panandreas line.'

'Which means,' Margaret said taking the package from Jason and handing it Michaelis, 'that this belongs to you. Dimitris Panandreas was your great grandfather.'

'I don't want it,' Michaelis said immediately handing it back to Jason. 'I only wanted freedom from uncle Aris. You people have given me that. So Panandreas or Tzankatis, it doesn't matter. I have no family now, the feud is over. You were meant to find this so you keep it.'

'Whatever,' Jason said vaguely. He had started to worry about interbreeding. He suddenly realised that he sounded ungrateful and changed his tone. 'I mean, whatever is it?'

'What's the other letter about pet?' Harriet pointed to it and Jason opened it.

Everyone waited patiently as he read it to himself, his eyes wide and his head moving from side to side. When he had finished he sat down again, confused.

'Well?' Margaret prompted. 'What does it say?'

'It is written in German,' Jason began quietly. He looked across at Margaret. 'You were so close.'

'Do explain Jason dear,' she prompted. 'Or read it out.'

Jason handed her the package now only loosely wrapped in material, the string having been untied. 'Open it,' he said, 'and I will tell you what The Golden Fleece is.'

As Margaret carefully unwrapped the parcel Jason translated the letter:

Venice, 1882

To my dear friends Christos and Maria Panandreas

I hope this letter finds you in better health than me. I have had trouble with my heart and I fear the strain of the last production has weakened it beyond repair. I fear that I will not be here for very much longer and I am therefore putting my affairs in order as best I can.

I owe you for many things. For your generosity, your patronage and of course, I owe you a huge financial debt. Would that I had the means to repay you these things.

I have thought long and hard how I was to achieve this and, in the end, could only think of one way to repay you for your faith in me.

It is enclosed. No one knows of its existence but us. I can not reveal it now and so entrust it to you. You will see, when you look through it, the reason I can not make it public. It tells what I truly feel. It reverses all those anti-Semitic ramblings of mine, it tells the truth about Parsifal, Tristan and the others. It attacks those people who financed me for their own gain. I only wrote what I wrote in the past because they paid me to. I was nothing more than a sham. But The Golden Fleece changes all that. It will, when the time is right for you to bring it to the attention of the world, rewrite the history books. It will show the world that I was not who the world believes I am; believed I was.

And I have written it for you. No more Teutonic themes, no more Germanic blustering and roaring! Soon it will be time for the world to revel in the glory of your Greek mythology.

Protect this from my critics and my followers. If they know I have 'double crossed' them all these years by not believing in what they thought I believed - what they paid me to believe - they will want to do only two things. They will destroy it and defame me. Let it into the world only when the time is right.

Protect The Golden Fleece, Christos, until the time is right for the world to know the truth about me.

Your dying friend

Richard Wagner.

P.S. The chest is the Benson and Pollack you gave me in Paris all those years ago. You remember the combination I trust? I suggest you reset that combination to a number of your own choice. R.

'It appears to be music,' Margaret said.

Everyone looked at her. On her lap she rested a large, leather bound book. Across the title page was written 'The Golden Fleece. An Opera in three acts by Richard Wagner. Venice 1882.' And a signature. She turned the pages carefully to reveal the score, orchestrations, lyrics and melodies. All were all written out in a thin though legible handwriting.

'It's an opera hon,' Cassie said as she read some of the music. 'An original opera by Wagner that the world has never known.'

'What's it worth?'

'Jason how could you…' Margaret tutted.

'Put this up for auction and you're looking at millions,' Cassie said. 'Assuming it's authentic of course.'

'Well it has to be surely,' said Polly. 'I mean why else would people have gone to so much trouble to hide it?'

'I'm sure the signature, ink and paper can be easily authenticated,' Oliver said. 'And Cassie is right. This is probably the most valuable musical find since the missing Brandenburg concertos came to light in a cupboard.'

'Most valuable and controversial,' Cassie replied. 'The letter said that this opera basically reverses everything that we believe Wagner stood for. His anti-Semiticism and all that crap. He's basically changing his mind on his death bed. That will upset a few people in the musical, not to say right wing political, world.'

'And it would have really upset the Nazis, had they ever found it,' Polly said.

Jason didn't understand everything that was being said. All he knew was that he did not currently hold any money in his hands. He was no better off than when he opened the worthless cigarette case. In fact he was worse off. He'd probably been fired by now. Slipe would be waiting back at the Villa to inflict the final humiliation. Jason would soon be packing his bags, saying goodbye to Michaelis at the quay side and getting on a plane back to England with his grandmother. What use was this book to him?

Margaret gave him the book but he would not take it. 'You should look after this,' he said. 'It belonged to granddad really. Besides, I wouldn't know what to do with it.'

'Well, put it back in your flight bag dear and we will discuss it later.'

Margaret left the group chatting excitedly about the find and filling Lesley in on the events of the previous evening. She walked away from the shade of the tree, out into the heat of the day and went to the outhouse.

Looking over her shoulder she imagined Dimitris Panandreas behind her, staggering into the chapel to die. She looked back at the outhouse door and tried to imagine Stanley's last view as he pushed it open.

She fought back tears and she walked across to the low wall and the iron railings. The sea was out there beyond; deep blue, dotted with tiny white waves and larger white boats. It stretched off to melt with the pale horizon at the edge of the world. Beneath her the mountain fell away to the sea. The breeze was stronger here; it would carry Stan off into nowhere and everywhere.

She unscrewed the lid of the urn and held the jar out through the railings. She thought of Jason and how he had found happiness, she hoped, with the young Michaelis. She thought of her daughter and her granddaughter neither of whom she would ever know again. She thought of her remaining family: Jason.

'Goodbye my love,' she said quietly to the urn. 'I will be with you soon. Until then I shall get used to being alone, I'm sure.'

The ashes caught in the wind and were quickly blown far out over the cliffs and the ocean, vanishing into the air.

Margaret wiped her eyes and turned back to the courtyard.

'You won't be alone pet.'

The others were standing behind her. Lesley was wiping her eyes, the rest stood with bowed heads and sympathetic looks.

Jason held out his hand to his grandmother. 'Come on love,' he said kindly. 'Let's be getting back shall we?'

EPILOGUE
Symi harbour
October 26th
9.55 a.m.

Dimitris was on the most important mission of his young life. He had to get the letter from the clock tower around to the ferry before it left and he had only five minutes to do it in. As soon as it was done he could head off to meet his friends for his name day party. The five euros the woman had given him for the errand would buy some extra bangers, if he could find some, then the party at the little church of Saint Dimitris would really go with a bang. His heart raced as fast as he did as he ran. He waved to the men selling sponges to the last of the season's tourists and jumped over the ropes that tied the fishing boats to the quayside. He could see across the harbour to where the last tourists were preparing to board the ferry. He could see piles of suitcases, crowds of people and a general mayhem that could soon cause him a problem.

The person who had given him the letter to deliver had said it was of the utmost urgency. Those were the strange words she had used. They had spoken English and Dimitris had not understood all of the words but he knew that they had been important ones. And he had understood the message: the boat must not leave until he had handed the envelope to the man.

He was at the bridge now. His watch showed he had four minutes to go. He jumped down the steps and ran to the corner. A motorbike blared its horn at him as it narrowly avoided hitting him but he ignored it. He also ignored the shop keepers and café owners who called to him to slow down. He was on a mission. He only hoped he would get to the ferry in time.

He was a good runner, he ran at school. When he went to the big school in three years time he would be in the running team. He was the only person that could do this urgent errand. He was proud to have been chosen by the rich lady who had trusted him with his task.

He turned onto the south side of the harbour and saw the throng of people up ahead. He looked for the blue and yellow uniform but could not see it at that distance. He tucked his head down and ran faster.

'I can't Michaeli, we've been through this before.'

'I don't understand, you said you would stay.'

'I can't. We have no money.'

Jason had seen the last of his guests onto the ferry. He had five minutes to say goodbye to the love of his life before he too lifted his bags on to the boat and left Symi. Possibly for ever. But Michaelis was not letting him have his suitcase and was holding it tight.

'I have the monastery now,' Michaelis was saying. 'It has become mine. I have the land around it and the goats. We will survive.'

'Please don't make this any more difficult than it already is.'

'Jason…'

The decision had not been easy for Jason to make. In fact the last six weeks had not been easy for him at all.

Since the discovery of The Golden Fleece his life had not changed as much as he had thought it would. O.k., so now he had Michaelis and the two of them had spent as much time as possible together but it wasn't the dream he had so often fantasised about. He still had to live at Villa SARGO and deal with groups of old folk while Michaelis lived and worked up at Stavros. He still had Slipe to put up with on a regular basis. He had often wished that he had been fired that day back in September.

He remembered Slipe's face when the group returned to the Villa under police escort. The way Slipe's jaw had dropped and then cracked into a smile. He had actually rubbed his hands together as he started to berate Jason for not returning his calls, for not being there to greet him and for bringing his guests back with injuries. But Margaret and the others had managed to keep him from being fired. They had enthused about the trip (while keeping most facts to themselves) and had said what good value for money it had been. Just in case this had not impressed Slipe, Margaret had threatened to get Slipe fired for the way he had spoken to her in Rhodes on her arrival and she had promised to speak directly with SARGO HQ on her return to England. Slipe had been beaten into submission by the Sargonauts and gone back to Rhodes with his slimy tail between his bandy legs.

But SARGO had not hired Jason for another season. He was leaving Symi today to find work in England. If he managed to save enough money he would come back and see Michaelis the following summer and pick up where they had left off. His dream had become a reality and it was not going to be plain sailing. But he had promised to write. The situation was in fact horrible and he was sick with himself for not having enough courage to simply stay and risk what happened.

'Is it alright to use the facilities while we are stationary?' A stray SARGO guest was shouting down at him from up on deck. 'Or is it like British Rail?'

'Use whatever you like,' Jason called back. 'I'll be with you in a minute.'

He checked his watch. Two minutes to go.

'So, bye for now and I'll see you...'

'Stay.'

'I can't! We can't afford it.'

'You said you loved me.' Michaelis lowered his voice just in case any of his ex-army mates were around. They wouldn't have minded too much, they thought it was o.k. to be in love with another man just as long as it wasn't done in public.

'I do.'

'Then we don't need money.'

'We do Michaeli. We need to buy food...'

'I grow food.'

'We need to pay bills, I need clothes... oh forget it. Let's not part like this.'

Their painful discussion was interrupted by the arrival of a small, red faced boy. He thrust an envelope towards Jason.

'What's this?'

'She said you must open it now.' The boy panted.

'Who did? Never mind I will read it on the boat.'

'Now!' the boy shouted.

'Ella Dimitri!' Michaelis cuffed his ear. 'What is so important?'

'I don't know,' Dimitris replied and ran off.

Jason gave the envelope to Michaelis and finally prised his suitcase from his lover's hand. 'You deal with it, it's probably my P45.'

He dragged his case up the gangplank and into the belly of the ship. He was just slotting it into place beside the pile of other luggage when he felt it being taken from him again.

Michaelis pulled the case and Jason back down the gangplank.

'What the fuck are you doing now!' Jason was well fed up with all this.

But Michaelis didn't answer. He pulled Jason clear of the boat and ignored his protests as the gangplank lifted.

Once Jason saw that the ferry was departing without him and had reached the point of no return, he resigned himself to not only never working for another holiday company again but also to the fact that Michaelis was just as controlling and unhinged as his uncle had been.

'Great, so you win,' he said as he waved goodbye to his bemused guests and future career. 'What's going on?'

'You will see. Come with me.'

Five minutes later and Jason found himself standing beside another gangplank. This one belonged to a boat that was moored over near the clock tower on the north side of the harbour. The boat was some kind of luxury yacht, all white and chrome. A large man in a boiler suit was scrubbing the decks with his back to Jason as they arrived.

'What's going on?' Jason said as he turned to Michaelis, his eyes lighting up. 'You arranged for me to go over to Rhodes on this?'

'You can go wherever you want on it pet.'

Jason looked up in surprise. The large man scrubbing the deck was in fact Harriet.

'What the...' Jason started but stopped.

Other people were coming out on deck and he recognised all of them.

'Mrs. Shaw? Oliver?'

'It's Mrs. Simpson now,' Lesley said as she sashayed down the gangplank in something gold, low cut and inappropriate.

'It's all so exciting,' Oliver enthused as he pumped Jason's hand. 'I picked her up in Rhodes and changed her name to Argo, the boat I mean not dear Lesley. We thought it appropriate. We raced over here as fast as we could. We hoped we would be in time.'

'The last few weeks have been such a whirlwind. We arrived just half an hour ago,' Lesley added. 'I am captain, Oliver is first mate and Harriet is the crew.'

'Us bitches are just here for the ride hon.' Cassie and Polly came down the gangplank and greeted the boys warmly. 'The new show goes into rehearsal in three weeks so we're doing a last minute cram on the script.'

'*Everything shows,*' Polly said. 'The title was her idea unfortunately but I've written the only funny parts.'

'Any high kicks?' Jason asked, completely overwhelmed.

'No darling, we have some rather stunning chorus boys to do that for us. And no high notes either,' Polly said looking pointedly at Cassie. 'They wouldn't insure us for that.'

'I don't understand what you are all doing here,' Jason said when all the greetings had been made.

'Did you not read the note pet?' Harriet had even washed her hands before slapping them on Jason's back by way of a hello.

'I read it,' Michaelis admitted. 'But I didn't tell him who it was from.'

'So?' Jason, stilled slightly dazed, turned to Michaelis. 'Who was it from and what did it say?'

'It doesn't matter now,' a familiar voice said. 'You're here, that's what matters.'

The group parted to reveal Margaret descending the gangplank. She was dressed in a light, designer two piece suit, her hair was neat and perfectly cut and she carried a black briefcase. She looked years younger, Jason hardly recognised her.

'Gran!'

He hugged her, she hugged him, Lesley hugged Michaelis until Oliver had to pull her away and everyone went up on deck so that Margaret could explain.

'We took Cassie's advice,' she said once Harriet had handed round champagne. 'We put The Golden Fleece up for sale and it was immediately bought by the Bayreuth opera house and Wagner museum. It has been authenticated, copied, and will get its first performance next year, on the anniversary of Wagner's death. We are all invited.'

'But the boat...?'

'I split the money,' Margaret went on, 'between all of us and a war veteran charity, as Stanley would have wanted. I am leaving some of my share to the island.'

'I sent some to the old folks' home and they dropped the charges,' Oliver said quietly.

'And we financed our revue,' Cassie explained.

'And in here,' said Margaret handing over the briefcase, 'are your shares. Plural.'

'I don't believe it.' Jason shook his head as he accepted the case. He sat on a very comfortable sofa and rested the case on his lap. 'How much is it?'

'Open it and see.' His grandmother smiled at him. Everyone else gathered around. Michaelis sat next to Jason and they looked at the case together.

'It's a combination lock!'

'I thought that appropriate dear.'

'What's the number?'

'You're so smart, you figure it out,' Margaret said and chuckled.

Jason turned the three dials to read two hundred and forty and the case opened instantly. 'Not very original gran...' he started to say but he shut up when he saw the money inside.

'The Golden Fleece turned out to be very valuable indeed,' said Margaret. 'But don't waste it. And half is for Michaelis.'

Michaelis was beaming from ear to ear and shaking his head in disbelief.

'It's for the two of you to live whatever life you want to live.'

That night the little monastery of Stavros hosted its first party in over one hundred and twenty years.

Michaelis had driven Jason and the Sargonauts up the mountain in his late Uncle's battered old truck, daydreaming of a new Nissan. They had stopped by the army camp and been joined by some of the soldiers who willingly carried the bags of shopping up the final path. Oliver was in charge of the barbeque, of course. When he was not dancing with his new wife he eagerly tasted the food on a regular basis. Michaelis and the soldiers had strung lights through the tree and over the railings, lanterns burned around the walls and Cole Porter sang out from the old gramophone.

Margaret and Cassie danced together, Harriet and Polly watched. Jason looked on, still unable to believe the events of the day. He suddenly had the means to stay on Symi, he had his perfect hideaway in the hills and he had Michaelis. The money was a bonus.

'Come and dance with me,' Michaelis pulled him up from his chair.

'Not in front of my grandmother,' Jason protested.

'If you don't dance with him I will never speak to you again,' Margaret said. 'Trust me.'

Jason and Michaelis took the floor and everyone applauded. Polly dropped the needle onto the old seventy-eight once more and the music started.

Only to be interrupted by Jason's new mobile phone ringing out 'we're all going on a (pause) summer holiday.'

'Bugger it!' He jumped back like the phone had bitten him. 'I forgot all about my bloody guests!'

He answered the phone, kept it pressed to his ear and hurried off to one side for privacy.

Everyone watched as he nodded, shook his head, said a few words and then turned the phone off. He looked back at Michaelis standing alone in the middle of the courtyard and suddenly looking very vulnerable. He was lit by the flickering lamplight, his face showing concern.

Jason walked across to the well and stood thinking.

'What's going on? Are you in trouble?' Margaret also looked concerned.

'That was SARGO HQ,' he said. 'They say Slipe has been sacked. He went mad when I didn't arrive in Rhodes this morning with my guests and hit one of them. They want me to be area manager next year.'

'Well that's good news dear,' Margaret said.

'It would mean I would have to live in Rhodes for the season,' Jason said weighing up the proposition. 'Good money of course and I'd kind of be my own boss.'

'It's what you always wanted lad,' said Harriet.

'Yes, I thought so too,' Jason replied and looked at Michaelis.

'You do what you think is right,' the Greek lad said. 'I'll stand by you whatever you decide.'

Jason looked at the group as they looked back at him.

'You should always follow your dream dear,' said Margaret.

Jason looked at Michaelis who nodded in agreement.

'Well,' Lesley said after waiting long enough. 'Don't keep a secret. What answer did you give?'

Jason didn't answer, he didn't need to. He just dropped the phone into the well.

The dancing continued long into the night. The soldiers went home, the lanterns flickered and died and one by one the group headed off into the outbuildings to make up makeshift beds for the night until only Jason and Margaret remained in the courtyard. They danced under the moon as the voice of Cole Porter drifted off into the night.

'In olden days a glimpse of stocking was looked on as something shocking but now god knows…'

An interview with James Collins

Working on Jason and the Sargonauts

Where did the idea come from?

In 1991 I had an idea for a thriller/mystery story involving a piece of coded music; a kind of 'The 39 steps' meets 'La Cage aux Folles'. It was to be a sequel to a Christmas present, a short novel I had written for and about a group of friends. It started at Heathrow, involved a group of Nazi villains and ended up with a drag queen racing through the canals of Amsterdam on her way to save the Opera House.

I didn't write it.

But the idea stayed with me.

Then, eleven years later when I moved to Symi, I had time to write. I had Symi to inspire me and plenty of characters to observe. I'd met a 'Jason' on holiday in Gran Canaria and, having met some 'SARGO' guests on Symi, I just kind of put two and two together. The rest fell into place, albeit slowly.

Is this your first novel?

It's actually my fourth. The first, *Other People's Dreams*, was also inspired by Symi (I was on holiday here in 1996 when I started it) although in that story I call the island 'Kalados' as I wanted to take liberties with it, artistic liberties I mean. There are two others, one a farce/comedy about the after effects of having your wishes granted, *You Wish* and the other a thriller about dual personality, *Into the fire*. I seem to bounce from thriller to comedy and back again; don't know why. I just like both genres I guess.

O.k. plug over. What were your influences in writing *Jason*?

Thinking about it I guess that the first person to influence me was a school friend from nearly 30 years ago. We were both musicians; me piano and composition and him just about everything else. He had a band called 'Another Language' and he always said that music was just that, another language. Maybe he's the Stanley Reah of the story, but the idea that music is a language lends itself completely to the idea of code. I've always liked crosswords, puzzles, anagrams, codes and so on and am always looking for the perfect twist or turn in a story. (By the way *Jason* was started long before we'd heard of *The Da Vinci Code* or any of the other copy-cat versions.) You don't have to understand music to enjoy Jason but you would have to be a musician to figure out the code for yourself; luckily the characters in the story do it for us.

And of course friends and people I observe have influenced the story, well the characters. Without naming names there are quite a few bits of people I know in the *Jason* characters, including myself. And the island of Symi is a great influence - such a lot of history for such a small place and so many perfect locations.

How factual is Jason and the Sargonauts?

I'd say about half of the facts stated are true, but there are many references to other facts that make up the background and don't get a big mention. Explain? O.k.:

It's a fact that 'W' (I'll call him W so that if you haven't read the story yet this won't spoil it for you - if you have read it you'll know who W is) it's a fact that W was in Venice and died there. He was also in Paris for some time. It is possible that Panandreas could have met him because sponge exporters from Symi did have offices and business in these places, and throughout Europe. (By the way, there are two chairs in a villa on Symi that once belonged to W, I've sat in them.)

Other historical things are factual: Widor - him of the famous Organ Toccata that people play after weddings - was professor of Organ at the Paris Conservatoire in 1890, as was Caesar Franck before him, students like Dimitris would have studied under them. There is a Panandreas theatre in Los Angeles. The British did invade Symi on July 14th 1944 and concerts were held on the island towards the end of the war, (though not necessarily on the date I used.) Benson and Pollack? Imaginary as far as I can find out.

So you see the story has a mixture of fact and fantasy. Certainly the places I have used do exist though Villa Sargo is actually Villa Papanikola, the SARGO office in Rhodes is Visa Travel and the trek from Vasilios bay to Stavros tou Polemou... well, you won't meet the soldiers and I wouldn't advise it - it's not as easy a walk as the story suggests.

And what about Jason and the Argonauts?

The first great hero/adventure story? Well, there are references to it throughout *Jason*, some obvious and some hidden. In my story we don't spend much time on the boat - I wanted the story to happen mainly on Symi rather than at sea, but there are other tributes to the original myth. Jason's throne was usurped by Pelias (anagram of A. Slipe), the broken sandal, the Golden Fleece and so on. Margaret's surname is Reah (anagram of Hera who helped Jason on his quest). Harriet has had many jobs and is strong: Hercules. Cassie and Polly the double act: Castor and Pollux the fighting twins of myth. Lesley's jewellery clashes with her outfit: the clashing rocks (a bit tenuous I know) and there is a reference to mosquitoes being Harpies that I couldn't resist. There are also other hidden references in there for you to think about if you have nothing better to do one day.

And who helped you in the writing of this story?

Ah, the acknowledgments section!

Well, many people have contributed thoughts and ideas. Neil spent many hours reading the manuscript and the original screenplay version. Hugo lent me his research material from Operation Tenement (July 1944). Dave lent me some books and a couple of ideas for Oliver's sub plot. As I said before various friends have (unknowingly) lent bits of their characters. And I should also thank Nicholas and Adriana, Carl, Jen and Terri for their proof reading. And anyone else I have forgotten to mention. I'm not doing an Oscar speech here but it is very difficult to write in isolation and so many people have had to put up with me blabbering on about the book that I'm bound to have forgotten some of the people I've bored with it.

And so what's next?

At the time of writing this I am actually suffering from the opposite of writer's block. I have so many ideas I don't know which one to start first. The next immediate task is *Symi 85600* which is a collection of writings I have done for www.symidream.com. Once that is complete, in early 2007 I hope, I shall be free again to stretch my imagination and put pen to paper, or rather fingers to keyboard. But whether it will be a comedy about ex-pats on a small Greek island or a fantasy farce about time travel, or a ghost story set in an old villa in the forest on Symi or something more serious… I will have to wait and see. Meanwhile the ideas notebook just keeps getting fuller.

Symi is that kind of place, it feeds one's creativity and, quite frankly, I am full up!

If you enjoyed Jason and The Sargonauts you can find more novels by James Collins at www.lulu.com in paperback and hardback.

Printed in Poland
by Amazon Fulfillment
Poland Sp. z o.o., Wrocław

51619891R00219